NEXT OF KIN

DAVID HOSP

MACMILLAN

First published 2011 by Macmillan
an imprint of Pan Macmillan, a division of Macmillan Publishers Limited
Pan Macmillan, 20 New Wharf Road, London N1 9RR
Basingstoke and Oxford
Associated companies throughout the world
www.panmacmillan.com

ISBN 978-0-230-75334-1

Copyright © David Hosp 2011

The right of David Hosp to be identified as the
author of this work has been asserted by him in accordance
with the Copyright, Designs and Patents Act 1988.

1 3 5 7 9 8 6 4 2

A CIP catalogue record for this book is available from
the British Library.

Typeset by Ellipsis Books Limited, Glasgow
Printed in the UK by CPI Mackays, Chatham ME5 8TD

Visit **www.panmacmillan.com** to read more about all our books
and to buy them. You will also find features, author interviews and
news of any author events, and you can sign up for e-newsletters
so that you're always first to hear about our new releases.

NEXT OF KIN

David Hosp is a trial lawyer who has spent a portion of his time working pro bono on behalf of wrongly convicted individuals. He finds time to write his novels on his daily commute by boat across Boston Harbour. He lives with his wife and family outside the city.

Critical acclaim for David Hosp

'Hosp hits the trifecta – brilliant, brawny, and totally believable'
David Baldacci

'Hosp is a born storyteller, a master of quirky character and detail who enthrals through the simple, but elusive, expedient of never seeming to write a dull sentence'
Daily Telegraph

'Brilliant . . . handled with page-igniting panache'
Daily Telegraph Top 50 Summer Reads 2009

'This is a knock out; Grisham with passion, even a touch of the great Michael Connelly thrown in . . . It crackles from the first page to the last and never lets up for a second'
Daily Mail

'A top-notch tale . . . Fast paced and gritty; Hosp knows his stuff and it shows in this suspense-filled novel'
Nelson DeMille

For my family.
Writing about characters who go through the world alone
makes me appreciate my own family even more.

PROLOGUE

1966

Winter came to New Hampshire early. By Thanksgiving the ground was dusted with an inch of loose, dry snow, the kind easily whipped into funnel clouds as the wind howled across the open fields leading to the Connecticut River.

The hospital stood at the edge of the river, looming out, its great gothic turrets defiant against the elements. It was an enormous stone structure, ill-suited to its purpose: impossible to keep warm and unlikely to provide comfort. And yet they came. In an endless stream, sent by dishonored families and desperate lovers, young and frightened and alone; it seemed nothing could stop them.

Emily heard the first scream shortly after midnight. A shriek of terror and agony echoing off the stone floors. She waited, eyes closed. One minute. Two. Three.

The scream came again, louder this time, panicked and desperate. 'Please! Somebody help me! Oh God, I'm bleeding! Somebody please help me!'

Emily opened her eyes and rolled to her side. She switched on the light next to the bed, checked the clock, shook the sleep from her head. Rising, she retrieved the dress from the chair next to her bed, pulled it over her head and looped a white smock around her neck, tying it to her waist. She

1

could hear the pitiful sobs coming from down the hallway. 'For goodness sake, I'm coming,' she muttered as she walked out of the room.

Emily knew who it was. She'd watched the one called Lizzie at dinner. Her movements were slow and deliberate, and she was shifting uncomfortably in her chair, her eyes downcast and worried. Her belly had descended. Emily recognized the signs.

She walked into the room and flipped the light switch next to the door. Each tiny dorm room had two beds, which were always full. Lizzie was sitting up, her back against two pillows, her knees pulled up under her armpits. Her sobs were now silent, rhythmic gasps, and tears streamed down her cheeks. 'Oh God, please help me,' she whispered.

'You'll be fine,' Emily said. Her tone was cold, and she felt a pang of guilt; after midnight her bedside manner suffered.

She walked over and lifted up the bottom of the girl's nightgown. It was pink with a silk hemline. Embroidered into the silk, white rabbits chased each other in an endless circle. Lizzie was no older than fifteen. Even in agony, though, she was beautiful. Most of them were. That was what got them into trouble.

'It's time,' Emily said. She looked at the girl in the other bed, who was watching with fascination. Her belly, too, was low, and Emily's intuition told her that she would be the next to go, perhaps even later in the day. She couldn't remember the second girl's name, not that it mattered; the names were fake. All the girls were given fake names when they arrived. That was the point, after all.

Lizzie screamed again. 'Oh, God, it hurts! Why does it hurt so much?'

'God punishes evil,' Emily said. It was cruel, but it was what she believed, and it was after midnight. 'It will be all right.' She didn't bother to infuse her voice with sympathy she didn't feel. 'I have to get the doctor.' She looked over at the second girl, and was tempted to tell her to hold Lizzie's hand. The second girl didn't seem the type to give sympathy easily, though. Emily supposed she had problems of her own. 'I'll be back shortly,' Emily said. 'Keep her calm; everything will be fine.'

As Emily walked away down the hallway, Lizzie screamed again, this time louder. Emily quickened her pace.

Lizzie opened her eyes. It took a moment for her to remember where she was; then it came flooding back, drowning her. She tried to turn so she could see the tiny window in between the beds, but her body shrieked in pain, and she lay still. Judging from the shadows on the far wall, the sun was almost down. It was late afternoon.

Out of the corner of her eye she could see that the girl in the bed next to hers was gone. She was glad of that; the two of them didn't get along well. Looking down, her feet were visible for the first time in months. Her belly had popped; the huge, round, heavy balloon she'd carried for so long deflating, leaving her empty. She tried to speak, but her throat was dry and the effort was agony. She swallowed twice and tried again.

'Is anyone there?' It came out as a croak.

She sensed movement at the doorway. Whispering shadows. One of them said, 'Go fetch Sister Emily.'

'Please, is anyone there?' Lizzie called again. There was no answer, and the shadows pulled away from the threshold.

A moment later, Emily came into the room, a whirlwind of German efficiency and Irish judgment. She walked over to Lizzie and picked a glass of water off the bedside table. There was a straw in the glass and she fed it into Lizzie's mouth. Lizzie drank, in spite of the pain, and realized how thirsty she was as the water spread through her. After half a glass, she let the straw fall from her lips. 'What happened?' she asked.

'It was a breach,' Emily said. 'That makes it much more difficult.' She put the glass down on the table. 'You had the doctor worried. You lost a lot of blood.'

Lizzie tried to turn again, but it felt as though her neck were held in a vise. 'My head hurts,' she said.

'That's normal,' Emily said. 'They had to use the ether to knock you out. It takes a while to wear off. You'll have a headache for a couple of days.' She looked down at the rest of Lizzie's body, a frown tugging at her lips, and Lizzie felt violated. 'You'll feel uncomfortable in other ways, too.' She picked up the glass again and offered it, but Lizzie shook her head.

Lizzie's lips trembled. 'What happened to my baby?'

Emily put the water back down on the table and stood. She flattened her smock with her hands against her thighs, straightening her back. 'That's none of your concern, now, is it?'

Lizzie felt the tears running down her cheeks. 'It is my concern,' she said quietly.

'Not anymore. The baby is better off with a family that can take care of it. With a real mother, who isn't wicked. That's what everyone agreed.'

'I never agreed.'

'You didn't have to.'

'Is my baby okay?'

'The baby's fine. But it isn't yours.'

Lizzie's head pounded. She worked to catch her thoughts, but they slipped just out of her grasp. 'Please,' she begged. 'Is it a boy or a girl?'

Emily folded her arms across her chest. 'Why do you want to know? You can never be a part of its life, you understand. You signed the papers. You agreed.'

'I know,' Lizzie said. 'It's just that . . .'

'It's easier this way, child. You don't understand how lucky you are. It will be as if this never happened at all. You can go back to your life. You can make something of yourself. You can be a good girl now. You should be thankful; not everyone in your situation gets to wipe the slate clean.'

'Please!' Lizzie cried. It felt as though her head had shattered, but she didn't care anymore. 'Is it a boy or a girl?'

Emily uncrossed her arms, then crossed them again. Lizzie could read the indecision on her face. 'It was a boy,' Emily said after a moment.

'A boy,' Lizzie repeated. She pushed herself up on her elbows, fighting the pain, until she was able to lean back on the pillow, inclined slightly. 'I want to see him.'

4

'No.' Emily shook her head; there was no hesitation this time. 'You can't.'

'I want to see my baby!' Lizzie screamed. Her anguish reverberated off the stone walls, echoing down the corridors until it was lost. 'Let me see my baby!'

'You can scream,' Emily said coldly. 'We are used to it here.'

Lizzie was racked, her body convulsing in pain as she cried out. 'I want to see my baby! Let me see him! Please, let me see my boy!'

Emily towered over her, her expression hardening, lips pursing angrily. 'I'll be back later, when you're feeling better and you can be civil. You'll see eventually. This is for the best.' She started walking out of the room.

'Wait! Please!' Lizzie called. Emily stopped at the door, keeping her back to Lizzie. 'What will happen to him?'

Emily turned and fixed Lizzie with a stare colder than the New England wind. 'He'll be happy,' she said. 'If you let him go, I promise you, he'll be happy.'

CHAPTER ONE

Scott Finn was not happy. Sitting in his brownstone office in Charlestown, he looked across his desk at Eamonn McDougal. Despite the expensive fabric and expert tailoring, McDougal's suit refused to sit comfortably on his working-class shoulders. The collar of his custom shirt cut into the fat of his neck; his Italian shoes looked painfully tight. He took a silk handkerchief out of his pocket and blew his round nose, rubbing vigorously before slipping it back into his jacket.

'I can't do it, Eamonn,' Finn said. He was taking a risk; McDougal was a dangerous man.

'Yes, you fuckin' can, Finn,' McDougal said. He still had the accent from the old country; the word came out as *fooken*. 'What's more, you will do it. I don't send you enough fuckin' business?'

'You send me business because I win,' Finn said. He was in his mid-forties and had established a courtroom record that justified the confidence. Tall and thin, with black hair and a face too lined to be called traditionally handsome, he had an ease and charm that juries trusted. All the charm in the world couldn't help him with McDougal, though. 'And when you send me a case that can't be won, I tell your boys to plead it out, or get another lawyer – take their chances with a jury and get ready for sentencing. I play straight; you know that.'

'That's all I'm askin' for here,' Eamonn said. He spread his hands in a gesture of assurance that was comically inappropriate.

'No, it's not. You and I both know it. This is your son we're talking about. You want a guarantee; I don't give guarantees. If I start cheating the system, I lose my credibility, and I won't be any good to you anymore.'

McDougal stood up and paced. The office had recently been redecorated, a sign of Finn's success and growing reputation. The walls had gone from scuffed-gray to eggshell-white. The prints hanging on the walls had been replaced with actual paintings purchased at some over-priced studio down the Cape. The wood floors were refinished and covered with rich, sound-killing Persian rugs. Nearly everything in the office had recently been upgraded, from the computers to the draperies to the chairs. The only thing that remained from the office's previous incarnation was Finn's desk, a beaten, blond-wood remnant he'd found years before at a second-hand office furniture shop. The decorator, a chain-smoking divorcee from Newton, had begged him to let her get an appropriate 'piece' for him. She argued he needed something to proclaim his authority – something huge and dark and masculine. He told her he needed something functional – something comfortable. The desk stayed.

The chain-smoker also wanted to put walls up in the open first-floor workspace to create separate offices for Finn and his associate, Lissa Krantz. He and Lissa preferred the shared office, though. They liked to yell at each other; walls would have interfered.

Given the opportunity, Lissa hadn't hesitated to pick out a new desk for herself. She'd chosen an antique Chippendale, with polished cherry wood and brass trimmings. She'd always had expensive taste; she was raised with money, and had plenty of her own. Finn didn't mind. The firm was doing well, and she was a big part of its success.

At the moment, Lissa was sitting behind her expensive desk on the other side of the room, watching McDougal rail at her boss with his chopped Irish accent and his tailored English suit as his tight Italian shoes sank into the thick Persian rug. She kept her mouth shut; a struggle for her.

'You sayin' no?' McDougal demanded from Finn. His eyes had gone dark; not a good sign.

'I'm saying your son won't take my advice. And the fact that he's your son doesn't change what my advice is gonna be.'

'You don't know nothin' about the case, and already you know what your advice is gonna be?'

'I know what I've read,' Finn said.

'Papers always get shit wrong,' McDougal said.

'And I know what you've told me.'

'I get shit wrong, too. You know that. Just talk to him. I don't want him fuckin' things up any more than he already has.'

'Ironic coming from you, Eamonn.' Finn knew he'd crossed a line as the words died on his tongue.

'You watch your fuckin' mouth, boyo.' McDougal wagged a finger at Finn. His face blossomed red, and he raised his voice. 'I do what I do. I make no apologies. And I make a lot of people a whole bundle of fuckin' money – including you. You wanna play Mr Clean, I let you play. But don't ever think that deep down you're anythin' different than me or my people, 'cause you're not.' He paced angrily for another moment, took a deep breath and sat down in front of Finn's desk again. He leaned forward, and regarded Finn with a menacing expression. 'We go back a ways, Finn. Not like family or nothin', but I remember you when you was a kid on the street. I remember when you got out of the life. I've done right by you ever since. Don't turn it wrong now. Talk to the kid for me.'

Finn looked at McDougal for a long moment before he answered. What McDougal was saying was true; he was one of the first who regularly sent Finn business, and was still a significant source of clients. The little firm could survive now without McDougal's support, but it might not flourish in quite the way it had. Finn wondered whether it was worth it. He didn't relish the idea of feeling indebted to a man like McDougal. 'I'm not cheating,' he said. 'You understand that?'

'Yeah, 'course,' McDougal said. 'Goes without saying. You lose your license, my boys lose the best goddamned defense lawyer in Boston. I want that?'

Finn watched the man's eyes. They didn't blink. 'Okay. I'll talk to him.'

McDougal stood. 'You're a good shit, Finn.'

'High praise.'

McDougal grunted. Turning around, he nodded to Lissa. She made a face. 'I'll see you, counselors,' he said. 'Keep up the good work.' He opened the front door and walked out into the crisp October air, to the Caddy double-parked on Warren Street. Two heavy-set men leaning on the fender stood when they saw him. One opened the back door for him; the other climbed into the driver's seat. Finn stood at the window, watching the car pull away.

'Way to be strong, Boss,' Lissa said. 'You set him straight.'

'What did you want me to do?'

'It's a bad idea, that's all I'm saying.'

'Yeah,' Finn agreed. 'It's a bad idea.'

A breeze blew withered leaves into piles in front of the three-story brownstone on Massachusetts Avenue near Melnea Cass Boulevard as Detective Zachary Long pulled up to the curb. He looked down at the address he'd jotted on his pad to make sure he had it right. Six-Seventy-Nine. He had it right. He leaned down below the dashboard for a moment, pulling a flask bottle from under the seat, tipping it to his lips, then putting it back.

Looking up, he could see that the stoops on either side of the building were crowded with faces of varying shades of brown. They regarded him warily as he stepped out of his car. Only one person was on the stoop of the building itself. Officer Ray Washington stood like a uniformed sentry at the front door, protecting the entrance, mirroring the uneasy resentment directed toward him from those hovering nearby.

Long looked up at the building. Removed from its surroundings and transported ten blocks north to the fashionable Back Bay section of town, it would have been a gem. It stood solid, with tall, arched windows in the four-story front bay, conveying a sense of sullen pride. Two doors down, a similar building stood vacant, boarded up and derelict. Ambulances crawled through the inner-city traffic, sirens screaming, carrying the unfortunate to the nearby Metropolitan Hospital. An argument was breaking out at the bodega across the street, anger shot through in heavy accents. Horns could be heard blaring from the nearby Southeast Expressway.

Long pulled a stick of gum from his pocket and popped it into his mouth, crumpled the wrapper and put it back in his pocket. It was habit more than anything else; he was almost at the point where he didn't care who knew about his drinking.

He walked deliberately, taking in the scene as he approached. As he got to the front steps, he paused and looked at those gathered near the entrance of the building next door, isolated the face of the biggest man there, and nodded to him. Those standing with the man on the stoop looked at their companion, eyes curious. The man seemed reluctant for a moment, his eyes darting to the ground, but eventually he nodded back. It was a good start; Long would need cooperation from the neighbors, and it was important to establish authority and acceptance as quickly as possible.

As he turned back toward the front door, Long caught a face in the crowd out of the corner of his eye. The face registered. He didn't quite recognize it, but it was familiar to him; like a phantom fading from a dream in the early moments of morning, hazy and distant. It was one of the few Caucasian faces in the crowd, framed by steel gray hair that matched the sky. A light pink scar in the shape of a 'v' marred the forehead. But what truly made the man stand out was the fact that he was looking directly at Long. While the others only looked toward him, the man with the scar was regarding him directly without the slightest hint of reservation. The image sounded an alarm in the back of Long's head. It was such a subtle thing that it took a moment for him to recognize the intuition, and he spun back to the crowd, his own eyes burning as they sought out the face again.

The man was gone.

Long gripped the stoop's rusting handrail, as he considered giving chase. But then he wondered: *Chase what? Chase who?* What had the man done to be chased? It was no crime, after all, to look out of place.

He took one last long look through the crowd before continuing his ascent.

Officer Washington looked nervously at Long. A light sweat had broken out on his forehead underneath his policeman's cap despite the cool of the October weather. Long understood why. 'Detective,' Washington said. 'You got here quick.'

'I was on the way in when I got the call,' Long replied. 'Just pulled off the highway.'

Washington looked at his watch and smiled uneasily. Long knew it was after eleven. 'You're just coming in? I gotta get myself into plain-clothes.'

'I was at a funeral.'

'Sorry. Anyone close to you?'

Long shook his head. 'My father.'

'Shit. I didn't mean to . . . I'm sorry.'

'So's he. What've we got in here?' Washington hesitated. Long could sense the man was gauging whether his apology had been suffi-cient. 'Don't worry about it. Just tell me what we're dealing with.'

'Neighbor called it in an hour ago. Name's Elizabeth Connor, apartment 2C in back. Fifty-nine years old. Lived here for the last

11

fifteen years. No one's seen her for a few days. They noticed the smell yesterday. Super showed up with a key this morning. Other than him, no one's been inside. I took a look, just to secure the place, but I didn't touch nothing. I told people in the other apartments to stay put until we get to them. Told 'em we might need to talk to them.'

Long nodded. 'What's it look like?'

'Looks messy. Lots of blood. Nothing you haven't seen before. Some sign of a struggle, but not much. Looks like it was on and over pretty quick.'

'Okay. Crime scene and backup should be here in a minute. Other than them, no one comes up, got it?'

'Yeah, all right.'

Long looked at the crowd on the nearby stoops. 'Once they get here, start gathering statements from these people out here. Doers sometimes like to hang out and observe the scene. If they don't have anything to say, at least get their names and contacts. Get a look at their licenses where possible, just to make sure you're not getting fake information. Tell them we may need to come back to them. Someone might'a seen something.'

'You think so?'

'In this neighborhood? No. Not really.'

'Okay. You going in?'

Long nodded. 'Might as well. I'm here, and I got nothing better to do.'

Reggie Hill arrived on time for the baby's noon feeding. Finn had no idea what qualified Reggie to take care of Lissa's son, but he seemed to do a good job, and Lissa depended on him. Outfitted like a sherpa to the armies of Hannibal, he blew through the door with three bags slung across his shoulder, an infant car seat hanging from the crook in his other arm. Finn marveled at his balance.

Lissa stood and took the baby in the car seat from him. 'How was he this morning?' she asked. She'd taken two weeks off after giving birth; there was never any question that she would come back to work. She was a caring parent, but not the stay-at-home type. Finn suspected that she and the baby would bond better with her at the office much of the day. She set the car seat down, and pulled the baby out. He was sleeping, and she put him over her shoulder, rubbing his back.

'He was a doll,' Reggie replied, setting the bags down on the floor. 'Always is. I swear, you could pull teeth if he had any and he wouldn't complain.'

'He takes after his father,' Lissa said.

'God forbid,' Reggie said. He shuddered. 'Let's aim higher than that, shall we?'

'Koz hears you talking like that, he'll fire you, Reggie,' Finn said.

'He wouldn't,' Reggie said. He sat in one of the leather chairs against the wall and crossed his legs above the knees. 'He secretly wants me. Most men do.'

Finn shook his head. 'He hears you talking like that, he won't fire you, he'll shoot you.'

Lissa chuckled.

Reggie said, clucking his tongue, 'Anyone that repressed is hiding something.'

'Trust me,' Lissa said, 'he's not repressed.'

'Maybe he's hiding his hatred of stereotypes,' Finn said.

'No, you di'ent!' Reggie falsettoed. 'I know you did not just call me a cliché.'

Finn smiled amiably. 'I think I did.'

Reggie reached down to a mahogany magazine rack and pulled out a newspaper, shaking it open with a loud flap. 'Lissa Krantz, I love this child, but if you think I'm going to take this sort of abuse for the pittance you pay me, you are sadly mistaken. I demand that you defend me.'

The baby was stirring. 'Apologize to Reggie, Finn,' Lissa said. 'Or I'll cut your balls off.'

'You wouldn't. I'd sue.'

'Fine, then I'll quit, and you can run this place on your own.'

Even in jest the thought made Finn's heart rate double. 'I'm sorry, Reggie,' he said. 'You are a beacon of masculinity in an insecure world.'

'Like you'd know.' Reggie folded the newspaper and put it back into the magazine rack. 'I'm going to Starbucks to get something to soothe my wounded pride. Anyone want anything?'

'I'll have a venti-non-fat-decaf-latte-skim-three-Equals,' Lissa said.

'Finn?' Reggie asked.

'Do they have coffee?'

'Heathen.'

'Skip it.'

Reggie opened the door and stepped out.

'Don't start,' Lissa said to Finn once the door had closed behind Reggie. 'He's got his quirks, but he takes fantastic care of Andrew. I'd be lost without him.'

'What? I didn't say anything, did I? I like the guy. And I'm pretty sure he's right; Koz has got a huge crush on him.'

'Funny.' The baby was fully awake now, and he started to grump hungrily. Lissa maneuvered him around so that his feet were on her knees, his nose to hers. 'Uncle Finn likes to take his life into his own hands, doesn't he, Andrew?' she cooed. 'Yes, he does.' She put him into his car seat and began rummaging through the array of baby bags, looking for a bottle. 'Speaking of taking your life into your own hands, are we really gonna represent the McDougal kid?'

'We'll talk to him.'

'There's a difference?'

'Maybe he won't like what we have to say, and we'll get out of it that way. You never know.'

'Yes, I do. And so do you.'

The door opened and both of them turned. The man standing there looked like something out of the imagination of Stephen King. He was in his fifties, with a thick head of grayish-brown, disheveled hair. His clothes were rumpled and stained. His face was dirty, though not enough to obscure the long, deep, jagged scar running from the corner of his eye down to just below his ear. He was solid and stocky, and he held a piece of grease-stained computer printout above his head. 'I got it!'

'Hi, hon, how was your evening?' Finn said.

'Fuck off.'

'Koz!' Lissa said sharply. She tilted her head. 'The baby!'

'Sorry, I didn't know he was here.'

She walked over and kissed him on the cheek. 'It's okay.' She crinkled her nose. 'You smell.'

'That's because I've been crawling around in garbage.'

'Everyone needs a hobby,' Finn said.

'Yeah, everyone does,' Tom Kozlowski replied. 'Mine is saving your ass. I spent the night watching Spencer's apartment, waiting to see how he would react to his partner's arrest.' Finn's interest was piqued. Will Spencer was the business partner of Carlo Manelli, a client who had been arrested for dealing drugs out of the restaurant the two of them owned. The case against Manelli looked solid.

'And?' Finn said. 'How'd he take it?'

'Not so well. First thing this morning, he comes out of his apartment with a cardboard box, and climbs into his car. He heads out to the restaurant, pulls around the back and tosses the box into the dumpster.'

'You climbed into a dumpster?' Finn said.

Kozlowski frowned. 'Don't be stupid. You think he wouldn't notice someone digging around in the dumpster out back of his restaurant?'

'Fair point.'

'I was gonna wait till late tonight, but it turns out today's trash day at the place; while I'm sitting there a big Waste Management truck pulls up and cleans out the dumpster. So I followed. At the next stop, I gave the guy a fifty to let me in the back of the truck.'

'Good thinking,' Finn said. He looked at Lissa. 'I can see why you love the man.'

'He's hard to resist.'

'So's the Ebola virus.'

'Keep it up,' Kozlowski said. 'I won't tell you what I found.'

'Sorry,' Finn said. 'Continue.'

'It's all here. Dates. Amounts. Customers. A whole second set of books. It all matches the drug buys the FBI is charging Carlo Manelli with. We got the guy nailed. It wasn't our client, it was his partner, Spencer, at the restaurant.'

'Weird,' Finn said, winking at Lissa. 'My money was on Colonel Mustard in the study with the candlestick.'

'You don't think this gets Manelli off?' Kozlowski demanded.

'How do we know they weren't in this together?' Finn pointed out. 'They're partners in the restaurant, why not in drug dealing, too? Why didn't Manelli notice the restaurant had a cash surplus every week? We go to the feds with this, they're just gonna indict Spencer and charge the two of them as co-conspirators, and they'll probably make it stick whether it's right or not.'

'So don't go to the feds with it,' Kozlowski said. 'Let them push the case against Manelli alone. When the trial goes forward, you pull this out on cross. It'll mess with the entire theory of the case the prosecutors have laid out for the jury, and *voilà*, you've got reasonable doubt.'

Finn considered this for a moment. 'It might work,' he admitted skeptically. 'It's better than anything else we've got to work with.'

'See?' Kozlowski said. 'Worth a night's work, fifty bucks and some new clothes. All of which I'm billing you for.'

'Fine,' Finn said. 'I'll charge it back to Manelli as trial preparation expenses.'

Kozlowski took off his jacket, rubbing a finger against a dark stain on the lapel. 'As long as I get paid.'

'What's a new sport coat go for at Wal-Mart these days, anyway?'

'Laugh if you want, but the people I deal with don't trust a man in a thousand-dollar suit. You want people to talk to you, you gotta look like one of them.' He rolled the jacket into a ball and tossed it into the garbage. 'Anything happen while I was out?'

'Finn agreed to represent Eamonn McDougal's son,' Lissa said.

'I did not,' Finn protested. 'I agreed to talk to him.'

'To give him legal advice?' Kozlowski asked.

'Yeah.'

'Isn't that representing him?'

'Technically,' Finn admitted. 'But it's not like I agreed to take the case to trial. And I told Eamonn that I'm not crossing the line. I'm treating his kid like anyone else. He accepted that.'

'You're a moron. You know that, right?'

'Your wife already pointed that out, thanks.'

'She knows what she's talking about. McDougal doesn't want you to treat his son like anyone else. He wants you to get his son off. No matter what. And if you don't, he's gonna be pissed.'

'I know,' Finn said.

'He's gonna be a real pain in the ass if he gets pissed. He's dangerous and unstable.'

'I know that, too.'

'So, why'd you agree to represent him?'

Finn shrugged. 'I guess I just believe that everyone is entitled to the best representation they can afford.'

'Bullshit. You agreed to represent him because it's a challenge.'

The door opened behind Kozlowski and Reggie walked in. 'I've got lattes!' he said. As soon as he stepped through the door, his face screwed itself into a frown. 'Ugh! Jesus Christ on a popsicle stick, what reeks in here?'

Finn and Lissa pointed to Kozlowski. 'Him,' they said in unison.

Reggie regarded Kozlowski with revulsion. 'What happened? Did you go swimming in garbage?'

'Yeah,' Kozlowski replied. He looked uncomfortable. 'Sorta.'

Reggie rolled his eyes and looked at Lissa. 'I swear, sweetheart, you don't have to live like this. Just say the word, and my people can have you and that child in a safe house in Provincetown within two hours. He'd never find you, I promise.'

Lissa smiled. 'Yes, he would,' she said. She looked over at her husband, still covered in a film of waste, his features rough and hard set, and her smile broadened. 'I'd die if he didn't.'

CHAPTER TWO

Zachary Long climbed the stairs to the second floor of the Massachusetts Avenue brownstone slowly, evaluating everything as he went. Judging from the edges, the carpeting on the staircase had once been beige, but that was a long time ago. Now it was mottled and brown and stained. The wooden railing was beaten and sagging, and the stairs themselves listed from the wall. Even at noon on a sunny fall day, the place was dark. A lamp hung from the wall on the second floor, dislodged and dangling from its wire. There was no bulb, not that a bulb would have been of much use.

As he approached the landing, he caught the stench from the back apartment. It became more pronounced as he reached the top, and he put his arm up to his nose. He wondered how no one had called it in before that morning. As he looked around, the door closest to the stairway, marked 2B, cracked open and a man stuck his head out. His eyes were too big for his face, he was gaunt and he had fringes of white hair around a bald, dark brown head. He was wearing a dress shirt buttoned to the top and a cardigan. Long judged him to be in his eighties.

The man nodded to Long. 'Safe to come out yet?'

'Safe, yeah,' Long said. 'But we need you to stay in your apartment for a little while longer.'

The man looked around the hallway, stuck his head out further and glanced down the stairway, frowning. 'We?'

Long pulled his shield out of his pocket, held it up. 'BPD,' he said. 'I'm Detective Long.' He tucked it into the breast pocket of his coat so it would be visible.

'I see,' the man said. He made a face. 'Bad smell.'

Long nodded. 'How long's it smelled like that?'

The man shrugged. 'Don't know. Don't go out much. I cook; my place always smells good. You wanna get the ladies, you gots to keep your crib fresh.'

'That work? With the ladies?'

'Hell yes, fool. Been workin' for me since before your daddy was born.'

'I'll remember that,' Long said. 'Someone will be back to talk to you in a little while, okay?'

'I got nothing to say.'

'Maybe you'll think of something. Till then, just stay in your apartment.'

The old man scowled and closed the door.

Long looked around the floor. There were three apartments. One in the front, one in the middle, one in the rear. The back and the middle were accounted for with the deceased and the old man. The third apartment, according to the mailbox in the entryway, was occupied by an individual or a family with the last name Wolfe. It was an open question in a place as run-down as this whether the mailbox was accurate and up to date.

He glanced around the stairway one last time. Seeing nothing of note, he walked toward 2C. He stopped before he entered and pulled out a flashlight, flipping it on and leaning down to take a close look at the doorknob. There were marks; fresh scratches on ancient copper. Moving up, he could see similar scratches at the keyhole for the deadbolt.

He pulled on gloves and turned the doorknob, being careful not to smudge any prints. It was unlikely that they'd get anything useful, but you never knew. The knob turned with little resistance and he pushed the door in. It swung free and easy on the hinges, and Long stepped into the apartment.

The stench was overpowering. The blinds were pulled and the place was dark; slashes of light cutting through at the sides of the window did little to aid his vision. The shelves along the walls of the living room had been cleared, the books and pictures were spilled on the floor. The coffee table was overturned, and a desk in the corner had been stripped, its drawers heaped nearby along with bills and papers and letters. A purse lay on the floor just in front of the front door, turned inside out, its contents in a loose pile. Elizabeth Connor's body lay in the middle of it all, splayed face down on the faded carpet.

Long stepped carefully around the debris and moved toward her. She was thin, with dark hair and fair skin. She was wearing blue slacks and a yellow blouse. A zebra-print shoe was still on one foot; the other had been knocked off and lay nearby. A long dark stain spread out on the rug from her head, and a fire poker lay to the left of the body. The fireplace was on the far wall, and Long could see the set to which the poker belonged.

He squatted and looked at the woman's face. Her eyes were still open, staring at the carpet, and he had to resist a natural impulse to close them. It wasn't his job, and he didn't want to touch anything until the coroner and the crime lab boys had been over everything. 'Sorry,' he mumbled to the body.

Long heard footsteps on the stairway. 'Doc's here,' Officer Washington called. He came up the stairs, breathing heavily, coughing from the smell. 'Truck's on the way, but Doc's coming up.' He was standing in the doorway, and Long could feel him looking around. 'You see anything interesting?'

Long stood and shook his head. 'No,' he said. 'Probably a junkie looking for enough cash to score his next high.'

'You think?'

Long shrugged. 'No way to know for sure until we do some more poking around, but it fits. Locks were picked. Place was tossed, but tossed quickly. Looks like he just hit the places where he'd likely find basic valuables.' He looked around at the mess and the furnishings. 'Probably didn't find much. Maybe enough to get high once or twice. Maybe not even that much. Most likely she was either already here, back in the bedroom, or she came home when it was going down. Perp grabs the easiest thing he can find – the fire poker – and gives her a whack. Then he's gone.'

'That's it?' Washington said. 'You think someone kills that easily?'

'Trust me,' Long said. 'People kill a lot easier than that.'

Finn and Kozlowski walked into Murphy's Law, a bar at the edge of the commercial district in South Boston. It was a long cement building with a bright red awning and dark tinted windows. At night the place served a decent cross-section of the community, from older locals and blue-collar stalwarts to some of the urban pioneers homesteading on office salaries from downtown in the business district. When Finn and Kozlowski walked in, though, it was still only two in the afternoon. At two in the afternoon, the only people in the place were those who had nowhere else to go.

Kevin McDougal was sitting in a booth at the far end of the bar with two others keeping him company. His companions were bigger than Kevin, which wasn't saying that much. Eamonn McDougal was over six feet tall, but his wife was tiny; no taller than five feet and no heavier than ninety pounds. Their son inherited her build. What he lacked in physical presence, though, he made up for in attitude. He worked out incessantly, and his muscles bulged under tight clothing. His arms, legs and neck were covered in tattoos that seemed to spread like vines, engulfing him further and further every month. He had a quick temper and a reputation for fighting dirty.

Finn and Kozlowski walked the length of the bar, Finn in front, toward the trio in the booth. Kozlowski nodded to the bartender as they made their way; the bartender nodded back.

The three in the booth noticed Finn and Kozlowski coming – in the quiet of the afternoon drinking crowd, they were hard to miss – and McDougal's two companions stood up, guarding the booth.

'Fuck you want?' one of them barked at Finn.

'I want to talk to your boy, there,' Finn replied. 'Kevin, right?' He extended his hand.

McDougal looked up at him. 'I don't know you, mutherfucka,' he said. He had a watch cap pulled low over his brow, and his street accent was exaggerated, as if to convince people he was tough.

'No, you don't.' Finn said. 'My name's Finn. We need to talk.'

'You cops?' the friend standing closest to Finn asked.

'No,' Finn said. 'We're not cops.'

'Then my boy don't need to fuckin' talk to you.'

'Yeah, he does.'

'Says who?'

'Says his father,' Finn said. That made all three of them pause. The two standing looked at McDougal, seeking direction.

McDougal looked down at the table. 'My father don't fuckin' run me,' he mumbled.

After a beat, the young man standing closest to Finn said, 'Yeah, his father don't fuckin' run him.' He took a step into Finn's face. He wasn't tall, but he was meaty, with thick shoulders and a layer of fat across a prominent brow that jutted out beneath a shaved head. A tattoo spread out from his neck up to his ear, reading, *Don't Mess*. 'He don't wanna fuckin' talk, he don't fuckin' talk. Get the fuck outta here.'

Finn looked the young man in the eyes. 'You kiss your boyfriend with that mouth?' he said, nodding toward the other man standing by the booth. The tattooed man moved closer, until his face was only inches away. 'You don't want to act tough,' Finn said. 'You want to sit down.'

'You wanna make me siddown, asshole?'

'Me? No.'

The young man reached up and grabbed Finn by the collar. He pulled back his other hand in a fist, sneering confidently. The look lasted only a split second, though. Before he could throw the punch, Kozlowski moved forward and grabbed him by the elbow. In one swift move, he twisted the young man's arm around far enough that the back of his hand was above his shoulder blade. The move forced the young man to let go of Finn's collar and double over as he gave a high-pitched squeal. Kozlowski used the momentum to drive the man's forehead down hard into the top of a nearby table, splitting the skin just above the nose. Leaning over him, Kozlowski used all of his weight to keep him immobilized. 'Man asked you to sit,' Kozlowski said.

'Fuck you!'

Kozlowski pulled the man's head off the table and slammed it down again. Then he pushed the man's arm up even further, drawing a fresh scream. 'Any more, and it breaks,' Kozlowski said. 'You wanna sit yet?'

People at the bar were watching, as were McDougal and his other friend, both of whom remained still. The bartender called over, 'Koz! Fuck's goin' on over there?'

'Young man here slipped,' Kozlowski said. 'I'm trying to make sure he's all right. Make sure he doesn't slip again.'

'Did he slip hard enough to need an ambulance?' the bartender asked.

'Not yet.' Kozlowski leaned down and spoke into the side of the man's face. 'What do you think, kid? You gonna sit, or are you gonna slip hard enough to need an ambulance?'

The young man was wheezing through the pain. 'Ahhh!' he yelled as Kozlowski applied additional pressure to the arm. 'Okay, I'll sit!'

Kozlowski eased up on his arm and spun him around into a chair at the table. He pulled a handkerchief out of his pocket. 'Wipe the blood off your face.' The young man sat there fuming, but remained in the chair. He took the handkerchief and put it to the top of his nose to stop the bleeding.

Finn looked at the other young man. 'You want to sit, too.' The young man didn't hesitate, and slid into a chair at the same table as his friend. 'Not there,' Finn said. 'Both of you, over there.' He pointed over toward the other side of the bar. The two of them hesitated. 'I'm Kevin's lawyer,' Finn explained. 'At least for now. That means whatever I say to him is privileged, as long as I say it to him in confidence. If you're close enough to hear what I say, the privilege dies.' The two of them looked at him, still not comprehending.

'Just move, morons,' Kozlowski said.

The two of them looked at McDougal. He didn't look up from the table, and after a moment they stood up and moved to the other side of the bar.

Finn stood at the opening of the booth, looking down at Kevin McDougal. 'Mind if we sit?'

CHAPTER THREE

Long stayed at the apartment while the coroner and the lab boys did their work. He didn't need to be there; he'd get a report when they were done, and he suspected he'd learn little from it. The case was likely to be over quickly one way or another. Either they would find a fingerprint that could easily be matched with someone already in the system and they would make an arrest in a day, or there would be nothing to point in any particular direction and the case would die on the vine in a week.

He'd work the case no matter the direction it took; he believed in working cases even when they looked hopeless. And there was always a chance that there was something more to the case than appeared on the surface. It was unlikely, though, and Long was resigned to the notion that there would be little to go on.

He sat on the chair in front of the woman's desk, watching the activity in the room. Pictures were being snapped from all angles; surfaces were being dusted with dark gray fingerprint powder; items were being catalogued for the evidence locker. In the middle of the room, Doc Murphy, the coroner, was performing his initial examination of Elizabeth Connor's remains. He leaned over her with a clinical precision that approached indifference, his tall, thin frame curled into a Dickensian stoop as he slid around the body, instructing his assistant where to snap images.

'What do you think, Doc?' Long asked as Murphy worked.

'Well, she's dead.'

'You're good. I can see why you're in charge. Any thoughts about how long?'

'Have to run some tests. At least forty-eight hours. That takes us back to Tuesday morning. Could've been Monday night. Probably was.'

'Cause of death as obvious as it seems?' Long asked.

Murphy shrugged. 'I assume. Looks like the lethal blow was a single whack to the head. I've been doing this for too long to put my reputation on the line until I've done the full exam. There are too many things her body may want to tell us.' He shifted position, examining her fingers. 'From the way her head bled out I can tell you that she was alive when she was hit. Poker's lying there with blood stains on it; looks like the head wound is consistent with the shape and heft of the poker. You draw your own conclusions. What's interesting are the other wounds.'

'Other wounds?' Long said.

Murphy lifted up the back of the woman's shirt so that Long could see the dead woman's back. It was covered with cuts and marks. 'You see these?'

'Yeah.'

'They look like they were made after she went down from the blow to the head. I count thirty in all, and from the look of them, some were made after she had bled out enough that she had to be dead. Look here.' He pointed to a few long cuts. 'No blood came out. Deep, violent slashes, but no blood. Whoever did this was still hitting the body in a rage minutes after she was already dead.'

Long frowned. 'Drug rage, you figure?' Long asked.

'Could be,' Murphy said. 'It's some sort of psychosis, that's for sure. No other reason to keep hitting the body that way.'

'When she was hit in the head, the first blow, was she facing her killer, or was she hit from behind?' Long asked.

'No way to tell at this point. Probably no way to tell ever.'

'You kidding? They figure out stuff like that on television all the time.'

'Yeah, I know,' Murphy conceded with a sigh. 'Those TV coroners are good. Maybe we should call one of them in, see if they'd be any help here. Unfortunately, she was struck on the side of the head. I may be able to tell a little more from the angle once I measure it, but it's not going to be conclusive. She could've been turning, she could've been ducking; there's really no way to tell. Does it matter?'

Long shook his head. 'No, probably not. Just curious.'

Murphy stood up and looked at his assistant. 'Bag her,' he said. 'We'll do the rest back at the morgue.' He looked at Long carefully. Long reached into his pocket without thinking, drew out a piece of gum and put it in his mouth. 'I'll let you know if we find anything else,' the coroner said. 'But I wouldn't hold my breath if I was you. It's probably exactly what it looks like.'

'Yeah,' Long said.

'She got any family?'

'Not that we've identified yet. Neighbors don't know of any.' He gestured to the mess on the floor. 'I still gotta go through her mail; maybe we'll learn something from that.'

'I hope she didn't have family,' Murphy said. 'Something this random . . .' he shook his head. 'Tough for a family to take. How are you doing?'

'I didn't know her.'

'No, not about her; everything else. You doing okay?' Long hated the question. He got it often these days, and he wasn't sure how he was supposed to answer it honestly. He didn't try anymore.

'I'm good.'

'You sure?'

'Yeah. Thanks.'

Murphy looked Long in the eyes, and Long looked away. 'If you ever want to talk, I know some pretty good guys. Department'll pay for it, too, y'know?'

'Yeah,' Long said. 'I know. Thanks, I'm good.'

'You change your mind, you know where to find me. You're a good cop,' he said. 'Don't let them take that away from you.' Long said nothing. The coroner looked around the room. 'I'll be in touch about this. Let you know what we find.'

'Okay, thanks Doc.' Long watched as Murphy walked out the front door. There were still a few of the crime lab boys left, taking some last snapshots and cleaning up their gear, but soon the site would be deserted. They all knew the odds of solving something like this; there was little enthusiasm in the air. Uniformed officers were canvassing, but as yet they had learned nothing helpful. No one saw anything, no one heard anything, no one knew anything.

God, he needed a drink. *Not yet*, he told himself. *Soon*.

He bent down and started gathering up the papers strewn across the floor. He had to go through them eventually, and there seemed no time like the present. The faster he worked the angles, the faster he could put the case behind him.

He found it an hour later. He'd been through nearly all of the correspondence – bills, mainly. A few catalogues from low-end discount retailers; no personal mail to speak of. He figured he was just about done.

It wasn't in the stacks on the floor or in any of the drawers or shelves; it was taped to the bottom of one of the desk drawers, which had been tossed on the floor. Carefully hidden, it blended in with the wood, and he might not have even noticed it, but he had trouble getting the drawer back into the desk and turned it over to see where the slides were.

As he pulled the envelope free, the cellophane tape pulled chips of wood off the bottom piece of the drawer. It was medium-sized, manila, with a flap at the top and a metal wing attachment that fit through a hole so the envelope could be opened and closed repeatedly. Long pulled the wings together and opened the flap.

There was a letter inside, old and yellowed. He held it up and examined it closely. Grimy fingerprints marred the outside of the envelope, and the postage mark was smudged. Long could just make out the date of delivery – July, 1991.

He read the letter twice. It was likely unconnected with the murder, but it complicated the investigation. At the very least, it would require an additional stop, or maybe two, along the road to putting the case behind him. That was fine with him; that's what they paid him for.

CHAPTER FOUR

'How old are you, Kevin?' Finn asked.

'Fuck you care?'

Finn looked at Kozlowski. 'You believe this?' He shook his head and turned back to McDougal. 'It's a simple question, dipshit. How old are you?' He feigned sign language as he asked the question.

McDougal stuck his chin out like an angry child. After a moment he said, 'Twenty.'

Kozlowski motioned to the bartender. 'I'm gonna have to tell Jimmy not to serve you anymore.'

'Fine,' McDougal said. 'I'm gonna have to slit your fuckin' throat. Then I'm gonna have to find a new bar.'

'You're not very bright, are you Kevin?' Finn said. 'It's okay, in my line of work I deal with a lot of guys who are dumb as stumps, so I'm used to it. I just like to know what I'm dealing with.'

Kevin said through his teeth, 'I'm only twenty and I'm smart enough to have my own crew. Smart enough to drive a fuckin' 7-Series and live in a duplex. Fuck do you drive, asshole?'

Finn looked over at the two young men sitting at the far end of the bar. One of them still had Kozlowski's handkerchief to his forehead to stop the bleeding. They were engrossed in a cartoon playing on the television over the bar and seemed to have lost interest in what was happening at the table. 'You call those two a crew?' Finn asked. 'Koz took them out in about ten seconds, and he's on Social Security. They make the stumps I deal with normally look like Rhodes Scholars. Get it straight, Kevin, the only reason no one's punched your card is because you're Eamonn McDougal's kid, and they're afraid enough of him to leave you alone. That doesn't make you smart, it makes you lucky.'

'I'm smart,' McDougal replied, though his head was down.

'No, you're not. You got busted selling crack to an undercover officer across the street from a middle school. If you were smart, you would have known that if you deal within two hundred yards of a school, jail time doubles. Now I come out here and find you with these losers in a bar while you're out waiting on a trial, when a condition of your bail was to stay off drugs and alcohol and to stay away from anyone with a criminal record. If you were smart, you would know enough to stay clean while you're out on bail. Nothing pisses a judge off more than finding out that someone they've let out is screwing up. It makes them look bad. But no, here you are with a couple of guys who, no doubt, already have some time on their sheet, tossing back Jameson's and High Lifes, lookin' for trouble. Not smart.'

'I—'

Finn cut him off. 'You wanna be smart? Listen; don't talk. Your father hired me because I'm good at what I do. I know the prosecutors and I can work this to get you the best possible deal. But only if you listen to me.'

'What kind of a deal?' McDougal seemed interested for the first time.

Finn shrugged. 'We'll have to wait and see. There's a budget crunch and the prisons are overcrowded. Drugs haven't been a major priority for law enforcement since Nancy Reagan was first lady, and since 9/11 nobody really cares unless there's some evidence that it's tied in to the financing of terrorism. Given all that, and the fact that it's your first bust, I may be able to get you six months in and probation after. That's if you're lucky.'

'Bullshit!' McDougal barked, slamming his beer down on the table. His two friends at the bar tore their eyes away from their cartoon and looked over toward the table. A glare from Kozlowski was sufficient for them to turn away again. 'I'm not goin' in.'

'To jail? Yes, you are,' Finn said. 'The only question is for how long. You listen to me, and it'll be for a lot less time. You don't listen to me . . .' he shrugged.

'For a first bust? I know plenty of guys got busted first time and got nothin' but probation. Why can't you get me that?'

'Two reasons. First, you got busted selling crack to an undercover who looked like she was twelve and who you thought was in the eighth grade. That pisses law enforcement types off. Second, because you're Eamonn McDougal's kid.'

'Fuck's that got to do with anything?'

'You really are stupid, aren't you? It's not like the cops and prosecutors don't know what your father does for a living, and most of them would give their left nut to put him away. Now they've got you – his son – jammed up. There's gonna be a lot of pressure to put the hammer down. Go for the max. That'd be fifteen-to-thirty when they roll all the charges together. It's gonna take some serious dealing to push through all that bullshit to get them to be reasonable. I can do it, but you're not gonna walk for free. You're gonna have to put in some token time. That's just the reality.'

McDougal picked up his beer and went to take a sip, but Finn caught his hand and pushed it back down to the table. 'You want to work with me, you stay clean and listen to me, got it?' Finn said.

McDougal let go of his beer and sat back in the booth. 'I'm not goin' to jail. You're supposed to be such a hot shit lawyer, why not take it to trial? That way I walk.'

'Because at trial we lose. I can get a deal because I can talk a good game with the DA's office, and I've done well enough against them that they'll get nervous. But in the end that's nothing but bullshit and bluffing. We get to trial, we lose this case. They've got the evidence, and there's no basis for excluding it. You do what I say, it's the best chance you've got to be back out on the street in time to drink legally.'

'This is bullshit.'

'Maybe,' Finn said. 'But it's your bullshit, not mine. I'm just here to try to clean it up. So the real question is: Are you smart or not?'

McDougal looked at Finn for a long moment. Then he picked his beer up and took a sip. 'I'll think about it,' he said.

Finn shook his head. 'Good. You think about it. Looks like your brain cells need the workout anyway.' He motioned for Kozlowski to slide out of the booth and they both stood up. 'You want to do this my way, you let me know,' he said. 'If not, I wish you all the luck you deserve.'

Finn and Kozlowski walked the length of the bar toward the door. As they passed McDougal's friends sitting at the bar, Kozlowski looked at the bartender. 'You used to get a better class of customer in here, Jimmy. What happened?'

'Economy's in the crappa,' the bartender replied in a thick South Boston accent. 'We gotta take what we can get.'

Kozlowski leaned in and spoke quietly to the young man with the handkerchief to his forehead. 'You boys be good in here, got it? If I hear you've been causing Jimmy any problems, I'll find you. Next time you fall down when I'm around, Kleenex won't stop the bleeding.' He stepped back and walked over to Finn, who was waiting at the door. 'Take care, Jimmy.'

The bartender nodded. 'Take care, Koz.'

Finn pushed the door open and the two of them stepped out into the sunlight.

CHAPTER FIVE

Sally Malley sat on the stone wall near the parking lot in the rear of Brighton School, a private enclave in Cambridge. She could feel the other students looking at her as they walked by, could smell their curiosity and distrust. She didn't care. She didn't belong there, but she wouldn't be intimidated. She'd been at the school for only a month and a half, but it had been enough time for her to understand that she was as smart as they were. School, she'd come to realize, was a game, and she was going to learn to play it better than anyone else. She figured she owed that to herself.

She looked out at the street, scanning for Finn's car. She hoped he would get there soon. Idle moments like these were the worst. When she was in class, she felt directed – and therefore protected. When she had no focus, she felt exposed.

She was looking out to her left when she felt a shadow cross her face. She turned her head and looked up at two girls from her class. She knew who they were; everyone knew who they were. They were the popular girls; the girls who, as sophomores, were dating juniors and seniors and claimed privilege as a result. That was fine with Sally. They had no idea what privilege was. Privilege could only be comprehended if you understood deprivation first. Sally understood deprivation; these girls never would.

'You're the new girl,' one of them said. Her name was Tyler, and she was precious. Sally said nothing. She craved a cigarette, but she knew she could get kicked out for lighting up. As far as the school was concerned, tobacco was worse than coke or heroin – a policy that illustrated the school's naiveté. 'Where do you get your hair cut?'

'I cut it myself,' Sally said. It was only partially true, but she enjoyed the shock value. She'd gotten it cut at a place in Charlestown before she started school. She had nice hair, she knew. It was jet black, straight and thick. They'd done a decent job with it. When she got back to the apartment and looked in the mirror, though, it seemed too even for her. She'd taken out scissors and cut the bangs diagonally across her forehead. She wouldn't go so far as to say that it looked better, but it definitely looked more like her.

The second girl laughed derisively. Her name was Tiffany, and she played a bit part in her own life. She didn't have the confidence to lead; she was focused on keeping her grip on an identity that depended on those around her. 'You cut it yourself?' she asked. 'Why?'

'Why not? It's my hair.'

'I think it's cool,' Tyler said. She was being polite; Sally's guard went up automatically. 'I heard you're from Southie. The projects?'

Sally eyed her. 'Grew up there. I live in Charlestown now.'

'Charlestown projects?'

Sally shook her head.

'Still,' the girl said. 'Charlestown . . .'

'What do you want?' Sally asked.

The girl hesitated. 'I'm having a party this weekend,' she began. 'I thought maybe you'd like to come.'

Sally was too smart to fall for it. 'Why?'

'You're new in school. Hanging out with us would make it a lot easier to fit in. I thought you might like it.'

It made little sense. 'Seriously,' Sally said. 'Why?'

Tiffany looked nervous. Tyler just stared at Sally, studying her; trying to figure out whether or not to be honest. 'We've got booze,' she said at last. 'We don't have other supplies, though. The guy who usually helps us out isn't around. We thought maybe you could.'

'What sort of supplies?' Sally asked. She already knew, but she was curious to see how Tyler would respond.

'Specifically?' Tyler asked.

'Specifically.'

'Blow. Maybe some H if it's good. I don't want anyone freaking out on bad shit. That'd suck.'

Sally said nothing. She felt a distant instinct to punch the girl, but knew it wouldn't go over very well in her new school. Tyler would lie about their exchange, and the teachers and principal would believe her. Besides, to her surprise, Sally didn't feel real anger toward her. She felt only pity.

'So?' Tyler asked. 'Can you help us?'

Sally shook her head. 'I don't do drugs.'

Tyler wasn't easily put off. 'You don't have to do them. You just have to buy them. I'll pay you double. Given where you grew up, you must know someone, and I'm guessing you could use the cash. I don't want to go cruising the streets to make a buy. It's too dangerous.'

'Sorry,' Sally said. 'Can't help you.'

'Can't? Or won't?' Tyler was clearly angry. She stepped in closer to Sally. 'Don't you understand what I'm offering? You want friends here, don't you? I can help you with that.'

'How?'

'I know a lot of people. I have a lot of friends. You help me with this, and my friends will be your friends.'

Sally frowned. 'That sounds kind of pathetic, don't you think?' She saw Finn's car pulling up the street and she stood.

Tyler grabbed her by the shoulder. 'I can be a great friend,' she said. 'But I can be a totally bitchy enemy.'

Sally leaned in close to Tyler and spoke evenly. 'I'm new here, and you don't know me, so I'm not gonna take offense. I don't do drugs.

I don't buy drugs. As far as you being popular, have you ever considered that's because you've blown half the hockey team?' Tyler looked shocked. 'Small school,' Sally said. 'Even the new kids hear the gossip. And when it comes to having enemies, you don't even understand what that means. You want a real enemy, you're messin' with the right girl. Where I come from, we don't do the Brady Bunch *you-won't-get-invited-to-parties* kind of vendettas. We keep it real. You think you're up for that, say the word.' She looked down at her shoulder. Tyler was still holding on to her. 'If not,' Sally said, 'then take your goddamned hand off me.'

Tyler dropped her hand without a word. She started to say something, but closed her mouth.

'Thanks,' Sally said. She looked at Tiffany, wondering what was keeping her on her feet. She looked like she'd already fainted. 'Nice meeting you. Maybe we can hang out after school sometime. Do each other's nails.'

Finn drove his battered MG convertible up the street that led to the school. It didn't matter how much money he made, he'd never get rid of his car. It was a part of him, like a friend or a dog.

The school was beautiful – bigger than the city college he'd gone to at nights, and more expensive. It was one of the few things he knew he could give Sally, one of the few things he couldn't screw up. She'd been with him for less than a year, and he still had trouble thinking of himself as anything like a parent. People who knew him assumed that she'd been foisted on him, that he'd never really had a choice. They were wrong; he wasn't the sort to be forced into anything. He'd accepted the responsibility of being her guardian willingly. In many ways she reminded him of himself at that age, a lean stray dog left alone to fend for himself. He'd made it out of that life, but he didn't want to see her go through the same struggles. Even if his nurturing instincts left something to be desired, he figured he'd be better than the streets.

The Brighton School was his idea of a back-stop. He figured even with his inevitable mistakes, she couldn't go too far wrong as long as she was at the right school. From his own experience when he was younger, he knew that the city public schools could be dangerous places where drugs and violence were always hovering. He didn't want that for her. A place like Brighton would keep her sheltered from those influences. It gave him some peace of mind, and helped ease some of the pressure he put on himself.

As he drove up, he could see her waiting for him on the stone wall, talking to two girls. That was good; he wanted her to make friends. If there was one thing about her that made him worry, it was that she could be prickly.

She stood up as he pulled to the curb. The two girls watched her climb into the car. 'Hey,' he said.

'Hey.'

'How was school?'

'Fine.'

Finn pulled out back into the traffic. 'I've got some work to do at the office,' he said. 'That okay?'

'Sure,' she replied. 'I've got a bunch of homework to do. I can do it there.'

'You're liking the schoolwork, huh?' he said. 'That's good.'

She shrugged. 'You're payin' for it. It's a shitload of money; I'd feel guilty if I wasted it.' He winced at her language. It was an issue he hadn't addressed with her yet. 'Besides,' she continued, 'the teachers aren't too bad. They're clueless about the real world, but they know their shit when it comes to the classes. That's kinda new for me.'

'What about the kids?' Finn asked. 'They okay?'

'They're assholes.'

'They can't all be bad,' Finn said. 'They're probably just different.'

'They're definitely different.'

'Different doesn't mean bad.'

'No,' she agreed. 'Not always.'

'In some ways, it can be good. You can meet the sort of people that can help you later in life. It can make things easier.'

He could feel her looking at him. 'Is that the way you got to be successful? By knowing the right sort of people?'

'Hardly. The right sort of people don't hang out with people like me.'

'So Lissa and Koz aren't the right sort of people?'

'That's different. I'm talking about people with connections. There are a lot of advantages to going to a school like this. Not just academically. It couldn't hurt to get to know some of the kids; who knows, you might even end up liking them.'

She looked out the passenger window. 'I kinda doubt it,' she said quietly.

He decided to change the subject. 'What do you want for dinner?'

'Whatever. Doesn't matter to me.'

'We could pick up some Chinese on the way back from the office. That sound okay?'

'Fine.'

Finn swerved through the Cambridge traffic on the way back into Charlestown. 'It's gonna be fine,' he said to her. 'Trust me, it's gonna get better.'

She pulled her eyes away from the passenger window and looked at him for a moment, then turned back to the window. 'Trust me, it already has,' she said.

CHAPTER SIX

The man with the scar on his forehead waited patiently as the owner of the garage snapped his fingers at the young mechanic finishing the work on the car. His expression concealed his impatience, but the garage owner knew enough to regard him nervously. Little about the manner in which the man presented himself to the world ever altered. He confined his expression to casual indifference. His close-cropped, steel-gray hair was never out of place. His clothes were simple, understated, unwrinkled. He'd reached an age where he viewed any change as the harbinger of decrepitude. He would never allow that. Past his sixth decade, he remained in better physical condition than most men half his age. It was necessary in his line of work.

'I'm sorry, Mr Coale,' the garage owner stammered.

Coale wasn't his real name. His real name had been lost to the wind decades before. All he had now was a series of identities. None mattered to him. As a name, Coale worked just fine.

'I was sure it would be ready,' the garage owner apologized again, this time with a weak smile.

Coale didn't smile back. 'Not a problem,' he said. There was no accent to his voice. He'd fought hard to lose the accent. 'I'm in no hurry.'

That was a lie. There was much to do.

Detective Long's appearance at the dead woman's apartment presented a challenge. Coale knew from Long's reputation that he was good. Tenacious. Bright, too. Bright enough to pick Coale out of the crowd. That had been careless. It bothered him; he was never careless.

Fortunately given the events of the past few months, it was unlikely that those in the police department would take Long seriously. Still, Coale had only survived this long because he refused to underestimate his adversaries. It was why he was the best.

The garage owner was now motioning frantically to the young mechanic to bring the car around, and as the gleaming wheels flashed off the fluorescent lights, Coale almost allowed himself a smile. The car was his one vanity. He lived simply in all other respects, but he always drove an exceptional car. Not flashy, his profession wouldn't permit that, but a quiet confirmation of class – elegance, even. His current vehicle was a gleaming black Mercedes S class.

He supposed it went back to the days of his youth. He'd been raised in sustainable poverty by a father who was a chauffeur to a wealthy Boston Brahmin family. His mother had died giving birth to him – the irony of his first kill – and he and his father had nothing. They lived in a two-room garage apartment, and the only objects of beauty in their lives were the cars. Three of them – two Rolls Royces and a Bentley. Someone else's cars, though his father had cared for them with a passion he'd passed on to his son. The appreciation for a beautiful automobile was something he and his father had shared.

The garage owner was pulling the mechanic out of the driver's seat, taking a chamois to the door handle and the wood finish on the steering wheel. Then he held his arm out, presenting the car to the man as though it were a gift. 'It's ready, Mr Coale,' he said, his voice cracking. Coale smelled fear on the garage owner's breath.

He reached into his pocket and pulled out a polished silver money clip stretched with bills.

'Oh, no,' the garage owner protested. 'I can't. Please. It wasn't ready on time.'

Coale pulled five one hundred dollar bills off the stack of cash, re-clipped the rest, folded the bills twice. As he walked past the garage owner, he tucked the bills into the man's breast pocket. 'You do the best work in the city, Hassan,' he said. 'You should be paid properly.'

'Thank you,' Hassan said simply.

Coale slipped into the car and eased on the gas in neutral. The sound of German engineering well maintained was gratifying. Sliding the car into gear, he looked over his shoulder. 'I'll be back next month, Hassan.'

Hassan nodded, and the Mercedes rolled out toward the street. Coale had much to do. Inattention to detail could be fatal. He'd made his reputation on attention to detail.

Before pulling into traffic, he glanced in his rearview mirror. Hassan was standing by the door to the garage, watching him go, leaning against the building and wiping the fear from his brow with a cloth.

CHAPTER SEVEN

Detective Long stood at the doorway to the townhouse near the top of Bunker Hill in Charlestown. It was a moonless evening, and a light autumn rain misted down on him. It smelled clean. Cleaner here, up on the hill, than down in the projects by the water. It was nice up here, he thought. Nice to be so high up that you couldn't smell the shit that coated the shoes of the little people. Nice to have a view that didn't force you to witness what others went through just to survive. Long could only guess at how nice that would be. It wasn't how he'd spent the first half of his life; it clearly wasn't how he was going to spend the second half.

He took a deep breath and checked his attitude as he rang the doorbell to the top apartment. Scott T. Finn, Esquire had done well for himself. *Good for him,* Long thought; he had no reason to hold it against him. From what he'd learned through a brief background check, it wasn't like the guy was born on a pile of gold. Finn had made it to the top of the hill on his own. More power to him. Long wondered whether the booze was affecting his judgment, but dismissed the notion quickly. Besides, he could afford to wait to pass judgment on the man. He was going to get a good, clear look into the man's soul. Stress was the best truth serum, and Long was about to dump a whole truckload of stress on Scott T. Finn, Esquire.

The doorbell speaker crackled. 'Yeah?' It was a man's voice.

'Is that Scott Finn?' Long responded.

'Yeah. Who is it?' There was an instinctive distrust in the voice.

'Detective Long, Boston Police. I need to talk to you.'

The pause lasted longer than necessary. 'I'll be down.'

'I can come up,' Long said. The box had gone dead, though. That was fine with Long; he could do this in stages. There wasn't any question in his mind that he'd be invited up eventually.

The door opened a couple of minutes later. Finn was standing in the doorway wearing jeans and an untucked button-down shirt. He looked to be about ten years older than Long, and a few inches taller. 'Detective,' he said, nodding. 'What can I do for you?'

'Can we talk upstairs?' Long asked.

Finn shook his head. 'I'd prefer not to. I try to keep my home life separate from my work life. Which one is this about?'

'Sorry?'

'I assume you're here about one of my clients? It may be easier to do this tomorrow at the office.'

Long shook his head. 'I'm not interested in any of your clients. I need to talk to you.'

The lawyer's eyes darkened. 'About what?'

'This really would be easier to do upstairs, Mr Finn.' Long knew he wasn't going to convince the man . . . yet.

'I don't think so,' Finn said. 'Why don't you just tell me why you're here?'

'Okay,' Long relented. 'I have to ask you some questions about your mother.'

Finn smiled, as though the visit were a mistake. 'You've got the wrong guy,' he said.

'I don't think so.'

Finn was still smiling. 'I don't have a mother.'

'Everyone's got a mother,' Long said, toying with him.

Finn shook his head. 'I'm an orphan,' he said. 'I never had parents.'

'Yes, you did,' Long said. He reached into his pocket and pulled out the letter he'd found taped to the bottom of Elizabeth Connor's desk drawer. He held it up so that Finn could see it. 'You wrote to her once.'

Finn's face went white, and he staggered back slightly, leaning against the door. 'Where did you get that?' he asked in a whisper.

'It was in your mother's apartment,' Long said. 'About five feet from her body. She was murdered last weekend.' The lawyer didn't respond. 'You look a little shaky, Mr Finn. You sure you don't want to discuss this upstairs?'

For a moment, Finn heard nothing. Not the patter of the raindrops tapping on the stoop; not the words the detective spoke after announcing the reason for his visit; not the pounding of his own heart. For a moment he was lost, overwhelmed by emotions he thought he'd put behind him many years before.

He managed to recover his composure only with significant effort. He had to, he knew. The lawyer in him understood that he had to let it go and refocus so that he could deal with the police detective at the door. 'Maybe it would be better if we discussed this upstairs,' he said at last.

Long nodded, and Finn thought he could detect the shadow of a smile cross his lips. 'Yeah, that's what I was thinking,' he said.

Finn led the way up the three flights of stairs to his apartment. He looked back twice to take some measure of the man. He looked to be younger than Finn, though there was wear around the edges of the eyes that testified to more experience than his age would suggest. He was a couple of inches shorter, maybe just shy of six feet, with a body that was neither thick nor thin. His light brown hair was rain swept, making him look, at first glance, disheveled and disorganized. The eyes were bloodshot but sharp, and they seemed to notice everything, taking it all in with the efficiency of a video camera, ready to play it all back later for analysis.

Finn opened the apartment door at the top of the stairs. The shock was wearing off, and underneath it Finn found a million questions.

'Come in,' he said, gesturing. Detective Long stepped in and Finn followed. He could see the man's head swivel, the camera still recording.

'You live here alone?' Long asked.

'No,' Finn said. They walked through the entryway and into the living room. Sally was sitting on the couch reading. She looked up. 'This is Sally,' Finn said. 'She lives here, too. Sally, this is Detective Long.'

Long walked over to her, and reached out his hand. His raincoat dripped dirty spots on the cream-colored carpeting. 'Nice to meet you, Sally,' he said.

She looked up at him, and then over toward Finn. 'It's all right,' Finn said.

She looked back at Long's hand, put her own out slowly. 'Hello,' she said. Long took hold of it and gave a firm shake, his eyes never leaving hers.

'Detective Long and I need to talk about something in private,' Finn said. 'Can you give us a few minutes? Go on back and read in your room?'

Sally got up and walked out. 'Nice meeting you,' Long called out behind her, but she didn't respond. 'Cute kid,' Long said to Finn after she'd left. 'I did some digging before I came over. Didn't know you had a daughter.'

'I don't,' Finn responded.

Long raised an eyebrow. 'Niece?' he asked. There was something untoward in his tone – the hint of a euphemism.

'Client's daughter,' Finn said. 'He died. I'm looking after her.'

'Tough break.'

Again, there was something in the detective's tone that Finn didn't like. 'What do you mean?'

'I mean having your parents die. Must be tough for her. Tough living without parents.'

'Her father's dead. Her mother's alive; she's just got problems,' Finn

47

said. 'Did you come here to talk about Sally?' Finn asked. 'I mean, is she connected to my mother?'

'No.' Long shrugged. 'Just making conversation. I didn't know about her. It made me curious, is all.'

Finn cocked his head and said, 'Is that really what you're curious about?'

'No,' Long said. It was clear that he was still studying Finn, trying to read him. 'Did you know your mother was dead?' Long asked.

'I didn't even know she was alive,' Finn answered. 'Who was she?'

Long held up the letter. 'She never wrote back to you?' he asked. 'You never found out who she was?' The detective walked over to the window and looked out at the view reaching down the hill to the shore.

'No,' Finn said. 'She never wrote me back, and I never found out who she was.' He felt his voice starting to rise, and took a deep breath to calm himself down. 'I've spent my entire life knowing nothing about my parents. You're telling me now that my mother was murdered. Sorry if I seem a little impatient. Who was she?'

It took a moment for Long to respond. He turned from the window and said, 'Sorry.' The way it came out made Finn want to knee the man in the groin, but he kept his composure. 'Her name was Elizabeth Connor,' Long said at last. 'Lived in Roxbury, just out past Metropolitan Hospital. You been out that way recently?'

'I'm in Roxbury District Court just about every week,' Finn said. 'You probably already know that if you did some background on me. How was she murdered?'

'Beaten,' Long said. He took a small notebook out of his pocket and flipped through the pages. 'With the poker from a fire set. Whoever did it kept hitting her even after she was dead. Looks like there was a lot of anger involved. The locks were picked, her place was tossed. We're not sure what she had there before, so we don't know what's missing.'

'And the letter . . . ?'

'Found it taped underneath a desk drawer. Interesting reading.'

'I was angry when I wrote it.'

'Yeah,' Long said. 'So I gathered. Understandable, I guess, given everything that you went through. You didn't have the happiest childhood after she gave you up, did you?'

'No, I didn't,' Finn said.

'Must've been tough.'

'Lots of kids have it tough,' Finn said. He narrowed his gaze at Long. 'How about you, Detective? How was your childhood?'

Long nodded with a bitter laugh. '*Touché*, Mr Finn. 'Course, neither of my parents were murdered, otherwise I'm sure some cop would've shown up at my door asking a bunch of annoying questions. Your mother, though . . .' His voice trailed off. 'How many foster homes did you go through? How many stays at state facilities before you hit the streets?'

'Too many,' Finn said. He fought to keep his mind from pointlessly traversing the past. 'It was a long time ago.'

'Yeah, it was,' Long admitted. 'Some wounds take a long time to heal.'

'Do you have something you want to ask me, Detective?'

Long turned his palms up. 'It's my job – you understand.' He looked at his notes again. 'Elizabeth Connor,' he continued, summarizing, 'lived alone; no evidence of any long-term attachments; not married; no children we know of – other than you, of course; fairly mundane job about ten blocks from where she lived. From what we know so far, she lived an unexceptional life.'

'Any leads on who might have murdered her?' Finn asked.

'Just an angry letter from a son she apparently never knew taped to the bottom of a drawer.' He waved the letter again. Finn looked away. 'Other than that, nothing. You understand why we have to follow up, I'm sure.'

'I'm sure,' Finn said. 'It's late, so I'll make this easy on you,

Detective. I wrote the letter a long time ago and sent it to the agency that placed me as a baby. They said they would forward it to my birth mother if she was willing to accept it. I never heard anything back. I never found out anything about my mother's identity until five minutes ago, and I had nothing to do with her death.'

Long was jotting down notes as Finn spoke. 'That it?' he said, looking up. 'Nothing else?'

'Not that I can think of,' Finn replied. 'Just a lot of questions about who she was and why she was murdered.'

'You never knew her, and she abandoned you,' Long said. 'Why should you care?'

'I don't know,' Finn said. 'Maybe I shouldn't, but I do. Is there anything else you can tell me?'

Long shrugged as he closed his notebook. 'It's not the best neighborhood. Chances are it was just a simple robbery gone wrong. Crackhead looking for something to sell for his next high.'

'Sounds like a logical theory.'

'Yeah. Maybe. I still have to follow every lead.' The detective looked down at the dark stains on the carpet. 'Shit, I dripped on your rug. Sorry about that.'

'It's water,' Finn said. 'It'll dry.' The silence dragged out for several beats, both men looking at each other from across the room. 'You got a picture?'

Long frowned. 'Nothing you'd want to see.'

'What do you mean?'

Long looked uncomfortable for the first time in the evening. 'It was taken at the morgue.'

'I still want to see it.'

Long reached into his jacket pocket and pulled out a Polaroid, glanced at it briefly. 'You sure?'

Finn reached out and took the photograph from him. She barely looked human. She was naked to the tops of her breasts, a sheet covering her below. The glare of the surgical light reflected off white skin that was pulled tight. Her hair was back, and Finn could see the splatters of blood coming forward from her scalp. It gave him little idea of what she might have looked like in life. At least her eyes were closed.

'I'm keeping it, okay?' Finn said.

'Why?'

'Because.'

Long nodded. 'I got others.'

'Anything else?' Finn asked.

'No, I guess not,' Long replied. He slipped the notebook into his jacket. 'Sorry to drop all this on you like this.'

'Like you said, it's your job.'

'Yeah. I'll find my way out.' Finn watched as Long headed down the hallway.

'Long?' Finn called after him as he reached the door. The detective turned to look at him. 'You've really got no other leads?'

Long shook his head. 'Nothing.'

'How long do you think you'll work the case?'

Long frowned. 'I assure you, Mr Finn, I'll work this case as hard as I can until there's nothing left to go on.'

'How long?' Finn demanded.

Long started to say something, but checked himself. He took a deep breath. 'Realistically?' he asked.

'Yeah,' Finn said. 'Realistically.'

Long shrugged. 'Unless there's some sort of break – something that gives me something to chew on – a week. Maybe more, maybe less. You understand how it works.' Finn stared at him, and Long nodded and opened the door. Then he was gone.

'Yeah,' Finn said quietly. 'I understand how it works.'

CHAPTER EIGHT

Eamonn McDougal had once loved bars. He'd spent most of his life cruising through pubs and taverns, flashing his smile at the women, and his fists at the men. It was where he'd made his reputation, where he'd built his life. He'd loved bars the way a sailor loves the sea or a pilot loves the sky.

His son had ruined all that for him.

Kevin McDougal began sneaking into bars at age fourteen. That fact alone wouldn't have bothered his father; it probably would have made him proud if the boy could carry forward the family's reputation. He couldn't, though. Where Eamonn was tall and broad in the chest and shoulders, Kevin was short and slight. The son had worked hard over the years at the gym to hang muscle from his thin bone structure, but for some reason that had only annoyed Eamonn even more. It made his son seem insecure, weak. Weakness was the thing in life that Eamonn hated most, and he saw it in abundance in his only offspring.

His son's greatest weakness had developed slowly over the past few years. Slowly enough that Eamonn had been able to convince himself that it wasn't really a problem at all. Eamonn had tried a little cocaine himself in his youth, after all, and it had never taken over his life. It was a mere dalliance that provided an added rush in his adrenaline-fueled life, and he was smart enough to know that anything more than dabbling would weaken his mind.

Clearly his son didn't share his strength or intelligence when it came to drugs. According to the rumors, Kevin had started with cocaine, but moved quickly through crack and heroin. Now the boy was using pretty much anything he could get his hands on. Selling, too. Eamonn had no moral problem with the drug trade, it had supplied him with a steady income stream over the years, but the notion of selling on the street depressed him. That's what the hustlers and the skanks and the immigrants were for. No one of stature sold on the street. If he was involved in a deal, it was at the wholesale level, and the cash on the table reached into seven figures at least. That his son had been picked up on the street selling ten-dollar bags of crack outside a schoolyard made him want to vomit.

So, notwithstanding his long-standing love of bars, it was with revulsion and near dread that Eamonn opened the door to the HotSpot in Southie, looking for his son.

The HotSpot was new to the neighborhood, and it didn't blend well. The black lacquer bar, modern abstract black and white photographs on the wall, and zebra-striped velvet curtains hanging at the back made plain that the bar was catering primarily to the yuppie scum who had invaded the South End in the past decade. For a terrifying moment Eamonn wondered whether it might be a gay bar, but the presence of numerous long-legged young women in tight cocktail dresses and expensive dye jobs set his mind somewhat at ease.

He looked around, his eyes adjusting to the lighting. Most of the patrons wore either business suits or the black-jeans-and-sweater uniforms of the Eurotrendies. He couldn't believe the locals hadn't burned the place to the ground yet.

Kevin was in the back, in an area of large, circular booths upholstered in the same velvet zebra trash that hung from the curtain rods. He was half reclined with two women and two of his 'crew'. The two women were attractive, at least, but even that couldn't temper Eamonn's annoyance. Kevin was wearing black leather pants and a loose-fitting white sweater that showed off his muscles. He sat up straight when he saw his father.

'We need to talk,' Eamonn said coldly.

Everyone at the table looked uncomfortable. 'Do you wanna sit?' Kevin asked.

Eamonn shook his head. 'I want you to stand.'

Everyone at the table looked at Kevin. He was pinned in at the booth by two people on either side of him. 'You heard him,' he barked at the others. 'Let me out.' All four moved instantly, and Kevin had the option of moving in either direction. He chose the route that took him furthest from his father. 'I'll be back,' he said to the others once he was out, and they all slid back in.

Eamonn took a few steps away from the table, making sure that no one was nearby to eavesdrop. 'You come here often?' he asked once his son had joined him. The tone in his voice made clear his judgment.

'Sometimes,' his son admitted. 'Why? What's wrong with it?'

'There's fuckin' zebras on the seats,' Eamonn said, shaking his head. 'You gotta ask me what's wrong with it?'

'What?' Kevin asked. 'The owner says zebra's the new black.'

Eamonn raised his hand, as if to hit his son, and Kevin flinched. The reaction was enough to make Eamonn feel better for a moment. 'You're a fucking idiot,' he said.

'Because I like this place?' Kevin asked.

'No, that's just tonight's confirmation.'

'What, then?'

'I got you a lawyer,' Eamonn said. 'One of the best. And you don't even use him? You give him attitude? I don't need this shite, you understand, boy?'

Kevin folded his arms defiantly. 'He wants me to take a plea that would put me in jail,' he said. 'I'm not going in.'

Eamonn McDougal sighed heavily. 'You really are stupid, boy. You think I'd let you go to jail?' He shook his head. 'It might be the best thing for you – show you what real life is – but you wouldn't survive. I know that.'

'But that's what the lawyer said,' the son protested.

'Shut the fuck up, and do as I say. The lawyer isn't going to let you go to jail, no matter what he tells you right now, you understand? He's gonna get you off. Period.'

'That's not what he told me.'

'Yeah, well, he'll change his mind.'

'How do you know?'

'Because I can be very persuasive.' He looked at the outfit his son was wearing and shook his head. He grabbed him by the shoulders and pulled him in close so that he could look into his eyes. They were red and watery, and they betrayed his recreational inclinations. If they hadn't been in public, Eamonn probably would have thrown his son through the wall. 'Get off the shit,' he growled.

'I don't understand,' Kevin said. 'What shit?'

Eamonn squeezed his son's shoulders with his massive hands until he grunted in pain. 'I'm deadly serious, boy,' he said. 'It's time for you to get right, you understand? If it doesn't happen now, it won't happen at all, and I'm not going to watch you put your mother through that. If it comes to that, I'll make it quick and painless, for you and for her, you understand? I shit you not.' He squeezed the boy's shoulders even harder. 'You understand?'

'Aaargh!' Kevin grunted, writhing out of his father's grip. 'Okay,' he protested. 'Okay.'

'Now, you get your ass back to the lawyer, and you tell him you're in. Tomorrow. You understand?'

'Yeah, okay.' Kevin rubbed his shoulders.

Eamonn nodded, turned on his heels and walked to the front door. As he passed the bar, he looked at the bartender. He was wearing tight-fitting black pants, a white T-shirt two sizes too small, and a black leather vest. He had three earrings in both earlobes. 'Tell your boss to make sure his insurance is paid up,' Eamonn said. The bartender frowned in confusion. He started to say something, but Eamonn held his hand up. He was in no mood. 'Just tell him.' With that, he pushed the door open and headed back out to his waiting car and driver.

Long sat in his car, scribbling notes into the small pad he kept with him. There wasn't a lot to write, but he worked hard to cram as much detail as he could onto the tiny pages. The key to his work was in following the details, keeping track of them, herding them into pad-docks to let them feed and interact and mate. Every once in a while, if you let yourself get to really know the details, you saw the patterns you were looking for, the inconsistencies that were the hallmarks of guilt.

So far, he'd seen none of those hallmarks in his brief conversation with Scott Finn. The man had been nervous, but the nervousness seemed born of the sheer scale of Long's revelation to him. Long could discern no prevarication. The only aspect of the lawyer's life that seemed out of place was the girl. Long would look into her situation, but his hunch was that it would lead nowhere.

When he was done scribbling in his notebook, he slid it back into the breast pocket of his raincoat. He reached down and felt for the bottle under the car seat. It was there, but when he brought it up to his lips, it was empty. He shook his head. It was a bad sign – he had no recollection of finishing it.

Finn was still sitting on the sofa, staring at the wall. 'You gonna stay like that for the rest of the night?' Sally asked.

He turned and looked at her. She was standing in the doorway wearing an over-sized T-shirt and leggings. She looked at him the way an oncologist might examine a patient in remission, searching warily for any sign of disease – some indication that the patient might con-vulse at any moment. 'You were listening,' Finn said.

'Yeah,' she replied without hesitation. 'I was.'

'So you heard.' He didn't like the fact that she'd been eavesdropping. His childhood abandonment was a window into his psyche he'd have preferred she hadn't looked through.

'That was the basic point of listening,' she pointed out. Finn closed his eyes and tilted his head back, but said nothing. He was exhausted. 'You didn't even know her,' Sally said. 'And from the way everything looks, she didn't want to know you. I say good riddance.'

Finn opened his eyes and looked at her. 'Is that what you'd say if it was your mother?'

'My mother?' Sally looked down, and for a moment Finn was sorry he'd asked the question. 'I knew my mother, so I could say a lot worse than that about her.'

'Would you?' Finn asked. 'Say worse?'

Her expression was serious. 'No. I probably wouldn't. My mother's such a fuckup, I'm not even really mad at her anymore, I don't think. We've all got our problems; she's got hers. The world turns. At least your mother sounds normal.'

'A normal mother who gives up her child?' Finn said. 'Doesn't seem possible to me.' He rubbed his forehead with the palm of his hand. 'You should go to bed,' he said. 'It's a school night.'

'What'd you say in the letter?' she asked. She had a way of asking the most personal questions directly and somehow making them sound reasonable. Finn admired that skill except when she directed it at him.

'I don't even remember,' Finn lied.

'Yes, you do.' He had to admit she was smart, and she could read people. She didn't take people at their word. It was probably one of the things that had kept her alive. 'What'd you say?'

Finn leaned forward. 'I told her she was going to hell,' he said. 'I told her about every bad thing I could remember that happened to me when I was growing up, and I blamed it all on her. I told her about the beatings; about the fights; about the gangs I used to run with and the terrible things I used to do.' He stood up and walked to the same window where Long had stood, taking in the view from the top of the hill. It was impressive. Sometimes it amazed him how far he'd come. 'I told her I hoped whatever she'd gone through was at least as bad, and that whatever was going to happen to her in hell would be even worse still.'

'Huh,' Sally said. He could feel her looking at him. 'So . . . not exactly a Hallmark card?'

He snorted an involuntary laugh. Thank God she had a sense of humor. 'Not quite,' he said. 'I called her every awful name I could think of. I was immature.'

'How old were you?'

'I was in law school at the time, and still dealing with some of the things I had to do to pull myself out of the street life. I wasn't entirely happy back then.'

'How about now? You happy now?' Looking at her, Finn could tell it was an honest question. He wasn't sure how to answer it honestly.

'I'm better now,' he said. That much, at least, was true.

'Law school,' she said, marveling. 'Isn't that, like, in your twenties?'

'Yeah,' he said. 'About there.'

She shook her head incredulously. 'You mean my childhood is gonna keep me fucked up for another decade?'

He smiled sadly. 'If you're lucky. If you're like the rest of us, it'll mess with you a lot longer than that.' He walked back over to the couch and sat down. He frowned at her as he spoke. 'You shouldn't have to deal with all of this. I'll be fine, you don't need to worry.'

'I'm not worried,' she said. 'I'd just like to help.'

'How?'

She shrugged. 'How about a yogurt?'

'You think that'll help?'

'It's got active cultures. Couldn't hurt.'

Finn shrugged. 'I'll give it a shot.'

She brought over two containers with two spoons, handed one of each to him. She pulled the tin foil top off hers, licked it, and began stirring the contents with the spoon, bringing the fruit to the surface. 'You ever find out anything about your father?'

'Nope.'

Finn watched her as she stirred her yogurt, her eyebrows crossed in thought like dueling swords. She was looking intently at her yogurt, and she didn't look up when she spoke next. 'This isn't over for you.' It wasn't a question, it was an observation.

'What isn't over?' he asked. It was foolish; they both knew what she was talking about. He kept forgetting that she'd crammed a lifetime of tragedy into her sixteen years. It gave her better insight than most people in their sixties.

'Your mother. Her murder,' she said. 'You're not gonna let it drop.'

'You don't need to worry about it,' Finn said.

'Like I said, I'm not worried; I want to help. But I also want to know why.'

Finn considered the question for a moment, and realized he had no good answer. 'She was my mother,' he said at last. 'I never knew who she was. I never knew where I came from.'

'So what?' she asked. 'Who cares who your parents were or where you came from? The only thing that matters is where you are now. Look at my parents: a murdered thief for a father, and a crack whore for a mother. If people think I'm gonna let them define who I am, they got another goddamned think coming.'

Finn believed her. 'Not knowing is different. I've lived my entire life with this question mark, and now there's a chance I can get some answers.'

'What if they aren't the answers you're looking for?'

'I'd still rather know,' he said. 'Besides, you heard the detective. No one's gonna lift a finger to find her murderer. He was right, I know how this works; they'll do some poking around, but unless something obvious pops up, this case will die before the weekend. She was my mother. I'm going to find out what happened.'

Sally scraped the last of the yogurt from the bottom of the container and licked the spoon clean. 'I understand,' she said.

He laughed ruefully. 'That makes one of us.'

'It's pretty simple,' she said. 'You're a decent guy. You think it's the right thing to do. End of story.'

He shook his head. 'I'm not a decent guy,' he said.

She stood up and walked over to the kitchen and threw her yogurt cup into the trash. 'Yeah, you are,' she said. 'Doesn't mean you're perfect. But a bad guy wouldn't take care of a pain-in-the-ass daughter of a dead client just because it's the right thing to do.' He looked up, but she was already headed out of the room, back toward the hallway. 'I'll see you in the morning,' she called back over her shoulder.

'Yeah,' Finn called. 'See you in the morning.'

Coale sat in the dark on the street outside the lawyer's apartment. He'd watched Long pull away after taking a pull from the empty bottle. That, at least, was a good sign. The more the detective unraveled, the less dangerous he became. Coale knew from his contacts that Long was barely hanging on in the department. If they discovered he was drinking, the BPD would have the legitimate grounds they needed to dismiss him. It was what everyone wanted.

It would solve some of Coale's problems, too. Drunk or not, Long had put Elizabeth Connor together with the lawyer. It looked as though his skills as an investigator were not as impaired as Coale might have hoped.

He frowned. The lawyer added additional challenges to the equation. He knew about Scott T. Finn, Esquire. The lawyer had a colorful past. He had a reputation for being stubborn. That wasn't what Coale needed at the moment.

He reached for his phone and dialed the number. Eamonn McDougal picked up on the second ring. 'It's me,' Coale said. 'I'm in Charlestown. Long just left the lawyer's apartment.'

'That was fast,' McDougal said. 'Not surprising, though. I can use it to my advantage.'

'How?' Coale asked.

'It's not your concern.'

'You hired me to do a job,' he said. 'Everything is my concern.'

'Just stick with Finn. Let me know what he does.'

Coale bristled. 'I don't take orders. If you don't like it, hire someone else.'

'You know that's not an option,' McDougal said. 'I'll double your rate.'

Coale considered the offer. 'I'll keep an eye on the lawyer,' he said. Realistically he didn't have a choice.

He closed his phone, opened it again. He had another call to make.

CHAPTER NINE

Long stared at the paperwork on his desk, trying to rub the pain between his eyes away with his thumb and index finger. It wasn't working. If anything, the pain seemed to grow and spread out from the bridge of his nose to the rest of his skull like an oil spill. Mornings were the worst, he was finding.

Elizabeth Connor's life was spread out before him. Bank records, utility bills, phone records, credit reports. Even when the interview notes from her neighbors and co-workers were added, it painted a thin, watery picture. From all appearances, the woman had lived on the edge, constantly in debt and falling further behind. She worked at a place called Rescue Finance, which was little more than a legal loan-sharking business that advanced cash on future paychecks for those in trouble at a twenty-one percent interest rate. Probably a money laundering racket for the mob, as well. It was a three-person office operation, the actual ownership of which was obscured in a corporate gopher warren. Her fellow workers seemed to know little about her; they described her as distant. Her neighbors described her as unpleasant. No one described her as a friend.

Digging through the woman's life depressed Long. It all seemed too familiar. Few would mourn the passing of Elizabeth Conner, and it struck Long that that probably put her in a solid majority of the population. Nobody really cared about anyone else in the end. You were born alone, and you died alone. At least that was how Long saw it through the lens of Elizabeth Connor's existence. All she'd left behind was a broken trail of paperwork.

He glanced at the yellowed sketch artist's drawing on the corner of his desk. He'd taken it from the bulletin board downstairs earlier in the morning. It had been hanging there for years, and he had passed by it every day without taking conscious note of it. And yet it must have penetrated his brain at some level, because there on the sheet was the image of a middle-aged man with gray hair pulled back from his forehead, revealing a light v-shaped scar. The man's eyes were bright, and his expression in the image was cold. It was probably a coincidence, but the man in the picture looked exactly like the man he'd seen in the crowd outside Elizabeth Connor's apartment.

'That the Mass Avenue job?' a voice behind him asked.

Long looked up. Captain Townsend was looking over his shoulder. He was short enough that he had to stretch his spine to see the desk. His interest seemed feigned. 'Yeah,' Long said. 'Not much, is it?'

'Anything worth following up on?'

Long shook his head. 'Probably not. Lab came back – no fingerprints, not even any from the murdered woman. Departed had a kid. Gave him up for adoption. He's a lawyer now in Charlestown. I went over there last night to check him out, but I don't think there's anything to it. He said he didn't know who his mother was, and I believe him. He wrote an angry letter back in the nineties, but there's no indication she ever responded. I can't find anything that ties them together other than the birth itself.'

'Nothing else?'

'Not really. There's a bar nearby where she worked, she used to go there a lot. Not the happy-go-lucky drinking type. More hardcore. Word is she had a little bit of a rep when she was younger, but that was a long time ago.'

'Explains how she ended up with a kid.'

'It does,' Long agreed. 'I've run her records and I haven't come up with anything solid to suggest she was a pro, but it wouldn't surprise me if she was a hell of an amateur for a while when she was young. There are a few phone numbers that I have to chase down, but I don't expect to find much. Chances are it's just a random robbery.'

'What's with the picture?' Townsend asked, looking at the sketch.

'Probably nothing,' Long replied. 'When I was outside Connor's apartment the other day I saw a man in the crowd who looked like this guy. Same hair, same eyes, same scar. I pulled this off the board this morning just to look at it more closely.'

The captain picked up the picture, laughed in a short, clipped grunt. 'He's not real,' he said. 'He's a ghost.'

'A ghost?'

'That's what we used to call him. This is a description given by a witness to four murders back in the nineties, before you were on the force. Ugly business, after the Winter Hill gang collapsed, and people were trying to fill the vacuum. There was a group run out of New York that was trying to move in. Some of the more established local players decided to send a clear message, so four guys from the New York contingent were targeted. They were picked off one by one in some of the grimmest murders we'd seen around here in a long time. The New York guys stayed away after that.'

'And this guy was behind it?'

'It was never clear. A snitch named Toby Shilow claimed he'd seen the guy who did it. He's the one who gave us the description. Said the guy was a freelancer hired by some of Whitey Bulger's crew. To hear Toby tell it, he was the coldest killer anyone had ever seen. The kind of a guy no one would fuck with. He did piecework as a cleaner and a button pusher. We looked hard into it, though, and we came up with nothing.'

'You think the snitch was trying to throw you off the real killers?'

'That's what we figured,' Townsend said. 'We'll never know for sure, though. A couple weeks later we found Toby in a suitcase. He'd been cut into about ten pieces. His eyes and tongue were missing. Doc was pretty sure they'd been cut out before Toby was killed.'

'Nasty.'

'Yeah, it was. We went back to looking for this guy, but we never found anything. If he ever existed, he disappeared. We started calling him the Ghost. For a while, whenever we came across a murder we couldn't solve, we blamed it on the Ghost.'

'Sounds melodramatic.'

'It was. He's more of a myth than an actual suspect in anything. Like Keyser Söze or Bigfoot. We only keep the picture up for our own amusement.'

'Well, like I said, it's probably nothing. Just my imagination.' Long's neck was starting to ache from looking behind him, so he turned back to his desk. He expected Townsend to leave, but it didn't happen. He turned around again. 'Something else, Captain?'

'Yeah,' Townsend said. He wouldn't meet Long's eyes. 'In my office.'

Long looked down at the papers strewn across his desk. There was a flask in the drawer; he was tempted to pull it out and have a drink. He could feel his arm reach in that direction, but reconsidered. No point in making matters worse. Not yet, at least. 'Sure, Captain,' Long replied. He'd known this meeting was coming at some point.

Tom Kozlowski listened as Finn described his meeting with Long from the night before. When Finn finished, Kozlowski sat back and thought for a moment.

'Did he tell you you're a suspect?' he asked.

Finn shook his head. 'No. But he wasn't particularly subtle when he said that I'm pretty much the only person they're following up with. Apparently the woman didn't have very many people in her life. And the letter I wrote . . .' Finn didn't finish the thought.

'Not good, I take it?'

'It explains the visit,' Finn said. 'I wasn't in the most loving frame of mind when I wrote it.'

'Did you make any actual threats in it?' Kozlowski asked. He was working the issues like a cop. 'Did you say anything that would suggest that if you found her, you'd do her harm?'

'Not directly,' Finn said. 'I told her I thought she was going to hell, and I said I hoped really bad things happened to her, but I never made any direct threats.'

'That's good, at least,' Kozlowski said. He stretched his feet out from his body, looked at his toes. 'In the end, you didn't have anything to do with her death; you didn't even know her, so you've got nothing to worry about.'

'Yeah, you're probably right,' Finn said.

'But you're not going to leave it alone, are you?'

'No,' Finn replied. 'I'm not.'

Kozlowski sat forward. 'No, I didn't figure you would.'

'Would you?'

He shook his head. 'Doesn't matter one way or another what I would do. She wasn't my mother, she was yours.'

'I still want your advice.'

'Bullshit,' Kozlowski said. 'You don't want my advice, you want my help. You don't listen to my advice when I give it to you.'

'I listen to it,' Finn corrected. 'I just don't always follow it.'

'Ever. You don't *ever* follow it.' Kozlowski let his head hang down between his knees. 'I swear to God, keeping your ass safe is becoming a full-time goddamned job.'

'Yeah, but it pays okay.' Finn leaned forward and looked at Kozlowski. 'You'll help me, right?'

'Have I got a choice?'

*

Long sat in Townsend's office. The captain was uncomfortable; most people were around Long these days. He wondered whether that would ever change.

Townsend shifted in his chair, a big black leather beast that swallowed him up, making him look even smaller against the huge dark backdrop.

'So,' Townsend began. He stopped, not seeming to know in which direction to take the conversation. 'We're still trying to figure out who to partner you with,' he said. 'It may take a little while.'

'That's not surprising.'

'No,' Townsend said. 'It's not.' He cleared his throat and shifted in the giant chair. 'I want to be clear with you here, Long. You've been one of the best detectives we've had on the squad. Your record speaks for itself. Three months ago, I would have pegged you as being a guy who was gonna sit in this chair someday.'

'Not anymore,' Long said with a sardonic smile.

Townsend frowned at Long's attitude. 'No, not anymore. The investigation into Cullen's shooting didn't find any wrongdoing. That's not the same as finding you didn't do anything wrong. You get what I'm saying?'

'Yeah,' Long said. 'You're saying people still think I was dirty. So much for the presumption of innocence.'

'Don't act so self-righteous. You're a cop. A jury gives a perp a pass, you generally assume he's innocent?'

'No,' Long admitted.

'No, of course not. Like everyone else, you assume he got off because someone fucked up.' Townsend leaned back in his chair and scratched his crotch. 'You sure this is still the job for you?'

'It's the only job I know how to do,' Long said. 'It's all I'm good at.'

'How about Internal Affairs, then? They could always use good people. I could put in a good word for you.'

'They think I'm dirty, too.'

'They think everyone's dirty, who the fuck cares? Besides, they're the ones who cleared you in the investigation. Why not let them eat their own shit?'

'Thanks,' Long said.

'You know what I mean,' Townsend sighed. 'Listen, I like you; I brought you in. But I also know how shitty your life is gonna be here now.'

'I want to chase criminals, not cops,' Long said quietly.

'That's not what you told IAD, was it though?'

Long pursed his lips tightly before he answered. 'That wasn't my decision. I didn't have a choice.'

'Maybe not,' Townsend admitted. 'But this job is about trust. The other cops in this department need to be able to trust you on the street. Maybe it's not your fault, but they've lost that trust in you. It's gonna make it hard to do your job.'

'I'll be fine,' Long said. 'I can still do the job.'

'Yeah,' Townsend said. 'I'm guessing you can. But is it worth it?' He stood up and paced behind the desk. 'Even if you can still do the job, there are things that could get you kicked off the force if you're not careful.'

'Like what?' Long demanded.

'Like I'm hearing some rumors about you and the bottle. Not the good kind.'

Long could feel his face darken. 'Who're you hearing these rumors from?'

'Does it matter?'

'To me, it does.'

Townsend shook his head. 'Not to me. The only thing I care about is whether they're true.' He came around the front of the desk and sat on the edge, leaning in toward Long. 'So, I gotta ask: Are they true?'

Long stood up. 'You think anything I do is interfering with the job, you put me on notice,' he said. 'I don't answer to rumors.'

'Fair enough,' Townsend said. He walked back and sat in the giant chair again. 'Think about it, though. If you need to take some time off, get yourself straight, let me know. I can make it happen.'

'I just got back from taking time off,' Long said.

'Did you do anything good?'

'I watched my father die.'

Townsend looked down at his hands. 'I heard,' he said. 'Sorry. Can't catch a break right now, can you?'

'Lucky for me I'm a glass-half-full kind of a guy.'

Townsend looked up and locked eyes with Long, and Long had the feeling he was searching for something. Answers, probably. Long knew the captain wouldn't find any, though, because there were none to be found. 'I'm on your side here, Long. But I can't protect you if you screw up now. People are looking to clear you out, even if it's only so they don't have to look at you anymore, you understand?' Long didn't respond. He didn't need to; they both understood. 'Think about IAD, it may be better than here for you now. Even a cushy job on the outside doing private security work; I've got connections out there – you say the word, I could hook you up.'

'I'm not a civilian,' Long said. 'You know that.'

'Yeah, I know that,' Townsend said. 'But everybody here is wondering whether you're still a cop?'

Finn was working on a motion to exclude a confession made by one of his clients when Kevin McDougal walked into the office. He seemed less full of bravado. The tattoos on his neck were just as pronounced, and he wore the same angry scowl, but now it seemed an empty threat.

Finn stared at him from his desk, waiting for McDougal to speak.

McDougal stared back. The standoff might have continued all day had Lissa not decided to break the impasse.

'Can I help you?' she asked from behind her desk.

McDougal had been so focused on Finn he hadn't noticed her, and her voice took him by surprise. 'Uh,' he said.

'I'm guessing you're Kevin McDougal,' she said, rising out of her chair. She came from behind her desk. 'I'm Lissa Krantz, I work with Mr Finn.'

He shook her hand and let himself be guided over to the chair in front of Finn's desk. 'I'm sure you two have a lot to talk about,' Lissa said. 'I'll be right over at my desk if either of you needs anything.'

She walked away, and Finn figured he'd secured enough of a victory to be gracious. He acknowledged McDougal with a nod. 'I take it you've changed your mind.'

'I'm here, ain't I?'

'Yeah, you are,' Finn said. 'You understand, we do this my way, right? You listen to what I say, and you do what I tell you to do. No more hanging out with the moron twins from the bar. No more drinking, particularly not in public. No drugs, and no pulling any jobs. Once this is behind you, you can do whatever you want, but until then, you're in voluntary lockdown.'

McDougal looked away.

'I'm serious, Kevin,' Finn said. 'I told your father I'd deal with this for you, but only if you play by my rules. If this thing gets fucked up, I don't want my name attached to it. You understand?'

'Yeah,' McDougal muttered.

'Good,' Finn said. 'Lissa will make contact with the DA's office to see what we can get done. You drive your 7-Series home and stay put in your duplex; it's the easiest way to stay out of trouble.'

McDougal stood and walked to the door.

'Kevin?' Finn said.

The young man turned. 'Yeah?'

'I'm serious. I don't care how much business your father brings me, I'm not trading my reputation for you no matter what it costs me.'

McDougal just stared at Finn. After a moment, an evil slit of a smile split his lips. 'You have no fuckin' idea who my father really is, do you?' he asked.

'I know exactly who he is. But if you screw me, I'll still dump your ass so fast it'll make your head spin, and you'll spend the next ten down in Walpole,' Finn said. 'Leave your phone number with Lissa so we have some way of getting in touch with you. We'll keep you informed.'

CHAPTER TEN

'You're kidding me,' Finn said.

'I'm not,' Kozlowski confirmed. 'That's the word from inside the department.'

'Long killed his partner? Holy crap.' Finn had no idea what else to say.

'That's putting it mildly. It's safe to say Long's not the darling of the force anymore.' They were headed toward Elizabeth Connor's apartment. Finn was driving his MG with the top up. His huge partner, who hated the tiny vehicle, gripped the dashboard in front of him, as if having a firm hold would save him in the event of an accident.

'How'd it happen?' Finn asked.

Kozlowski shook his head. 'Everybody I know clammed up when I tried to get into details. It was like bad juju or something.'

'You didn't get anything? You're an ex-cop, for Christ's sake, how could you not get any information?'

'Yeah, I'm an ex-cop,' Kozlowski agreed. As Finn pulled around the corner from Massachusetts Avenue onto Melnea Cass Boulevard, he could see Kozlowski's grip on the dashboard tighten. 'Sometimes people focus on the *ex*.'

'What good are you, then?' Finn asked.

'Not much on this, apparently. You wanna fire me, you go right ahead,' Kozlowski replied.

'I can't,' Finn said. 'I cut you out, and I lose Lissa. Can't risk it.'

'Then shut up.'

Finn pulled into a parking space across the street from the apartment building, shut the engine off, reached over and pulled up the emergency brake. The loud clacking seemed to startle Kozlowski, and Finn was afraid he was going to put his enormous fingers through the dash. 'We're here,' he said. 'You can let go now.'

'You make enough goddamned money to get a decent car,' Kozlowski grumbled.

'I'll get a decent car when you get a decent suit.'

Police tape hung from the doorknob, but it no longer barred the door. It was dark on the landing at the top of the stairs, and Finn felt like he was in the middle of a nightmare. 'What do you think?' he asked Kozlowski.

Kozlowski shrugged. 'I think it's ambiguous,' he said. He put on leather gloves. 'Let me check something.' He reached out and tried the knob, which refused to turn. He gripped it and turned harder; Finn heard a loud crack as the lock's internal workings shattered. The doorknob turned with a grinding sound. 'It's not locked,' Kozlowski said. 'Must be okay.' He gave a push.

The door swung open. Finn waited, but nothing happened. Kozlowski took a step back and swung his arm forward, inviting Finn to lead the way into the apartment. Finn hesitated. 'You really want to look into this, we gotta start here,' Kozlowski said.

Finn nodded and stepped into the apartment. Other than the mess, there was nothing remarkable about the place. There was gray fingerprint powder smudged on most of the surfaces, and a dark stain on the floor where Elizabeth Connor had bled out, but other than that it looked like thousands of other apartments in Boston. It was one-bedroom with just enough room to live. An old television offered the only apparent escape from the monotony of an overlooked life. A chair was pulled up close to the screen with a cheap table in front of it, where most meals were probably eaten alone. Everything about the place depressed Finn.

He walked around, looking for something – anything – that might give him some insight into the woman who'd brought him into the world. There was nothing, though. No pictures. No mementos. Kozlowski moved around the apartment efficiently, poking into the closets and cupboards. After several minutes, he looked up at Finn. 'We need to go,' he said.

'There's got to be something,' Finn replied.

'If so, I don't see it. Cops must have had a dozen men search the place. Anything of importance may be gone.'

Finn scanned the apartment again. 'There's nothing here that tells me anything about her. Nothing personal. How is that possible?'

Kozlowski shrugged. 'This is how some people live. Work, TV dinners, nothing much else. It's how I lived before Lissa.'

'So why was she murdered?' Finn asked.

'Maybe she was just in the wrong place at the wrong time. Crackheads don't care who they steal from.'

'Maybe,' Finn said.

'If we stay here much longer, the cops will show up and we'll have some 'splaining to do,' Kozlowski said.

Finn nodded and the two of them walked out, closing the door behind them. As they turned, the door to 2B creaked open. An eye peered at them. 'Whachu doin' here?' a voice said, muffled by the door.

'I'm Elizabeth Connor's son,' Finn said. 'I was just looking around.'

The eye frowned. 'I called the cops,' the voice said.

Finn looked at Kozlowski, who gave a reassuring nod. 'Detective Long?' Finn asked. 'He came to see me last night, to tell me about my mother's murder.'

The crack widened and Finn could see an ancient black man,

nattily dressed, well coiffed, looking back at them. 'You know Detective Long?'

Finn nodded. 'Like I said, I'm Elizabeth Connor's son.'

The man made a face. 'Didn't know she had a son,' he said. He looked more closely. 'I see it now. You must have some of your father in you, too, though.'

'I wouldn't know,' Finn said. 'I was adopted.' The man took that in, and said nothing. 'What was she like?' Finn asked after a moment.

'Your mother?'

'You lived next door. You must have known her.'

The old man leaned against the door frame. 'She was an unhappy person,' he said. 'That's the nice way to put it. Others might not be so generous, even to her son, you know?'

'Not really,' Finn said. 'Tell me.'

The man looked uncomfortable. 'She wasn't a good person,' he said, looking at the floor. 'You want me to tell you the truth, I'll tell. It's up to you.'

'I want to know,' Finn said.

'She moved in here probably five years ago. When I first met her, I thought she was a racist. Mean as a snake to me, that one was. Treated me like I was somethin' to be scraped off her shoe. Took me a while to understand it wasn't because I was black, it was because I was human. She was a cruel, bad person. That's as far I'm willin' to go. She's dead, after all, an' I don't like talkin' ill of the dead any more than I have.'

Finn nodded. 'I appreciate that,' he said.

'I'm sorry about your mama,' the man said.

'I never knew her.'

'Still, she was your mama. That counts for somethin', I guess.' The old man started back into his apartment. He paused, and turned back to them. 'I wasn't lyin'; I really did call the cops. They'll be downstairs I 'spect by the time you get out there.'

'It's okay,' Finn said. 'I really am her son.'

The man shrugged like it wasn't any of his business. 'If that's true, you make sure you find your own place in this world. Don't go makin' all her mistakes over again.'

Long was just pulling up in front of the townhouse when Finn and Kozlowski walked out the front door. He seemed agitated as he got out of his car. 'What are you doing here, Mr Finn?' he demanded.

Finn and Kozlowski walked down the stoop. 'Detective Long,' Finn nodded. 'Do you know Tom Kozlowski, former detective out of District D4?'

'I remember him,' Long said. Kozlowski put his hand out, but Long kept his attention focused on Finn. 'I still want to know what the hell you're doing here. This is a murder investigation, and you crossed a police line.'

'There was no tape across the door,' Finn said. 'It was lying on the floor. Looked like the investigation was over.'

'Bullshit,' Long said. 'There was tape on the door, and the door was locked.'

'All I did was turn the knob,' Kozlowski said. 'Maybe the lock was old. There was no padlock, no chains. We figured it wasn't a problem to look around; Mr Finn is next of kin, far as we know, right?'

Long finally looked at Kozlowski. 'You figured it wouldn't be a problem,' he repeated. 'After twenty-five years on the force, you didn't see a problem with contaminating a crime scene? You didn't see any problem with interfering with a police investigation?'

'Didn't seem like there was much of an investigation to interfere with,' Kozlowski said. There was a challenge in the tone.

Long took a step toward Kozlowski. 'You don't have a badge anymore. I could take you both in, charge you with obstruction.'

'Charges would never stick,' Finn pointed out.

'Maybe not,' Long said. 'But it'd be a hell of a pain in your ass, and it would keep you out of my hair for a while.'

The three men stared at each other for a moment. Finally, Finn said, 'We didn't touch anything. We just wanted to see the place. She was my mother.'

'I understand that,' Long said. 'But I have an investigation to run, and I can't have you interfering. I'll let you know what we find when and if it's appropriate, but you're just gonna have to stay patient until then. And you're gonna have to stay out of the way. You understand what I'm saying?'

Finn looked at Kozlowski. Neither of them said anything.

'I'm dead serious,' Long said. 'I'll overlook it this one time. But if you fuck with me, I'll run you both in. I'll mess with your lives like you won't believe. You got that?'

'Yeah,' Finn said. 'We got that.'

'And you'll drop this?'

Finn held his hand up. 'Promise,' he said. 'We'll drop this.'

Long's eyes narrowed and he shook his head as he climbed back into his car. 'I'm holding you to that,' he said as he pulled out.

Kozlowski and Finn watched his car drive away. 'You had your fingers crossed, right?' Kozlowski asked.

'Toes, too,' Finn replied. 'Where to next?'

'From what I've been able to dig up, there were only two other places where she spent any time,' Kozlowski said. 'The place where she worked and the place where she drank.'

'Either one close by?'

Kozlowski nodded. 'Both. She worked at a little place that rips people off a few blocks up around the corner. She drank at a dive a couple blocks from there.'

Finn looked at his watch. It was ten forty-five. 'Probably too early for people to be drinking,' he said.

'Not too early at this place, from what I remember,' Kozlowski said. 'This used to be my beat.'

'Let's start at the place where she worked anyway,' Finn said. 'If I start drinking now, I might not stop.'

CHAPTER ELEVEN

Long was back at the station house within five minutes. As he pulled up the street, looking at the cops milling about, he considered driving past and leaving it all behind him. A part of him no longer believed in the mission. He was just going through the motions now; he'd lost the passion and the belief that what he was doing was right.

He didn't drive by, of course. It wasn't in him to abandon his duty. In many ways, that was the root of his problem.

As he pulled into a parking spot and got out of the car, he could feel those around the building go tense just from having him nearby. He was getting used to it. He was like the survivor of some horrible, socially unacceptable disease; people treated him with an odd combination of fear, revulsion and awe.

He walked up the steps, into the building, and down the hall to the detective bureau. There were two voicemail messages waiting for him. The first was from Human Resources. He'd failed to sign some insurance form upon returning to work, and the woman on the message was warning that the consequences could be dire. He deleted the message before he'd even heard the extension to call back.

The second was from an assistant in the technology department named Julie Racine. She was in her late twenties with long red hair and a naive attraction to those on the right side of the fight for justice. She and Long had been involved several months before. It'd been mainly physical and the duration had been short, but it hadn't ended badly. She'd dated cops before, and sensed when it was over. She broke it off before he had to, which allowed them to maintain some affection for each other. He hadn't talked to her since he'd returned from leave.

'Zach, it's Julie,' the message began. 'I should have called earlier, just to see how you were doing. I probably should have gotten in touch with you when you were out on leave, too, but I figured you'd want to be left alone.' Her voice was halting, searching for the right words.

'Anyway,' she continued. 'I just wanted to let you know how sorry I am. If you ever need . . .' her voice trailed off. 'Well, I'm here,' she finished. Long couldn't tell whether she was offering more than professional sympathy. Not that it mattered; it wasn't the right time to mess up someone else's life. He almost put the phone down, thinking she was done.

'I wasn't calling about that though,' the message continued. 'I pulled the request you submitted to have a couple of unlisted numbers off the Connor phone records run. I'm still trying to chase down one of the numbers – there's a strange block on it. I've never seen anything like it. The other one is interesting, though. I came down to give it to you myself, to see how you're doing, but you weren't there, so I left it on your desk. Call me if you want to.'

The line went dead. Long stared at the handset for a moment before putting it down. He suddenly couldn't remember why he'd let her get away.

He took a breath and let out a long sigh, turned to the report on the telephone records. It was short; Elizabeth Connor hadn't been particularly sociable. She placed few phone calls, and received fewer. There were a couple to her place of business, and a few to credit card companies – probably responding to debt collections, Long figured. Other than that, there were only two numbers that were called more than once, both unlisted.

Long flipped to the end of the report, and his eyes widened. The first unlisted number, which Elizabeth Connor had called five times in the month before her murder, was owned by the 355 Water Street Corporation. The company name meant nothing to Long, but Julie had written a note beside the entry: *Zach – did a quick check, 355 Water Street Corp. is owned by Joseph Slade.*

Joey Slade was a name that Long knew well. He'd grown up in Dorchester, the son of a loading dock union supervisor with ties to the local Irish mob. Joey had followed his father into the business, and had done very well for himself. There was little 'organization' left in Boston's organized crime. La Cosa Nostra's New England offshoots had been crippled in the 1980s, and Whitey Bulger's Winter Hill gang had collapsed when Whitey fled prosecution in 1994 after it was revealed that he had been an FBI informant for years. Joey Slade was one of the leaders in what remained of Boston's criminal underworld.

Long picked up the phone and dialed Julie's extension. She answered on the second ring. 'Racine,' she said.

'Julie, it's Zach,' he said.

He could hear the intake of breath on the other end of the line. 'Zach,' she said. Another deep breath. 'How are you doing?'

'I'm fine,' he said, more abruptly than intended. He could hear the pity in her voice, and he didn't want that from her. 'Is this right?'

She didn't say anything for a moment. 'Is what right?'

'The phone listing. The company is owned by Slade?'

'Oh, yeah.' She sounded reoriented. 'The phone records are right. I checked twice. Figured you'd find it interesting.'

'I appreciate it.' The pain between his eyes was back, but he fought it off. 'What possible connection could she have to Joey Slade?' The question wasn't addressed to anyone.

'I don't know,' Julie said. 'Not my area. I do research, you do investigation.'

'It doesn't make sense,' Long muttered.

'Well, if you think that's odd, you'll love this,' Julie said.

'What?'

'I mentioned I was having trouble getting information on a second number?'

'Yeah?'

'I found out why. The information is protected at the federal level.'

'What does that mean?' Long asked.

'Honestly, I don't really know,' she said. 'I've never come across anything like this before. All I know is that I had to submit an official request from BPD with an explanation to the Department of Homeland Security to get anywhere. They said they'd get back to me.'

'Weird,' Long said.

'It's more than weird,' Racine said. 'I highlighted the calls on the phone records for the mystery number and for the number for 355 Water Street Corp. Take a look.'

Long flipped to the front portion of the phone records report. The two numbers were highlighted – one in pink, one in yellow. It was hard to miss the pattern. 'So both numbers were called five times in the past month,' he said. 'The unlisted number first, then the number for 355 Water Street within minutes after hanging up.' The headache fought back and gained ground.

'That's what the records say,' Julie said.

'What's the connection?' Long muttered.

'Who knows? The best I can do is get you the information on the other number. After that, it's your job,' Julie replied. 'That's why we've got guys like you on the payroll.'

The thought didn't make Long feel any better. 'Right.'

'You're still on the payroll, right?' Long heard the pity in her voice again.

'Why? What have you heard?'

'Nothing,' she said. 'I just figured with everything . . . you know . . .' She ran out of things to say, and bailed.

'Thanks for this, it's helpful,' he said.

'It's my job.'

'Yeah,' Long agreed. 'Still, thanks.'

The silence that followed was awkward. 'Do you want to get dinner sometime?' she asked.

Pity again, he figured. 'Sometime, sure,' he replied. It wasn't a rejection, but it wasn't an acceptance either. He figured it would give him some leeway. 'Let me see how it goes down here on the job. I've got a bunch of stuff going on right now.'

'I understand,' she said. He couldn't tell whether it was relief in her voice, or disappointment. 'Give me a call if you think it would work.'

'I will.' He hung up. He hated lying.

The Asian woman behind the desk at Rescue Finance eyed Finn and Kozlowski with open hostility. 'I already talked to the police,' she said.

She stood behind the counter in a tiny storefront office no bigger than a Western Union. The posters on the grimy walls offered all sorts of financial services, from advances on paychecks to wire delivery services, to credit card applications. On each of the posters, pictures of smiling, scrubbed-faced people promised that every problem could be solved with ready cash: a college student receiving money from home for books; a father beaming at his daughter as she opened Christmas presents; a young man sitting without a care in the world, his leg up in a cast, his mind relieved of all worries by some sort of transaction from Rescue. The images formed a checkerboard of every ethnic group imaginable, enjoying the benefits of easy money borrowed, not earned.

The office was near the courthouse, so there was also a notice that certified checks for bail should be made out to the Roxbury District Court. There was no picture on the notice, and Finn marveled that no marketing genius had been able to spin joy into that particular financial service.

'We're not the police,' Finn said to the woman. He guessed she was Vietnamese; there was a significant population in the area.

'I talked to the police already,' she repeated. 'I'm not talking to anyone else. You go 'way now.' She was in her late fifties; first generation from the accent, though she had been in the country long enough to pick up all of the warmth of a native New Englander. 'You go 'way,' she repeated, making a face like Finn and Kozlowski reeked.

'I just want to ask you a couple of questions about Elizabeth Connor,' Finn said. 'Then we'll leave.'

'I'm working,' she replied. 'You leave now.'

Finn looked around the tiny storefront. There were no customers. It was the beginning of October, and Finn figured business on paycheck advances probably didn't pick up until the second or third week of the month. 'Please?' he said. 'I won't take up much of your time.'

'Why?' she demanded.

'She was my mother,' Finn said.

The woman's demeanor changed instantly. She suddenly viewed him with great sympathy and kindness. 'Oh,' she gasped, her hand grasping Finn's over the counter. 'I'm so sorry,' she said. 'She never said she had children.'

'I'm trying to find out what happened to her,' Finn said.

The woman behind the counter was nodding, and Finn felt for a moment as though she'd accepted him into some sort of circle of trust. 'You worked with her?' Finn asked.

'Only few times a month,' the woman replied. 'We have only one here most times. Sometimes, middle of the month and month end, we need two, but not very often. Three of us split time – two now.'

'But you knew her?'

The woman was clearly saddened by Finn's story, though her sadness did not appear to extend to Elizabeth Connor's absence itself. She gave a half shrug. 'Not really,' she said. 'We talked only a few times. I don't think she like me; she keep to herself mostly.'

'Did anyone else work with her more often?'

The woman shook her head. 'No one here knows her well. She not the type to let people know her.'

'What about your boss?' Finn asked.

She frowned. 'No boss.'

Finn raised his eyebrows and looked back at Kozlowski. 'What do you mean *no boss*? Someone owns the business.'

The woman shrugged her shoulders.

'Who hired you?' Finn asked.

'You go now,' the woman said quietly, her compassion gone. His membership in the Vietnamese version of the *Joy Luck Club* had been revoked.

'I need to know,' Finn said. 'Please.'

'You go now!' She yelled the words this time, loud enough to make Finn back up a few feet. 'Now! Now! Now!' she yelled. 'You go now or I call real police!'

Finn put his hands up and backed away. He passed Kozlowski, still standing near the door to the place, and walked out onto the street. Kozlowski stayed for a moment, looking at the woman.

'You go!' she yelled at him.

He nodded. 'Thanks for your help,' he said, following Finn out the door.

Long sat at his desk, staring at the phone records for several minutes. There was a part of him that was tempted to let it all go. After all, who really cared about the death of someone as unimportant as Elizabeth Connor? He didn't need the hassle.

And yet the case nagged at him. There were too many things about it that didn't make sense. For example, the forensics report indicated that no fingerprints were found anywhere in the room in Elizabeth Connor's apartment. Not even any of the victim's own fingerprints. That suggested that the place had been professionally cleaned. If

Elizabeth Connor was so unimportant, why had such effort been spent to wipe the place clean of any evidence? It certainly didn't feel like something a junkie would do. Was it possible that Joey Slade had something to do with the murder? And, who was the man with the scar Long had seen outside Connor's apartment? That was the question that bothered him most; he couldn't get the man's face out of his memory.

He picked up the ancient composite sketch from the bulletin board, looked at the face closely. The Ghost. That's what Townsend had called the man.

He opened the bottom drawer to his desk; the top of a flask bottle was leering at him. He looked at it twice, trying to decide. If he got caught drinking at the station house, his career would be over. It would be the excuse everyone was looking for to let him go. Still, a drink would take away the pain, and with the pain gone he might actually be able to think again.

He reached down, leaning with his entire body to obstruct the line of vision of anyone who might be nearby. As he was over the drawer, he pulled out the bottle and tucked it into his jacket pocket. He closed the drawer, stood, and headed to the men's room.

Once there, he stepped into a stall. Hanging his jacket on the back of the door, he reached in and took out the bottle. He unbuttoned his pants and dropped them to his ankles – he had to keep up the pretense, at least – and sat on the toilet.

He hadn't looked closely at the bottle before he put it in his jacket. It was rye – not his favorite. Also not a great choice for drinking on the job. Like most dark liquors, the rye would smell. He wished he had some vodka. Vodka would be better.

He twisted the top off the bottle, held it under his nose, inhaled deeply. He'd always enjoyed a drink, but he couldn't remember exactly when he'd crossed the line. It was recently, since he went out on leave. He raised the bottle to his lips, tipped it back. It felt good. He didn't need much more; just another taste would be fine. He could already feel the pain receding.

He put the top back on the bottle and stood up, tucking it back into his jacket pocket. After pulling up his pants and tucking his shirt in, he opened the door to the stall.

He half expected Captain Townsend to be waiting for him outside the stall, holding out his hand, ready to accept Long's badge and gun from him. It would serve Long right, he knew.

The captain wasn't there, though. The bathroom was empty.

He walked over to the sink and washed his hands, continuing his pantomime for an empty room. The water was cold, and he cupped his hands, lowered his head and splashed it on his face. When he looked up, he caught his reflection in the stainless steel mirror. He looked old and tired.

Taking a handful of paper towels, he dried his face. He looked back in the mirror and straightened his tie. The pain in his head was gone. Once it had subsided, the thoughts came quickly, and he knew what he was going to do.

CHAPTER TWELVE

Finn and Kozlowski sat at a tiny bar called High Life, around the corner from Rescue Finance. The uneven stools rocked back and forth unsteadily with every shift of their weight. It was lunchtime, and the place was half full. The menu was limited and cheap: two types of sandwiches – ham and cheese, and roast beef – neither of which could entice Finn or Kozlowski. From the look of those at the bar, the clientele was far more interested in the beverage service.

Four televisions mounted over the bar blinked out at the patrons. Three of them showed Keno, and many of those gathered around the bar were playing. The fourth television had the local midday news, the volume down low.

'You believe this fuckin' guy?' the man sitting next to Finn said. He looked to be in his forties, with a well fed build. A yellow construction helmet sat on the bar in front of him next to his beer. Finn looked up at the television. They were interviewing James Buchanan, one of two Massachusetts senators. 'He's talkin' 'bout fighting terrorism. You think this guy served in the fuckin' military?' Finn wasn't sure to whom the question was addressed, but after a moment the man turned to him. 'I served in the fuckin' military,' he said. 'First Gulf War. Two tours in Iraq in the second with the reserves.' The man nodded toward the television. 'This guy up here? I guaran-fuckin'-tee he's never seen action. You think someone pointed a gun at him at Hah-vahd? I don't fuckin' think so. Not with his family's money.'

'Probably not,' Finn agreed. He glanced over at Kozlowski, who shook his head.

'You like this guy?' the construction worker demanded. He looked Finn up and down, taking note of his suit. 'You like him?'

'I don't follow politics very closely,' Finn said. He was desperate to extricate himself from the conversation. The only person he wanted to talk to at the moment was the bartender. If anyone at the bar was likely to have information about Elizabeth Connor, it was the man who poured the drinks.

The construction worker snorted. He grabbed his beer and finished the last half of it in one swig. 'It's people like you make me wonder what the fuck I was fightin' for,' he said. He threw a few bills on the bar, stood up, and walked away.

Finn looked back at Kozlowski. 'Making friends, I see,' Kozlowski said.

'I love all mankind,' Finn replied.

'Mankind doesn't love you back,' Kozlowski pointed out.

The bartender moved toward them, eyeing them warily. 'Can I get you guys something?' he asked.

Finn and Kozlowski both ordered a beer. When the bartender put the glasses down in front of them, Finn said, 'I'm also looking for some information about a woman. Elizabeth Connor. You know who she is?'

The bartender cleared the used glasses from in front of the empty stools next to Finn and Kozlowski. He was thin and wiry, with veins bulging out along his wrists. His long brown hair was tied back into a ponytail, and he had a thick beard covering most of his face. He wore a T-shirt that hadn't been washed any time recently. He looked like a roadie for a seventies rock band. He glanced sideways at Kozlowski. 'You drinkin' on the job?'

Kozlowski shook his head. 'We're not cops.'

'I've seen you around before, a long time ago,' the bartender said. 'You're from the station house around the corner.'

'I used to be a cop,' Kozlowski admitted. 'Not for a few years.'

The bartender nodded. 'Okay, you say so. Who's this?'

'I'm Elizabeth Connor's son,' Finn said.

The bartender evaluated him. 'Name doesn't ring a bell,' he said.

Finn reached into his coat pocket and pulled out the Polaroid he'd taken from Long. He put it on the bar, facing the bartender, who looked at it briefly – too briefly not to have already known what he'd be looking at. 'She was my mother,' Finn repeated.

'I've seen her,' the bartender admitted. 'She's looked better. Didn't know her name.'

'Now you do.' Finn leveled a hard stare at the bartender.

'Yeah,' the bartender said without irony. 'I guess now I do.'

'What do you know about her?' Finn asked.

The bartender fidgeted uncomfortably. 'Not much,' he said with a shrug. 'She was in here, I don't know, two, maybe three times a week. Sometimes for lunch. The liquid variety, usually. Sometimes after work.'

'What else?' Finn demanded.

'She liked Scotch. Cheap stuff when she was alone. Single malt when someone else was buying.'

'Who else was buying?'

The bartender gave a cruel laugh. 'Not that many people recently,' he said. He recognized that neither Finn nor Kozlowski appreciated his humor, and he shifted in his stance. 'Hey, c'mon, guys,' he said. 'The bloom was off that rose a while ago, y'know?' He looked apologetically at Finn. 'Not that she wasn't once attractive, I'm sure. It's not the years anyways, it's the mileage. They say she had a lot of mileage on her.'

'Who says?' Finn asked.

'*They*,' the bartender responded. 'You know, people. Look, I know she was your mother, but she was bad news. I don't mean no disrespect, but it's true.'

Finn considered this for a moment. 'When's the last time she drank single malt?'

The bartender sighed as he searched his memory. 'A few weeks ago. She was in here, and a guy comes in. Older guy, nice suit.' He took a finger and bent his nose so that it was askew. 'Looked connected. Didn't look like a happy conversation.' He pointed over to a corner table. 'They sat over there, talked for a little while, and he calls over for the drink. Single malt. He paid, then he left.'

'You ever seen him before?'

The bartender nodded, looking around to see whether anyone was eavesdropping. 'Once or twice. Don't know his name.'

'What did he look like?'

'He looked like the kind of a guy who'd cut my nuts off and stuff 'em down my throat if he knew I was talkin' about his business.'

'Anyone else ever buy her drinks you can recall?'

The bartender's eyes darted toward a man at the end of the bar. Finn looked over and frowned. The guy looked to be in his eighties. He had disheveled white hair, and he was hunched over his ham and cheese. Two empty shot glasses were next to the paper plate, and his gnarled hand was wrapped around a twenty-ounce beer. As Finn looked at him, the old man snorted loudly, cleared his throat and swallowed hard.

'Him?' Finn asked.

'You didn't hear it from me,' the bartender said. He smiled greasily and made an obscene gesture with his fist. 'Years ago, from what I hear.'

'Seriously? Him?' Finn asked again.

'That's nine-fifty for the beers,' the bartender said.

Kozlowski took out a twenty and threw it on the bar.

'Thanks,' the bartender said. He didn't offer any change.

91

Finn looked at Kozlowski, then back at the fossil at the end of the bar.

Kozlowski shrugged. 'There's no accounting for taste,' he said.

The offices for 355 Water Street Corp. were located, appropriately enough, at 355 Water Street in Chelsea. Long crossed the bridge from downtown Boston in the off-blue unmarked sedan, ducked under the elevated highway, and followed a broken maze of streets down to the waterfront.

It was a strange place for corporate offices. The building was a long, one-story cinderblock structure near the harbor. There were no windows and a nondescript front door, which Long approached with caution. Part of the building was sided in corrugated steel, rusted at the edges, and there was a heavy lock and alarm system at the front door, neither of which was engaged at the moment. The surrounding area was deserted except for three men in coveralls working across the street, breaking down wooden palettes and feeding them into an oil drum fire. They looked up and watched Long as he approached the building.

Long reached into his jacket and unsnapped the restraint on his shoulder holster. He pushed the door open and stepped inside.

The reception area surprised him; it actually resembled an office. It wasn't opulent, but it could pass. The floor was covered with gray industrial carpeting, and the stains were reasonably contained. A small table with outdated magazines was surrounded by metal chairs in a waiting area. A young woman sat at a desk at the far end of the reception room, in front of a door that led to the back. She looked up at Long and snapped the gum she was chewing. 'Can I help you?' she asked.

'I hope so,' Long replied. 'I'm looking for some information about a woman.'

The girl at the desk took an extended, evaluative look at Long, leaned forward seductively and smiled. 'Any particular woman?' She had tinsel blond hair and dark eyes. The top three buttons on her blouse were undone, revealing the bridge between the cups of her bra. From the size and angle of her breasts, it appeared that the bra was a marvel worthy of engineering accolades.

Long smiled back. 'Elizabeth Connor,' he replied.

The smile vanished from the girl's face. 'So sad,' she said. She sat back in her chair and pulled her arms forward, reducing the cleavage.

'You knew her?' Long asked.

'No. I never met her. Never even spoke to her. Still, it's awful what happened.'

'If you never met her, how do you know what happened to her?'

The girl looked confused. 'I handle the books. I deal with payroll. It'd be hard for me not to know who she was.'

'She worked here?'

'Well, not here, exactly,' the girl said. 'She worked in Roxbury at Rescue, but it's a related company, and we do all the back office for them.' She frowned, as though she'd said too much. 'What kind of information are you looking for?'

Long pulled out his wallet and flashed his badge. 'Any information I can get,' he said. 'Boston Police Department; I'm investigating her murder.'

'Shit,' the girl said. 'You need to talk to my boss.'

'I'd like to keep talking to you,' Long said.

She shook her head. 'I don't need that kind of trouble,' she said. 'And I don't know nothing about nothing. You need to talk to my boss.'

'Who is your boss? Joey Slade?'

'Who?'

'Joey Slade. He owns the company, doesn't he?'

'I wouldn't know,' she said. 'I never heard of him. I'm going to get my boss. You wait here.' She stood up and walked to the door behind her. Long couldn't help but notice how tight the girl's pants were. They made it difficult for her to walk, and instead she shimmied, swaying her hips from side to side to generate enough swing in her legs to propel her forward.

While the girl was gone, Long wandered around the reception area. There wasn't much to it. The walls were a gray two shades lighter than the carpet, and there were two framed prints hanging on one wall. They were standard, innocuous office fare; outside scenes of boats for one, a farm landscape for the other. Neither gave any hint as to what the business was really all about.

Long was looking at the print of the boats when he heard the door open behind him. 'Can I help you, Officer?' a male voice asked.

'Detective,' Long said as he turned. The man standing in front of him was dressed in a tailored English suit, polished cap-toed shoes, and an expensive silk tie. All the clothes in the world, though, couldn't disguise the coarseness of the man's physique and demeanor, and his face was familiar to every Boston cop. 'Eamonn McDougal,' Long said.

The man smiled humorlessly. 'See, Janice,' he said to the woman behind him. His girth nearly hid her from Long's view. 'I told you the cops know me.' He turned back to Long. 'What can I do for you, *Detective?*'

Something about the way the man carried himself lit the anger in Long. He stood there in his four-thousand-dollar suit, his hair swept back from his forehead, smiling as though there were nothing that anyone could do to touch him. Long instantly felt the desire to bring him down.

'I'm here investigating the murder of Elizabeth Connor,' Long said.

The smile never left McDougal's face. 'Seems like a pretty serious issue,' he said. 'You should probably come into my office to talk.'

CHAPTER THIRTEEN

Finn leaned into the bar at the empty space next to the old man. 'You mind if we talk?' he asked.

'I don't know you,' the old man said. He didn't look at Finn.

'No, you don't,' Finn said. 'But you knew her.' He took out the photograph of Elizabeth Connor at the morgue and laid it on the bar in front of the man.

'Aw, shit,' the man said. His hand went to his mouth, and his eyes went to the empty shot glasses in front of him. 'Frank,' he called out to the bartender. 'I need another.'

The bartender raised his eyebrows, but took a shot glass off the shelf behind the bar and reached for a bottle.

'You knew her,' Finn repeated. Up close, the man looked younger than he had from across the bar. He was in his seventies, probably.

'So you say.' He looked at the Polaroid again. 'Frank, you got that shot?' he yelled.

The bartender walked over and put the shot down in front of the old man. 'Four bucks, Jack,' he said.

The old man looked up sharply, but Kozlowski threw a five on the bar before any harsh words could be exchanged. The old man turned and looked behind him. 'Much obliged,' he said. He hoisted the shot glass, paused and tipped it slightly toward the picture.

'It's not a question,' Finn said. 'I want to hear you say it.'

The man put his head down and sighed. 'Fine,' he said. 'I knew her. I didn't do that to her, if that's what you're getting at. I didn't even know she was . . .' he paused. 'I didn't know until you put that in front of me.'

'What's your name?'

The man made a face, as though he wasn't going to say, but another quick glance behind him at Kozlowski changed his mind. 'Howland,' he said. 'Jack Howland.'

'How long did you know her? How long were you two involved?' Finn asked.

'Who are you, and why do you give a shit?' the man responded.

'I'm her son.'

The old man turned and took a good look at Finn for the first time. 'I wasn't *involved* with her long enough to be your daddy,' he said after a moment. He reached over to take a sip of his beer.

'Imagine my relief,' Finn said. 'How long did you know her?'

The man shrugged. 'Long time, that's for sure. Most of my life.'

'What was she like?'

'She was a fuckin' pistol,' he said. 'At least she was when she was younger, back the first time we got together. Like I said, that was a long time ago. Back then, I had some juice. Might not know it to look at me now. I had cars, I had women, I had anything I wanted.'

'What happened?' Finn asked.

'Real estate. I made some bad plays even before things really hit the shits. Got overextended, and I was off balance when it all came down. I got out with enough to live on, if you call this living.'

'How did you meet my mother?' Finn asked.

'We both grew up around Dorchester. Two kids from the neighborhood, but I was older, and I'd made it out. She was always lookin' for some angle to get her where she thought she should be.'

'Which was where?'

'Anywhere but here.' He looked around the bar and gave a subtle shudder.

'Bartender says you still bought her drinks,' Finn said.

'Bartenders should shut the fuck up,' Howland said loudly. The bartender glared at Finn, but Finn ignored it. Howland let his head hang down another inch or two. 'I still bought her drinks,' he admitted after a moment. 'Not that it would've done me any good at this point. Even at her age, even with our history, she wouldn't let anyone near her without cash. She was like that her entire life, even when she was a teenager. If she thought you had juice – if she knew you had money and she might be able to get at it – she was willing to go anywhere, do just about anything. Without it, though . . .' he held his hand up in a fist, then opened it to show it was empty. 'Nothing. Not even for her favorite Scotch.'

'At least she had standards,' Finn muttered.

'Oh, she had standards,' Howland said. He looked over at Finn again, examining him from head to toe. 'They might not reach up to yours, from the look of you, but she definitely had standards. She was always looking for a big score, always thinking that just a little more money would fix her. Truth is, money wasn't what was broke about her.'

'What was broke about her, then?' Finn asked.

'Beats the shit outta me,' Howland said. He took another sip from his beer. 'She told me about you, once.'

Finn raised his eyebrows.

'Not in the way you think. We were drunk once, way back. Out on the town, tearing it up the way we used to do. I remember we were laughing, laughing so hard we were crying, I can't remember what about. And suddenly I realized she wasn't laughing anymore, she was just crying. I figured it was the booze, and that was part of it, but there was more, I could tell. She told me she had a son. Said she'd had a boy who'd died after he was born. I guess she was only telling me part of the story.'

'She gave me up for adoption,' Finn said.

Howland nodded. 'Makes sense. I can't imagine her with a kid.'

'Do you know who could have been the father?' Finn asked. 'Was there anyone she was dating forty-five years ago?'

'She didn't *date*.'

'You know what I mean.'

Howland shook his head. 'That's a long time ago, and she wasn't the type to keep to one attachment at a time. Whoever he was, though, you can bet he had some money. That was her rule.'

Finn thought about that for a few minutes. 'You know anyone who would have wanted to kill her?'

'Not specifically,' Howland said.

'What does that mean?'

Howland looked at Finn. 'Look, I'm trying to be diplomatic here, okay? She was your mother, even if you didn't know her. I don't wanna say anything that's gonna piss you off.'

'You can't say anything about her that would piss me off,' Finn said. 'I just want to find out what I can.'

Howland looked up at the ceiling. 'Fine, you wanna know, I'll tell you. Your mother was a first-class bitch. I mean, I liked her, 'cause she was such a pistol, but she treated people like shit. That's just the plain truth. She could try the patience of the saints. So, yeah, I could see lots of people gettin' pissed off enough to take a swing at her. But do I know of anyone in particular who was that mad at her? No.'

'Nothing more specific than that?'

'No. You wanna talk specifics, you got the wrong guy. I didn't even really know her anymore. I'd see her sometimes in here. If I had money, I'd buy her a drink, just for old time's sake.' He frowned, as though reconsidering. 'I do know she was into her company for a pretty penny.' Finn flashed him an inquiring glance. 'I never trusted that place. Other than that, there's nothing I can tell you.'

Finn stood up and threw a twenty on the bar. 'I'll buy the next round,' he said.

'Much obliged,' Howland said again. Finn turned to leave, but Howland caught him by the arm. 'You were probably better off,' he said. 'Putting you up for adoption; that was the right thing for her to do. She was a selfish person. She wasn't the kind of person you would have wanted as a mother.'

'I wouldn't know,' Finn said.

'No, but I would.' Howland pushed the twenty to the edge of the bar. 'Frank!' he called out to the bartender. 'Gimme another shot and a beer!' He nodded toward the twenty on the bar. 'Thanks again,' he said over his shoulder to Finn. 'Good luck with whatever you're lookin' for.'

'You too,' Finn said.

Howland smiled sadly. 'My lookin' days are over. If I haven't found it by now, I'm pretty sure it doesn't exist.'

'Long, was it?'

'Detective Long, yes.'

McDougal pushed the intercom button on his desk phone. 'Janice, could you bring some coffee for Detective Long?' He took his finger off the button. 'How do you take it, Detective Long?' The emphasis in the question offended Long. He was pretty sure it was intentional.

'Nothing for me,' Long replied.

'You sure?' McDougal asked. 'Maybe you could use a little pick-me-up. You look a little frayed at the edges, y'know?'

'Nothing, thanks,' Long said. It occurred to him that one disadvantage to carrying a gun was how often he had to fight the inclination to use it.

McDougal clicked the intercom again. 'Never mind, Janice. The detective will tough it out.' He took his finger off the phone and sat down. They were in a windowless room. The rug was the same industrial turf from the reception area, but the décor was a step and a half above. McDougal's desk was large and ornately carved. The green leather desktop matched the upholstery on the chair. The pictures on the walls showed McDougal with a wide range of Bostonians of varying infamy. Politicians featured prominently; Long could name only a few of them, but their faces were familiar enough from the papers for him to know they were men of local significance. The centerpiece was a signed photograph of McDougal with Kurt Schilling from 2004. McDougal noticed Long examining it. 'Game six of the Yankees series,' he said. 'That picture was taken right after. I had tickets with some of Menino's boys. Great game.'

'Yeah,' Long said. 'I remember.'

'You there?'

Long shook his head. 'I've got to ask you some questions about Elizabeth Connor, Mr McDougal.'

'What's your first name?'

'Detective.'

'Is it some matter of national security?'

'Zachary.'

McDougal nodded. 'I knew the name was familiar. You're the cop who killed his partner. Shit, it's good to meet you.' He smiled and stuck his hand out.

Long ignored the hand. 'I'm going to need whatever information you have on Ms Connor,' he said. 'All her employment records, any correspondence the company has had with her. Everything.'

'I'll have Janice put that together for you just as soon as she gets a chance,' McDougal said. 'You looking for anything in particular?'

'Yeah,' Long said. 'I'm particularly looking to find out who killed her and why.'

'I guess that narrows it down,' McDougal said.

'What's Joey Slade's interest in the company?' Long asked.

'Careful, Detective,' McDougal said. There was menace in his tone, though he was still smiling. 'You don't wanna be pissing off the wrong people.'

'He's listed with the Secretary of State's office as one of the owners. Is there a reason my knowing his role here would piss him off? Seems like that would only be the case if someone was trying to hide something.'

The smile on McDougal's face vanished. 'I know you, Detective,' he said. 'I know who you are. You're a man who'd rather stand on principle and shoot his partner than look the other way. I admire that. I admire Don Quixote, too, but the windmills still beat him every time.'

'I'll ask the question again,' Long said. 'What's Joey Slade's involvement in this company?'

McDougal looked down at the desk. After a moment's thought, he said, 'Mr Slade is an investor in the company. He is, for all intents and purposes, a silent partner in the operations.'

'He trusts the operations to you?' Long asked.

'He does. I'm very reliable.'

'Does he keep an office here?'

'No. I'm not sure he's ever been to this building. Only Janice and me work here. The rest of it's a warehouse. Like I said, he's a silent partner.'

'How about Elizabeth Connor?' Long asked.

'How about her? She's dead.'

'Had she ever been to the offices here?'

'How should I know?' McDougal responded. 'I don't know all the people who work for me. I never met the woman, so I wouldn't know her if her ghost walked through that door right now.'

'You ever talk to her? Even over the phone?'

'No. Why?'

'No reason,' Long said. He reached into his pocket and pulled out his cell phone along with the copy of Elizabeth Connor's phone records. He dialed the highlighted number.

'What are you doing?' McDougal asked.

'Checking something.'

101

The phone on McDougal's table rang. He looked at it, looked at Long. On the second ring, Janice picked up from out in the reception area.

'355 Water Street,' she said sharply.

'Thanks, Janice,' Long said. He closed his phone. 'Funny thing, Mr McDougal. Elizabeth Connor called this number five times in the month before she was killed. In each case, the call lasted more than five minutes. In two cases it lasted more than ten. You tell me that there are only two people who work here – you and Janice – but both of you say you've never spoken to her. How is that?'

'It's time for you to leave,' McDougal said.

'We could do this down at the police station,' Long said.

'That's fine,' McDougal said. 'You just call my lawyer any time you want me. I'll come running.' He reached into a drawer and pulled out a business card. 'His number's right there on the front. One of the best in the city. He'll have me out of the police station in a matter of minutes.'

Long looked at the card and frowned. It was heavy card stock with embossed lettering that read *Law Offices of Scott T. Finn*. Long felt like he might throw up.

'Something wrong?' McDougal asked.

'I'll be in touch, Mr McDougal,' Long said, standing. He walked to the door. When he got there, he turned. 'One last question, Mr McDougal: What did you and Ms Connor talk about when she called?'

'Go fuck yourself,' McDougal replied.

CHAPTER FOURTEEN

'There has to be more to this,' Finn said. He and Kozlowski were back at the office in Charlestown. Finn was sitting behind his desk, staring into the computer screen, running searches for any public information regarding Elizabeth Connor. There were over a thousand women in the United States with the name, and most of the other nine hundred and ninety-nine seemed to have led more interesting lives than the one who was murdered in Roxbury.

'Why?' Kozlowski asked.

'Because,' Finn said. 'People don't just get murdered.'

'Yeah, they do,' Kozlowski replied. 'After baseball, murder is America's favorite pastime. People "just" get murdered all the time.'

'Not my mother.'

Kozlowski grunted. 'Listen to yourself,' he said. 'You're talking like you knew her. Like you have any idea who she was.'

'She was my mother,' Finn said. 'I must know her at some level, right? Even if it's buried. Isn't that the way this is supposed to work?'

'Only in Hollywood. This look like Hollywood?'

Finn said, 'There's got to be something we're missing.'

Kozlowski shook his head. 'There isn't. At least, there's nothing you're gonna find on the Internet. I've got access to search engines that blow anything you've got working on Google or Yahoo. I ran her name through all of them, culled through the results, limited what I had to what was relevant to this particular Elizabeth Connor. Know what I came up with? Nothing. A big fat goose egg. You're not gonna do any better tapping away on your computer, trust me.'

Finn pushed his chair away from the desk in frustration. 'What do you expect me to do?' he demanded. 'You expect me to just give up?'

Kozlowski shook his head. 'Not in your nature.'

'What, then?'

'Start in the past,' Kozlowski said. 'And start with what made her different.'

'What the hell is that supposed to mean?'

'From everything we've learned, only two interesting things happened in Elizabeth Connor's life: she was murdered, and she gave up a child for adoption forty-four years ago. We haven't had any luck finding out anything about her from her murder, so start at the other end and find out whatever you can about the adoption.'

'From who?' Finn demanded.

'For starters, from the adoption agency and the place where you were born. It's up in New Hampshire, right?'

'Yeah,' Finn said. 'A couple of hours north.'

'So, go there. Start asking questions,' Kozlowski said.

Finn considered the suggestion. 'I've got to pick up Sally from school at two-thirty today. Then I'd have to figure out what to do with her while I go up there.'

'Take her with you,' Kozlowski suggested. 'It'd be a nice little father-daughter bonding experience.'

'She's not my daughter,' Finn said.

'She's more your daughter than Elizabeth Connor was your mother. Besides, you'll seem a lot less intimidating if you've got a daughter with you when you get there. It'll be a lot easier to get information that way.'

Finn shook his head. 'I don't want to get her involved.'

'She's involved already,' Kozlowski said. 'She's a part of your life; this is your life.'

'She shouldn't have to deal with this kind of crap,' Finn said.

'She's dealt with worse,' Kozlowski said. 'A lot worse.'

Kevin McDougal's duplex apartment was on L Street in South Boston, looking out on Pleasure Bay, toward Castle Island. Across Boston Harbor, airplanes approached Logan Airport parallel to the horizon on the narrow peninsula jutting out from East Boston. Eamonn McDougal had his driver pull the car up to the building. He took out his key and slid it into the front door, letting himself in.

His son's apartment took up the second and third floors. Eamonn had paid for it a year before. Now, he wondered whether he'd done the right thing. He'd never demanded enough from his son; he'd allowed the boy's mother to coddle him in a manner that would have been unthinkable when Eamonn was young.

He slid a second key into the apartment lock, turned the knob and opened the door.

The first thing that hit him was the smell. It was the sweet, sharp, synthetic odor of burnt chemicals. He recognized the stench, and understood what it meant. The fury grew in his chest as he stepped into the apartment.

There were five of them sprawled out on the endless Corinthian leather sectional for which he'd paid top dollar. His wife had said she didn't want their son living without the best that money could buy. Sal D'Ario, nicknamed 'Dorito', and Peter Alred, the two idiots Kevin McDougal considered his 'crew', were fully reclined at either end of the couch. Dorito's eyes were partially closed, rolled up into his head. Alred was staring at the television, which was playing a cartoon about a bright yellow talking sponge. There were two women – girls, really – sitting between them on the couch. Whores, no doubt, from the way they were dressed, though Eamonn knew that fashion had gone in such a radical direction that it was ~~now~~ often hard for him to tell. They both seemed to be sleeping.

His son was in the middle of the couch, his shirt unbuttoned, bare chest showing, staring idly up at the ceiling. On the coffee table in front of him a bent spoon balanced precariously on the edge of a glass. A butane lighter lay on its side next to the glass, and a dozen small vials of brown powder were lined up in the center next to a length of rubber tubing and two hypodermic needles. Three empty vials were overturned on the floor next to the table.

Alred was the first to notice Eamonn standing before them. 'Oh, fuck,' he said, struggling to sit up. 'Fuck, Kev.' He stood unsteadily, knocking into the coffee table, spilling the remaining vials onto the floor. 'Mr McDougal,' he stammered as he bent down to pick up the vials, chasing them around the hardwood floor with his fingers as they skidded and eluded his grasp. 'I'm sorry,' he said over and over. 'I'm sorry.'

Eamonn ignored him, keeping his focus on his son. 'Kevin,' he said, 'tell these people to leave.'

His son looked at him, and it took a moment for the gravity of the situation to register. He stood up and pulled his shirt closed in front of his chest. 'Dad,' he said quietly. 'I didn't know you were coming. I'm staying in the apartment; I'm doing what you told me to.' At least he wasn't shaking, Eamonn thought. He wondered whether the drugs were lending him courage.

'Tell them to leave. Now.'

Dorito and the two girls were awake now, and they were looking nervously back and forth between Eamonn and Kevin, unsure what to do. Alred was still on his knees, scooping up the drug paraphernalia.

Kevin walked around the coffee table, toward his father. 'It's . . . it's okay,' he babbled, his confidence waning. He didn't even come up to Eamonn's chin, and though he was well muscled, it was all fake. It wasn't the hard, lean build that came from real work; it was the round,

106

puffy muscle that came from leisure time at the gym. Everything about the boy was for show: the car, the clothes, the tattoos, all of it. All carefully cultivated in the hope that people would overlook the fact that he was a squirt of a child, quite literally half the man his father was. For just a moment, Eamonn thought he was going to be sick at the sight of him. 'I swear,' Kevin was repeating, 'I'm doing what you told me to.'

Eamonn waited as his son approached him until he was just within range. Then without warning, and with the speed and force of a man half his age, he swung his fist in a solid arc into his son's face. He was surprised at the satisfaction he took from the boy's shocked expression. He didn't go down, but he staggered to his right, off balance, his hand going to his bleeding lips, his eyes spinning.

The others in the room were still and silent, their mouths agape. Eamonn ignored them and chased the visceral pleasure that had come with the first punch. He took two steps toward Kevin and grabbed him by the shirt, spinning him around. With the boy so far off balance, it was easy to generate momentum, and Eamonn gave a heavy shove as he let go of him, sending him headlong into the glass shelving along the wall. The whole apartment seemed to shatter, and Kevin crumpled to the floor. Eamonn's wife had paid over a thousand dollars for the shelves that now lay in shards on top of her son. For the first time, Eamonn felt they were worth every penny. He wasn't done yet, though.

He stepped through the glass, grabbed his son by the shirt and hauled him up onto his feet. The boy was bleeding, but not badly enough to be in any imminent danger, and not enough to douse Eamonn's anger.

Holding his son's face close to his own, Eamonn yelled, 'I'm not going to say it again! Tell these people to leave!'

Kevin was too incapacitated to say anything, but it no longer mattered. The room was immediately thrown into motion. The two girls were on their feet, tripping as they fled to the front door. Dorito and Alred were right behind them, grabbing armfuls of their belongings, not bothering to pull on their shoes and jackets. No one said a word – not to Eamonn, not to Kevin. Within a matter of seconds the door slammed behind them and the apartment was still.

Eamonn was still holding his son dangling helplessly in front of him. All at once he felt tired, and he let the boy slide to the ground. He walked over to the kitchen and pulled a beer out of the refrigerator, twisted the cap off and took a long drink. There was a dishrag on the counter and he picked it up, ran cold water over it in the sink. Reaching into the freezer, he pulled out some ice, wrapped it in the wet dishtowel, and tied off the end. Her picked his beer back up and walked out into the living room.

Kevin was still lying on the floor, looking up at him. 'Get up,' Eamonn said.

His son didn't move. 'Do as I say, boy,' Eamonn said, throwing the ice pack at him. 'Don't make me angry again.'

Kevin struggled to his feet and made his way over to the sofa, holding the ice to his lips.

'I need you clear headed now,' Eamonn said. 'I catch you with any of this kind of shit again, and I won't have a son anymore. Do you understand?'

'I understand,' Kevin mumbled through the ice.

'Good.' Eamonn sat in a chair across the coffee table from his son. 'The police came to talk to me. They wanted to know about a woman who worked for me. She was murdered.'

Kevin stared at his father. 'Is that bad?'

'There's good and bad in everything,' Eamonn said. 'It's all in how you look at it, and what you're willing to do with it.'

The boy said nothing, and it was clear to Eamonn that he didn't understand. At least he was learning to keep his mouth shut; Eamonn supposed that was the best he could hope for at the moment.

'I may have some work for you to do, boy,' Eamonn said. 'You keep your head clear and your mind on what you're doing, I may just be able to keep you out of jail. You think you can do what you're told?'

Kevin took the ice pack away from his lips and examined it. The blood had soaked through the dish towel, turning it a deep, dark crimson. He looked up at his father and nodded.

'Good,' Eamonn said. He finished the rest of the beer in one swallow. 'Maybe we can turn this fuckin' mess to our advantage.'

CHAPTER FIFTEEN

Long slammed open the door to the brownstone office building in Charlestown. The doorknob hit the brick wall in the entryway hard enough that he wondered whether the glass would shatter. He didn't care if it did; breaking a door might make him feel better. For the first time in months the booze hadn't. He'd downed half a bottle of vodka to settle his mood after his meeting with McDougal. But rather than settling him, as it usually did, it had thrown his equilibrium off. He was determined that his inebriation wouldn't stop him from getting answers from McDougal's lawyer, though.

A young black man holding an infant poked his head around the corner from the office. 'Excuse me, can I help you?' he demanded angrily.

'Who are you?' Long demanded back.

'I'm Reggie,' the man replied. 'Who are you?'

Long wondered whether he had burst into the wrong building. 'I'm looking for Finn,' he said.

'He isn't here,' Reggie said. The man's attitude was obdurate. 'Can I give him a message? What do you want with him?' He stood there with the child on his hip, looking defiant.

Long pulled out his badge, held it up. 'None of your goddamned business,' he said.

The badge didn't seem to intimidate the man, who simply squared his shoulders, as if to block Long from passing. 'Lissa,' he called over his shoulder, back into the office, 'you may want to come out here.' Reggie's eyes never left Long's, and Long was tempted to escalate the confrontation. He was in no mood to be challenged. He wasn't sure what he'd do with the child if he tried to frisk the man, though, so he stood there, a feeling of inebriated impotence growing within him.

A moment later a woman came around the corner. She looked at Long, noting the badge he still held aloft. 'Officer,' she said with a hint of steel.

'Detective,' Long corrected her. 'Detective Long.'

She nodded. 'Detective. I'm Lissa Krantz, Mr Finn's associate. Can I help you?'

'I'm looking for Finn,' he said. He could feel himself sway ever so slightly.

'As Reggie just said, he's not here right now,' she said calmly. 'Can I give him a message when he gets back?'

'Where is he?' Long demanded.

'I couldn't say,' the Krantz woman responded. It was a carefully worded response.

'How about Kozlowski?' Long asked. 'He here?' As he asked the question, Kozlowski came around the corner from his office in the back of the building.

'Long,' he said when he saw the police detective. 'What are you doing here?' He frowned as he got a closer look at Long. 'You all right?'

Long didn't ask what the man meant. He scowled and took two steps forward. 'I'm here to find out what the hell is going on,' he said. His voice sounded loud to him.

'What are you talking about?'

'I should have run you two in this morning when I found you at the Connor woman's apartment. I should have my head examined for letting you go.' He shook his head. 'You played me!' he yelled. 'Now I want some goddamned answers!'

'Back up,' Kozlowski said. 'You're not making any sense. Answers to what?'

'Answers to this,' Long said. He took the business card McDougal had given him out of his pocket and flipped it at Kozlowski.

Kozlowski picked the card off the floor and looked at it. 'It's one of Finn's business cards,' he said. 'So what?'

'Eamonn McDougal gave me that card,' Long said.

Kozlowski said, 'So? He's a client. Why were you talking to him?'

'Because he's a scumbag,' Long replied. 'And he's also Elizabeth Connor's former boss. And he's also one of the few people Elizabeth Connor called in the days leading up to her murder. You gonna tell me you and Finn didn't know any of this? You gonna tell me this is all a big fuckin' coincidence?'

Kozlowski's face turned to stone. 'Calm down,' he said.

'So, I gotta wonder,' Long continued, 'why is this scumbag's lawyer – the son of the victim, who's already expressed his hatred for the departed in a letter – going to the woman's apartment, trying to take over the investigation? Is it possible he's looking to make sure the investigation is steered away from him and the scumbag client?'

Kozlowski shook his head. 'You've got it wrong,' he said. His face was still expressionless, though. Long couldn't tell whether or not he was hiding something.

'Yeah? Give me some reason to believe you, then. Tell me where Finn went.'

He could see the muscles in Kozlowski's jaw flex. 'He's not here,' he said simply. 'We'll call you when he gets back.'

'That's it?' Long said. 'That's all you've got?'

'For now. You need to go calm down.'

'What the fuck does that mean?' Long hollered. Looking up, he suddenly realized he was still holding his badge in the air. He stuck it back in his pocket. He didn't give Kozlowski time to answer the question; he didn't want to hear the response. 'You tell him that if I find out he's pursuing this investigation, I'll bust his ass for obstruction. And if I see you anywhere near this, I'll have you brought up on charges so fast you won't know what the hell happened. I'll get your god-damned pension stripped if I can. You got it?'

Kozlowski was still working his jaw slowly. 'We'll call you as soon as Finn gets back,' he said.

'You better,' Long said. His mouth was turning dry. 'If I don't hear from you, I'm coming after you with everything I've got.' He turned and stormed out of the office building before Kozlowski could say anything else.

Route 2 wound north from the Brighton School, through Cambridge, past Alewife, and out toward Lexington and Concord. Just past the prison in Concord, the road broadened into a highway that slashed north of Worcester, through Leominster and past a dozen other towns only New Englanders would pronounce correctly. On Friday nights during the winter, the road was bumper-to-bumper with wealthy suburbanites, fleeing the city for skiing in the mountains of Vermont and New Hampshire. In October, though, there was no skiing to be had, and the road was deserted. It made for a pleasant drive.

'How far is it?' Sally asked.

'Not too far,' Finn replied. 'Another hour and a half, maybe.'

'When was the last time you were up at this place?'

'Forty-five years ago.'

'You've never been back up here since you were born?' She sounded surprised.

'No. Why would I have been?'

She shrugged. 'I don't know. Maybe you could've learned some-thing sooner. It's a long time to wait before returning to the scene of the crime.'

'Thanks.'

'You know what I mean.'

Finn said, 'Are you sure you're gonna be okay with your home-work?'

'It's Saturday tomorrow,' Sally reminded him. 'Besides, I'm ahead in every class. I can work if I need to when we get home.'

'It may be a little late.'

'How late?'

'I don't know,' Finn admitted.

She glanced at him, hesitated before asking the next question. 'Is what we're doing dangerous?'

It took Finn by surprise. 'No,' he said emphatically.

'Is it illegal?'

'Of course not!' Finn shook his head. 'You really think I'd get you involved if it was illegal or dangerous?'

She shrugged. 'It'd be okay if you did. It's not like I've never done anything dangerous before. And my parents taught me how to break the law and get away with it when I was just a little kid. It's no big deal. Besides, I told you I wanted to help.'

'It *is* a big deal,' Finn said. 'I don't want you doing things that are dangerous or illegal, you understand? Not for me, not for yourself.' He glanced over at her; she looked surprised. 'That's not your life any-more.'

His eyes were back on the road again, but he could feel her looking at him. 'What is my life now?' she asked.

He frowned. 'I'm not sure,' he said.

'Let me know when you figure it out, okay?'

'Yeah, no problem.'

They drove for a few miles without talking. That was fine with him; it was a beautiful autumn day, the height of the season in New England, and the foliage was putting on an explosive display of color. The landscape, filled with reds and yellows and oranges dotted with evergreens, made for a relaxing drive. The road was virtually empty; the only car Finn had seen in ten miles was a heavy black dot a few miles back, and he only caught sight of that on the long straight-aways. Other than that, they were alone on a ribbon of smooth asphalt cutting through the crisp wilderness. He really couldn't ask for anything more.

'You can help me,' he said after a while.

'How?' she said.

'When we get there, listen to what people say. Pay attention to how they say it. You're a good judge of character; I'll be curious to hear what you think.'

'You serious?' she asked. 'That's it? No stealing files or breaking into offices?'

'That's it,' he said. 'It's important, though.'

She shrugged. 'Sure. If that's all you need.'

'That's all I need,' he said.

They were almost there; another twenty minutes. He watched the highway signs, looking for the exit. In his rearview mirror, the dark dot of the car reappeared occasionally. He figured it was probably some venture capitalist coming up to check on his ski house before the season started.

The big black Mercedes cruised along the highway, following the little MG convertible. The engine growled angrily at the restraint; it was used to traveling at much greater speeds. There was no need to catch up to the lawyer, though; keeping him in sight was sufficient. Even if the Mercedes fell back a little and lost contact, that was all right. There was little question where Scott Finn was headed.

The darkened windshield of the Mercedes reflected the sun at the top of the mountains to the west as it purred along Route 2, and then split off north up Interstate 91. Coale's eyes were almost as impenetrable as the tinted windshield, hiding from view his determination and resolve.

So many questions remained, the answers hidden in the past. And yet the danger was now greater than ever, as were the stakes. In the face of that danger, Coale's eyes revealed no hesitation. After all, in the gathering storm of uncertainty, only one thing remained clear: There was no turning back now.

CHAPTER SIXTEEN

Finn half expected to feel some sort of emotional epiphany upon seeing the place of his birth. He'd prepared himself for a lightning bolt of recognition; the staggering impact of a homecoming long delayed.

It didn't happen, though.

The place had a gothic aura, no question, and the architectural style was suggestive of the supernatural. But the guts of the place had been so efficiently institutionalized that the ghosts had fled, leaving behind only a first-rate medical facility.

When Finn was born, the place had been called the New Hampshire Home for Wayward Girls. Now it was called the New Hampshire Health Services Center. Catholic Charities had sold the place to a medical non-profit in the 1990s. The place still provided reproductive counseling, birthing and adoption resources to indigent and single women, but the need for the two-month-long stays for pregnant girls had vanished with the changing times, and the abortions that were now performed at the center were out-patient procedures requiring relatively little space. Three quarters of the facility was currently dedicated to drug and alcohol rehabilitation. It had both in-patient programs and out-patient services, and it catered principally to the children of the upper and upper-middle classes who, deprived of actual life challenges, had built their own obstacles to overcome.

The driveway presented well, in a deliberate way. Immaculately manicured hedges and close-cropped lawns conveyed a sense of order and stability that must have been comforting to those depositing loved ones for extended recovery stays. Giant signs with bright, easy-to-read lettering directed visitors to the various medical destinations with anxiety-reducing clarity. The place's exterior had the feel of an antique castle lovingly updated with all modern amenities, keeping only the outline of the classic structure.

Finn parked in a visitor's spot near the front of an endless parking lot.

'You ready?' he asked Sally.

'For what?' she responded as she opened the door. 'We're just asking some questions.'

Inside the building, architectural authenticity had been completely abandoned for convenience. The reception area struck a careful balance between the sterility of a modern medical facility and the welcoming comfort of a 1980s rumpus room. The reception desk was scrubbed, shiny Formica, well ordered and neat. A broad expanse of spotless hospital tile covered most of the floor. Off to the side, there was a section that was covered by red carpeting. On the carpeting, bright leather chairs of a low-slung, curving modern design in all the colors of the rainbow gave a hint of orchestrated whimsy.

Finn and Sally walked up to the reception desk. 'May I help you?' the woman behind the desk asked. She was in her thirties, her hair was more tossed than brushed, like a salad, and it fell in unruly tangles into her face. Her sweater was a large, loose-knit sack of undyed wool, and she had two studded hoops through each nostril.

'I hope so,' Finn said. 'We're looking for someone to talk to about adoption.'

The woman immediately looked with sympathy at Sally. 'Of course,' she said. 'We have a wonderful group here, they're really special.' She lowered her voice conspiratorially. 'They'll also be able to tell you about your *other* options.'

'No,' Finn started to say, then decided to skip the explanation. He thought they would face less resistance if the woman had some sympathy for them. 'Where can we find someone to talk to?' he asked simply.

'I'm not pregnant,' Sally interjected.

The woman behind the desk looked confused. 'You're not?' Finn watched her face as her mind ran through the other possibilities and settled on the most bizarre. 'You aren't looking to adopt, are you?' She regarded Finn as though he were a pedophile; he'd been instantly transformed into the enemy.

'No,' Finn said. 'It's a long story. Is there someone we can talk to?'

The woman frowned. 'Adoption Services is down the hall to the left.' She nodded to a hallway that ran off the reception area. 'They can help you down there.'

'Thanks,' Finn said. He and Sally headed down the hallway.

'You were going to let her think I was pregnant,' Sally said. She sounded angry.

'I figured it was too much of a hassle to explain it to her,' Finn said. 'Is it a big deal?'

'Yeah,' Sally said. 'It is.'

'Why?'

'I don't want anyone thinking I'm pregnant.'

Finn looked at her. 'So you wouldn't mind doing something illegal – acting as a lookout, or breaking into someplace – but it's over the line to give someone the misimpression that you're pregnant?'

'That's right,' she said.

'I don't get it.'

'Growing up in the projects, it's what you hear all the time. *You're gonna end up pregnant before you can drive. Either that or crack-whoring for some asshole and a fix.* It always pissed me off. That's not who I am; that's not who I'm ever gonna be. If I'm gonna fuck up my life, I'm gonna do it my own way. You understand?'

'Yeah,' Finn said. 'I do.' They had arrived at a glass door with the words 'Adoption Services' stenciled on it. 'I'll be more careful in the future.'

'Good.'

Coale put the time to good use. Sitting in the Mercedes in the parking lot of the great Gothic building where Scott Finn had been born, he tapped away at his laptop computer, researching all of the personnel in the Adoption Services Center. Once he had the names from the Center's website, he began a detailed search using the most powerful information retrieval tools available. It took less than an hour for him to have everything he needed.

He derived no pleasure from this part of his job. Still, it was necessary, and he'd given up squeamishness long ago. Too long ago. He would do what needed to be done one last time.

CHAPTER SEVENTEEN

Long was unsteady when he left the lawyer's office. It had been months since he'd felt really drunk. A hovering level of inebriation had become his status quo, but he'd always felt in control. The booze usually provided some equilibrium. Now he felt lost, and his tongue felt two sizes too big for his mouth.

His plan had been to go back to the station house to continue his investigation, but he understood that was not an option. He knew that if he returned to the station in his current condition his career would be over. Driving back from Charlestown, he looked at his watch; it was after four. It was early to call it a day, but he didn't have much of a choice.

Suddenly, tires screeched and horns blared. He raised his eyes back to the road to see that he had strayed over the double-yellow line, and cars were swerving to avoid a head-on collision.

Long jerked the wheel to the right, and his car hopped back into his lane. He almost overshot the mark and narrowly missed colliding with another car in the second lane headed south on Massachusetts Avenue. Horns sounded again, and through his window he could hear the obscenities yelled in a thick, heavy stream. He needed to get home, and he would have to pay attention to get there. He headed toward the Southeast Expressway, where the traffic at least traveled in only one direction.

Long lived in a condominium complex in Quincy, just south of Boston. The place was called Louisburg Square South, a rip-off of the most swank and expensive block on Beacon Hill in Boston, where the élite had their townhouse mansions. Quincy's version was more modest. Several developments in brickface lined the main thorough-fare that ran from the edge of Dorchester out toward Wolliston Beach. Long had a one-bedroom rental with a view of the parking lot. It was fine. The place was clean and reasonably well maintained; the kitchen had been redone sometime in the 1980s. More importantly, it was affordable, and it was right off the highway, which made it an easy ten-minute trip to the station house.

By the time he got to the apartment his legs were buckling, and he knew he'd been lucky to get off the road alive. It took him three tries to thread the key into the lock, and when he tried to push the door closed behind him he didn't make enough of an effort for it to catch. Instead it remained resting on the latch, neither opened nor closed.

Fuck it, he thought, looking at the door. He was drunk, he was a cop, and he had a gun. He'd pity any burglar with the misfortune to choose his apartment to rob at this particular moment.

He wanted a drink.

No, he needed a drink.

Needed not in the sense that he felt a desire to be more inebriated; he wasn't sure that was possible. The need now came from someplace that was divorced from the actual physiological impact of the alcohol. It was more of an obsession. It was a compulsion, and for the first time he understood how it was possible for the bums down in the shelters to drink themselves to death – to continue pouring grain alcohol into their bodies until the cellular structures were too overwhelmed to continue the fight for survival, or to pick up a bottle of antifreeze, close their eyes and pretend it wasn't pure poison.

He stumbled to the kitchen and opened the cabinet above the

utensils, where he kept the bottles. Grabbing a fifth of Stoli, he pulled out a glass and started to pour. The upended bottle yielded nothing, though; it was empty.

He slid the bottle into the sink and pulled out another, not even checking to see what it was. Unscrewing the top, he lifted it to his lips and tipped his head back.

Nothing.

He threw the bottle at the sink, and it connected with the empty Stoli bottle, both of them shattering. He ripped open the cabinet again, this time hard enough to hear the wood crack. There were several bottles still there, and he went through them one by one. As each one proved useless, he threw it into the sink until the shards of glass started to spill over onto the counter.

Finally, the second to last bottle answered his angry prayers. It was a flask bottle of Jägermeister someone had given him a long time ago as a gag gift. He hated the stuff; it tasted like cough medicine to him, and he'd often bitched about the under-aged girls and metro-sexual assholes at bars who drank the crap.

Now, though, looking at the bottle, he had trouble imagining anything else that might taste as good.

He twisted off the cap, closed his eyes, and drank a quarter of the bottle – four full swallows – without pausing. He lowered the bottle, sighing heavily as he opened his eyes.

Suddenly he realized he wasn't alone. Someone was standing by the door, inside the apartment, looking at him. His vision was blurred, both from the alcohol and from how tightly he'd shut his eyes. Panic shot through him, and he started reaching for his gun. His hand was tugging on the butt before his vision cleared enough to recognize Julie Racine standing there, looking at him with an expression that fell somewhere between horror and disgust.

'Shit, you scared me!' he barked. 'How long have you been standing there?'

'I was waiting for you in the parking lot,' she said. 'I tried calling you a few times at the station house earlier; tried email, tried your cell phone. I was just waiting, and I saw you pull in.'

Long looked over at the sink. Broken glass was everywhere. 'How long?' he asked again.

'Long enough,' she replied.

He noticed she was holding a bottle of wine and a folder. 'You brought wine.'

'I didn't know,' she said. He half expected her to run. She didn't, though; she stood her ground. He had to give her credit for that.

'What were you going to do?' he asked, his tone angry and defensive. 'Get me drunk and take advantage of me?' He was leaning against the kitchen counter, and he stood up to take a few steps toward her, veered off into the living room. 'I've already taken care of the first part.'

'I thought you might want someone to talk to,' she said.

'You need wine to talk?'

'Apparently not like you do.'

He smiled viciously. 'Yeah, well wine is all right, but if you want real conversation, there's no substitute for Jägermeister.' He held the bottle up in toast, then guzzled a good portion of the remaining contents.

'What are you doing?' Julie demanded. 'Seriously, what the fuck are you doing? Wallowing? Is that really the best you can do? Is that all you've got left?'

He was looking at her, and the sight was devastating. He'd forgotten how beautiful she was, or maybe he'd just never really noticed before. Her thick red hair fell seductively over her bright green eyes, and he could get a good sense of her lean, athletic build under her cotton shirt. He savored the memory of being next to her body, touching her freely. He'd taken that for granted. When they'd been together before, he'd been the department's superstar. Now his career had disintegrated, and the rest of his life was falling apart. He slumped onto his couch. 'What do you want, Julie?' he asked wearily. 'What could you possibly want with me now?'

'I want to know what happened,' she replied.

He shook his head. 'I can't.'

She walked into the room. On some shelves near the window a few pictures caught the waning sunlight. She picked one up; it showed Long with an older man. Both were in uniform, both were smiling broadly, squinting into the camera with the same eyes. 'I'm sorry about your father,' she said.

'Yeah, well,' he shrugged.

'I'm serious – that must have been hard. Particularly with everything else you were dealing with.'

'It was only fair,' he said. Looking up, he could see the question in her eyes. 'He told me I was dead to him,' he explained. 'I guess now we're even.'

'Don't,' she said. 'Please don't.'

Suddenly Long felt so tired he could barely move. 'I appreciate your coming out to check on me,' he said to her. 'Really, I do. But as you can tell I'm not in the best condition for a heart-to-heart right now. I'd like to be alone.'

Julie nodded. 'Fine,' she said. 'But I didn't come out here to check up on you. I have some more information on the Connor case. I thought you should have it right away.' She dropped the folder in her hand onto the coffee table in front of him. He was too exhausted to open it, and he wasn't sure his eyes could focus enough to read.

She didn't let him off the hook, though. 'It's the report on the other unlisted number,' she said. 'Homeland Security cleared the release. They just needed to know that it was for a genuine police investigation.'

'Why?' Long asked reflexively.

'Because the number traces back to the home of a United States senator. I guess it's just a precaution.'

His brain struggled to fight off the alcohol. 'Who?' he stammered.

'James Buchanan,' she replied. 'It's the number for his townhouse on Beacon Hill.'

Long stared at the file in front of him. He couldn't even form words that made sense anymore.

'You asked what I wanted from you before,' she said. 'For now, I'd settle for you doing your job.' Without another word, she was gone. The door closed behind her, and he was alone on the sofa. The bottle of Jägermeister was nearly empty. Leaning over, he rested his head on the arm of the couch and closed his eyes. He was out cold in a matter of seconds.

CHAPTER EIGHTEEN

'I'm sorry, there's not that much I can do to help you. I wish you'd called first.'

The stenciled metal plaque on her door announced her name as Shelly Tesco, and she sat behind her desk in a small office in the New Hampshire Health Services Center. The head of the Adoption Services division of the Center was a well-kempt woman who looked to be in her early sixties. Her hair was solid steel gray brushed neatly into a ponytail. She was thin, and the wrists that stuck out of her white peasant blouse displayed a wire of sinewy muscles.

As near as Finn could tell, the Adoption Services division consisted of three rooms: Ms Tesco's office, a waiting area with a desk for her secretary, and a file room.

Finn said, 'All I want is access to my records.'

'I understand, Mr Finn, but – as I would have told you over the phone – first, your file must be located. As I'm sure you can understand, given that your adoption records are more than forty years old, that it is not necessarily an easy task.' She pointed to the room behind her with all of the filing cabinets. 'You see those? They represent only a fraction of our records. Everything from the past five years is on computers; everything else must be dug out of there, or out of the state records center.'

'So, dig,' Finn replied.

She frowned at him. 'We will,' she said. 'But that may take some time. We generally try to respond to requests within two weeks.'

'Two weeks? What could possibly take that long?' Finn demanded.

'Well, as I was saying, finding the file is merely the first hurdle. Once the file is found, we have to pull out whatever information we can give you.'

'What do you mean, "pull out"? I want the entire file.'

Ms Tesco sat back in her chair. 'I understand that, but I can't give you all the information in the file.' Finn stared back at her intently, waiting for more of an explanation. The roll of her eyes made clear that she found him tedious. 'You said you were a lawyer, didn't you, Mr Finn?'

'I did.'

'Then you know I have to follow the law with respect to any information I give out. And under New Hampshire law, the only information I can give you about your parents is what's known as "non-identifying" information. That includes things like any medical histories, allergies, general descriptions – anything that doesn't identify *who* your parents were. You were born back in the 1960s, and those were the days of closed adoptions, when people had the right to conceal their identities. It's only more recently that the trend has been toward open adoptions.'

'But I already know who my mother was, and she's dead. I'm just looking for any additional information about her.'

'I understand, but I can't give you anything beyond the basics.'

'She's dead, for Christ's sake,' Finn said, his voice starting to rise. 'Who's gonna complain?'

She nodded. 'I understand your frustration,' she said. 'But that's not the way the system was set up. For right or wrong, the system was designed to protect people's privacy – to ensure anonymity. It seemed reasonable at the time.'

'Why?' Finn asked.

'Because of how important adoption was to the country back then,' she replied. 'Particularly in the 1950s and '60s, adoption was very common. The domestic adoption rates in this country went from around ten thousand per year before World War Two, to over one hundred and fifty thousand per year after the war. There was literally an explosion of babies being born to unwed mothers at the time. Placing those babies was a societal priority.'

'Why were there so many more unwed mothers?' Finn asked.

'Times were changing,' she said with a shrug. 'It was inevitable, I suppose. People talk about the sexual revolution in the 1970s, but the real sexual revolution happened in the 1940s and '50s – it's just that no one bothered to notice. Women got a taste of freedom when the men went off to war and they went into the workforce. Economic freedom leads to all other forms of freedom, including sexual freedom.'

'What's that got to do with my getting information about my mother?' Finn said.

'Because the system was set up to prevent you from getting any information,' Ms Tesco said with a sigh. 'As more children born were to single mothers – young mothers – the adoption laws were changed to address the problem. You couldn't have that many single mothers out there; society wasn't ready for that. So a system was developed to make it acceptable for these young mothers to give up their children. That system also had to encourage people to adopt these children. One way to accomplish both goals was to sever all ties between the birth mother and the child when the child was put up for adoption. That way, the new parents never had to worry about the birth mother coming back looking to claim rights to the child. And the birth mother never had to worry about the child she gave up tracking her down. She could live her life as if she never made the mistake that led to the pregnancy. So the adoption laws were designed to make it very hard for anyone involved to get any information.'

'Great,' Finn said in a hollow voice. 'Everyone got what they wanted. Except for the kids.'

'And the mothers, in many ways,' Ms Tesco said quietly.

Finn frowned at her. 'I don't understand. Like you said, the mothers got to get rid of their mistakes. It's exactly what they wanted.'

She shook her head. 'In most cases, it turns out that's not true. The girls – and these are *girls* we're talking about for the most part – were usually never informed that they could keep their children. That was never an option. They were told that the only way that they could have any sort of a life was to give up the child to adoption. Sometimes they were told that they were evil for what they had done, and were unfit to care for a child.'

Finn scoffed. 'Name-calling wouldn't stop a mother from keeping her baby if she really wanted to,' he said. 'That's a cop out.'

Ms Tesco's eyes flashed at him. 'I can understand your anger, Mr Finn. I'm sure people have told you over and over that your mother didn't want you, that she gave you up because she thought her life would be better without you. That's always been the party line – the story that's been sold to adoptees and adoptive parents and the public for decades – it's all okay, because the birth mothers didn't want their children anyway.'

'I've learned a little bit about my mother in the last day. It sounds like it was pretty true in my case,' Finn said.

'Maybe,' Ms Tesco said, grudgingly. 'I'm sure it was true in some cases. Not in a lot of others, though. Trust me.'

Sally had been quiet throughout the conversation, just watching Ms Tesco as she spoke. Now she said, 'You gave up a child.' The words came out simply and plainly, without judgment. She could have been commenting on the woman's jewelry.

Ms Tesco was taken by surprise. She looked at Sally as though she'd forgotten she was in the room. 'No,' she said quickly.

'That's why you work here now, isn't it?' Sally said.

Ms Tesco looked back at Finn. 'I'm just trying to explain the law to you. It has nothing to do with . . .' She took a deep breath. 'There is only so much information I could give you, even if all of the information was there, which it likely isn't.'

Finn looked back and forth between Sally and the older woman. 'Is she right?' he asked. 'Did you give up a child?'

'Does it matter?' Ms Tesco said.

'Maybe, maybe not,' Finn said. 'But I want to know.'

The woman looked away, her hands clenched, the wiry cables of muscle on her wrists flexing nervously. She nodded. 'Yes, it's true. I gave up a little girl for adoption when I was young.' She drew her lips in tight to her teeth and closed a file sitting in front of her. 'Now, if you'll excuse me, I have a lot of work to do. I will put in your request, and we will try to get back to you in two weeks.'

'Great,' Finn said slapping his thighs in anger. 'So the system is set up to prevent adoptees from finding their real parents, and just to make sure the system works, people like you with a vested interest in keeping their secrets are made the gatekeepers. That's just wonderful.'

She turned on him angrily. 'I have no secrets, Mr Finn,' she snapped. 'And I would give anything in the world – *anything* – to find my daughter. To talk to her, even once. To know whether she was happy growing up, whether I did the right thing. You have no idea what it's like to give up a child. In some ways, it's worse than having a child die; at least when your child dies, you know where they are – you have closure.'

'Except that giving up your baby was your decision,' Finn pointed out.

'You have no idea what you're talking about,' Ms Tesco said. 'None of it was my decision. I lost control over everything in my life the moment I got pregnant. In many ways I still haven't gotten that control back.'

Finn said, 'You had all the control, and you still do.'

'I didn't,' Ms Tesco said. 'And I don't. I don't expect you to understand.'

'What happened?' Sally asked. 'What wouldn't we understand?'

Ms Tesco looked at the girl. 'There were no choices back then,' she said. 'Things are different now. If it ever happened to you, you could make your own decisions.'

'What's different?'

'Everything.' She shook her head angrily. 'I was a good girl, you understand? A good, upper-middle-class girl. I was a straight-A student. Things like that didn't happen to girls like me. They happened to *other* girls. *Bad* girls. At least, that's what they told me.' She looked down at her hands, but her demeanor remained steely, her voice clipped. 'My father hit me when he found out. My poor father, the most mild-mannered, non-violent, decent man I've ever known, and he hit me. Hard enough to knock me off my feet. I could tell he was sorry about that, but he never said so; that's how awful it was. A young, unmarried daughter getting pregnant?' She shook her head. 'It was enough to destroy a family. I could see that in my father's face; I could see his fear that we would lose everything he'd worked so hard to build. He was a vice-president at a local bank, and something like this, if people had found out, could have destroyed his career. We were Italian, and he always felt like he was under suspicion as it was. He felt like my pregnancy would confirm all of the unspoken prejudices.'

'What did you do?' Sally asked.

Ms Tesco looked up at her. 'I did what I was told to do,' she said. 'I did what hundreds of thousands of other *good* girls did back then when they got into trouble. I kept my mouth shut and kept to myself for months. I wore baggy clothes to hide the changes. And then, when the baggy clothes weren't enough to keep people from noticing, I went away.'

'You ran away?'

She shook her head. 'No,' she said. 'Not ran away, *went* away. It was all arranged. It was what girls did back then. I went far away to a place where I could give birth without anyone knowing. I *went away*. That was what they called it back then.'

'Where did you go? Here?'

'Goodness, no,' she said. 'My family lived two towns over from here. You never went away to someplace nearby; someone might see you, someone might find out. I went to another place in western Massachusetts.'

'For how long?' Sally was fascinated, Finn could tell.

'Three months,' Ms Tesco said. 'For three months I was alone, literally a prisoner. My family didn't give me any choice. My father told me that I would either do what I was told, or I would be thrown out of the house and disowned. I was sixteen. I didn't think I would survive. Probably wouldn't have.'

'What did your mother say?'

'Not much.' The older woman laughed bitterly. 'She prayed a lot. That was her reaction to most things that were difficult for her to deal with. She prayed, and she told me to listen to my father. We were a very traditional family.'

'You must have been pretty pissed at your mom,' Sally said.

Tesco shook her head. 'That's just who she was. At least she visited me once when I was at the home. My father never did. She came and she brought me a Bible. She told me it was to mark my rebirth. She told me that when "it" was done – everyone referred to my pregnancy, the birth, my baby, as "it", as if they couldn't use real words to describe what was happening – when "it" was done, I could start life over.' She closed her eyes. 'I can remember sitting there, wanting to scream at her. Wanting to tell her that I didn't want to start over. Wanting to beg her to save me, take me back home.' She breathed heavily. 'I didn't, though. Because that's not what *good* girls did. Good girls did what they were told to do.'

'So you gave up your baby,' Sally said.

She nodded. 'I gave up my little girl. I remember when labor started, I was so happy because it was finally going to be over. They didn't tell you anything about what childbirth was like, though. They never told me anything to prepare me. It took fourteen hours, and I kept screaming in pain, asking why, and they said it was a punishment. They told me, *This is what happens when you're bad.* And I believed them.

'All through the birth, I kept promising God that I'd be good from then on. I promised that I would do what I was told, that I'd give up the baby and go back to being a good girl. And then it was over, and I heard her cry. My heart broke when I heard my daughter cry that first time. All I wanted was to make everything okay for her. And they put her on my stomach and she stopped crying. Just like that, she stopped crying and clung onto me. I looked up at this one young nurse who'd been there with me the entire time – she was a nun, and she was so nice, so kind, she couldn't have been more than five or six years older than me – and I said, "She knows." I was crying, and I said, "She knows I'm her mommy."

'And this nurse smiled at me, and said, "She does. She'll always know you're her mommy. Even if she doesn't remember, she'll always know."' A tear trickled down Ms Tesco's cheek, only to be brushed aside with the flick of a wrist. 'I thought, *That's something, at least.* At that moment, I even thought maybe that was enough.'

'But it wasn't?' Sally asked.

Ms Tesco shook her head, wringing her hands nervously. 'Some of the other girls never spent any time with their babies. They encouraged that at the home – complete separation from the start. Sometimes they didn't just encourage it, they enforced it. They said it made it easier. I don't think they were right, but I wouldn't know, because I didn't take their advice. I spent three glorious days with my daughter, telling her how much I loved her, and how I was doing the right thing for her. It was all lies, I knew it the entire time, but I said it anyway. Because I was a good girl, and that was what they told me to say.

'And then, three days later, they came to take her away. They had papers for me to sign, and I screamed at them and told them that I wouldn't sign them. I told them that I was keeping my baby. Oh, I made such an awful scene, they had to bring in orderlies. And then the man who ran the place came down to talk to me. He was very calm; I got the feeling he'd had this conversation before with other girls. He explained to me how much better it would be for my little girl to be adopted. He called her *the girl*, because we weren't allowed to name our children – that was up to the adoptive parents – but I named my little girl anyway. I called her Christine, and I would talk to her and tell her to remember me, and remember that her real name was Christine. Anyway, he told me that *the girl* would be better off with a real family. He said that he'd called my father, and my father had told him that I couldn't go home with a child. He said my father told him that they wouldn't come get me. I told him I didn't care.

'Then he nodded, and asked how I would pay. I said to him, "Pay for what?" And he told me that I hadn't been charged for the three months board and the medical care and the hospital stay because that was all covered if the baby was being adopted. But if I didn't intend to give the child up for adoption, then I had to pay. It came to almost a thousand dollars, which might as well have been a million, as far as I was concerned. I told him I didn't have any money, and he said he would have to turn the matter over to the police. And while they got all that sorted out *the girl* would have to go into foster care with the state because if I couldn't pay them, I clearly couldn't take care of the child.'

'What about the father?' Sally asked. 'The boy who got you pregnant?'

Ms Tesco laughed in surprise. 'Oh, no,' she said. 'He never got involved. That was the accepted double standard; he was never really affected by any of this. Back then it was considered the girl's problem, not the boy's. If anything, it probably helped his reputation. I didn't hear much from him after I told him about the pregnancy. It didn't matter, he certainly wasn't in any sort of position to offer an alternative – he was only seventeen.'

'So, what happened?' Sally asked.

'I didn't know what else to do, so I signed the papers. They told me I had five minutes to say goodbye. Can you imagine? Five minutes to say goodbye to your child? She was still tiny, but she had that three-day-old chubbiness that babies get, and I held her close to my face and I whispered to her the whole five minutes. I can't remember everything I said to her, but I know I told her over and over how much I loved her, and that I was sorry. I promised that I would find her. And then they came and they took her.'

'And you've never found her?'

She shook her head. 'I came to work here a decade ago, thinking it might give me some sort of advantage in my search, but it hasn't worked out that way. The law is the law. Even for me.'

The room was silent for a few moments. Then Sally said, 'That sucks.'

Ms Tesco nodded. 'Yes, it does. I think the worst part, though, was afterward. When I got home, everyone expected me to be okay. My parents, my friends, everyone. They all thought I should be fine and just step back into my life like nothing happened. They even thought I should be grateful to have a second chance. I wasn't allowed to talk about it. I tried – I tried talking to my parents, but they refused to discuss the topic. "That's all in the past," they would say. "It never happened." Except that it did happen. I wanted to shake them and scream, *It did happen!* I didn't, though.'

She looked at Finn. 'So, when you talk about your mother as if you know what she went through – remember, you may not know the whole story.'

'That's why I'm looking for more information,' Finn said. 'That's why I'm here, but you're telling me you can't give me that sort of information. Why? Maybe you're right. Maybe my mother didn't want to give me up, but that doesn't seem to fit with what people have told me. From what I've learned so far, she was exactly the kind of person who would willingly give up her child for her own convenience.'

'Maybe she was,' Ms Tesco said. 'But I can tell you from having worked here for the last ten years – from dealing with women searching for their children ten, twenty, fifty years after giving them up – my story is far more common that you would ever think. I've talked to hundreds of women who never recovered from giving up their children. They spent years in torment. Some were so broken from the experience that they could never let themselves be happy.'

'Maybe,' Finn said. 'But I'll never know if that's what happened to my mother because you won't give me whatever information you have in my file.'

'I can't,' Ms Tesco said, shaking her head. 'The law –'

'Fuck the law,' Finn blurted.

Sally leaned forward. 'Ms Tesco, I've only known Finn for a year, but he's one of the few really good people I've ever met. He took me in when my father was killed and my mother left me. He just found out who his mother was, and that she was murdered. If you were the one who'd been killed, and it was your daughter searching for information, what would you want the person on your side of the desk to do?'

'I don't know.'

'Yes, you do.'

Ms Tesco looked at Sally for a long moment. 'It may take some time to find the file,' she said.

'We understand.'

'I'm not promising anything,' she said. 'But I'll think about it.'

Sally nodded. 'That's all we can ask.'

CHAPTER NINETEEN

Finn was still adjusting to Saturdays. During the week, he was so busy working and taking care of Sally he had no time to think; he had to keep his feet moving just to keep things from falling apart. When the weekend came, though, there was time to draw breath and consider the complications of being the guardian to someone else's child. It was that time that scared him most – the time he was most afraid of screwing up.

That Saturday, Sally slept later than usual. They'd stopped to get dinner on the drive back from New Hampshire and had gotten home later than anticipated. Finn woke up at five-thirty, as was his habit. He would have liked to sleep later, but his body wouldn't let him. It was one of the great ironies of growing older: it seemed the more sleep he craved, the less his body tolerated.

He threw on a pair of running shoes and a tattered T-shirt and headed out for a morning jog. He'd never been a devotee of exercise for its own sake, but there was something about the city early on a Saturday morning that he loved. It was all his. There was a stillness to it as he swept through the early morning mist – down Bunker Hill, along the waterfront, then back up along the Charles. The Boston skyline slumbered off to his left. The brownstones along the river, with their multi-million dollar views, were dark and quiet; the office towers behind them gave no signs of life. It felt as though he were the last man alive, and it all belonged to him – the only one who truly knew the place for all its faults and beauty and grace. It was like watching a lover sleep – an exquisite moment of unrequited intimacy.

By the time he crossed back into Charlestown the city was beginning to stir. Delivery trucks rolled slowly down toward the commercial district, and an occasional taxi passed him, lacking its accustomed weekday hurry. The spell had been broken, and once again he had to share the city he loved so much.

He could see Kozlowski waiting for him on the stoop as he turned the corner at the bottom of the hill and headed up toward his apartment. The raincoat gave him away.

'I rang the bell,' Kozlowski said as Finn approached.

'I was running,' Finn replied. He slid the key into the lock and opened the door.

'Sally?'

'Sleeping,' Finn said. 'She's a teenager. A terrorist attack wouldn't wake her on a Saturday morning.' Kozlowski didn't crack a smile. 'What's up?' Finn asked.

'Detective Long came to visit the firm yesterday. He wasn't happy.'

Finn frowned. 'He found out we're still looking into my mother's murder?' Kozlowski nodded, and Finn's frown deepened. 'That's gonna cause some problems.'

'There's more,' Kozlowski said.

'What?'

'He was out questioning McDougal.'

'Eamonn?' Finn said. 'Why?'

'Because McDougal was your mother's boss when she was working at Rescue Finance. She called him a bunch of times before she was killed.'

Finn frowned. 'My mother worked for McDougal?'

Kozlowski nodded. 'Apparently.'

'And you needed to tell me about this at six o'clock in the morning?'

'I was nervous,' Kozlowski said. 'I figured if McDougal had some reason to kill your mother, and he found out that you had been up in New Hampshire yesterday poking around, who knows? Maybe he'd think he had some reason to come after you. Stranger things have happened.'

Finn finally understood why Kozlowski had been concerned that the doorbell had not been answered. His eyes widened. 'Oh my God,' he whispered. 'Sally.' He turned and bounded up the staircase to his apartment in a panic.

Long woke up on his couch. His arm was hanging off the edge, numb, and his face was mashed so far into the corduroy fabric that he could feel the pattern impressed on his skin. Pushing himself up with his one working hand, he caught a glimpse of the stain of his drool, spreading out on the sofa cushion like a map of Florida from the spot where his mouth had lolled open for most of the night.

He closed his eyes and rubbed his forehead. The pain was intense, and radiated out from behind his eyeballs toward his temples.

The sunlight was streaming through the windows, and opening his eyes to behold the mess from the night before was agony. The bottle of Jägermeister lay on its side on the coffee table, nearly depleted, a thin puddle having dribbled from the top onto the light-colored wood, like his own mocking, inanimate doppelganger. Even from where he sat, he could see the pile of broken glass spilling out from the top of his sink. For a moment, he wondered whether he should vomit but the impulse was not urgent enough to give in to just yet. Perhaps later.

The events of the day before came back to him in disjointed flashes. The interview with McDougal; his abrupt and unsuccessful visit to the lawyer's office; Julie Racine's intrusion into his apartment. The shame of it all tormented him, and he let out a low, tired moan.

He reached out and took hold of the bottle of Jägermeister. There was still some left. Not enough to get drunk; maybe just enough to stop the pain.

Bringing the bottle to his lips, he held it there for a moment. *Just a little*, he thought. *Just enough to get through the day.*

As he began to raise his arm to take the sip, he looked over the bottle and saw a folder on the coffee table. One corner was soaking up some of the alcohol that had spilled the night before. His forehead wrinkled as he struggled to remember. It was there, in his memory, just out of focus. Julie had brought the folder, hadn't she? Why? It came back to him in dribs and drabs. The Connor case. Phone records. Homeland Security.

Just as the alcohol reached the lip of the bottle, the memory came clear.

Senator Buchanan.

He put the bottle down without taking the sip and reached for the file. The soaked corner stuck to the table, and tore when he picked it up. Inside the folder, the records were there, the information clear in black and white. Elizabeth Connor had called Senator James Buchanan five times in the weeks leading up to her death. Each time, after hanging up, she had immediately called Eamonn McDougal.

Long stared at the information in the folder for a few moments. His mind grinded like rusted machinery. The questions were multiplying to the point at which they could no longer be ignored. What was the connection between McDougal, Connor and Senator Buchanan?

He didn't even realize he was standing. Instinctively, he was headed toward the bathroom to shower, shave, and brush his teeth. His mind was consumed with planning out the attack, thinking through various approaches, and considering the consequences. It wasn't until he reached the hallway that led back to the bathroom that he turned and looked back at the coffee table.

The bottle was still there. Sitting open on the table. Three fingers full, waiting for him.

He took a step back, toward the bottle. It wouldn't hurt, would it?

It might even make it better, make his mind clearer. It might even be the right thing to do.

He hesitated, then turned toward the bathroom and went in. The bottle would be waiting for him when he got out of the shower. Maybe then.

Finn poured a cup of coffee. His hand was still shaking. 'So, what now?' Kozlowski asked.

The two of them had rushed up the stairs in a panic. It took two tries for Finn to get the apartment door unlocked, and once accomplished he slammed the door open and sprinted down the hallway to Sally's room. It was amazing how quickly it had become *her* room. For years it had been the guest room. Even when she first moved in, that was what he continued to call it for a while. But now there was no doubt – it was her room, and she belonged there.

He threw open her door, and yelled, breathlessly, 'Sally!'

She was there. Still stretched out, asleep, under the covers, oblivious to the world. His scream shocked her out of her slumber.

'Jesus! What the hell!' she screamed.

Finn held up his hands. 'Oh, sorry,' he stammered. 'I thought . . . I just . . . Sorry.'

He could feel Kozlowski in the doorway behind him, shaking his head.

'What's wrong?' Sally had demanded.

'Nothing,' Finn lied. 'Just go back to sleep. Sorry.'

'Jesus,' Sally repeated. She threw the blankets back over her head, and Finn had closed the door gingerly.

'Sorry,' he'd said once more.

He and Kozlowski had gone into the living room and reported to each other the events of the previous day. Finn made the coffee as Kozlowski described Long's visit to the office. The adrenaline from his panic over Sally was still coursing through Finn's veins when Kozlowski asked about next steps.

'I don't know,' Finn replied, taking another sip of his coffee. He heard Sally turn on the shower, and he knew they only had a few moments to talk before she came out. He didn't want to alarm her any more than he already had. 'Howland said my mother was borrowing tons of money from her boss. If Long is right, and Eamonn was her boss . . .' Finn blew out a heavy breath.

'Eamonn doesn't like it when people don't pay him back. It makes him testy.'

'Testy enough to kill?'

Kozlowski shrugged. 'Depends on how much money she owed, I suppose.'

'I need to confront Eamonn.'

Kozlowski's head bounced from side to side, as he assessed the idea. 'Maybe,' he said. 'You accuse him of murdering your mother, though, and it's gonna strain the attorney-client relationship.'

The shower stopped, and Finn could hear Sally moving around in her room. She wasn't the primping type, and Finn knew their time was almost up. 'I can't just let this go,' Finn said. 'Besides, he's gonna realize I know eventually. He'll take one look at me the next time I meet him and he'll see it in my eyes.'

'Yeah, that's probably right,' Kozlowski agreed. 'When do you want to do it?'

'Today,' Finn said.

'He may not be at his office,' Kozlowski pointed out.

'I've got his cell number,' Finn said. 'I'm representing his son. He'll show up if I call him and tell him I need to talk to him.'

'You're not meeting with him alone. I'm coming.'

'He may insist I come alone.'

'He can insist all he wants,' Kozlowski said. 'It's not gonna happen.'

Finn nodded. 'Can Lissa watch Sally this morning?'

'Yeah,' Kozlowski said. 'She may want to know why, though.'

'You gonna tell her?'

'Some, probably,' Kozlowski said. 'Not all. Not until we know for sure.'

The door to Sally's room down the hall opened. 'I don't want Sally to know about any of this,' Finn said quietly.

Kozlowski nodded.

She was in the kitchen a few seconds later. 'Okay,' she said. 'Somebody want to tell me what that was all about?'

Finn and Kozlowski looked at each other. 'It was nothing,' Finn said.

'I'm not an idiot,' Sally replied.

'I was out running when Koz got here, and you didn't answer when he rang the doorbell,' Finn tried again. 'I was just concerned that something had happened to you.'

'That wasn't concerned, that was freaked out.'

'Seriously, don't worry about it, okay?' Finn said. 'Lissa wants your help with the baby this morning. Is that cool with you?'

'As long as you tell me what's really going on.'

Finn ignored the ultimatum. 'Around noon?' he asked Kozlowski.

'Sounds like a plan.'

'Okay.' Finn clapped his hands together to signal the end of the conversation. 'I'm gonna go take a shower.'

'I'm going back to the apartment,' Kozlowski said.

Sally looked back and forth between the two of them. 'Great. I guess I'll just sit here by myself and try not to think about whatever it is that the two of you aren't telling me.'

CHAPTER TWENTY

Long found the connection between Elizabeth Connor, Eamonn McDougal, and Senator James Buchanan quickly. All it took was a single Google search, and the top link took him to a website dedicated to tracking the political contributions reported by politicians. Connor and McDougal were both contributors to the senator's campaign. Alone, that might have seemed inconsequential. But as Long continued to dig, he discovered that they were not only contributors, but significant contributors. In fact, they had both given the maximum amount allowed under the law in both of Buchanan's elections – two thousand, four hundred dollars.

For McDougal it was a paltry sum. No one knew how much McDougal actually made for a living – most of it was obtained illegally – but it was well into the millions. Long had seen the apartment where Elizabeth Connor lived, though. It was not the sort of place where most residents gave thousands of dollars to politicians. It didn't make sense, and yet it hardly seemed enough of a motive to justify murder.

Long continued to dig.

A half hour later he noticed another abnormality. It seemed that all of the employees of the 'legitimate' companies controlled by McDougal had maxed out on their contributions to Senator Buchanan. From the managers to the janitors, each and every one of them had given the same amount.

Long went back to Google and put in a search for the Federal Election Commission. When he arrived at the website, he pulled up the phone number for the local office. The phone rang a dozen times before it was answered. 'FEC,' the tired bureaucratic voice on the other end of the line said.

'Hi,' Long said, 'this is Detective Long of the Boston Police Department, homicide division. I need to speak with whoever is in charge of investigations into campaign finance violations.'

Coale was parked on the street, watching the two men in the tiny convertible. The MG was a terrible car from an engineering standpoint, he reflected. It handled okay, but the engine wasn't powerful enough to provide the kind of spunk that usually made tiny convertible cruisers fun. When any pressure at all was applied to the gas pedal, the tiny four-cylinder engine had to work so hard an automotive critic had once likened it to driving an old biplane without wings.

Still, as a man who understood the role of emotion in automotive enthusiasm, Coale appreciated the lawyer's devotion. It took a particular sort of person to stay loyal to something that defied rationality as completely as a forty-year-old two-seater with few comforts and fewer practical advantages.

He slipped the Bluetooth over his ear and dialed. McDougal answered even before Coale heard it ring. 'They're here,' Coale said.

'They?'

'He's with the ex-cop.'

'Outside?'

'Yes. They're going in.'

'Did they stop anywhere on the way over?'

'The lawyer picked up the ex-cop. That's it.'

'Are you staying outside?'

'No,' Coale said. 'I'll tail them again once you're done with them.

146

Right now I'm going to the lawyer's office. Keep them busy for fifteen minutes, and I'll have eyes on his computer and ears on his phone.'

'Make sure you don't lose them when they leave here.'

'Are you telling me my job?' Coale didn't care how much McDougal was paying, at his age there was a limit to his patience.

'No,' came the response. 'I hired you because you know your job. I expect you to do it.'

'They're getting out of the car,' Coale said. He disconnected the line.

Finn and Kozlowski sat in the parking lot of the corrugated building in Chelsea that housed Eamonn McDougal's office.

'You know what you're gonna say to him?' Kozlowski asked.

'Not really,' Finn said.

'You better get it figured out or he'll tear you to shreds.'

They got out of the tiny MG and walked over to the building's entrance. The chain was off the steel door and they opened it and stepped inside. Finn was surprised to see McDougal's assistant sitting at her desk. She was dressed more casually than normal, which is to say that her eye shadow was two shades lighter, and her heels were of the two-inch, not the four-inch variety. Looking up, she smiled, taking out her gum and slipping it into the trash can under her desk. 'Hi Finn,' she said with enthusiasm.

'Hi Janice,' Finn responded. 'Working on a Saturday?'

She shrugged. 'I'm here when he's here. That's the rule. Besides,' she leaned forward seductively, 'when I heard he was meeting with you, I didn't mind. How's everything goin'?'

'Been better, actually.' Finn often enjoyed her flirtations. At the moment, though, he had no patience for them. 'He in his office?'

She nodded. 'Uh huh. Girl trouble?'

'Can we go in?'

She looked hurt. Glancing up at Kozlowski, she said, 'I think he's only expecting you. I don't think he knew you were bringing someone.'

'We work together.' Finn walked by the side of her desk to the door that led to the back.

'Wait!' she objected. 'Let me tell him you're here!' It was too late, though. Finn was already through the door with Kozlowski following close behind. As Janice rose to block them, she bounced off Kozlowski's shoulder and dropped back into her chair. 'You can't just go in!' she yelled.

Finn walked through the door to McDougal's office. McDougal was standing at a filing cabinet, placing some folders into a file. He heard Finn enter the room, and he slid the cabinet shut and locked it with a key. Then he turned and looked at Finn. His eyes narrowed. 'Must be important.'

'What?' Finn said.

'Whatever it is you need to talk to me about,' McDougal responded. He walked over to his desk and sat down. 'It must be very fucking important for you to come barging into my office. Other circumstances, barging in like that could be dangerous. You'd do well to remember that, Finn. You'd do very well.' He nodded to Kozlowski standing in the doorway behind Finn. 'And you brought the muscle. Must be very important indeed.'

Finn and Kozlowski walked into the office. Finn sat in the chair across the desk from McDougal. Kozlowski stayed standing.

'Kozlowski.' McDougal nodded a greeting. 'You wait outside while Finny and I have a conversation.'

Finn answered for Kozlowski. 'We work together.'

McDougal looked at Finn. 'Careful with your tone, boyo. You'll have me thinking you don't trust me. Relationships are based on trust. We lose that . . .' he shrugged. 'Who knows?'

Finn leaned in toward McDougal. 'You wanna talk about trust?' he demanded. 'Why didn't you tell me about Elizabeth Connor?'

McDougal frowned theatrically. 'Elizabeth Connor,' he repeated. 'Now why does that name seem so familiar?' He closed his eyes, as though thinking hard. Then the eyes flashed open and his brow cleared. 'Ah, yes. Of course, I remember now. She worked for me. In fact, I have her file right here.' He pulled a manila file toward him, opened it. 'You know, lots of employers just keep the basics about their employees in their files. That's not how I work. I like to know everything about the people who work for me. You'd be amazed what kind of information you can dig up on people.'

'Did you kill her?'

McDougal didn't flinch. In fact, he didn't move at all. He just sat there, staring at Finn, his expression inscrutable. Finally, he asked, 'Are you asking as my lawyer? Or are you asking in some law enforcement capacity.' He nodded to Finn's chest.

Finn reached down and grabbed the hem of his shirt, lifting it up to reveal his bare chest. 'I'm not working for the cops, and I'm not wearing a wire.'

McDougal nodded toward Kozlowski. 'What about him? I don't see him showing me what's under his shirt.'

'You haven't bought me dinner,' Kozlowski responded.

'We're here on our own,' Finn said. 'I heard she was into you for a lot of money. I just want to know if you killed her.'

'Why do you care?' McDougal asked. 'What's it to you?'

Finn could see the smile tugging at the corner of the man's lips. At that moment, he was almost overcome by the desire to launch himself across the desk and grab him around the neck. He found himself wondering what it would be like to strangle him; to feel his life slip away, to hear his last breath. 'You know why,' was all he said.

McDougal's eyes were almost black. They reminded Finn of pictures of great white sharks he'd seen. 'I want to hear it from you.'

'She was my mother,' Finn said.

The smile spread from the corner of McDougal's mouth to his

entire face. 'That's in the file, too,' he said. 'Goddamn, it's a small world, ain't it, Finny-boy?'

'Did you kill her?' Finn asked. He was seething, and he wondered what his reaction might be if McDougal said yes.

Instead McDougal shook his head. 'No. I didn't. She wasn't important enough for me to kill. I have a pretty good idea of who did, though.'

'Tell me.'

'It's all right here in her file.'

'Then let me see the file.'

'If only life was that fuckin' simple. It's not, you know? Life is never that simple.'

'Why not?'

McDougal shrugged. 'There are other considerations to take into account. I'm not a rat, by nature.'

'Bullshit,' Finn said. 'You'd send your mother away if it gave you an advantage.'

'Be careful bringing up a man's mother,' McDougal said. 'I know you're not used to it, but it cuts close to home.'

'So I'm learning,' Finn said.

'I guess you are. You want to know who killed your mother? That's fine, but you've got to do something for me, first.'

'What do you want?' Finn asked.

'You know what I want. I want my boy off the hook,' McDougal said.

'I'm already representing him,' Finn said. 'What more do you want from me?'

'I want you to do what needs to be done!' McDougal thundered.

'Like what?'

'That's the fuckin' question, now, isn't it?' McDougal said. 'You've been in this game, what, fifteen years? You must have favors you can call in, people you can lean on. Right now, you're not doing *all* you can, and you and I both know it. Right now, you're playing by the rules. I know you, Finn; when you want to you take care of things, you do. When you want to fix things, you find a way. But right now, you don't want to fix this thing for me bad enough. Well, maybe now I have something to trade.'

Finn shook his head. 'You're wrong. There's nothing I can do outside the law. Even if I wanted to, there's nothing I have to trade, no favors I have to call in.'

'I don't believe you,' McDougal said.

Finn stood up, leaning over the desk. 'I don't give a shit what you believe; I want to know who killed my mother!' he screamed.

McDougal pushed his chair back from the desk against the wall to create some space between Finn and himself. His right hand had been concealed beneath the desktop, but now Finn could see that it was gripping a large shiny semi-automatic pistol. McDougal pulled his hand up so the gun was resting on the top of the desk. 'You just back away, Finny-boy, right this goddam second.' He looked at Kozlowski. 'And if I don't see both of your hands in the next two seconds, your friend here's dead, got it?'

Kozlowski pulled his hand out of his coat pocket. 'You pull a gun, you better be ready to use it,' he said in a low tone.

'No problem there, Mr Kozlowski. Try me, if you'd like.' He stood and walked over to the filing cabinet, unlocked it and slid the file in. 'I'll make this easy on you. My son's case gets dismissed in the next two weeks, and I'll give you the file. I'll even answer any questions you've got – though after you see the file, I'm sure you won't have many. And as a bonus, I won't kill you.'

'Lucky me.'

'My son's case is still around in two weeks, though, and you can ask your mother who killed her yourself. You understand?'

'This isn't over,' Finn said.

'No,' McDougal answered. 'I guess it isn't.'

CHAPTER TWENTY-ONE

Senator James Buchanan's was the largest townhouse in Louisburg Square – the real one on Beacon Hill, not the Quincy imitation where Long spent his lonely evenings. Buchanan didn't really live there most of the time, though; he stayed there when he was in Boston, which was less than a third of the year. He split the rest of his time between a mansion on embassy row in DC, a chalet in Park City, and a beach compound in Newport, Rhode Island. Rumor had it that he also kept an apartment about which his wife had no idea.

Long had called ahead to confirm that Buchanan was in residence. Congress was on a one-month break, theoretically to allow the members to take the pulse of their constituents, to argue issues, and to return with a better feel for how to represent those who had elected them. In reality, the recesses were used to raise funds to bankroll the next campaign. The cost of running for the Senate in the United States had gotten so high that even the wealthy relied heavily on fundraising, rather than paying for campaigns themselves. Buchanan had offices in the Kennedy Building downtown, but he ran his operation out of an office suite in his home.

The door was opened by a young woman in a stylish business suit. She was nearly as tall as Long, and she had a stunning figure and a beautiful face. 'Can I help you?' she asked.

Long showed her his badge. 'Detective Long, BPD,' he said. 'I called a little while ago about an investigation.'

She nodded. 'We're expecting you,' she replied. She stepped back from the door and extended her arm in an invitation to enter. 'I'm Sonia Harding, one of the senator's personal assistants.'

'He has more than one?'

'He's a very busy man.'

'I'm sure.'

She shot him a cautionary glance. 'He's on a call, and he'll be down shortly. He asked me to have you wait in the library.'

She led him into a room that was out of an English country manor. Mahogany bookcases with ornately carved moldings lined the walls up to the ceiling, towering fifteen feet above them. Two ladders on wheels attached to a brass rail that ran along the top edge of the shelves allowed access to the books. The furniture was leather, including the tops of two reading tables.

Two walls were covered with ancient lithographs showing some sort of excavation. They caught Long's attention, and he walked over to get a better look.

'Landfills,' Sonia Harding said.

'Pardon?'

'Landfills.' She motioned to the images on the walls. 'They show the landfills in progress. More than seventy-five percent of what is today the city of Boston was once covered in water. Most of the city is built on landfills.'

'I didn't know it was that much.'

She nodded and pointed to one particular sequence of prints. 'This is the Back Bay landfill. The senator's great grandfather was an engineer. He was in charge of the process by which nearly six hundred acres between Fenway and the Charles River was turned from a swamp into a fashionable neighborhood. For nearly forty years, a train car's worth of earth and gravel was dumped into the Back Bay every ten minutes, twenty-four hours a day. It doubled the size of the city at the time, and made the senator's family one of the richest in the country.'

'You seem to know a lot about it.'

'I try to know as much as I can about the senator.'

Sonia Harding motioned him into a tall wingback chair that looked like it had cost the lives of several calves to make. The personal secretary sat across from him in an identical chair, crossing her legs discreetly.

'How long have you worked for the senator?' Long asked her.

'Three years,' she replied.

'Do you like it?'

'It's better than what I was doing before.'

'Which was?'

She smiled. 'You didn't say what this meeting was about when you called.'

'I didn't.'

'Can you tell me now? It may save some valuable time for both you and the senator.'

'It's something I need to talk to Senator Buchanan about directly.'

'Are you sure? I may be able to help you while we wait.'

'Never let it be said that I turned down an offer of assistance,' Long said. 'You may be able to give me some background. You work out of the office here?'

She nodded. 'This is where the senator prefers to work. We keep a couple of people at the downtown office, but most of the important work goes on here.'

'Does that include work on the reelection campaign?'

'Some. We're very careful, of course, because there are rules about who can work on the campaign. We don't want to be accused of using taxpayer resources to run the reelection, but yes, many of the campaign staffers are located here.'

'Who is in charge of the campaign's finances?' Long asked.

She hesitated. 'I should probably know, but I don't. I don't deal with the finance people at all. I handle the senator's calendar. I do some typing, too. It's a pretty traditional role, I guess.'

'Nothing wrong with a traditional role,' Long said. 'Is he a decent boss?'

She frowned. 'What do you mean?'

'I don't know,' Long said. 'I thought it was a pretty straightforward question. Is he a decent boss? Is he nice? Does he treat you well?' He noted her hesitation.

'He treats me very well,' she said, though her expression didn't lighten at all.

'He has a reputation,' Long said. It was non-specific; he could have been referring to a good reputation or a bad one. He wanted to see how she would interpret it.

'I don't know what you're referring to,' she said, crossing her arms. 'And I think I resent the implication.'

'I wasn't implying anything,' Long said. The two of them looked at each other in silence. 'Are my questions making you uncomfortable?'

'No,' she said, though her arms remained crossed. 'It's just that –' She cut herself off abruptly. Long's back was to the door, but he recognized the change in Sonia Harding's posture as an indication that someone had entered the room. She stood. 'Senator,' she said.

Long stood up as well and turned toward the door. The man lingering in the doorway cut an imposing figure. He was tall, six-three at least, with the broad shoulders of an ex-athlete who worked hard to keep at least the vestiges of his former physique. He had thick dark hair framing a prominent forehead, and carved, attractive features. He smiled and his cosmetically enhanced teeth gleamed. 'Detective,' he said, ignoring his personal secretary.

'Senator,' Long said.

'Thank you, Sonia,' Buchanan said without looking at the woman, 'you can get back to your work.' She nodded and walked out without a word. Buchanan didn't look at her until she'd already passed, and then he turned to follow her retreat. Long noticed his eyes track her below the waist. He turned back to Long. 'What can I do for you, Detective . . . ?'

'Long.'

'Detective Long.' Buchanan advanced to shake Long's hand. 'You were cryptic over the phone. I might have put you off, but you piqued my curiosity.'

'I just have a few questions,' Long said.

'About what?'

'An investigation I'm pursuing. It's probably nothing.' Long wanted to put the senator at ease; not that he appeared to be the type who was easily rattled.

'Well, I'll help in any way that I can.'

'I appreciate that. Are you familiar with a man named Eamonn McDougal?'

Buchanan frowned. 'I'm not sure; the name sounds familiar, but maybe that's just because it's a familiar-sounding name.'

'Eamonn is familiar-sounding?'

'McDougal,' Buchanan said.

'Ah,' Long said. He let the silence linger. 'Or, maybe the name sounds familiar because he was one of your largest contributors. He gave the maximum amount allowed by law.'

'Really? I wasn't aware.' Buchanan's tone was conversational but guarded.

Long nodded. 'It's amazing how much information is accessible now, with the Internet.'

Buchanan shrugged. 'There were many people who gave the maximum to my campaign. I wish I could say that I knew every one of them. The truth is, I know very few of them.'

'I understand,' Long said. 'It's hard to keep track. On the other hand, every single one of the employees at the companies he runs gave the maximum as well. Right down to the janitors. Doesn't that strike you as odd?'

The senator cleared his throat. 'Perhaps, but not unheard of.'

'When else have you heard of it?'

'It feels like you have a point to make, Detective,' Buchanan said. 'Maybe it would be helpful if you shared it with me.'

'Well, it just occurs to me that if McDougal has been using his employees to conceal campaign payments to you above the legal limit, that would be a serious violation, wouldn't it?'

'I suppose it would.'

'And given the fact that you're on the Banking and Finance Committee, which controls the regulations that impact several of the financial companies McDougal controls, that would look pretty bad for you, too, right?'

Buchanan didn't answer. Instead he smiled. 'I'm sorry, Detective Long, I must have missed the session of Congress where we assigned jurisdiction over campaign finance to the Boston Police Department. My understanding was that this was a matter for the federal authorities. Which, of course, would mean that you are investigating a matter without any proper authorization. I just mention this because I wouldn't want you to get yourself into any trouble.'

'Thank you for your concern, Senator. But you don't need to worry, I'm not investigating campaign finance violations.'

'Then what are you investigating?'

'Murder.'

Long kept his eyes trained on Buchanan, evaluating his reaction. The senator would have made an excellent poker player, but Long could see the immediate twitch of his eye and the involuntary movement of his jaw.

Buchanan asked, 'Who was murdered?'

'A woman named Elizabeth Connor,' Long said. 'She lived in Roxbury.'

Buchanan shook his head. 'I don't believe I knew her. I don't spend much time in Roxbury.'

'I wouldn't have thought so,' Long replied. 'Which was why I found it so interesting that she called you five times in the weeks before she was killed.' With that, Buchanan went white. 'What seems even stranger to me,' Long continued, 'is the fact that each time she got off the phone with you, she immediately called Eamonn McDougal. She worked for him at one of his businesses. Oh, and I should also mention that Eamonn McDougal is one of the principal figures in organized crime in New England. So, when you put together the phone calls, the campaign contributions, and the murder of Ms Connor, I'm sure you can see why I have to ask a few questions.'

For a moment, Long thought Buchanan had swallowed his tongue. He stood there, gaping, his jaw slack, his eyes bulging slightly. 'I'm sorry, Detective,' he said. 'I have a call scheduled that I must take. It shouldn't take too much time – if you'd care to wait?'

Long nodded. 'Of course, Senator,' he said. 'I'm not going any-where.'

CHAPTER TWENTY-TWO

'Finn's in trouble, isn't he?'

Sally was sitting in Lissa's kitchen watching her struggle to get some of the mashed banana from the jar of baby food into her son's mouth. It was Reggie's day off, and from the look of things Sally suspected that if he ever took an entire week's vacation the baby might starve.

'Why would you think that?'

It was an annoying lawyer's non-answer. Lawyers answered questions with questions; they probed, they never committed. The baby bobbed and weaved and Lissa tried to keep up with the spoon. A large dollop of banana fell to the floor.

'He wouldn't give me a straight answer this morning. Then he ditches me off on you.'

'He had some work to do.' Andrew spat a mouthful of banana.

'Don't give me that. If he just had work to do, he would have told me,' Sally said. 'If he just had work to do, he wouldn't have taken Koz with him.'

'Who said Koz is with him?'

'He's not here, is he? I'm not a moron.'

Lissa scraped some of the mush off her son's face with the spoon and aimed again for his mouth. 'No,' she said with a sigh. 'You're clearly not a moron.'

'So? He's in trouble?' Sally clenched her fists underneath the counter.

'Not really,' Lissa said. 'Not in a way he and Koz can't handle.'

'How can you be so sure?'

Lissa gave up on the feeding and started to clear the mess away. 'I can't. But you've got to believe, and you've got to let them work it out. They're men – they see a problem, they need to fix it.'

'What if we can help?' Sally asked.

'If you could, you would. Right now, though, they have to handle this on their own. Besides, Finn is responsible for you now. He doesn't want to put you in any sort of a position where you can be hurt. You've got to let that be his call.'

'That's not how it's supposed to work,' Sally said. 'Where I come from, if someone you care about is in trouble, you're supposed to stand up for them.'

'Is that the way it's worked for you?'

Sally shook her head again. 'No. That's the way it's supposed to work, though. That's what my parents never understood.'

Long waited in the library for what seemed like an eternity. Pacing back and forth on the heavy oriental rug, he began to wonder whether he'd played it right. He could have called the senator down to the station house for an official discussion, but that would have gotten the brass involved. Once that happened, he'd likely be taken off the case. The last thing the higher-ups wanted was the departmental burnout poking around in the affairs of a man as powerful as James Buchanan. In all likelihood, the connection between Buchanan, McDougal and Elizabeth Connor would be covered up in the regular course of political horse-trading that went on at the highest levels of the law enforcement bureaucracy.

He walked over to the window and looked out on Louisburg Square. It was a patch of grass less than half the size of a football field surrounded by four-hundred-year-old cobblestone streets so uneven that any vehicle other than the highest-end luxury SUVs wouldn't survive regular use in the area. The streets could easily have been made more accommodating, but that would detract from the atmosphere of nineteenth-century privilege and gentility the residents preferred. The tiny plot of green, reserved for those with townhouses on the square and fenced off against the rabble, represented the last stand of a world all but disappeared.

'I need to borrow a car,' a voice came from behind him.

He turned. The light was streaming in from the street through the ten-foot-high window, casting him in silhouette. The woman in the doorway squinted to see him. 'You're not my father,' she said after a moment.

'No, I'm not,' Long agreed.

She was tall, with James Buchanan's dark hair and chiseled features. There was no mistaking her for anyone else's child. And yet there was something different about her. She was dressed in a short skirt and a sheer, loose-fitting T-shirt.

'Who are you?' she asked.

'Police,' he said. 'I'm here to talk to the senator. He's your father?'

She made a face and nodded in a reluctant sort of way. He was guessing she was in her late twenties, though she presented younger. 'What are you here to talk to my father about?'

'It's confidential,' he said.

'Everything my father does is confidential,' she said. 'Makes it hard to have a conversation around here sometimes. I'm Brooke.'

He nodded to her. 'Detective Long.'

'That's a very formal name.'

'Comes with the badge.'

'Too bad.' She walked over to the side table where two decanters of liquor stood. 'Can I get you a drink?' She reached down and opened a bookcase; Long was surprised to see a small refrigerator hidden behind a set of false book spines.

He looked at his watch; it was eleven-fifteen. 'It's a little early for the hard stuff, isn't it?' he asked. He felt like a hypocrite as he spoke. There was a part of him that was screaming to join her.

She tossed a few ice cubes into her glass, turned and smiled at him again. 'It's never too early for the hard stuff.' She took the elaborate stopper out of the crystal decanter of Scotch. Her pour was ostentatious, filling the glass until the booze just topped the rim, enough to bulge slightly above the glass, but not so full that it spilled. Long's mouth went dry. Raising the glass, she held it up to him in toast, took an extended swallow. She wiped her mouth with the back of her hand. 'Is my father in trouble?'

'What makes you ask that?'

'You're a cop.'

'I am.'

'That suggests that someone is in trouble.'

'Maybe,' Long said. 'Do you know a woman named Elizabeth Connor?' It was a shot in the dark, but he figured it couldn't hurt.

She shook her head. 'No. Should I?'

'Not necessarily.'

'Who is she?'

He shook his head. 'Nobody. She was murdered recently.'

Brooke Buchanan seemed intrigued. 'Really. A murder? I would have expected my father to be caught up in something more white collar. Maybe I underestimate him. What does he have to do with it?'

'Nothing that I'm aware of,' he said, truthfully.

'And yet, here you are.'

'I'm just here to ask some questions.'

He was watching her, mesmerized, when the spell was broken by a shout.

'Brooke!'

He turned. Standing at the door was a striking older woman. She was in her late fifties, dressed in an understated tailored silk suit. An endless string of pearls hung loosely from her neck, and the diamond ring on her left hand looked heavy enough to weigh down her arm. She was shorter than the young woman in the T-shirt, but she stood straighter, and she had a regal bearing.

'Mother, I just . . .' Brooke looked at the glass as though it might tell her what to say.

'Put that drink down!' the older woman said.

Brooke looked embarrassed, and she hesitated.

'Please,' the older woman said. Her voice was softer, and Long could see the change in Brooke Buchanan's posture.

'What does it matter?' she said.

'It matters,' the older woman said.

Brooke put the glass on the table next to the decanter.

'Go to the kitchen and we'll talk in a moment,' the older woman said.

Brooke left the room without looking at Long.

The older woman advanced. 'I'm Catherine Buchanan,' she said, her hand extended.

'Detective Long.'

The woman raised her eyebrows. 'Police detective?'

'That's correct, ma'am,' Long replied.

She turned and walked over toward the table with the bottles on it. 'I apologize for my daughter,' she said. 'She doesn't normally drink before noon here. She's acting out, I think. Campaign season has been a hard time for all of us. We kept a much lower profile during the first election. Neither one of us is used to it.'

'I can see how it would be hard,' Long said. 'How many more weeks left until the election?'

'Three and a half,' Mrs Buchanan replied. 'It can't come fast enough.'

'Last poll I saw looked pretty good for your husband.'

'It did,' she agreed. 'Of course, that can change instantly,' she said.

Long nodded. 'All it takes is a scandal, I suppose.' He watched her closely.

'I'm sorry?'

'All it takes is a scandal,' he repeated. 'Isn't that right? An undocumented nanny,' he nodded toward the door, 'a daughter who drinks before noon? Maybe a campaign finance issue. I would imagine anything like that could turn the outcome of an election.'

She looked at him carefully. 'I'm sorry, Detective, why is it that you said you are out here?'

'I didn't say, actually.'

'Would you like to now?'

'I was discussing it with your husband. We were interrupted.'

'What were you discussing?'

'Elizabeth Connor,' Long said. 'Have you heard that name?'

She shook her head.

'She was a contributor to your husband's campaign. She was murdered recently.'

'How ghastly.' She turned away.

'Are you sure your husband never mentioned her?'

'If he did, I don't remember.'

'She's contributed the maximum amount to his campaign. It's hard for me to believe that your husband wouldn't have known, and that he wouldn't have mentioned it to you.'

'My husband has literally tens of thousands of donors.'

'Maybe he just didn't want to worry you.'

Mrs Buchanan put the top back on the decanter of Scotch. 'Maybe that's right. I know my husband doesn't tell me everything. To be honest, I don't really want to know *everything*.'

'No?' Long let his surprise show. 'Where do you draw the line?'

She shot him an angry look. 'I let James draw the lines,' she replied.

'I suppose that's your choice. I guess that means I'll just have to continue the conversation with your husband.'

She straightened the bottles so they were lined up perfectly. Picking up her daughter's glass, she took a sniff, crinkling her nose at the smell, letting out a slight grunt of disgust. She put the glass back down. She said, 'I'll go see what's keeping him.'

As she started walking toward the door, Long said, 'It must be hard.'

She turned to look at him. 'What must be?' she asked.

'Sharing your husband.'

She was frozen, staring at him. 'I have no idea what you're talking about,' she said.

'With the job,' Long replied. 'It must be hard sharing him with such a demanding job. It must require a great deal of sacrifice.' He took out a business card. 'If there's ever anything you'd like to discuss, maybe share some of that sacrifice, I'm more than happy to talk.'

She took the card and looked down at it. 'I don't think that's likely, Detective,' she said.

'Why not?' he asked. 'I'm a good listener.'

She looked up at him again, and her face was fully composed. She appeared ready to go on stage as the dutiful wife at a political fund-raiser. 'Because, Detective,' she said, 'I'm quite sure that you would never truly understand the sacrifices my life requires.'

He looked at her, saying nothing. After a moment Sonia Harding walked into the room. 'I'm sorry, Detective,' she said. 'The senator asked me to give you a message. An emergency has come up, and he has no more time today. If you call his office, he'll be glad to set up another appointment.'

'It must be something very important,' Long said.

Sonia Harding didn't respond. She looked at the senator's wife. 'Mrs Buchanan, he also wants you to go to his office as soon as possible. You two have an event tonight and he has a few questions he needs to ask you.'

The assistant stood there, waiting for Mrs Buchanan to leave the room. 'It was a pleasure meeting you, Detective Long,' Mrs Buchanan said. She shook his hand and left the room.

'The senator asked me to show you out,' Sonia Harding said. The pleasant smile she'd greeted him with at the front door earlier was gone. He suspected he would never see it again.

He nodded. 'I'm sure he did.'

James Buchanan was in the study off his bedroom on the second floor. Officially it was still called a guest room, but that was just for appearances; James hadn't shared a room with Catherine for years.

Catherine lingered at the door for a moment before going in, her stomach turning with anxiety. He was sitting at his desk, flipping through papers. It was just an act, though. She'd lived with him for long enough to tell. He was moving too quickly through the papers to actually be reading; he just wanted to seem busy.

She took a deep breath, steeled herself, and walked into the room. 'You wanted to see me,' she said. Even to herself, her voice sounded more like a domestic servant than a wife or a partner.

He looked up sharply, as though diverted from something of far greater importance. 'No,' he said.

'I'm sorry. Sonia said –'

'I didn't want you talking to the police anymore. I don't want anyone in the household talking to them.'

'Why not?'

He stood and crossed to the credenza near the door, closer to her. 'I just don't.'

She stood there, watching her husband, a man she didn't know. Though they were only feet apart, they had never been more distant from one another. Her arms were crossed. 'What is it?' she asked.

'It's none of your business.' He couldn't even pull his head up to look at her.

'It is my business,' she insisted. 'If it has anything to do with this family, it is my business.'

The back of his hand came without warning, as it always did. A swift motion, a smooth arc, and it connected with the side of her face, knocking her back into the doorway. 'I said, it's none of your business!' he yelled.

She kept her feet. It wasn't the same thing as keeping her dignity, but she'd learned to accept a life of limited victories. She felt the familiar warmth and sting on her cheek where he'd hit her and knew from experience that it was already beginning to swell. She would have to put some ice on it shortly.

She said nothing, just kept staring at him. He was less than a foot away, and stared back with a look of such revulsion and hatred it made her blanch. She fully expected the hand to come again.

It didn't, though. They just stood there, staring at each other for several more beats. Then he turned and went back to his desk. He resumed flipping through papers, faster this time. After another moment he said, without looking up, 'We have a dinner tonight. You should fix your make-up.'

CHAPTER TWENTY-THREE

'Who's the DA on Kevin McDougal's case?' Kozlowski asked.

He, Lissa and Finn were walking along a path through Boston Common. It was Sunday morning, and the season was teetering. The leaves were losing their grip and tumbling off the trees, the wind was blowing a little stronger and colder by the day. Still, autumn was putting up a good fight, and the sun cut through the crystalline air, warming their faces. It was sweater weather; the kind of fall day that defines New England better than any other. Sally was walking ahead of them, pushing Andrew in the stroller.

'Mitchell,' Lissa said.

'Straight shooter,' Kozlowski commented. 'Not the best for working a deal.'

'He's political,' Finn said. 'ADA is a stepping stone for him. You don't go to Harvard and then take a job making thirty thousand dollars a year in Roxbury District Court without having a plan. He'll make a deal as long as there's something in it for him, and as long as he can be sure his ass is covered if things go to hell.'

'You think?' Lissa said.

Finn nodded. He looked up at the State House, looming over Boston Common with its gold dome blinding in the sunlight. 'He wants to be up there someday,' he said. 'You don't get to the governor's office without making a few headlines. The question isn't whether he'd make a deal; the question is: what do we have to offer?'

'The question is whether you're ready to risk your career by coloring outside the lines,' Kozlowski said.

'We're not virgins, Koz,' Finn said. 'Let's not pretend.'

'No, we're not,' Kozlowski agreed. 'But we've always been in the right. At least, that's what I've always thought. We've never bent the rules for someone who was guilty. And we've never done it for our own benefit. We do this, and we leave that behind.'

'Depends on how we do it,' Finn said.

'You've got a way that leaves room to maneuver?' Lissa asked.

'No,' Finn admitted. 'I'm still working on it.'

Sally turned back to look at them. 'He's smiling!' she called. She gestured to Andrew, who was looking at Sally, a long line of drool hanging from his lower lip as he giggled up at her.

'He likes you,' Lissa called back. 'You're like his big sister.' She lowered her voice again, so that Sally couldn't hear. 'Is it worth it?' she asked. 'Things are pretty good right now; you really want to risk it all?'

'She was my mother,' Finn said. 'What am I supposed to do? Just let it go?'

'Maybe,' Lissa said.

He shook his head. 'I'll find a way,' he said. 'I can't let this drop.' They walked on in silence, listening to the laughter of the city kids as they exhausted the last of the outdoor weather before the long, hard winter.

'Okay,' Kozlowski said at last. 'How do you want to handle Mitchell?'

Finn looked at Lissa. 'Set up a meeting for me with him on Monday. Lunch. Someplace nice, but not too obvious.'

'What are you gonna say to him?'

Finn shrugged. 'I'll figure something out.'

They were crossing Charles Street, heading into the Public

Gardens. The swan boats were still in the water, and smiling people paddled them through the pond.

'Look, Andrew, swans!' Sally called.

The baby babbled.

Lissa looked at Finn. 'Just make damned sure it's worth it,' she said.

Julie Racine lived in Boston's South End. Once it had been an area that shaded toward sketchy, inhabited by a mixture of gays and Hispanics and those on the outer fringes of societal acceptance. But that was decades ago, before being gay and Hispanic was fashionable. Now the established residents mingled easily with the yuppies and the home-steaders who had gutted run-down buildings to make multi-million dollar duplexes. The neighborhood had managed, somehow, to retain some of its historic flavor and edge, and was one of the few areas in the puritanical city that might be considered hip as opposed to quaint.

Racine lived in an apartment in one of the dwindling number of buildings that had, as yet, escaped renovation. It was off Berkeley, past Washington Street, out where the homeless shelters still burdened property values. Her apartment was on the top floor of a fifth-floor walk-up, but she was fit and the rent was reasonable.

She was alone on Sunday when there was a knock on the door. She glanced through the peephole and sucked in a breath. She was tempted to pretend she wasn't home. She knew it wouldn't work, though. She unlocked the door and opened it halfway.

Long was standing there in jeans and a sweat shirt. The file she'd left at his apartment was tucked under his arm. It looked thicker than when she'd left it with him.

She blew a strand of hair out of her face. 'What do you want?'

'Thanks for opening the door, at least,' he said.

'You're a cop. You would've picked the lock or kicked it in,' she said. 'I didn't feel like paying the landlord to have that fixed.'

'It's not like that.'

'No?'

'I just wanted to apologize. And to thank you. Is that all right?'

She put a hand on her hip. 'Depends. You sober?' His shoulders sagged, and she winced at the thought that she'd hurt him. She tried to harden her resolve.

'I deserved that,' he said quietly. 'I'll go.'

As he turned to walk back down the stairs, she softened her stance. 'What happened to you?' she asked. 'People used to joke that you were bulletproof.'

'You know what happened to me.'

She shook her head. 'I don't. I only know what they *say* happened.'

'What do they say happened?'

'Depends on who you talk to,' she said. 'Half say you were just as dirty as Jimmy. That you were into the drugs, too, and you killed him to save yourself from being found out. They say you set the whole thing up.'

'And the other half?'

She shrugged. 'The others say you betrayed him. That you found out about the drugs and you were looking to make a name for yourself. They say you could've helped him, and instead you shot him.'

'And you? What do you believe?'

He was leaning against the wall, looking lost. She wanted to go to him, but she held back. The images of him from two nights before flashed through her mind. 'I don't believe anything. I have to hear it from you, then I'll decide what I think the truth is.'

He looked at the floor. 'The truth . . .' He said the words as though they had no meaning; as though he were talking about a phantom. 'The truth is that they're right. All of them. Deep down, in the ways that really matter, I'm just as dirty as Jimmy was. Maybe we all are. The truth is that I should have helped him, and I couldn't, or I didn't.'

'That doesn't answer the question.'

'It's as much of an answer as I think I'll ever have.'

'So that's it?' she asked. 'You're beyond redemption?'

He gave a sad smile. 'That's the last thing my father said to me. He told me there was no salvation for what I'd done. When you're a cop, your partner is your brother. My father told me I killed my brother, and there's no coming back from that. He couldn't forgive me. He called it the world's greatest sin. That was two days before he died.'

Her heart was breaking for him. She stepped forward and took hold of his sweat shirt. He let himself be pulled, and she wrapped her arms around his back. She felt him lower his head onto her shoulder.

They stood there quietly for several minutes. Finally she stepped back and looked at him. He seemed so tired. 'Come on,' she said, motioning toward her apartment door. 'You can come in.'

'Are you sure?' he asked.

'No,' she said. 'I'm not sure.'

He nodded.

She turned and walked back into her apartment. It took a moment, but eventually he followed her.

The phone rang at Finn's apartment that night. When he answered it, he was surprised to hear the voice of Shelly Tesco, the director of adoption services at the Health Services Center in New Hampshire. 'Mr Finn, I have your records,' she said.

'Will you give them to me?'

'That would be illegal,' she replied.

'Then why did you call?'

'You misunderstand, Mr Finn. It would be illegal for me to actually give them to you. And if I give the actual records to you, people will know I was the one who handed them over. I'm not going to risk that. I will let you look at them, though. Only up here, and just you.'

Finn's heart beat a little faster. 'Okay,' he agreed. 'I can't make it tomorrow, but how about Tuesday night?'

'That's fine.'

'Should I meet you at your office?'

'No,' Tesco said. 'I don't want anyone seeing you here again. I'll pick a place and I'll call to let you know where.'

'Okay.'

'I should warn you, Mr Finn, there are some irregularities in your file.'

'What sort of irregularities?' Finn asked.

'I don't want to discus it over the phone. You should just know that it may not have all the answers you're looking for. There may just be more questions. I'm still doing some checking, but it's one of the more unusual cases I've come across.'

'You can't tell me about it now?'

'No,' Tesco said. 'Tuesday.'

'Tuesday, then,' Finn said.

When Coale slept, which wasn't often, it was in a small loft in a converted warehouse in the leather district, sandwiched between Chinatown and the business district, on the edge of what had once been known as the combat zone. He could have afforded a much larger place; in fact, he could have afforded several larger places, but he had no interest in ostentation. His needs were minimal, and his desires virtually non-existent. His was a wholly purpose-driven life, the purpose changing with the whims of his clients and the demands of his current employment.

He was in the loft on Sunday night to shower and sleep for a few hours. He would need the sleep now; he had work to do the next day. He'd been listening to the conversation between Finn and Shelly Tesco through the bug he'd placed in Finn's phone while the lawyer was meeting with McDougal two days earlier. There was no question about what had to be done. First he had to drive out to western Massachusetts, then up to New Hampshire. It would be a long day, and he wasn't looking forward to it, but it was part of the job.

He'd spent the weekend tailing the lawyer, watching him as he spent time with the detective and his wife and kid. He'd watched the way Finn interacted with the Malley girl. A quick search of state records on the Internet had revealed her history. It was a miracle she wasn't curled up in an alley somewhere with a needle sticking out of her arm.

Watching them for a few days, it had struck him how foreign their lives were to any reality he'd ever known. He wondered what it would have been like for him if he'd been allowed such a life. Not that it mattered; that had ended for him long ago.

He sat on the edge of his bed, the only piece of furniture in the loft, and let the water from the shower drip off his hair into the towel wrapped around his waist. A few hours' sleep would be good.

He looked over at the large suitcase in the corner that held most of his worldly possessions, wrestling with his impulses. It was pointless, he knew; the past was gone, and it wasn't coming back. And yet he couldn't fight the compulsion to pick at the ancient scabs, to peel them back and let the wounds bleed again, if only so that he could feel something – anything.

The pictures were tucked away in an interior pocket of the suitcase, wrapped in plastic to protect them. They were all that was left of his past. Even the memories had faded to the point where they were only fleeting impressions.

He pulled the photographs out. His breathing quickened. There were only two, but they'd been cared for well, and the images had only yellowed slightly. The first was a picture of his father, standing in front of one of the cars – the black Rolls with the maroon trim. It had been his favorite. He'd worked tirelessly to keep it in immaculate shape. Even after he'd been fired, he went over it one last time: cleaning the exterior with soft soap and drying it with a chamois; rubbing on two layers of wax and buffing it to a brilliant shine; wiping down the tires and treating the interior leather. When he'd finished, he'd hung the keys on a nail at the entrance of the garage, walked up to the garage apartment he and his son had shared for seven years, thrown a rope over a rafter and hanged himself.

Coale had found him an hour later, and he'd screamed as he tried to lift the weight of the body off the rope, crying desperately as he tried to cut his father down without letting the body sag back onto the noose. Finally the gardener heard the screams and came running. He'd cut the rope with his shears, and the boy had collapsed from exhaustion and grief.

Coale looked at the picture for a long time, rubbing his thumb over the image as he allowed himself to remember.

After a while he flipped the picture and looked at the second. This one held the image of a young girl, smiling at the camera. The sun was in her eyes, and she squinted slightly, but there was no mistaking her intimate joy. He only glanced at this picture for a few seconds. Some memories were too painful to dwell upon.

He wrapped the pictures back up in the plastic and put them away in the suitcase. Then he lay back on the bed and closed his eyes. He only had a few hours to sleep. Then he had to get back to work.

CHAPTER TWENTY-FOUR

Assistant District Attorney Peter Mitchell was a man of the people. He'd grown up in Dorchester, the son of a pipe fitter with Jamaican roots and a nurse whose parents had emigrated from Ecuador. At the local public school where more than two thirds of the students were failing, he was exceptional. In his valedictory speech on graduation day he'd attributed his success to his parents' determination. After attending UMass Boston on a full scholarship and again graduating at the top of his class, he was accepted at Harvard Law School. The competition there was more rigorous, but he still managed to graduate in the top quarter of his class, and to be named an editor of the *Law Review*. When it came time for him to pick from any number of jobs that were waiting for a new lawyer of his academic achievement and cultural background, he chose to join the District Attorney's Office.

To some it seemed like a bizarre choice. In private practice he could have made five times his thirty-thousand-dollar salary as an ADA. He knew, though, that he would never survive in the rarified air of one of the city's old-line, white-shoe firms. It wasn't that he lacked the intelligence. He had as much book smarts as anyone coming out of the Ivy League, and he'd put his common sense well above that of any of his silver-spoon contemporaries. Most of them had never experienced real life.

But he would never have survived because he was, at his core, an angry young man. He'd spent his entire life doing what people expected of him. He'd studied and smiled and worked his ass off to live up to the standards that others set for him. The very idea that he would spend the next seven years buttering the buns of a bunch of middle-aged white assholes who would inevitably assume him to be a product of affirmative action was enough to make him consider a trip to one of the local gun shows out in western Massachusetts to make a purchase. He knew he would have lasted all of a month before he punched someone in the face.

And so, rather than put himself in a position to fail, he put himself in a position where he could exploit all of his natural gifts. The DA's office was perfect for him. He was smart and motivated and political. It didn't hurt that he was black, and he could talk to jurors in a way that made sense. He was marked for greatness the moment he stepped into the office, and three years later it was only a matter of what he wanted to do now.

He'd been given the Kevin McDougal file as a reward for all the hard work he'd put in. Kevin was a bit player of little importance in the grand scheme of things. His father, though, was a star in Boston's shadowy mob world. Putting his son in jail for a significant time would be a coup.

Both Peter Mitchell and Scott Finn knew all this as they sat across the table from each other at the Capital Grille on Newbury Street out near Massachusetts Avenue. The restaurant had been chosen carefully. It was far enough out that it was reasonably close to the courthouse in Roxbury. It was nice, but not too nice, with thick steaks and dark wood that bespoke a male-dominated world where deals were expected.

They had engaged in the obligatory small talk throughout the lunch as they dug into their porterhouses, trading tidbits about judges and politicians and other lawyers, establishing their bona fides and setting the boundaries of male camaraderie, if not quite trust. It wasn't until the plates were cleared away that the real conversation began.

'I'm representing Kevin McDougal,' Finn said as the coffee was served.

Mitchell nodded as he stirred his cup. 'I saw that on the docket. Lissa Krantz talked to my assistant.'

'Any idea what you're thinking on plea bargain?'

Mitchell smiled. 'I wasn't thinking about any plea bargain,' he said. 'I was thinking about taking it to trial.'

'You serious?' Finn said, shaking his head. 'Your witness is for shit. She's, what, six months out of the academy? It was entrapment.'

Mitchell laughed. 'Your boy walked up to her next to a school playground and offered her a couple rocks. You think the jury's gonna buy into an entrapment defense?'

'After I get done with her?' Finn let out a slow whistle. 'She'll be lucky if the jury doesn't convict her. She's never been on the stand before, has she?'

Mitchell shook his head. 'Nope. Doesn't matter; she looks like she's fourteen. The jury'll take one look at her, and they'll be so pissed off at your client, they won't even listen to your cross. Either that or they'll get pissed at you for attacking her.'

'You've never seen me work, have you?' Finn said.

'I have. It's impressive, but it won't be enough. Not in this case.'

'You sound so sure, but I can see a little doubt in your eyes. You've got a great career ahead of you; you can practically write your own ticket if you don't screw things up. The only sort of thing that could derail you is an acquittal in a case like this.' Finn sipped his coffee as he let that sink in. 'I don't tend to lose.'

Mitchell stirred his coffee quietly. 'What did you have in mind?' he asked after a moment.

'I can probably get my guy to cop to a possession charge, B-class misdemeanor, eighteen months probation.' Finn said the words as though he were offering the ADA a gift.

Mitchell dropped his spoon, and it made a loud ringing sound off the china. 'Thanks for the lunch, Finn,' he said, 'but if you were just bringing me out to fuck with me, we could have gone someplace closer to the courthouse.' He started to stand.

'Wait, wait,' Finn pleaded. 'Sit down.'

'Why? So you can insult my intelligence some more? Your boy's facing fifteen-to-thirty hard time with a two and a half year minimum on a case a first year law student could win, and you think you can get it bumped by buying me a nice lunch? Don't call me again.'

'Please,' Finn said. He motioned to the chair.

Mitchell shook his head as though he were crazy to even consider sitting down with Finn again, but he pulled out the chair and took a seat anyway. 'What?' he asked. 'You gonna buy me dessert now?'

'I need this case to go away,' Finn said quietly. It was almost a whisper. His tone was desperate, and the words made him wince. It seemed hard to believe they'd even made it past his lips. 'I need you to *make* this case go away.'

The young ADA looked at Finn quizzically. 'You're putting me on, chief, right?' He looked around the restaurant. 'Where's Ashton Kutcher, because I know I'm getting punked here.'

Finn shook his head. 'I'm not joking. I need your help.'

Mitchell frowned. 'I can't give you this kind of help, you know that.' He leaned in close. 'We're off the record, okay?'

Finn nodded.

'I don't like what you do,' Mitchell said. 'You should know that. Defense lawyers get rich by getting their clients off even when they're guilty. And don't give me the "everybody has a right to a defense" bull-shit. I've heard this rationalization; it doesn't fly. To me, that's all a bunch of soul-soothing crap meant to justify the money your kind makes.' It might have been a campaign speech were it not for the fact that the words came out with real venom. He checked himself and continued more calmly. 'But as defense lawyers go, I've always thought of you as one of the good guys. One of the guys who wouldn't break the rules. So I'm sitting here wondering why the hell you're asking me to throw a case. Is it for money?'

Finn shook his head again. 'It's got nothing to do with money.'

'No, I didn't think so. So what is it, then?'

'All I can tell you is that I've got a good reason.'

'That's supposed to move me somehow? Sorry, but you're gonna have to do a lot better than that.'

'Fine. My mother was murdered last week.'

'Jesus, I'm sorry.'

'It's okay, I never knew her. But I still need to know what happened.'

'And?'

'And the only way I may be able to find out what happened is if Kevin McDougal walks.'

Mitchell rubbed his forehead in confusion. 'You're gonna have to explain the connection to me.'

'I can't. All I can say is that this is a hell of a lot more import-ant than some punk selling a little crack. I'm not excusing Kevin McDougal, he's a slimy little shit, but if it wasn't him out there, it would've been someone else – you and I both know that.'

Mitchell scratched his head. 'Let's assume I believe you. Let's assume you might actually learn something about your mother's murder. You're forgetting how people on my side of the courtroom feel about this kid's father. People are looking for him to go away, and for real time. They haven't been able to nail his father, but now that they've got his kid by the balls, they're not gonna let go until he's singing alto in the Vienna Boys' Choir. Even if I wanted to do you a favor on this, I wouldn't get sign-off from anyone in my office. Not without something in return.'

'Like what?' Finn asked.

'Like Eamonn McDougal,' Mitchell said. He sat back in his chair. 'Fair's fair. You want me to cut the son loose, I gotta have the father.'

'He's a client. I can't.'

'Oh, I see,' Mitchell said. 'It's okay for me to compromise my principles, but not for you? Fuck you.'

'It's not that,' Finn said. 'But anything I give you would be excluded. It would all be protected by the attorney-client privilege. Even if I was willing to do it, it wouldn't get you anywhere.'

Mitchell used the linen napkin to wipe his mouth. 'Then I guess we've got nothing more to talk about,' he said.

'No?' Finn asked.

'Not unless you've got something else to offer.'

'Nothing that you can use. There's no other way?'

Mitchell stood up. 'Without something to trade, there's nothing I could do for you even if I wanted to. You figure something out, though. You find a way to give me the big fish and I'll be all ears, I'll take it as high as I have to in the office.' He took out his wallet and tossed two twenties onto the table.

'I've got the bill,' Finn said. 'It was my dime.'

'Nah, I don't think so,' Mitchell said. 'I don't want anyone getting the wrong idea, thinking that you were buying me a lunch for some illegal purpose here. You understand me?'

Finn nodded. 'Perfectly.'

'Good. You let me know if we've got something to talk about when you've had a chance to think about it.' Mitchell turned and walked out of the restaurant without looking back.

The place was in a sagging brownstone in a run-down area north of Springfield. Everything about it was depressing. Coale sat in his car outside on the street, watching. A few of the passers-by had slowed to admire his car, but a sharp look had been enough to warn them off.

The man stepped out of the building shortly after noon. He looked younger than Coale would have expected. Coale knew from the records that he was in his forties, but Coale was expecting a weathered forties – someone with a pot belly and a receding hairline in a moth-bitten sweater. It would have fit the area better. Instead, the man looked young and vibrant, with thick brown hair and a thin, athletic frame. Coale got out of his car and approached him.

'Mr Altby?' Coale said.

The man was headed up the street. He looked around.

'Mr James Altby?' Coale said again.

'Yes,' the man replied.

'You're the director of the Springfield Adoption Center?'

The man smiled uneasily, looked up at the building. 'I am.'

Coale put his hand out. 'I'm Joe Wilson. I'd like to talk to you for a few minutes, if you can spare the time.'

Altby shook the hand. 'I'm actually heading out to lunch,' he said.

Coale motioned toward his car. 'I can drive you,' he said. 'It will only take a few moments. It's important.'

'What's it about?'

'Shelly Tesco,' Coale responded.

Altby nodded sympathetically. 'I'm familiar with Ms Tesco,' he said. 'Is this about her adoption records?'

'It is.'

Altby shook his head. 'As I've told her, there's really no information I can give her. I wish things were different, but the law is the law. I was under the impression that she understood that now.'

'I'm sure she does,' Coale said. 'I'd still like to talk to you. Where are you going to lunch?'

'Down at Martingano's, over on Main Street.'

'I can give you a ride. Please, get in my car.'

Altby looked doubtful, but moved toward the Mercedes. 'I'll take the ride,' he said, 'but I can assure you, there's nothing you can say that Ms Tesco hasn't already said before. There really is no information I can give you.'

Coale smiled at Altby. 'I don't know about that,' he said. 'I think you'll find that I am far more persuasive than Ms Tesco.'

'Am I off the case?' Long demanded.

Captain Townsend looked to the sky for help. 'Jesus, you just don't get it, do you? We're talking about a goddamned senator here. Not to mention one of the richest men in the Commonwealth. You can't just go out there and start making accusations!'

'I didn't make any accusations,' Long said. 'And you still haven't answered my question – am I off the case?'

'No!' Townsend shouted. 'You're not off the goddamned case! But you will keep me in the loop on whatever you're doing. And the next time you want to go out to talk to someone at Buchanan's level, you're taking me with you, you got that?'

'I need a babysitter now?'

'You need a witness, you jackass! Buchanan's people were on the phone all day yesterday and this morning, raising hell with anybody in the city who would listen. You're on a short leash as it is; you get into a situation where it's your word against his, guess who loses?' Townsend rubbed his forehead. 'I swear to God, Long. Ya know?'

'Yeah, I know,' Long conceded. 'As long as it's still my case.'

'It's still yours,' Townsend said. 'I don't know why you want it. I know I don't want it.' It looked like the man was going to have a heart attack. He took a deep breath. 'This angle on the campaign finance got legs?'

Long shrugged. 'Don't know. Something messed up was going on with McDougal's employees and the senator's fundraising. The Connor woman made the calls to both McDougal and Buchanan before she was murdered. You put those things together –'

'And it doesn't prove anything about her murder,' Townsend said. 'It could just be a coincidence. As far as we know, this could still be some crackhead and a random break-in. It still makes the most sense.'

'It could be,' Long said. 'There's one other thing, though. There were no fingerprints at the crime scene.'

'How does that help us on anything?' Townsend asked.

'You don't understand,' Long said. 'There were *no* fingerprints at the scene. Not even prints from Elizabeth Connor. Not from anyone. The whole place had been wiped clean. I mean professionally. The way people hired by Eamonn McDougal would clean a place.'

Townsend rolled his eyes at Long. 'You're still thinking about the man in the composite sketch, right? The ghost. You're stuck on the idea that he was at the Connor woman's apartment.'

'I saw what I saw,' Long said. 'You've got a better explanation?'

'Yeah, you're imagining things. That's a better explanation than the idea that a phantom from two decades ago showed up to whack Elizabeth Connor. What's she got to do with anything that would get her killed?'

'I told you; she knew things she might have been using against the wrong people.'

'So we're going with the campaign finance angle for now?'

Long shrugged. 'I gotta chase it down at least. See where it goes.'

'Yeah, you do,' Townsend said. 'Just chase carefully.'

Sally was in the apartment alone when Finn and Kozlowski arrived. She'd had two free periods at the end of the day, so she'd cut out of school early. Normally she headed straight over to Finn's office, but with the extra time, she'd gone to the apartment first to drop off some of her books and enjoy a few moments of solitude. It was one of the few things she missed about her old life. Before, nobody cared where she was or what she was doing. If she disappeared for a day just to be by herself, no one even noticed. Now, with Finn and Lissa and Kozlowski in her life, she rarely got a moment's peace. They constantly wanted to know what she was doing, and where she was doing it, and with whom it was being done. It was alien to her, and it meant that she no longer had the option of solitude when she wanted it. She wouldn't go back to her old life given the option, but it was nice to have a moment to herself.

She was sitting in her room doing her homework when she heard the door to the apartment open. She recognized the voices. Her first inclination was to go out to say hello, but something about their tone made her reconsider. She went to the door to eavesdrop.

'What'd you expect?' Kozlowski was asking. 'Did you think he was gonna thank you for giving him the opportunity to dismiss a high profile case against a confirmed scumbag who also happens to be the son of a major player?'

'No, I didn't think that,' Finn responded. 'But I thought he might consider trading a drug dealer for a murderer.'

'Maybe he would have, if you could have given him that. But you don't know what you can give him. For all you know, McDougal is just playing you to get his son off.'

'I don't think so,' Finn said.

'Why not? Because you trust him? Bullshit. He's a crook and he'll always be a crook. More than that, he's a sociopath. He doesn't play by your nice clean rules.'

There was a long moment of silence, and Sally wondered what was happening. Then Finn spoke again. 'So, what do you suggest I do?'

'Not you; *we*. We take this into our own hands. We get McDougal's file on your mother ourselves.'

'How?'

Kozlowski shrugged. 'It's in that filing cabinet at 355 Water Street Corp., isn't it?'

Finn frowned. 'You want to break in and steal it? You're crazy.'

'No, I'm not. It's not all that hard. We could be in and out in fifteen minutes.'

'Breaking into a client's office to get confidential information? Not the best move for my professional standing.'

'You got a better idea?'

There was another long moment where nothing was said. Sally wished she could see into the living room, to get an idea of what the two men were really thinking from their expressions. Finally, Finn spoke again. 'When?'

'Tonight.'

'Lissa's gonna have to take Sally again while we do it,' Finn said.

'I can arrange that.'

There was silence again, and Sally strained to pick up any sound at all. 'How do you want to work it?' she heard Finn say.

'We go in after McDougal leaves this evening,' Kozlowski said. 'Quiet and quick. With luck, he'll never know anyone was there. You got what you need?'

'Yeah, I just forgot the brief I was working on. Let's get down to the office so we can talk to Lissa before Sally gets out of school.'

Then they were gone. Sally heard the apartment door close, but she stayed where she was for a few minutes, a thousand thoughts racing through her mind. She looked around the room. Finn had painted it a pale pink when she moved in and picked up matching bed covers at some high-priced specialty linen store. Sally hated pink, but she appreciated the fact that he'd cared enough to make an effort. Now that she'd been there for a year, the room was filled with her personality, her things, her spirit. She stood there for a few moments, thinking about all that Finn had done for her. Then she picked up her book bag and headed out to Finn's office.

CHAPTER TWENTY-FIVE

Coale was in New Hampshire before four in the afternoon. He had plenty of time; the Health Center was open on Mondays until six. Add in commuting time, and Shelly Tesco wouldn't be home for well over two hours.

He found her place without difficulty. It was a small Cape house on a quiet street just outside of town. He parked his car around a corner, where it would draw less attention, and walked back.

The lawn was overgrown and a gutter needed fixing, but other than that it looked like a pleasant place. There was a large unruly garden in the back, with a patchwork of assorted fall vegetables in various states of harvest or decay. Online records indicated that the house had previously belonged to a Giuseppe and Maria Tesco – Shelly's parents.

He considered breaking a pane of glass in the back to let himself in, but thought better of it and searched briefly for a key outside. It took less than five minutes. The key was tucked into a small metallic box attached magnetically to the back of the water meter – a common spot. Ms Tesco probably assumed that there were few risks in a town as rural and friendly as hers. It was a dangerously flawed assumption.

He let himself into the house and began the search. Again, it took little time. The file was in the top drawer of a desk in the living room, clearly marked. Coale flipped through the papers to make sure it was what he was looking for.

Satisfied, he walked through the house, planning out the second half of the job. Fortunately, the place was far enough away from any neighbors that they were unlikely to be disturbed. Glancing at his watch, he saw that it was just after five o'clock. He had more than another hour to wait.

He sat down on a wooden chair and breathed deeply. He'd always been a patient man.

It was dark by six o'clock in Chelsea. Finn and Kozlowski were standing in the doorway of the warehouse across from 355 Water Street, watching. A biting wind blew up from the harbor, carrying with it the stink of dead fish and diesel. The place was silent, and it felt like the entire waterfront was deserted. It was an eerie, deceptive feeling; the fiercest creatures tended to move freely in the darkest places.

They'd been in the same spot for more than an hour, dressed in dark clothes, watching. They'd dropped Sally off at Lissa's apartment at four-thirty, and gone back to change at the office. Finn had told Sally that they needed to keep a client's wife under surveillance for the night. She'd simply nodded and said, 'Okay.'

At five-thirty, Janice, McDougal's secretary, pulled out of the parking lot in her bright white Camero. McDougal followed soon after, climbing into the back of his waiting Cadillac. It had been twenty minutes since they'd departed, and there'd been no further activity in the parking lot. Finn would have been tempted to move in by now, but Kozlowski said to wait. When asked why, Koz responded, 'Because.' He'd never been much of a conversationalist.

Now Kozlowski looked at Finn. 'I'm going to do a little reconnaissance,' he said. 'Stay here for a minute.'

'You're not going in without me.'

'No, I'm not,' Kozlowski agreed. 'But I want to have an idea what we are dealing with before we go for real. Then I'll come back and we can make a plan.'

'Fine,' Finn said. 'But if you go in without me, I'm gonna kick your ass.'

'Right.' Kozlowski didn't seem intimidated. 'I'll be back.' He slipped away, walking close to the building with his shoulders hunched over. He had on a black watchman's cap. He would be difficult to notice in the dark, and if he was spotted, he would look like a longshoreman completely at ease in the environment. He'd attract little attention.

He was gone for five minutes that seemed more like fifty to Finn. When he returned he was frowning. 'There's good news and bad news,' he said.

'Gimme the good news first.'

'They've got a sophisticated alarm system.'

'That's the good news?'

'Yeah. It's sophisticated, but old. I was trained on it when I was on the force and I'm pretty sure I can disable it.'

Finn nodded. 'That is good news. What's the bad news?'

'I don't think I can get us through the front door. I'm pretty good with my fingers, but the locks they've got on it are monsters. I won't get through them.'

'Crap,' Finn said. 'You're gonna give it a try, though, right?'

'If I need to,' Kozlowski said. 'There's a back door that looks a little more reasonable. That's the other good news. We'll start there.'

'Now?'

Kozlowski nodded. 'Now.'

They headed out along the building, in the same direction from which Kozlowski had just come.

The meeting was set for six-thirty. Long arrived early, Captain Townsend in tow. He felt like a child bringing his father to the principal's office, but he understood it was the only way he was going to stay in charge of the case.

Long had instructed Buchanan to show up at the station house –

189

this was a murder investigation, after all. That mandate was quickly rejected, which caused Long to resort to threats. As it turned out, United States senators are relatively impervious to threats from local law enforcement officers. Long was informed that if the police wished to talk with Buchanan, he would make himself available for the half hour between six-thirty and seven at his lawyer's office. There would be no negotiation on the matter, and the senator would leave as soon as the clock struck seven. Long didn't like taking orders from suspects, but there was little he could do about it. Captain Townsend told him to be grateful. He also told him that the two of them would be going to the meeting together.

The lawyer's office was in the heart of the financial district, in a tower of pink marble, steel and glass. To get into the building, Long and Townsend had to stop at the front desk, where their credentials were checked and they were issued a building pass. The process made Long feel as though the proper order of the universe had been flipped, and the police were the ones under suspicion.

Up in the law firm's reception area, they were kept waiting for another ten minutes, looking out from the floor-to-ceiling glass windows onto a view that made plain how important the attorneys at the firm were. Townsend's face acknowledged how impressive it was. Long looked away.

Finally they were led into a conference room with a similarly stunning view out of a different side of the building. Buchanan was already there, along with a stout, balding man in his fifties in a dark suit and bright blue tie. The second man stood, breathing heavily as he lifted his bulk off the chair. 'Gentlemen,' he said. 'My name is Spencer Carleson. I represent the senator.' Buchanan didn't bother standing, and no one shook hands. 'Sit,' Carleson ordered. 'It's my understanding that you'd like to talk to the senator with respect to a murder investigation?'

'That's right,' Long said. 'We –'

Carleson cut him off. 'The senator is, of course, more than happy to cooperate in any way he can with the police. There are some ground rules, however.'

Long looked at Townsend. 'Ground rules?'

'I'm sure you understand the politically sensitive nature of this discussion,' Carleson said. 'Senator Buchanan is in the middle of a reelection campaign that has less than a month to go. If word of the senator's connection to this matter leaked out, it could lead to all sorts of wild speculation. The senator's opponent would no doubt use it to imply some sort of wrongdoing. We can't have that.'

'We can't?' Long said.

'No,' Carleson said, with particular emphasis. 'We can't.' He let a beat pass to allow that to settle in. 'So, here are the ground rules. I will be present for all the questioning. Anything I believe is inappropriate, I will instruct my client not to answer. The interview will last no longer than a half hour, and when it is over, nothing about this meeting will be divulged to anyone. Not to the press. Not to others in the department.'

'We can't talk to other cops?' Long was well into a simmer.

'Once word spreads internally, it would undoubtedly be leaked,' Carleson said. 'I will not let this be used for political purposes. Besides, Detective Long, according to my internal sources, you don't have many people in the department who are talking to you these days anyway. It's not as though you have a partner, is it?'

Long came out of his chair. 'You wait a goddamned minute!' he yelled.

Townsend remained sitting, but his face had turned crimson. 'You're outta line, Carleson,' he said.

'I don't think so,' Carleson said. 'I'm not convinced the right man is investigating this case. Certainly if this outburst is any indication, Detective Long may not have the right temperament to handle such sensitive matters.'

Townsend looked at Long and motioned to him to sit down. Long lowered himself back into the chair, his eyes never leaving Carleson's, his instinctive distrust for the lawyer growing. Townsend said, 'This is Detective Long's case. He will not be replaced. If you have a problem with that, you will just have to deal with it.'

Carleson pursed his lips. 'Very well,' he said. 'Do we have an understanding with respect to the ground rules?'

'Fuck your ground rules,' Long growled.

Townsend put a hand up to cut him off. 'We will keep the conversation confidential for now,' he said. 'We will not let that confidentiality prevent the full investigation of this murder, however.'

Carleson nodded again. He looked at Long. 'Ask your questions, Detective.'

CHAPTER TWENTY-SIX

It was dark when Shelly Tesco got home. She'd been held up at work, explaining the adoption process to a couple who'd recently learned they were infertile. She could have told them to come back the next day; they walked in just as the office was closing, and she didn't get paid enough to justify overtime. But she felt like she couldn't leave without helping them. It seemed as though she could read the entire range of human emotions on their tired faces, from desperation to hope. She couldn't just send them away. Besides, it wasn't as though she had anything important waiting for her at home.

She noticed the Mercedes parked up around the corner, but paid it little mind. The Shumleys a few houses over had a son who was an investment banker in New York; he was probably visiting and eager to show off a new toy to his parents. Shelly wouldn't hear the end of it the next time she ran into Mildred. Bragging about her son's money had become the woman's full-time job, almost as though it made up for all the disappointments in her own life.

Shelly parked her car in the driveway. Soon the real weather would arrive, and she would need to park in the garage. But it wasn't here yet, and she'd have to put in a full day's work clearing out the single-car space to make room. She'd promised herself she would get to it last weekend, but just hadn't been able to muster the necessary motivation. *Next weekend*, she told herself. *There would always be next weekend.*

She opened the back door to the kitchen. Sometimes she wondered why she even bothered to lock the place up when she left in the morning. There hadn't been any real crime in the town in more than five years. It would be difficult to find a safer place to live. Reaching out, she flipped the light switch and it gave a loud clack, but nothing happened. She flipped it back and forth three times. 'Goddamned circuit breakers,' she muttered to herself.

It had happened before. Too often. Her electrician had told her that she should upgrade her system and replace the board, but she had no money for that. If it meant that she had to venture into the basement a few times a month to reset the circuits, so be it. It was better than spending money she didn't have.

She felt her way around the cabinets in the kitchen until she reached her utility drawer and pulled out a flashlight. Pressing the switch and having the beam of light to guide her provided some comfort. It was silly; she hadn't been afraid of the dark since she was a small child.

She walked over to the basement door and pulled it open. It was an unfinished space, cold and damp. The darkness was so complete that her flashlight barely penetrated it. She walked slowly down the ancient wooden steps, each of them creaking under her weight.

The circuit breaker panel was located over in a corner. Even knowing where it was, it took a moment for her to find it. She opened the panel and shone her light on the switches, frowning at what she saw. Normally, there would be one, maybe two, that had been tripped. Looking at the rows of switches, though, she could see that they were all thrown to the wrong side.

One by one, she flipped the switches back into their proper places. Then she turned to head back up to the kitchen. She swung her flashlight around, searching for the staircase, but it was blocked. A man in a dark suit was standing in front of her, only a few feet away. She tried to scream, but the shock had winded her, and all that came out was a petrified whimper.

The flashlight found his legs first, and as she raised it up his body. She saw the knife next, dangling casually from his hand. Finally, the light reached his face. He had neat gray hair, penetrating eyes, and a light scar on his forehead. Under different circumstances, she would have found him attractive, but her terror had overwhelmed her senses.

He stepped toward her, the knife raised slightly. 'I need to know about the file,' he said.

Finn watched as Kozlowski worked. They were standing at the back of the building down in Chelsea. A small flashlight was held between Kozlowski's teeth, aimed at the alarm keypad next to the door. With a small screwdriver he was removing the faceplate. Once the screws were out, he pulled the plastic off, careful not to separate any of the wires that clung to the keypad.

'They taught you this on the force?' Finn asked.

Kozlowski grunted. The flashlight prevented him from speaking, though Finn guessed he wouldn't have answered the question anyway.

Kozlowski pulled a small pair of wire clippers out of his pocket, and Finn watched as he counted the number of wires coming off the computer board. In the movies, the wires were all different colors. Apparently the movies weren't always right, because all the wires on the keypad were black.

Kozlowski counted them down, then paused between the third and the fourth wires. He moved the clippers back and forth between the two of them for a moment, looked behind him at Finn and raised his eyebrows.

'Don't look at me,' Finn said.

Kozlowski turned back to the keypad. The clippers zeroed in on the third wire. Then at the last moment, they moved down to the fourth, and cut the wire. Finn closed his eyes, waiting for the scream of the alarm. It didn't come. After a moment he opened his eyes again. Kozlowski looked satisfied. He was packing up his wire clippers and pulling out his lock pick. The flashlight was still in his mouth. He started working on the lock.

'Wait,' Finn said, holding up his hand.

'What?'

Finn cocked his head, listening intently. 'What was that?'

'What was what?'

The sound came again, a faint scrape against the steel siding around the corner of the building. 'That,' Finn said. 'What was that?'

Kozlowski had clearly heard the sound; he crouched as he slipped his lock-pick kit into his pocket and pulled out his gun. 'Stay here,' he said.

'Bullshit,' Finn replied. Kozlowski ignored him as he set out to find the source of the noise. He moved back along the building, his gun pointed into the darkness. As he rounded the corner, he saw movement in the shadows and his gun tracked it. 'Don't move,' he said, his finger tightening on the trigger.

'How well did you know Elizabeth Connor?' Long asked Buchanan.

James Buchanan glanced at his lawyer, who gave a permissive nod. 'I didn't,' Buchanan said.

'She was a donor to your campaign,' Long said.

'As I told you the last time we spoke, I have many donors,' Buchanan said. 'There is simply no way I could know all of them.'

'All of them don't give the maximum contribution.'

'That's true. But many do, and even for them there is no way I can personally keep track.' Buchanan's expression never changed as he answered Long's questions. If he was lying, he'd been well coached. Long had to find a way to break his confidence.

'You talked with her on the phone,' he said. It wasn't a question.

'You're wrong,' the senator said.

Long reached into the file he'd brought with him and pulled out a stack of papers. He laid them out on the table. 'These are Elizabeth

Connor's phone records,' he said. He was gratified that Buchanan's face seemed to turn a shade grayer. 'Do you see these entries here?' He flipped pages, identifying highlighted phone numbers. 'These are outgoing calls from her home phone. Do you recognize the number?'

Buchanan swallowed hard. 'That's my number.'

Long nodded. 'You still sticking with your story that you never knew her?'

Buchanan looked at his lawyer. Long couldn't read the signals exchanged, but there was clearly something there, because after a moment Carleson said, 'My client has answered the question, Detective. Move on.'

'*Move on?* Fuck you, move on. This is a murdered woman we're talking about. She called the senator repeatedly, and he expects to just sit there?'

'Perhaps one of the senator's staff took the call. There's nothing to prove that the senator ever actually spoke to the woman. She may have tried to reach him, and simply been turned down by one of his secretaries.'

Long shook his head. 'Take another look,' he said. 'Two of these calls lasted more than fifteen minutes. All of them lasted over five minutes. You telling me it takes fifteen minutes for his secretaries to hang up on someone?'

'My client has answered your question. These records prove nothing. Move on, Detective.'

'These records prove he's lying,' Long said.

Carleson's face turned magenta. 'Captain Townsend, I will not tolerate those kinds of accusations against my client. He is a United States senator, may I remind you!'

Townsend dismissed the lawyer with a wave.

'How about Eamonn McDougal?' Long demanded, remaining focused on his attack. 'How well do you know him?'

Carleson held up his hand to stop Buchanan from answering. 'I want to know what this has to do with the murder investigation before my client answers that question.'

'I'm sure you do,' Long replied. He looked at Buchanan, waiting for an answer.

'Understand, Detective,' Carleson growled, 'the senator doesn't answer any questions if I don't instruct him to. You want information? Then I'm going to have to be satisfied that it is relevant to the investigation. I will not allow this bullying to continue.' Long had to give the rotund little man credit, he could bark.

'Mr McDougal was Ms O'Connor's boss,' Long said.

'So?' Carleson said. 'That's hardly a justification for this line of inquiry.'

Long pointed to the phone numbers listed after each of the calls to the senator's residence. 'You see these?'

'Yes.'

'This number here, which was dialed immediately after each call she made to the senator's home, is the office number for Eamonn McDougal. Are you really suggesting this is a coincidence?'

'We're not suggesting anything, Detective,' Carleson said. 'It's not our responsibility to suggest anything. It's your job to convince me that any of this is relevant to this woman's murder. So far, it doesn't appear that there is anything to justify the kinds of questions you are pursuing.'

Long looked over at Townsend. 'Is he kidding?' he asked. 'Nothing to justify the questions?' He turned back to Buchanan. 'Senator, all due respect, but we have the phone records, we have the connection between the Connor woman and McDougal, we have records that show that each and every one of McDougal's employees donated the maximum amounts allowed by law to your campaign funds in each of the past four years. And we have Ms Connor's body lying dead in a pool of blood. Are you really going to tell the press that you have no comment about this?'

'This is unacceptable!' Carleson yelled, rising out of his chair. 'Captain Townsend, our ground rules were clear, this will not go to the press!'

Long was standing now, too, and he was several inches taller than the lawyer. 'You said he would answer questions!' he hollered back into Carleson's face. 'You didn't live up to your side of the bargain, so your ground rules don't mean shit to me!'

Carleson looked at Townsend. 'Then both your careers are over!'

'Wait, wait!' Townsend insisted. 'Just hold on, everyone!'

'You think I can't do it?' Carleson yelled. 'Just try me. You'll both be out on the street on your asses so fast and so hard you'll be shitting asphalt for a month! You think about that, Captain Townsend, before you let this maniac run loose!' He stood up and ushered his client out of his chair. 'Come on, Senator,' he said. 'You don't have to subject yourself to this anymore.'

'Yes, he does,' Long said. 'Whether it's here or down at the station later, he does have to answer these questions.'

Carleson smiled at him. It was a cold, humorless smile. 'Try to call him down to the station. I dare you. I would give anything to see what happens to you.' He looked at Townsend. 'I'll send my secretary to show you out.'

Long and Townsend were left alone. They were both standing, hunched over the table, like sprinters trying to catch their breath. Townsend looked over at Long. 'Well, that went well,' he said.

CHAPTER TWENTY-SEVEN

Kozlowski almost pulled the trigger. Someone with less experience would have started shooting as soon as they saw the shadow back behind the warehouse move again. He hesitated, though. His finger was tight to the trigger, but he allowed a moment for the shadow to take shape. When it did, he let out a loud sigh and put the gun down. 'Jesus Christ, Sally,' he whispered. 'I almost shot you.'

She was crouched down behind a stack of wooden palettes.

'Come out of there,' Kozlowski hissed.

'What is it?' Finn asked from behind him. He peered around Kozlowski and saw Sally emerge. 'What the hell are you doing here?' he demanded.

'I came to help,' she replied.

'What are you talking about?'

'I heard you. This afternoon at the apartment. I heard you saying you were breaking in here tonight.'

'How are you going to help? By almost getting yourself shot?'

She frowned. 'I can help,' she said stubbornly.

'You don't even know what this is about.'

'I don't need to. I know you're in trouble.'

Finn shook his head. 'What happened to Lissa? Why aren't you with her?'

'I told her I was going to do some homework in the guest room, and then I slipped out.'

Finn looked at Kozlowski. 'Call her; she's probably freaking out by now.'

Kozlowski already had his phone out. 'On it.'

'How did you get here?'

'Duh, I took a cab.'

'To this neighborhood?' Finn looked around.

She rolled her eyes. 'It's a much safer neighborhood than any of the places I grew up.'

Finn realized it was probably true. 'You have to go back. You can't be here.'

'Why not?'

'Because you're a kid. You can't be screwing up your life getting involved with something like this.'

'Look who's talking,' she replied. 'If I get caught, I'm a minor, so I'd get a slap on the wrist – maybe two months in juvie in a worst case, which gets wiped off my record when I turn eighteen. You get arrested out here, it's for real. Who's taking the bigger risk?'

Kozlowski hung up the phone. 'Okay, at least Lissa knows she's all right.' He looked at Sally. 'You may want to avoid her until she cools down; she's not exactly happy with you right now.'

'Sorry,' Sally said. 'But I'm not leaving.'

'Yes, you are,' Finn said.

'How?' Kozlowski asked. Finn looked at him. 'It's not like there are any cab stands around here.'

'We're not taking her with us,' Finn said.

'It's up to you,' Kozlowski said. 'But I'm not coming back tomorrow night. The alarm's disabled already, and I can't reset it. Chances are they'll notice tomorrow. They may just assume the circuit was tripped, but maybe not. Anyway you look at it, we're not coming back after tonight.'

'You can't seriously think it's okay for her to be involved.'

'No,' Kozlowski said. 'It's not okay for us to be involved, either. We're gonna be in and out in a matter of minutes. One file, that's all we're looking for.' He looked at her. 'You can be quiet, right?'

She nodded.

''Cause if you make a sound, I might have to shoot you, which would be a pain in the ass for all of us, you understand?'

She nodded again.

Kozlowski looked at Finn. 'Your call, but I say we get it over with.'

Finn felt completely outnumbered. 'Fine,' he said. He looked at Sally. 'But you do exactly as you're told. If we say run, you run like never before, and don't look back – got it?'

'Got it,' Sally replied.

'Okay,' Finn said reluctantly.

The three of them crept to the back door. It took Kozlowski less than a minute to pick the lock.

'Can you teach me how to do that?' Sally asked.

'No, he can not,' Finn answered.

Kozlowski looked at her and shrugged. 'We'll talk about it later.'

'No, you won't,' Finn said.

Kozlowski nodded toward the door. 'It's open, at least.' He turned the knob and pushed. The door swung inward a foot or so, and then stopped abruptly. Kozlowski pushed the door harder, but it didn't budge. 'It's blocked,' he said.

Finn stepped forward and threw his shoulder into the door, but there was no give whatsoever. He tried it again, with the same results. 'Whatever's blocking it is heavy,' he said. He reached his arm through the opening and tried to squeeze through. It was wide enough to get his head in, but his torso jammed. He tried sucking his ribcage in, but it was no use. After a couple of tries, he gave up and pulled his head back out. 'So, we try the front door now?' he said.

Kozlowski shook his head. 'I got a good look at the locks there. I'll never get through them.'

'There's got to be a way,' Finn said.

'There is,' Kozlowski said, looking at Sally.

Finn stared back at him. 'Other than that.'

'You got a better idea, I'm all ears.'

Sally piped up. 'I don't mind.'

Finn shook his head. 'I'm not letting you do it.'

'Why not?' Sally asked. 'You need to get into this place. I'm small enough to get through, I can find the front door and unlock it. Boom, we're all set. What's the problem?'

'The problem is that it's breaking and entering.'

'You already crossed that line,' she pointed out.

'Yeah, but you haven't.'

'I crossed that line when I was nine.'

Finn looked at Kozlowski for help, but found none forthcoming. 'Like I said before, it's your call,' the ex-cop said, 'but she's making sense.'

'What if she can't find the front door?' Finn asked. 'What if the back section is locked?'

'No sweat,' Sally said. 'Then I come back out the way I went in, and no one is the worse for it.'

'I still don't like it,' Finn said.

'Deal with it,' Sally said. She didn't wait for a response; she ducked past both men and slipped through the half-opened door.

'Wait!' Finn objected. His arm shot through the door to grab onto her, but she was already out of reach. 'Get back here!'

'No,' her voice answered from the darkness. 'Where's the front door?'

'In the front,' Kozlowski replied. He looked at Finn, who shot him a death stare. 'What? It is.'

'Which side?' Sally asked.

'Front right,' Kozlowski said. 'Knock three times when you get there. I have to disarm the alarm on the front door. When we knock back three times, it means the front alarm is disabled and you can unlock the door.'

'If I'm not there in ten minutes, come back and find me; I'll be here.' She was gone, and Kozlowski closed the door behind her.

'This isn't right,' Finn said to Kozlowski. 'She shouldn't be doing this.'

Kozlowski replied, 'If you want to find out what happened to your mother, we don't have much of a choice.' He nodded toward the corner of the building. 'Let's go out by the front door. We don't want to keep her waiting; she reminds me of Lissa, and I don't want her pissed at me.'

They slid along the rear of the building, walking quietly, staying in the shadows. Kozlowski reached the corner first and started around toward the front door. He came up short, though, and Finn bumped into him from behind. Kozlowski pushed him away from the corner. 'Shit!' he hissed.

'What is it?' Finn asked.

'McDougal.'

'What about him?'

Kozlowski glared at Finn. It was the first time Finn had ever seen even a hint of panic in the man's eyes.

'What about him?' Finn demanded again.

'He came back,' Kozlowski answered.

Spencer Carleson sat in his huge corner office in the top floor of the tallest building in downtown Boston. It wasn't the tallest in the city – the Prudential building in Back Bay held that distinction – but Carleson preferred the downtown area. It was closer to the water and it had better views. It was also closer to the courthouses. Of course, whenever he was forced to go to court, he felt as though he'd already

failed. He was a master of compromise, and an astute political opera-
tive. No one in the Commonwealth was better connected. His job, as
he saw it, was to keep his clients out of court.

That was looking like a difficult task with Buchanan.

'You were great, Spence,' his client was saying. 'I really appreciate
it.' It sounded like he actually meant it.

Carleson's secretary had met them at the door to the office when
they returned from the conference room. She had a tray of warm, damp
face towels in a silver tray, and she handed one to each of them, using
tongs the way they do in first class on transatlantic flights. Carleson
saw Buchanan raise an eyebrow, but he didn't care. A warm towel after
a tense meeting refreshed him. Right now he needed refreshing.

'Seriously,' Buchanan continued, 'I thought that detective was
going to come across the table at you. That would have been perfect.
I can't imagine I'll be having much of a problem with him from now
on.'

Carleson was rubbing the towel over his face, savouring the last of
the warmth. 'Thank you, Senator,' he said. 'I appreciate your confidence, but I wouldn't start the celebrations just yet. All I've done is
delay an inevitable confrontation.'

Buchanan looked stricken. 'You can't be serious,' he said. 'You
really think they will pursue this?'

'I'd count on it.'

'But you were so clear in there. They have no right –'

'They have every right,' Carleson cut him off. 'What I said in there
doesn't mean a thing. It was a bluff. They have a dead woman in
Roxbury. That gives them the right.'

'But I'm a United States senator.'

'Dead women trump political office every time,' Carleson said with
a sigh. 'If anything, the fact that you're a senator puts you in a more
vulnerable position. You can't dodge as well as a private citizen might.'

'I can't believe this. Isn't there anything we can do?'

Carleson threw the towel on the table. 'Maybe,' he said. 'Perhaps we can exert a little control through back channels. Try to get Detective Long off the case and delay the investigation at least until after the election.' He evaluated his client's face. 'Is there anything I need to know before we start? Anything you want to tell me? I'm your attorney, anything you say is protected.'

Buchanan put his head in his hands. 'Long is right about McDougal,' he said. 'He's donated to campaign ever since the beginning. So have his employees.'

'And he was reimbursing his employees for whatever they donated to you,' Carleson added. 'It's one of the easiest ways around the campaign financing laws. One of the most illegal, too.'

'I don't know what he was doing with his employees,' Buchanan said, raising his head. 'I never asked.'

'You just assumed that janitors and secretaries liked you enough to give up ten percent of their wages in the hope you'd be elected?' Carleson shook his head. 'Come on, Senator, you can see how that looks.'

Buchanan shrugged. 'I assumed, but I didn't know for sure. McDougal claimed to be responsible for over a million dollars in contributions, but I never asked how.'

'What was he getting in return for his money?'

'Access. Like everyone else.'

Carleson rolled his eyes. 'He gave you over a million dollars, and all he got was "access"?'

'Nothing more,' Buchanan insisted. 'He wanted the inside track on a series of government contracts that were awarded this summer. I told him I would see what I could do. Turns out, it wasn't much. I'm a first-term senator, and there were too many people lined up at the trough ahead of me. McDougal's companies didn't get any of the contracts. Not a single one. You can look it up.'

'That must not have made him happy,' Carleson said, stroking his chin.

'That's putting it mildly. If I didn't already have security, I'd have gotten some after the way he read me the riot act.'

'So the question is, what does all this have to do with Elizabeth Connor's death?'

'Nothing,' Buchanan said. 'I swear to God, Spence, I have no idea what happened to that woman.'

Carleson stared at the man. He considered himself an expert at reading people. It was a part of what made him a great lawyer. But in this case, Buchanan was a riddle, and Carleson realized after a moment that he wasn't going to be the one to solve it.

In the end, it didn't matter. Guilty or not, the man was a client. A wealthy, influential client at that. That was all that really mattered. 'Okay, then,' Carleson said. 'Let's put our heads together and see what we can come up with.'

Mildred Shumley walked her dog in the little New Hampshire neighborhood every night. It was one of the few things left in her life that she still found bearable. Everything else seemed to be falling apart.

Life was supposed to get easier as she got older. She and her husband had planned carefully for their retirement, making sure that they had enough to carry them through. It wasn't working out the way she had planned. Much to her dismay, Robert was living far longer than she had expected. By the time they were ready to retire, his cancer had spread and the doctors had assured them that he had a year, maybe eighteen months at the outside. That was two years ago, and her husband appeared to be making a miraculous recovery, thanks in large part to the miracles of modern medicine that were rapidly eating through their savings. Add to that the impact of the stock market crash, and Mildred was unsure how she was going to survive once Robert finally checked out. At one point she thought her son might help them out. But his fancy title hadn't protected him when his investment firm went belly up. Now he was talking about moving home. That was all she needed.

She was cataloguing her troubles as she passed across the street from Shelly Tesco's house. The place was dark, and Mildred assumed that her neighbor was out for the evening. Good for her. Maybe if she could find a man, Mildred would have something worthwhile to gossip about. That was really her only remaining pleasure in life.

As she glanced at the house, a man came around the corner from the back. At first he looked like a shadow; dressed all in black, he moved without making a sound. But he had a thick head of gray hair and his face was too light to stay hidden. She felt the tingle of something juicy to talk about, and ducked back into the shadows of an overhanging tree. He was the right age from the look of his face, probably early sixties, though he moved like he was much younger. Perhaps Shelly had found a man after all.

Mildred dismissed the thought after a few seconds' observation. He didn't move like someone leaving a tryst. He walked with purpose to the low, heavy sport sedan parked around the corner, never looking back at the house. Not only that, but the house was dark. Not the kind of dark where people are trying to conserve energy, but really dark. *Dead* was the word that came to Mildred's mind as she looked at her neighbor's house. The house looked dead.

The car's engine started, and the man pulled away. He didn't speed, but there was no let-up in his pace.

Mildred watched the car disappear into the darkness of the unlit street before she stepped back out into the street light.

She pulled on the leash, and walked her dog up the walkway to Shelly Tesco's front door. She rang the bell ten times and waited three full minutes before she gave up. She should leave it alone, she knew. It was none of her business – that was what Robert would say when she got back. Maybe Shelly was on vacation, and the man was a friend or a relative sent to check up on the house.

That certainly wasn't her impression, though.

She decided to wait. She'd call over to the house in the morning. Maybe again tomorrow evening. If she didn't get an answer, then she would ring the police no matter what her husband said about it. After all, what good were neighbors if they didn't keep an eye on one another?

CHAPTER TWENTY-EIGHT

'We've got to get her out of there,' Finn said. He started around the corner, but Kozlowski blocked him with a hand to his chest.

'I gotta think,' Kozlowski said.

'Think fast, then. Do you have any idea what he'll do to her if he finds her in there?'

'She's smart,' Kozlowski said. 'She'll probably stay hidden.'

'Probably?' Finn hissed. 'To hell with probably.' He ran to the back door and shoved it. It gave no ground. He stuck his head in and hissed, 'Sally!'

No answer.

'Sally!'

He pushed the door harder, and it groaned. Kozlowski was behind him, and pulled him away. 'Making noise isn't going to help her. The more commotion we make, the more likely it is that she'll get caught.'

Finn was in full panic now. He headed back toward the front of the building. 'I'm going in.'

Kozlowski grabbed him. 'If we go in there now, we're all screwed. Eamonn'll call in his boys and in a matter of minutes, this place'll look like a Sinn Fein meeting. Her best hope is that he does whatever he needs to do and leaves without ever knowing she's there. I don't think she's gonna show herself, and I don't think he's gonna find her.'

'You willing to bet her life on that? Because that's what we're doing.'

Kozlowski stared hard at Finn. Then he nodded.

Finn paced back and forth, agitated. Finally he said, 'Fine. But we're getting ready in case something goes wrong. We hear any noise in there – anything that doesn't sound right – and we're going in. Period.'

Kozlowski nodded again. 'You got a gun?'

Finn shook his head.

Kozlowski reached down his leg and pulled a .38 out of his ankle holster. 'My spare,' he said, handing it over to Finn. He reached into his jacket and pulled out his .357 Magnum. 'I'm gonna slide up closer to the door on this side,' he said. 'You circle around the building and come at it from the other direction.'

'Okay.'

'Be careful,' Kozlowski said. 'There's a driver in the car, and for all we know there may be others. Probably not, but be ready for anything.'

Finn nodded. 'If I hear anything unusual, anything at all, I'm going in,' he warned his partner.

'You don't have to tell me,' Kozlowski said. 'I'll beat you in there myself.'

It was pitch black and slow going inside the warehouse. Sally felt her way along the wall, stepping carefully to keep her balance. She hated the dark, and a part of her wished she'd stayed with Lissa at her apartment. Finn needed her help, though, and that gave her no choice.

It hadn't occurred to her that she might have trouble finding the front of the building. She had a good sense of direction, and she figured she could feel her way along the wall until she came to the right door. If she'd thought about it, she would have taken the flashlight from Koz, but she had moved too quickly, in part to cut short any protest from Finn. She regretted it now.

She checked her pocket for her cell phone, but realized it was in her bag back at Lissa's apartment. There was nothing left to do but press through the darkness.

Following the wall turned out to be impossible. There were steel shelves lined up all along the main walls of the warehouse, and there were crates and boxes stacked in front of the shelves. After twenty feet or so, her passage was blocked, and she was forced to turn right. She assumed the turn was ninety degrees, but there was no way to be sure. After another ten feet she tripped over a low cardboard box, rolled on the floor and bumped her head on what felt like a metal filing cabinet. She swore as she got up, and looked around in the darkness. There didn't appear to be any windows in the place, and there wasn't even enough light to make out shapes.

She started to move forward again, but tripped over another cardboard box. She was disoriented from the fall, and she'd lost all sense of direction. She reached out to feel the objects around her. The filing cabinet was to her right now. All of a sudden she was struck by the musty odor in the place. She hadn't given it a second thought when she entered the back portion of the warehouse, but now, lost in the darkness, the place closed in around her. In the darkness the air grew heavier, almost too thick to breathe. If she'd been able to figure out from which direction she'd come, she would have headed back, if only to get the damned flashlight from Kozlowski and to breathe fresh air for just a moment. Her heart beat wildly in her chest.

She began moving again. Driven by fear, she dropped to her knees and began crawling to keep from falling, desperate to find some way out. Every time her fingers clawed their way into a new obstacle her panic deepened, but she forced herself to keep going, forced her fingers to keep groping in the dark. At one point they dug their way into some sort of coarse fabric wrapped around a solid, curved shape that initially felt like a human shoulder. She nearly screamed, but managed to bite her lip. After a moment, she realized it was a rolled carpet.

She pushed herself forward.

Suddenly, like the dawn after a storm, a light appeared in front of her. It was just a crack at the bottom of a door, not nearly enough to let her see anything around her with any clarity, but enough to guide her; enough to sketch the outlines of the obstacles between her and the door.

She was hyperventilating by the time she reached the light, panic and relief sweeping over her in successive waves. Deprived of oxygen, she was beyond clear thought. She turned the knob and pushed the door open.

She was in an office with gray carpeting and a large wooden desk. There was a sofa next to a filing cabinet. Two chairs faced the desk. The light was blinding after coming from complete darkness, and she had to shade her eyes for a moment. Once they had adjusted, she saw a man standing at the far side of the desk, his back to her.

The possibility that there might be someone else in the warehouse had never crossed her mind; it wasn't in the realm of conscious possibility, and so at first she was disoriented. She started to open her mouth, but before she could the man spoke.

'Hello,' he said. She didn't recognize the voice. It was calm, even a little friendly. It was at that moment it occurred to her how much trouble she was in.

Finn was crouched by the northwest corner of the building, twenty feet from the front door, like a sprinter on his mark. Kozlowski's spare gun was gripped tightly in his right hand, and his muscles were tense. From his angle, he could see into McDougal's car. There was one man, the driver, seated at the wheel, his head tipped back against the head-rest, eyes closed, mouth open. It looked like he was taking a nap.

McDougal had entered the building alone, which meant there were only two – a fair fight in terms of numbers for him and Kozlowski, unless Eamonn called in backup. It might be wise to move now; they would certainly be able to take out the driver quickly enough, having the advantage of surprise. The prospect of storming the front door, where McDougal could pick them off easily, was less attractive.

Besides, Kozlowski might be right. Sally might be safely hidden away, and McDougal might come back out any moment and drive away.

Finn cursed himself for not being strong enough to keep her from going into the building. The truth was a part of him had wanted her to go in. It was the only way to find the information he needed about his mother's death. Crouching in the dark, Lissa's words came ringing back to him: *Make damned sure it's worth it.*

The driver stirred; he reached into his pocket and pulled out a phone. Finn's finger found the trigger to Kozlowski's spare gun.

Eamonn McDougal hadn't intended to return to the office. When he pulled out of the lot for the evening, he thought he was done. Halfway home, he realized he'd forgotten Coale's phone number, and the only place it was kept was in the file. Normally, he would have programmed it into his cell, but phones could fall into the wrong hands, and he couldn't risk someone else getting hold of the number.

When he got back to the office, he told his driver to wait outside. He unlocked the front door and disarmed the alarm on the front door, then went in. The file was in the cabinet in his office. It took him only a moment to unlock the drawer and pull out the folder. The number was on the inside of the manila file, written backwards as an added precaution in case the wrong eyes should ever fall upon it.

He dialed the number and waited. He was facing the wall behind the desk, looking at all the pictures of him with various celebrities and politicians. He'd led a remarkable life for someone born and raised in poverty in the outskirts of Belfast. As a child, he never imagined that he would be where he was now. He was the true definition of a self-made man, and no one was going to ruin that.

Coale answered on the second ring. 'Hello,' McDougal said. Lost in a self-congratulatory haze, he might have sounded a little too upbeat. 'Is it done?'

It took a moment for Sally to realize that the man hadn't seen her. At first it sounded like he was greeting her, that somehow he'd been waiting for her. Then she saw the phone in his hand.

She looked around, heart pounding. It might have made the most sense to back out of the room slowly, but her momentum was carrying her forward, and fear had sapped too much of her strength to allow her to change direction. She looked frantically for someplace to hide. The sofa to her right had an angled back, creating a narrow space against the wall, partially hidden. It looked just big enough, and she let her momentum carry her down in a silent dive. She shimmied her skinny body behind the sofa. Rolling onto her back, she looked down to make sure her feet weren't sticking out. She could see only a narrow section of the room – out to where the door to the warehouse stood open.

She held her breath. There was nothing else for her to do.

CHAPTER TWENTY-NINE

'It's done,' said Coale over the phone. His voice conveyed no satisfaction.

'Was it clean?' McDougal asked. Everything seemed to be falling into place; he couldn't have any slip-ups now.

'I said, it's done. You don't have to worry.'

'I do have to worry,' McDougal barked. 'The lawyer made contact with Tesco. I need to know that there are no loose ends.'

'It was clean,' Coale said.

'Good. Call me when you get back.'

McDougal hung up the phone and turned around. He sat heavily in his chair. *Lemons into lemonade*, he thought. That was the way he lived his life. Take the bad and make it good – or if not good precisely, at least turn it to your advantage. He closed his eyes. With luck it would be over soon, and when it was, he would be better off.

When he opened his eyes, he was looking straight ahead, his vision slightly blurred from the pressure to his ocular muscles. Something didn't seem right, and he blinked several times to get his vision to clear. When it did, he frowned.

The door to the warehouse was open.

He stood and walked around the desk. His office was little more than a dry-walled cubby carved out of the main storage area. The door to the back was almost always closed. There was nothing of consequence or interest that he needed to get at, and the place had a damp musty stench to it that, while not unbearable, was unpleasant enough to make him keep the door closed.

He walked over to the door and poked his head through, flipping on the lights. The place was a mess of bric-à-brac, with tires, old mattresses, carpets, boxes of paper, and documents stacked up to the twenty-foot ceiling. It had become a convenient dumping ground for all those things accumulated in life and business that were no longer worth keeping, but seemed too substantial to be discarded.

Stepping into the damp, cavernous space, he strained to detect any sound. 'Hello?'

He crept down the haphazard aisles created by the random stacks of junk. 'Hello?' he said again.

There was no answer, no sound at all, and after a few moments he headed back toward his office. When he got to the door, he turned and gave one last look back toward the warehouse, then shut the lights off and closed the door.

He stood there in his office, his hand still against the door, running through his afternoon, doing a mental check to recall whether he had opened the door that day. He didn't think so.

As he stood there, the shadow in the space between the wall and the sofa caught his attention. It was the only place where someone could hide, and he turned his head slowly. He moved two steps to his left, pulled his gun out of his pocket. When he was level with the back of the sofa, he ducked down in one swift motion, the gun pointing into the space, and he yelled, 'Don't move!'

Nothing. There was no one there.

Feeling foolish, he shook his head and stood up. He walked over to the desk and picked up the file. He thought briefly about putting it back in the cabinet but reconsidered. He wanted to go over the information one more time. Things were moving in the right direction, but now was not the time to lose track of the details.

He tucked the file under his arm and headed back out to the front of the building.

Finn watched as McDougal exited the building. The waiting was worse than anything he could remember. He'd lost people he cared about before. People he'd called friends. People he'd called more than friends. Life on the street was a daily roll of the dice, and the street was where he'd spent his youth.

That was different, though. On the street, the rules were the rules and couldn't be changed. If you played the game, you knew the risks; everyone was equal in that respect. Even when people in his crew had gone down, there was regret and anger, but no guilt. No shame at having been unable to change the rules by which they all lived their lives.

Now, as he crouched by the side of the building, gun in his hand, muscles tight and aching with the lactic acid building in them, he understood for the first time in his life what it was like to have someone depend on you for all they were and all they would become, and to fail them.

As soon as McDougal's car pulled out of the driveway, Finn stood up and moved quickly to the front door. He wanted to break into a full run, but he knew better. There were still dangers. The more attention they drew to themselves, the more likely it was that they would all be in peril. He forced himself to walk.

Kozlowski was approaching from the other direction. 'It's a good sign,' he said.

'What is?'

'He came out. Alone. If he'd found her, there would have been complications. There would have been activity. She's okay. She made it.'

'You seem sure.'

'I am.' Kozlowski pulled out his tools and began unscrewing the plastic case to the alarm keypad. 'We want to be ready,' he said as he went to work.

The office was still and dark for several minutes after McDougal left. Then slowly, silently, Sally slid her legs one at a time out from under the desk. She stood, shaking, her arms weak, afraid to move further. Holding her breath, she listened carefully for any sound, any sign that the man might be coming back.

She'd moved quickly as soon as she saw him walk through the door to the warehouse. The sofa provided marginal cover at best, and with the man's suspicions aroused there seemed little doubt that she would be discovered as soon as he returned.

Under the desk was the only alternative. It was a calculated risk – if he sat down again, or even walked behind the desk, he would have seen her. She figured the odds were fifty-fifty. Still, she liked those odds better than staying behind the couch.

She let herself breathe again after a moment, in short shallow bursts, afraid the sound might be enough to bring the man back. Nothing happened, and soon she was breathing normally again. Another minute and she felt confident enough to begin moving toward the door. Finn and Kozlowski were still out there, waiting for her, she hoped.

The door at the other side of the office led out into a reception area. At least, that's what it looked like in the dark. She couldn't be sure. There were windows, but it was a moonless night, and only faint glimmers from distant streetlights made their way through. It was enough to make out shapes, but nothing more.

She moved through the room slowly, carefully, convinced at every step that someone was lying in wait. She made it to the door at the far side of the room. It felt like she'd been in the place for an hour, though it had probably been fewer than ten minutes. She knocked three times on the door. There was no response.

'C'mon!' she hissed into the darkness. 'Don't do this!' She knocked three times again, this time hard enough to hurt her fists.

Then it came. A single knock from the other side of the door. She reached out to unlock the door and throw it open. Something in the back of her head stopped her, though. She ran through her memory, trying to recall what Kozlowski had said. She remembered him telling her to knock three times, and he would do the same. She waited, her hand on the knob, fighting every impulse she had to pull the door open.

It took another minute or two, but finally the knocks came again. This time there were three. She breathed a heavy sigh of relief, unlocked the door and pulled it open. Kozlowski and Finn slipped in, closing the door behind them. Kozlowski still had the flashlight, and he switched it on, pointing it at her.

'You all right?' Finn demanded. She could hear the tension in his voice.

'Yeah,' she said, as composed as possible. 'What took you guys so long?'

They moved quickly through the filing cabinet. Picking the lock took less than thirty seconds, and there were only three drawers. It didn't take long for them to realize that there was no information about Elizabeth Connor.

Finn said, under his breath, 'It's not here.'

'Are you telling me I almost got myself killed for nothing?' Sally asked.

Kozlowski was still flipping through one of the files. 'It's gotta be here,' he said. He gestured to the file with his flashlight. 'He's got files on everyone he's ever dealt with. Jesus, it looks like Eamonn has a little insurance on everyone.'

Finn looked over his shoulder. 'He must have taken my mother's file with him.'

'These files have an unbelievable amount of information,' Kozlowski said. 'Names, numbers, payoffs. There's enough here to put half of Boston away. He's even got tape recordings. Your mother's file has got to be here.'

'It's not,' Finn said. 'We've been through the entire cabinet. He must have moved it.'

Kozlowski continued flipping through another file. 'Would you look at this?' He showed the file he had in his hands to Finn. 'It's unbelievable.'

Finn didn't want to look at it; all he wanted was the information about Elizabeth Connor. He glanced over, however, and something on one of the sheets of paper caught his eye. He grabbed the file.

'Hey, what are you doing?' Kozlowski protested.

'Give me that for a minute,' Finn said. He read through the file, the gears in his mind turning. 'This is it,' he said. 'This is the answer.'

'What's the question?' Sally asked.

'The question is: who murdered my mother?' Finn said.

'And the answer is here? In files that have nothing to do with her?'

'Not the answer, but a way to get at the answer.' Finn rifled through the rest of the folders and picked out three. 'There's a copier in the other room,' he said. 'It shouldn't take more than a few minutes to copy these. I want to look through the tapes, too. Pick out a couple of those.'

'What are you going to do with them?' Kozlowski asked.

'I'm going to turn them into answers,' Finn said.

Long and Townsend were back at the station house, sitting in the captain's office. They were staring at each other. 'What an asshole,' Townsend said.

'Buchanan or his pit bull?'

'Both. I was talking about Carleson, though.'

Long nodded. 'I'd like to wipe the smug look off his face. Sitting there, looking at us like we're powerless against him and his client. It pissed me off.'

'That's what he was trying to do,' Townsend said. 'He wants you mad; he wants you so mad that you'll make a mistake. That's how he thinks he'll win.'

'So what do we do?'

Townsend leaned back in his chair. 'We need to be careful. We move forward and we build a case so solid it can't be ignored. Can you do that?'

'Yeah,' Long said. 'It may take a while, but there are too many people involved for them to keep it buttoned up. Every single one of Eamonn McDougal's employees gave money to Buchanan. If we can find a few who will swear that they were paid by McDougal to do it, that's the hook.'

'How do you get them to talk?'

'I lean on them. Some of these people must have pressure points we can exploit. We figure out where to push, they'll give.'

Townsend looked skeptical. 'If I were in their shoes, I'd be way more afraid of McDougal than I'd be of the cops. That's the sad reality.'

'Maybe. We'll see.'

Townsend shot Long a look. 'Don't lean too hard, Long,' he said. 'You're already being watched. People around here get a whiff of anything improper, you won't last a day.'

Long put his hands up. 'Don't worry, Cap. I won't cross the line.'

'You'd better not.' Townsend stared at Long for a few seconds. 'What happened between you and Jimmy? For real.'

Long stood up. 'It's in my report,' he said. 'I've got nothing else to say that I didn't put down on paper.'

CHAPTER THIRTY

Coale pulled his black Mercedes into the garage shortly after ten o'clock that night. He was amazed at how tired he was. More tired than he could ever remember being in his life. Not the pure physical exhaustion that comes from exertion or lack of sleep, but the endless soul-searing weariness that saps the strength more completely. For the first time in his adult life, he craved sleep not just to recharge, but to escape.

The garage was two blocks away from the loft. It was a trek he'd made more than a thousand times, and yet tonight it seemed different. He noticed the stores, noticed the people. He'd taken note of them all before, to be sure. It was a requirement of his profession to be aware of everything around him. If necessary for a job, or if pressed, he probably could have rattled off a description of every single building, every single storefront on the route. He probably could have described all of the locals and given an accurate account of their general habits – their morning commuting schedules and their evening routines. But he'd never really *noticed* them before as anything more than pieces of his environment. Tonight, somehow, something was different. They seemed like actual living, breathing beings.

Halfway between the garage and his loft, he passed a bar and glanced through the window. There was nothing unusual or notable about it; it was just like a thousand establishments in Boston. Wooden booths, a long mahogany bar fronted with well-worn stools, four-fifths empty on a Monday night. And yet something about the place caught his attention. Perhaps it was the way the bartender propped himself against the cash register, so comfortable in his conversation with two of the regulars. Maybe it was the couple in the booth, leaning in toward each other as though it had been a year since they'd last seen each other, so desperate were they to drink in every last word. Whatever it was, he paused in front of the place, opened the door slowly, and stepped inside.

Everyone in the bar looked up when he walked in, and he could feel them all recoil. He was used to that. He had carefully cultivated an aura that inspired fear and kept people distant. Kept people from approaching him. Kept people from questioning him. He never would have survived for this long any other way.

He walked slowly over toward the bar. He didn't sit; that would have been going too far. Instead, he put his hands on the counter and turned to look at the bartender, who abandoned the regular and walked over.

'Help you?' he asked.

'Yeah,' Coale said. 'You got Scotch?'

'It's a bar,' the bartender said. Coale gave him a look and the bartender shrugged apologetically. 'What kind?'

'Macallan still good?'

'Top shelf.'

The man nodded. 'Neat.'

The bartender retreated to pour the drink.

Coale could remember the last time he'd taken a drink. It was more than forty years before, on his eighteenth birthday. That was what people said you had to do on your birthday – get drunk. If his father had still been alive at the time, he would have taken the boy out. His father had liked his drink. He would sit in their bare garage apartment with a bottle, reading, the aroma from his glass the only texture to the place. As a boy Coale had loved that smell. He would have enjoyed a drink with his father on his birthday, but by the time it came his father had been six months in the ground.

At eighteen he was alone, homeless, penniless. The booze hadn't made anything better, and he didn't enjoy being out in public. Watching all the people around him swirl with their friends, their lovers, their lives, had only reinforced his loneliness. Soon after the hangover had worn off, he resolved to remove himself from all social contact. If he was to be alone, he wouldn't torture himself with meaningless interaction. If he was to be alone, he was going to take advantage of the solitude. And so he made himself into the perfect sociopath. Divorced from all feeling, all empathy, all mercy. And that had made him powerful.

The bartender returned with the Scotch. 'Twelve bucks,' he said. Coale frowned at him, and the bartender shrugged again. 'Top shelf,' he said.

Coale reached into his pocket and pulled out a tight roll of bills. The smallest he had was a hundred. He peeled it off and put it on the table. The bartender's eyes widened ever so slightly as he watched. He picked it up and went to the register to make change.

Coale stared at the glass for what seemed a long time. The booze was golden brown and it danced and sparkled even in the dim, chalky light of the dive. He picked up the glass, breathed in the aroma. It was foreign, after all the years. Sharp and stinging and dangerous, and yet somehow warm and alive at the same time.

He raised the glass to his lips and took a sip. Not even a sip, really; just a taste. The liquid settled on his lips, crept only far enough into his mouth for the flavor to roll over on his tongue, no more. He sat there, closed his eyes for a brief moment, lost in the memory of the life he'd given up.

Then he pulled himself back and put the drink down. The bartender returned with the change. Coale looked at him, and once again saw only an object, not a person. He could easily have pulled out a gun and shot him in the forehead without thought or remorse. It would have meant nothing.

He looked at the change on the bar, looked at the drink.

Without another word, he backed away, turned, and headed out.

CHAPTER THIRTY-ONE

Finn stood at the back of Courtroom D at the Roxbury District Courthouse. It was an arraignments session – a cattlecall of the accused, pulled from the holding pens filled from the previous evening and weekend. At the right of the courtroom, a Plexiglas box held the accused, who spoke only through a six-inch circular pattern of air holes at the front of the box. The holes were set low enough to allow the shortest defendants to respond, which meant that anyone of normal height had to stoop down to answer any questions. It wasn't a huge imposition. Few answers were required. A 'yes' when asked whether they had met with their court-appointed attorney, a 'not guilty' when asked how they wanted to plead to the accusations against them. Then a schedule was set, and they were whisked away, replaced by the next defendant. It went on like this for hours.

Peter Mitchell stood at the front of the courtroom, moving through the docket with dispassionate efficiency. For each case, he rattled off the facts embodied in the police report. Sometimes they were straightforward, sometimes sad, often shocking. A young woman was accused of burning her three-year old with a cigarette when the child wouldn't stop asking to watch television; a young man was accused of stabbing his girlfriend in the shoulder for looking at another guy; a sixteen-year-old boy was charged as an adult for beating a schoolmate nearly to death while stealing his bicycle. The parade of horrors went on from ten o'clock until just before noon, and it left Finn with the familiar acrid taste of despair and disgust at the back of his throat.

Finally, visibly worn out by the mundane tragedy of it all, the judge called the break for lunch, crawled off the bench, and headed back to chambers for a brief respite.

Mitchell packed up his files and headed toward the back of the courtroom. Finn caught his eye. 'What do you want?' Mitchell asked as he hurried past.

Finn fell in line to keep up. 'We need to talk,' he said.

'We talked already,' Mitchell said. 'I didn't like what you had to say.'

'Maybe you will now.'

Mitchell turned to Finn, exasperated. 'You for real? Or are you wasting my time?'

'Gimme five minutes, and you can decide for yourself.'

They took a conference room down the corridor from the courtroom. Mitchell put his briefcase on the table. He didn't bother sitting. 'I've got an hour to make about ten calls and try to get something to eat,' he said. 'You've got two minutes. Are you giving up Eamonn McDougal?'

'I can't,' Finn said. 'He's a client.'

'Then I'm leaving. We've got nothing to talk about.' Mitchell picked up his briefcase.

'You told me I had two minutes.'

'That's when I thought you were gonna say something I wanted to hear. Doesn't sound like that's gonna happen.'

'So I guess you wouldn't be interested in busting Joey Slade?' Finn asked.

Mitchell already had the door open, but he stopped. He didn't turn around, he just stood there, hand still gripping the handle, looking straight ahead. 'Don't mess with me.'

'I'm not messing with you.'

'You serious?'

Finn opened his briefcase and took out a file. He put it on the table. 'Judge for yourself.'

Mitchell turned around to look at Finn. His hand remained on the door. 'If you're bluffing, this is the last time we talk.' He let go of the door and walked slowly back to the table. He put his briefcase on the floor, his attention on the folder. He reached down and flipped it open.

He didn't touch the pages at first. He examined them while still standing. By the time he got to the bottom of the stack, he looked up at Finn, an expression of awe and wonder on his face. Finn just made a gesture for him to continue with his reading. He sat down, leaning over and flipping through each page in succession. 'Are these what I think they are?' Mitchell asked.

'What do you think they are?'

'It looks like documents that show a huge amount of money being funneled to Joey Slade. And a bunch of papers that show payoffs going to politicians.'

'Then they are what you think they are.'

'Where did you get these?' Mitchell demanded.

'I can't tell you that.'

Mitchell's eyes narrowed. 'Eamonn McDougal,' he said. 'He gave these to you, didn't he?' He flipped through the documents again. 'Eamonn is pretty much the only high-level scumbag whose name isn't on any of these documents. He's looking to trade Joey Slade for his boy?'

Finn shook his head. 'Eamonn McDougal has no idea that I am here, or that I have these documents. Eamonn's name isn't in these documents because he's a client, and it would be unethical for me to turn anything over to you about his business. He's not involved in this at all.'

Mitchell looked through the materials again. 'Well, that's too bad,' he said. 'Without any sort of corroboration or testimony about these documents, Slade will simply say they're all lies. Forgeries. They're useless without testimony.'

Finn pulled out a handheld tape recorder. He held it up and pressed play. A voice, clear and calm, came from the small speaker. 'It's not enough,' the voice said. 'You want a guarantee that this goes through, a hundred and fifty grand isn't gonna do it. You're talking about putting a thirty-story complex on protected land. I gotta buy off the state legislature as well as the city council. Plus I got the unions, I got the police, and all the others who are gonna be holding their fuckin' hands out. You want this to move, I need five hundred. Either that or . . .' Finn stopped the tape.

'You want to hear more?'

Mitchell was nearly drooling. 'You're telling me that was Joey Slade?' he said.

Finn nodded.

'How do I know that?'

'Because I'm telling you that.'

Mitchell frowned. 'You know what I mean. How do I prove that?'

'You get an expert,' Finn said. 'You do a voice comparison. It's not that hard.'

Mitchell considered this. 'Maybe,' he said. 'Still, he's gonna say the thing is a cut job. Someone duped his voice, edited some other conversation.'

'Yeah,' Finn said. 'He'll say a lot of things, but the tape is genuine, so he'll have a problem with that. I've got others, too,' Finn said. 'Talking about worse things – drug deals and distribution, things like that.'

Mitchell shook his head. 'But you don't have testimony.'

'Slade doesn't know that. You play this for him, show him the documents, he'll assume you've turned someone on the inside. He'll give it up quick in exchange for a deal. Then the whole house of cards starts to fall.'

'How are you so sure?'

'Because,' Finn said. 'Joey Slade's been on a winning streak since he was nine years old. He doesn't know how to handle defeat.'

Mitchell considered this. 'So, what are we talking about?' he asked. 'I drop everything on the McDougal kid, and I get it all?'

'That's not it,' Finn said.

'What else?'

'I have some conditions. First, my name stays out of it.'

'You don't want your clients to know you're working with the DA's office?'

'Something like that. Second, you wait a couple of days after the charges are dropped against Kevin McDougal before you go after Slade.'

'Why?'

'I have some things I need to take care of before the shit hits the fan.'

'Like what?'

'You don't need to know. All you need to know is that this is the way it has to be if you want a chance to make the bust of the decade. Do we have a deal?'

Mitchell shook his head. 'I can't make a deal like this on my own. I need to get approval.'

Finn nodded. 'So get it. But get it in the next few hours, or the deal goes away.'

'Give me your cell number,' Mitchell said. 'I'll call you.' Finn pulled out a business card and wrote his cell number on the back. 'When this is all over,' Mitchell said, 'I want to know what this was all really about.'

Finn shook his head. 'I wouldn't count on it. Get back to me soon.'

He looked at the number on the card. Finn could tell that, in his mind, Mitchell was already writing the speech he would give at the press conference when the first arrests were made. Either that, or he was already rehearsing his stump speech for when he ran for governor. 'I will,' he said. 'I definitely will.'

Finn got back to his office before one o'clock. Lissa looked up from her desk when he walked in. 'Well?' she said.

'We'll see,' Finn replied.

'That's it?'

'For now.'

Kozlowski walked in from his office in the back. 'What's the word?' he asked.

Finn shrugged.

'What, exactly, did he say?' Lissa pressed.

'He said he didn't have authorization to make this kind of a deal. He said he has to go back to his superiors for sign-off.'

'But he seemed interested?' Kozlowski asked.

'Oh yeah, he seemed interested. I thought his eyes were gonna come out of his head when he heard the tape. You could watch him playing out his entire political future as he thought about what this could lead to.'

'He'll make the deal,' Lissa said. 'I know he will.'

'Maybe,' Kozlowski said. 'It's gonna take a lot of convincing to get the top brass to give up Eamonn McDougal's kid without something that's a slam dunk. This isn't a slam dunk; it's a really good lead. They play it right, they may take down a whole bunch of people. They play it wrong, and they get nothing. That'd be hard to live with.'

Lissa shook her head. 'He's gonna take the deal,' she repeated.

'Maybe,' Kozlowski said. 'There's nothing to do but wait and see.'

'There's one other thing to do,' Finn said. 'I've got to get back up to New Hampshire tonight to meet with the woman from the adoption agency, take a look at my adoption file. Did she call?'

Lissa shook her head. 'It's been quiet.'

Finn sat behind his desk, picked up the phone. He pulled Shelly Tesco's card out of his wallet and dialed the number. It rang three times before her secretary picked up.

'Adoption Services.'

'Can I please speak with Shelly Tesco?'

'I'm sorry, Ms Tesco is not in; can I take a message?'

'What time do you expect her?'

The woman on the other end of the line paused. 'I'm not sure,' she said. 'She was supposed to be in this morning. Who's calling?'

'Scott Finn. She and I have an appointment for this evening, but she never told me where to meet her.'

'I don't see you on her calendar,' the secretary said.

'No, she might not have written it down. It probably doesn't qualify as a work appointment. She and I were going to meet after she left the office. All I need to know is where and when to show up.'

'I'm sorry, I'm not sure what to tell you. I've tried her home and her cell, and I haven't been able to reach her. What were you supposed to be meeting with her about?'

Finn wasn't sure how to answer. 'It's a personal matter,' he said. 'I was adopted, and I had some questions for her.'

'Why isn't that a work appointment?' the woman asked. She sounded suspicious. 'That's what she does.'

'Can you ask her to call me back when you talk to her?' he asked. There was no point in trying to answer her question; he had no decent answer. He gave her his phone numbers.

'Okay,' she said. She didn't sound confident, though. 'I'll have her call as soon as she gets in.'

The tiny New Hampshire town had only four police officers in the entire department. As a result, even Chief Steven Bosch had to take calls from time to time. He'd left the NYPD ten years before, determined to find a more reasonable lifestyle for his family. For the most part, it had worked out well enough. At the moment, though, sitting at his desk with the phone pressed against his ear, he wished he was back in the big city.

'What can I do for you, Mrs Shumley?' he asked in his most polite tone. He wondered how long the call might last; Mildred Shumley was a notorious talker.

'I'm worried about my neighbor, Shelly Tesco,' Mrs Shumley said.

'Oh?' Bosch tried to sound interested, but unalarmed. 'Why is that?'

'I don't think she was home last night,' Mrs Shumley said.

'And that worries you?' He kept the exasperation out of his voice.

'Well, normally it wouldn't, but I saw a man coming out of her house.'

'Ah,' Bosch said. 'And you don't think that's normal?'

'Clearly not. Not if she wasn't there.'

'And if she was there?'

'Well, that would be a different issue entirely.'

'But still inappropriate?' What was the point of having to put up with calls like this if Bosch couldn't have a little fun?

'That's not my point,' Mrs Shumley said. 'As I said, I'm worried about her. What if she was the victim of foul play?' The breathlessness of her voice on the final two words caused him to roll his eyes.

'She'd be the first since I got here to town,' Bosch said.

'I still think you should check up on her.'

Bosch sighed heavily. 'She's a grown woman, Mrs Shumley,' he said. 'I can't go disturbing her every time she has a gentleman caller.'

'But –'

'If she's still not around in a couple of days, call back and we'll look into it,' Bosch said. 'Thank you, Mrs Shumley. Take care.' He hung up the phone before she could say anything else. Sometimes he longed for the days when he was dealing with actual crimes, rather than the overactive imaginings of a bored and nosey little town.

234

CHAPTER THIRTY-TWO

Brighton lay at the outskirts of Boston, five miles to the west of Copley, midway between the campuses of Boston University and Boston College. The neighborhood coveted the bohemian aura of Greenwich Village and Haight Ashbury, and tried in vain to capture the same edge. The streets were lined with tattoo parlors and cut-rate furniture stores with names like Futon Palace and Just the Basics. The sidewalks teemed with students and people in their early twenties, guitars slung over their shoulders, heads shaved proclaiming their disdain for all things bourgeois.

Long stood on Brighton Avenue, looking up at an apartment that hung over a second-hand music shop. He checked his notebook again to make sure he was in the right place, headed over, and walked up the stairwell.

He'd spent most of the day going through records, making notes on political donations, checking addresses, doing the crucial research necessary for his job. Eamonn McDougal and his partners presided over a vast, disparate empire of legitimate and quasi-legitimate businesses, seemingly with no unifying theme. In addition to Rescue Finance, 355 Water Street Corporation owned controlling interests in two garages, a pizza parlor, an Italian deli, several tenements that rented rooms and efficiencies on daily and weekly schedules, and a sporting goods store, among other enterprises. Long now had a list of over fifty employees, along with their addresses, their history of political contributions, and a general idea of their salaries and lifestyles. He'd visited five of them so far, looking for anyone who might confirm his suspicions about the campaign finance violations without any luck. Three weren't home. The other two wouldn't talk. He wasn't giving up, though.

Matthew Pillar was an office manager at one of the garages owned by McDougal and his partners. According to the information Long had collected, he was a recent graduate from the undergraduate business program at Boston University, where he was a mediocre student at best. He was also the bassist for a local bar band that called itself No Way To Live, a name Long was sure appealed to angst-ridden twenty-somethings.

The door to the apartment was in desperate need of fresh paint, and the carpeting in the hallway stank of beer and pizza grease. Long knocked, waited. He could hear nothing. He'd called the garage to see whether Pillar was working, but had been told that it was his day off. He knocked again, and heard a groan and a crash as something was knocked to the floor inside the apartment. A voice called out, young but ragged. 'Hold on!'

'Mr Pillar?' Long called. Then he reconsidered. 'Matt?'

'Hold on! I'm coming!'

Long waited, relaxed, leaning against the wall. The door was pulled open and a young man was standing in front of him, his shaggy mane impressed with restless sleep, his eyes still adjusting to daylight. 'Yeah?' he said.

'Are you Matt?' Long asked. He kept his voice friendly, as though he'd been sent by a mutual friend. He smiled. 'Matt Pillar?'

'Yeah,' the young man said. He still seemed disoriented, but Long's demeanor put him somewhat at ease.

Long pulled out his badge, kept the smile on his face. 'I'm Detective Long, Boston Police. You mind if I come in and talk to you?'

*

Eamonn McDougal was leaning back in his chair; his fingers were linked, resting on his prodigious belly. 'You did it, Finny' he said, beaming. 'You golden bastard, you really did it!'

Finn didn't smile back. 'I did it,' he said.

Peter Mitchell had taken less than an hour to get back to him. Finn was sitting at his desk, pushing paper around, accomplishing nothing when the phone rang. 'You've got a deal,' Mitchell said. 'We get the documents and the tapes, and we'll drop the charges against Kevin McDougal.'

'How soon?' Finn asked.

'As soon as you want. You get me the stuff, I'll file a *nollo* today.'

'My name stays out of it?'

'Yeah,' Mitchell said. 'Your name stays out of it.'

'And no one moves on Joey Slade for two days.'

'You've got tomorrow,' Mitchell said, hedging. 'Plus tomorrow night. My people want to move in on Thursday. We want to announce the arrest before the evening news. That gives you a day and a half.'

Finn understood the thinking. Friday was a news black hole. The District Attorney wanted to make a media splash before the weekend. He calculated the time in his head. If the case against Kevin McDougal was dismissed that afternoon, he would be fine, he figured. He was in the DA's office twenty minutes later, and the papers ending the prosecution of Kevin McDougal were filed twenty minutes after that. Finn headed straight for McDougal's office in Chelsea.

'How'd you pull it off?' McDougal asked. His smile threatened to swallow his face.

'Does it matter?' Finn asked.

McDougal's expression darkened, but only for a moment. 'No,' he said. 'No, I guess it don't. You want your secrets, you can keep 'em. It's a hell of a job, though. You deserve to be congratulated.'

'I didn't do it for congratulations,' Finn said. 'I did it because we had a deal. A deal I expect you to live up to.'

McDougal nodded, waving a hand at Finn as though the man had nothing to worry about. 'I always honor my bargains,' he said. He stood and walked over to the metal filing cabinet. Pulling his keys from his pocket, he took out a manila folder. 'Here you go,' he said. He tossed the file at Finn, then walked back and sat behind his desk again.

Finn held the folder in his hands for a long moment, looking at it without opening it. He took a deep breath, flipped it open and began reading.

There were only a few sheets of paper; little more than a tally of figures going back more than a decade. Marks in a ledger. 'I don't understand,' Finn said. 'You said all the answers were in here.'

'And they are, Finny, they are.'

'All this shows is that she owed you money.'

McDougal nodded. 'Aye,' he said. 'That she did.'

'So you killed her?'

'No,' Eamonn said. 'I didn't.'

Finn waved the pages from the file at Eamonn. 'Then what –?'

'That's not why she was killed,' Eamonn said, gesturing toward the file. She'd been borrowing from me for more years than I should have allowed, and she was over her head. She knew judgment day was comin' and she couldn't take it. So she found a way to pay me back. *That's* why she was called.'

'I don't understand.' Finn said.

'Blackmail. The surest way to mark yourself as a target is to make yourself dangerous to someone else. Tell someone who has something to lose that you'll reveal a secret. *The* secret. The one thing that person doesn't want people to know. That person then has two choices: pay, or . . .' Eamonn opened his hands, as though revealing a surprise.

'Who?' Finn demanded.

'A very powerful man. Powerful and rich.'

'Who is he?'

'James Buchanan,' Eamonn said. 'He killed your mother, Finny.'

'The senator?' Finn's voice was little more than a whisper. 'Why?'

'Because he's your father.' McDougal leaned back in his chair and let out a belly laugh that ripped the paint off the walls. He howled, throwing his head back. 'Can you believe it, Finny? You? The bastard of an American prince. Fuckin' new-world royalty, you are. How does that make you feel?'

Finn shook his head. 'No,' he said. 'It's not right. It can't be.'

'Oh, but it can,' McDougal said. 'It was your mother's last play. When I told Lizzie that I was coming to collect one way or another, she told me she had a way to get the money. She told me she had a secret – a secret that could bring down the richest man in the Common-wealth. I didn't believe her at first; Lizzie was a slippery bitch, and she could bullshit with the best of them. So I had it checked out. She was telling the truth, and she started to collect. Made the first two payments back to me, even looked like she was getting in the black. Then, on the night she was to make the last payment to me, she disappeared. Poof.'

'I don't believe you,' Finn said.

'You can believe me or not, but it's the truth,' McDougal said. 'I thought she was stiffing me, so I went to her apartment that night. Found her on the floor. Almost shit myself. I'd been to the apartment before, so I knew my fingerprints were there. I couldn't be dragged into that – imagine the hard-on that would've given the fuckin' coppers – so I called in a man named Coale to fix the situation. A specialist. He cleaned the place, made sure that there was no evidence that I'd been there. He left the police nothing more than a victim of random urban violence.'

'Buchanan killed my mother?' Finn still couldn't digest it.

'He's an evil one, that man,' McDougal said. 'Crossed me, too. I paid more than anyone will ever know to get him elected, and then when I needed him, he was nowhere to be found.'

'So now you want me to expose him? You want me to get your payback?'

McDougal's face became somber. 'You do what you need to do, Finny,' he said. 'You kept my son out of jail. You lived up to your end of the bargain; now I'm living up to mine. However you want to use the information is up to you.'

Finn felt as though the ground were shifting under his feet. He put no trust in anything Eamonn McDougal said; the man was devoid of any sense of morality, and would lie without thinking. And yet, somehow, what he was saying rang true. There was a symmetry to it that made sense. McDougal was using him, Finn knew, but it felt like he was using him with the truth.

Finn stood, shaking.

'One thing, Finny,' McDougal said.

Finn looked at him. It seemed as though he were looking through a gauzy lens. He felt distant, disconnected from everything around him. It felt like he'd lost whatever identity he'd ever had, and that the new identity that had been picked out for him didn't fit. 'What?' he asked. He could barely hear his own voice.

'Do whatever you want with the senator,' McDougal said. 'This is between you and him now. But keep me out of it if you go public. If you tell the police you got this from me, I'll come after you. I'll send the same man who cleaned up after Buchanan when he did your mother. Except he won't leave a body if he comes after you. There won't be enough to identify you with if it comes to that, you understand?'

Finn thought about the deal he'd cut with the DA's office. His life depended on the hope that there would be no leaks coming from that office. 'Yeah,' he said. 'I understand.'

He turned and walked to the door. As he placed his hand on the doorknob, he heard McDougal laughing behind him. 'Cheer up, Finny,' he said. 'You may have lost your mother again, but at least you've found a father.'

*

240

Coale sat in his Mercedes outside McDougal's office. He was in the back of the parking lot, toward the water. He had an apple in his hand, and he sliced through it with his knife, the blade touching the pad of his thumb with every pass.

The lawyer exited the building, looking lost. He wandered toward his car, turned around and headed back toward the building. He made it halfway to the front door before he stopped, standing there looking back and forth between the door and his car, the indecision etched on his face. It took several moments before he made up his mind and moved with any sense of purpose. When he did, it was in the direction of his car. He climbed in, started the engine and pulled out.

Coale put a last slice of the apple in his mouth, chucked the core out the window and followed at a safe distance. McDougal had told Coale what he was going to say to Finn, so he had a good idea where the lawyer was headed now. He would stay close, observing, but he would only intercede if he absolutely had to.

Eventually it would become necessary, he knew.

CHAPTER THIRTY-THREE

The sun was sliding down the front side of Beacon Hill when Finn pulled into Louisburg Square. It chased the afternoon clouds toward Cambridge, the Back Bay and Newton on its daily journey out to the newer parts of the country. On the Square, though, none of that existed. It was almost as though the place were trapped in an earlier time, when power and privilege were birthrights passed from generation to generation.

Finn should have been a part of this world. By rights, he should have grown up safe and secure and happy. But he hadn't. Instead, he'd struggled for every scrap and crumb. He'd been cast out to fend for himself. Even before he'd drawn his first breath he'd been deemed unworthy, and as he climbed out of his car in front of the Buchanan mansion, the anger was building inside of him.

He climbed the front steps and rang the bell. He had no idea what he was going to say or do; all he knew was that he had to confront James Buchanan. His father. The man who had murdered his mother.

He rang the doorbell again, reached up to the great brass door knocker shaped like a lion's head and began slamming it down as loud as he could. He was still holding onto the lion's head when the door swung open.

'What?' the woman on the other side demanded.

Finn was startled. The woman who stood before him was young

and casually dressed, but she had about her the air of confidence that comes from growing up with unchallengeable wealth.

It took a moment for Finn to recover his composure.

'What?' the woman demanded again. 'You're banging loud enough to break the door, you must want something.'

'I need to talk to Senator Buchanan,' Finn finally managed to say.

'Yeah, you and everyone else in the world,' the girl said. 'Do you have an appointment?'

'No,' Finn said. 'But I still need to see him.' As he spoke the words, he realized how insane he sounded. Maybe he was insane.

The woman looked at him with an expression that made clear that she, too, thought he was insane. A voice came from behind Finn. 'Is there a problem, Ms Buchanan?' Finn turned around to see a bulky gentleman in a dark suit and sunglasses. A wire trailed from his ear into his jacket.

The woman looked at the man. 'No, Maurice. This man was about to leave.' She turned back to Finn, gave him a pitying look. 'Isn't that right?'

Finn hesitated, and the man moved in toward him. 'Are you his daughter?' Finn asked. The question lit a fire under the security guard, who took two quick steps and hooked a hand under Finn's arm.

'Okay, sir,' he said. Security was always polite, even when they were kicking the crap out of someone. 'It's time for you to leave.'

The young woman pushed the door. Before it could close completely, though, Finn yelled, 'Wait!' He pulled his arm free. 'I'm here about Elizabeth Connor! I'm her son!'

The door slammed shut, and the security guard reestablished his grip, this time digging his fingers into Finn's arm. 'I said, it's time for you to leave, sir,' he said, his voice harsh. Finn could see the bulge under the man's jacket where his holster rested against his side.

'I just want to talk to him,' Finn protested, clearly not helping the situation.

'The senator is a busy man,' the security guard said, speaking to Finn as if he were a five-year-old. 'I don't want to call the police, but I will.'

The door swung open as quickly as it had shut. The young woman was looking at Finn with renewed curiosity. 'The woman who was killed?' she said. 'The woman the police were asking my father about?'

The security guard was still dragging Finn away. 'It's okay, Ms Buchanan,' he said. 'I can take care of this.'

'That's right,' Finn called to her, struggling to get free from the larger man's hold. 'The woman who was killed. I didn't know about the police.'

'Let him go,' the young woman said to the security guard.

'You know him?' he asked her, looking doubtful.

'I said, let him go,' she said, more sharply this time, with a tone that made clear she was rarely questioned or disobeyed, particularly by someone as lowly as a security guard.

The man released Finn, giving him a hard shove to punctuate his annoyance. 'Is your father here?' Finn asked the woman.

She nodded slowly. 'He's in a meeting. What do you want to talk to him about?'

Finn shook his head. 'You don't need to be involved. I . . .' he stammered, looking for the right words as his world spun out of control. 'It's something between him and me.'

She looked at the security guard. 'Search him, Maurice, please.'

The guard spun Finn around and pushed him up against the Range Rover parked at the curb. He spread Finn's hands and kicked his feet apart, ran his hands over Finn's body, looking for weapons. He pulled Finn's wallet out of his back pocket.

'Hey!' Finn protested.

'Easy,' the guard said, pushing a fist into Finn's back between the shoulder blades. He looked up at the young woman. 'He's a lawyer,' he said. 'Name is Scott Finn. No weapons.' He checked in Finn's other pockets and pulled out the Polaroid of Elizabeth Connor's corpse. 'Nice.' He held it up.

'Let me see it,' the girl said.

The guard flipped it to her without letting up on Finn.

'Your mother?' she asked.

Finn nodded. 'Yeah.'

She looked at him closely, almost as though there were something familiar in his face. It could have just been his own paranoia, but he looked away. 'You can come in,' she said. 'You can talk to him after his meeting. On one condition.'

He looked back at her. 'What's the condition?'

'Tell me what's going on.'

She led him through the house, toward the back. Under different circumstances Finn might have marveled at the rooms they passed through, with their towering ceilings and ornate crown moldings and beautiful artwork. At the moment, though, the surroundings washed over him unnoticed.

'There was a detective here the other day to talk to my father,' the young woman said. 'He asked me if I'd ever heard of Elizabeth Connor. I looked her up on the Internet, and I saw what happened to her. I'm very sorry.' She didn't look at Finn as they walked; her eyes stayed focused ahead of her. 'I'm Brooke, by the way.' She didn't offer to shake hands.

'I'm Finn.'

'Maurice said Scott, right?'

'Nobody calls me Scott.'

'Oh. Anyway, I heard my father talking to his chief of staff the other day, saying that he had to go back and talk to the police again. I heard them mention your mother's name again.'

'Did you hear why?'

She shook her head. 'Do you know why?'

245

They had arrived at the kitchen. It was huge, with granite countertops and an endless rolling butcher-block island. Glass sliders led out onto an expanse of teak decking.

'You should ask your father,' Finn said.

She rolled her eyes. 'My father doesn't tell me anything.'

'Maybe he's just trying to protect you,' Finn offered. 'He's your father.'

'I don't want to be protected, I want to know what's going on.' She looked out at the patio. 'It's been a difficult election,' she said quietly. 'My father is not himself. He . . .' She hesitated. 'He scares me.'

'I'm sorry.' Finn had no idea what else to say. He was beginning to think coming was a bad idea.

'What does he have to do with your mother's murder? Did he kill her?' she asked.

'I don't know. That's why I'm here.'

She nodded. 'What will you do if it turns out that he did? He can be a very dangerous person; will you try to put him in jail?'

Finn opened his mouth to answer, but stopped when he saw the door to the kitchen swing open. He recognized the tall, imposing figure of James Buchanan from news footage. An attractive older woman stood behind him, her hands fretting the sides of her skirt.

'Who is this, Brooke?' Buchanan asked. His tone was polite, but sharp and threatening at the same time. 'It's almost dinnertime.'

'This is Scott,' Brooke replied.

'Finn,' Finn added.

'Right. Finn,' Brooke said. 'No one calls him Scott. He says he needs to talk to you.'

'He does?' He said the words as though there were nothing more normal than for strangers to show up randomly, simply because they needed to talk to their senator. 'What does he need to talk to me about?'

'I'm Elizabeth Connor's son,' Finn said.

Buchanan looked like he'd been slapped. 'Are you?' he said.

'Yes.'

The silence that followed felt deadly. It was the older woman who broke it. 'We're very sorry for your loss,' she said. It sounded like she meant it, but her husband turned on her and gave her a nasty look.

'Brooke, why don't you take your mother into the dining room. I'll join both of you shortly.'

'I'd rather stay,' Brooke said.

'Catherine,' he said to his wife. She hesitated. 'Now!' he yelled.

She jumped at the sound of his raised voice. A protective hand went to her face. She moved quickly forward and took her daughter by the arm. 'Come, Brooke,' she said. 'Your father needs to talk to this man.'

Brooke resisted at first. 'No!' she said. 'I'm staying.'

'No, you're not,' Buchanan said. He stared at her, and she wilted within seconds. She walked over to the door and she and her mother walked out of the kitchen.

Then they were gone, and Finn was alone with Buchanan. He looked at the man and saw that he was smiling. It was the most humorless smile Finn had ever seen.

'So, Mr Finn,' Buchanan said, 'what would you like to talk about?'

CHAPTER THIRTY-FOUR

'He admitted it?'

Julie Racine was sitting cross-legged on the floor of Zachary Long's apartment, a plate of Chinese food balanced on her knee, as she shoveled a mouthful of fried rice into her mouth. Long was giving her a quick summary of his afternoon with Matthew Pillar, the manager of McDougal's garage.

'He did,' Long said from the kitchen. 'Do you want something to drink? I have the wine you left the other night.'

Her heart nearly stopped. 'Are you having any?'

He looked sharply at her, and she averted her eyes. She knew he could tell what she was thinking, but she didn't want him to see the confirmation in her eyes. 'No,' he said. 'I'm not.'

'I won't either.'

'I'm not saying I'm never drinking again,' Long said. His voice was sharp. 'I just don't want a drink right now.'

'I'm not saying you can't drink again.'

'Good.'

She wondered whether there was an appropriate thing to say. Some words of encouragement or support that would actually help and not make matters worse. She didn't think so. Long wasn't the sort of man who would admit to a drinking problem out loud. It wasn't in his nature. And yet the silence between them was unbearable. 'So, what happened?'

He frowned. 'With my drinking?'

She shook her head. 'With Matthew Pillar.'

'Oh, that.' His frown disappeared and he came over toward her with his own plate, piled a heap of General Gau's chicken on it, and topped it off with a couple of spare ribs. 'I don't know that I've ever seen anyone so scared,' he said. 'He's a kid. Musician. Still asleep at five in the afternoon. I'm pretty sure he dropped a load in his boxers.'

'He knew why you were there?'

'No. He thought I was there about his closet.'

She gave him a quizzical look. 'I don't get it.'

'Hydroponics,' Long said. 'He had a forest growing in his closet, and it wasn't evergreens.'

'Pot?'

'Yeah, and a lot of it. Not enough for him to be a real player. Enough for his own personal use, maybe some friends. Still, he assumed he was looking at serious time when he opened the door and I showed him my badge. Stupid kid – didn't even know enough to tell me to screw off. He could have. I didn't have a warrant. But no, he's too scared for that. He let me in, and I could tell right away that he's hiding something. So I asked him if I could use the bathroom, and on my way, I poke my head into the rooms. There's this bright purple glow coming from the crack under one of the closets. I looked at him and I said, "What's that?" I thought he was gonna keel over. He just looked back at me, looking all sick, and said, "What's what?" So I pointed to the closet and said, "That. Mind if I take a look?" He just shrugged. He was crying before I even opened the closet door.'

'I almost feel bad for the kid,' Julie said.

'Me too,' Long said. 'I told him to relax, I wasn't there about the pot. I didn't even care about it, as long he told me the truth about his job and his campaign contributions.'

'And he did?'

Long nodded. 'I don't think he has any idea that there's anything illegal about it. He said McDougal told everyone at the garage to write a check for twenty-four hundred to Buchanan's campaign. That week, everyone got an envelope with the same amount with their paycheck. He never asked why. He didn't even know there were campaign contribution limits; he just figured they wanted it to look like lots of people were supporting Buchanan, instead of just a few heavy hitters. Even after I left, I don't think he had any idea how badly he screwed McDougal.'

'He did, though, didn't he? He's screwed him?'

Long nodded. 'It's a felony. Your average Joe could get up to two years, but with a background like McDougal's, it could go to four. They've put lots of people away for it.'

'So he could really go away just for giving money to a senator?'

'Hey, they put Capone away for tax evasion. Whatever you can get one of these guys on, that's what you get them on. The only thing anyone cares about is getting them off the streets.'

'It won't help Buchanan's political career at all, either.'

Long said, 'Clearly. Something like this breaks in the last few weeks before the election and at a minimum he loses his bid for reelection. At worst, he's sitting in the cell next to McDougal for a year to eighteen months.'

'Elizabeth Connor knew what was going on. You think she decided to see what she could get out of it?'

'It's possible,' Long said. 'Any way you look at it, it's a good motive for either one of them to have her killed.'

'I know the truth,' Finn said to Buchanan.

His heart was beating so hard he thought his chest might explode. He'd spent the first thirteen years of his life in orphanages and in foster homes, living under the constant threat of catching a beating or worse. He'd spent the next seven years on the streets, running with people who would stab you in the heart just to break the monotony of a dull day. Even as a lawyer, he'd had his nose far enough into the wrong people's business that his life had been threatened, a few times so directly he'd found himself looking down the barrel of a gun. Through all of that, though, he'd never known a fear comparable to the one that pounded in his chest now. Looking at the man who gave him life more than four decades ago and then walked away without ever looking back, there was no way to describe the range of emotions he was feeling. For whatever reason, fear predominated.

'What truth do you know?' Buchanan asked. He walked slowly over to the sink, passing within a foot of where Finn was standing. Close enough for Finn to touch him. Buchanan pulled a Tiffany glass from the cabinet and filled it from the small spout on the side of the sink that delivered chilled spring water. 'What is it you think you've discovered, Mr Finn?'

'You killed her.'

Buchanan shook his head. 'You're mistaken. I killed no one. What would even put such an idea in your head? Have you been talking to Detective Long? He has all sorts of strange notions.'

Buchanan was calm. So calm it fueled the rage in Finn's heart. 'No,' Finn said. 'I've been talking to Eamonn McDougal.'

Buchanan was taking a sip of his water, and Finn could see him hesitate, the glass at his lips, pausing as he swallowed hard. Finn could tell that he was beginning to chip away at the façade, beginning to tear down the protective barrier that had surrounded the man his entire life. It felt so good. 'He's a client of mine.' Finn was going to take his time.

Buchanan said nothing for a moment. Then he picked up his glass and tipped it toward Finn, gave a weak smile, and said, 'Congratulations, I'm sure he keeps you busy.'

'He does,' Finn replied. 'And I keep his people out of prison. I kept his son out of prison. That means he owes me.'

'Does he? And how does he propose to repay that debt?'

'He's done it already,' Finn said. 'He gave me what I needed.'

'What did you need?'

'I needed answers. I needed to know why the mother I never knew was murdered. He told me. He told me you did it.'

Buchanan smirked, but sweat beaded on his forehead. 'He repaid you in false currency. I did nothing. Mr McDougal and I have known each other for a number of years. He's been a supporter, as have many of his employees. None of that has anything to do with that woman's death, as far as I know. In any event, I had no involvement whatsoever. I will not allow Eamonn McDougal to drag me into his gutter, do you understand?'

'I understand,' Finn said. 'You'd never let someone drag you off your perch, would you?'

'I've done nothing wrong,' Buchanan said. 'This notion that I killed anyone is simply absurd. Why would I? What possible benefit could come from it for me?'

'She was blackmailing you,' Finn said.

'With what?' Buchanan demanded. 'What information did this woman have that would give her any ability to blackmail me?'

Finn leveled his glare at the man standing in front of him, his jaw set tight as he said the words, 'She was blackmailing you with the fact that you are my father.'

Buchanan looked like he'd been hit in the chest with a nine-iron. His eyes went wide and his mouth hung open, bobbing slightly as though he were searching for words or oxygen or both.

Finn continued, 'That's the truth I know.'

'Get out.' The words came from Buchanan in a whisper. His lips were quivering, and he was ashen, but the sound of his own voice seemed to inject some resolve. 'Now!' he said. 'I want you out of this house right now!' he yelled.

Finn nodded at him. 'I'll go,' he said. He walked toward the kitchen doorway, headed to the front of the house. Before he left the room, though, he turned. 'I know what I know,' he said. 'I'm going to prove it.'

Coale was sitting in his car up the street from Buchanan's mansion when Finn came out. He looked determined as he walked to his convertible, never glancing back at the senator's house. Coale gripped the wheel. The fact that the lawyer was getting this close was a problem. It put all of Coale's planning in jeopardy.

Finn pulled out, and Coale hesitated. There were too many moving pieces at this point – too many ways to approach the problem. After mulling it over for a few moments, though, Coale came to see that the lawyer was at the center of it all. He was the key, and the only way to keep control was to keep the lawyer in his sights.

He started the car and pulled out after Finn.

CHAPTER THIRTY-FIVE

'What now?' Kozlowski asked.

Finn shrugged. 'I don't know.' The four of them were in Finn's apartment in Charlestown. Finn was sitting on the sofa, his chin in his chest. Kozlowski sat on a stool at the counter that separated the living room from the kitchen. Lissa and Sally sat on chairs across the room from Finn. No one knew what to say.

'I let him know this wasn't over,' Finn said. 'Maybe I lied.'

'You didn't lie,' Lissa said. 'It isn't over.'

'It isn't? What do you suggest I do? All I have is the word of Eamonn McDougal that's he's my father. That's not enough to do anything no matter what I *believe*. Let's assume I even want to push this –'

'Are you saying you don't?' Lissa demanded.

'I'm saying, like it or not, I'm living a fucking Greek tragedy here, and my options aren't as simple as they might seem.'

'I know,' Lissa said. 'But you can't let him get away with it. He murdered your mother.'

'Again,' Finn said, 'all I have is Eamonn McDougal's word on that. I don't have anything else, and it's not like Eamonn's gonna testify.'

'Buchanan had a pretty strong motive,' Lissa pointed out. 'If he's really your father can you imagine what that news would do to him politically?'

Finn shook his head. 'We can't prove it.'

'There must be a way,' Lisa said.

'DNA?' Sally offered.

'We'd never get it. We'd need a warrant, and no prosecutor in his right mind would ask a judge for a warrant to take a senator's blood without some other evidence.'

'What about your adoption file?' Kozlowski asked. 'There may be something in that.'

'There may be,' Finn agreed. 'The head of the agency hasn't gotten back to me. She was supposed to call me this morning – we were going to meet tonight, but she was out sick.'

'So call her,' Kozlowski said.

'I'll call her in the morning,' Finn agreed.

'The morning?' Kozlowski let out a low whistle. 'You're gonna let this all slip away, aren't you? You really want to find out what this is all about, you need to get on the phone now.'

'All I have is her work number.'

'Judas frickin' Priest, you've got her name. You know where she lives. You really need to have a private detective in your apartment to tell you how to get her number?'

Finn looked at the three people in his apartment; the only three people in his life who really mattered to him. Each one of them was nodding at him. It was Sally who spoke. 'You need to do this,' she said.

Finn closed his eyes, took a deep breath, and walked over to the counter to pick up the phone.

Janet Washburn had arrived at the New Hampshire Health Services Center two years before, at the age of twenty-three, looking like a lost puppy. In the previous two months she had broken up with her boyfriend, lost her job, and relocated to a new state. She wasn't close to her family, and she knew virtually no one. She went into the Center to get birth control pills. She had no immediate prospects for a relationship, but she was so lonely she knew she was vulnerable to even the slightest male attention. She understood herself well enough to realize that she had little willpower, and she didn't want to deal with the unwanted consequences of an inevitable bad decision.

Her fifteen-minute appointment turned into a two-hour heart-to-heart with one of the case workers, filled with tears and regret. She left that day without birth control, but with a new job and a new cause to serve. As it turned out, she was an organizational dynamo, and the Center needed someone to help organize the adoption services section. She had been working as an assistant to Shelly Tesco ever since. Shelly had become more of a surrogate mother than a boss to her, and there hadn't been a weekday in two years when they hadn't talked.

Until today.

After work, Janet used the extra key Shelly had given her to open the house. She'd rung the doorbell several times, but there had been no response. Worried, she decided she needed to see whether there was anything wrong.

She opened the door slowly. 'Shelly?' she called out. There was no response.

The house had a classic Cape layout with three bedrooms upstairs and a quartered floor plan on the ground floor – living room, dining room, family room, and kitchen set out in nearly even proportion. It didn't take her long to explore the downstairs, and there seemed nothing out of order. She half expected to find Shelly's lifeless body, dead of a heart attack at too young an age; she was relieved, at least, that wasn't the case.

She crept upstairs. 'Shelly?' The house was silent. The sun was down, and it was a moonless night, so no light filtered in from outside. She turned lights on as she went.

The first two rooms at the top of the stairs were guest rooms. One had been converted to an office. She stuck her head into one and then the other. Looking around carefully, she could discern nothing out of place. Perhaps Shelly had simply been called away on some sort of family emergency. It was unlike her not to check in, and she had no family Janet knew of, but anything was possible.

By the time Janet reached Shelly's master bedroom, she'd opened her heart not just to hope, but to optimism. That optimism vanished as soon as she pushed open the door to the bedroom.

The place was a mess. The bed was askew, two chairs were overturned, and the sheets were rent from the mattress in an apparent display of panic and violence. The closet and the drawers were open, and clothes were strewn about the room. The floor was littered with papers and personal belongings. It looked as though a fight for survival had taken place in the room, and Janet felt her stomach churn just looking at the mess.

She stumbled around for a moment, feeling disoriented, trying to fathom the implications. As she made her way unsteadily into the room, her eyes came to rest on a dark shape on the center of the mattress. It looked at first like a giant spider, resting malevolently in the middle of chaos' remnants, pleased with whatever evil had visited the place. As she looked closer, though, she realized that it wasn't living; it was a stain. It was crimson, with its tendrils grasping in desperation. It took another moment for her to realize that she was looking down at a single bloody handprint.

She screamed, and as she did the phone next to the bed rang. She whirled around and knocked it to the floor. It continued to ring, and she approached it with dread, picked it up and held the handset to her ear. 'H-Hello?' she stammered.

'Ms Tesco,' a male voice said. 'It's Scott Finn.'

'It's . . . it's not Shelly,' Janet said. It all felt like a dream now. 'It's her assistant, Janet.'

'Oh, I thought I dialed her house.'

'I have to go,' she said, her panic growing.

'Wait,' the man said. 'You and I spoke earlier this morning. I was calling to follow up with Ms Tesco about our meeting. Is she there?'

'No, she's not. I have to go. I have to call the police.'

'The police? Why?'

'Because I think Shelly's in trouble.' As she said the words, Janet began to cry. It started as a gasp and a few tears, but within seconds it had turned into shocked wails as the enormity of what had happened in the bedroom washed over her and she gasped for breath.

The voice was shouting into her ear. She could hear it, but it took a moment for her to be able to process it. 'Talk to me!' the voice was saying. 'Tell me what happened!'

She gulped air, gaining control of herself again. She began to tell him what she could see.

CHAPTER THIRTY-SIX

Long sat in Townsend's office the next morning. The captain looked at him from behind his desk. The dark circles under his eyes appeared more pronounced; the red within the irises had overwhelmed the white. He looked down again at Matthew Pillar's sworn statement. 'He really signed this?'

'Yeah, he did.'

Townsend leaned back in his chair, the springs screaming with the shift in his weight.

'It gives Buchanan a motive, Captain,' Long said.

'For murder?' Townsend frowned. 'Feels like a stretch.'

'We're not talking about a misdemeanor,' Long pointed out.

'He'd never be convicted.'

'Maybe not, but he'd sure as hell lose the election. It ties him to a conspiracy to violate campaign finance laws, plus it links him with one of the heads of organized crime. You really think he survives that politically?'

Townsend rocked in his chair. 'Maybe not. But so what if Buchanan lost the election? What does he care? He's rich.'

'A guy like that doesn't like to lose. Plus I read he spent more than five million of his own money on the campaign. He's not gonna walk away from that.'

Townsend shook his head. 'We're gonna need more than this to take this guy on.'

'Why not call him in?' Long suggested. 'Get him down here this time, rattle his cage a little?'

'Because the cage he lives in doesn't rattle. Without more than we've got, we'll have lawyers and politicians all over our asses.'

'I'm telling you, this guy's dirty,' Long said. 'And he probably had Elizabeth Connor killed.'

Townsend nodded. 'You may be right. But you need more than this to prove it.' Townsend's secretary knocked on the glass door and poked her head in. 'What is it?' he grumbled.

'There are two men here to see Detective Long,' she said. 'They say it's an emergency.'

'Did they say what it was about?' Long asked.

She shook her head. 'One of them is named Finn. He said you'd want to talk to him right away.'

Townsend and Long looked at each other. 'You think they got something?' Townsend asked.

'Only one way to find out.' Long stood and walked to the door.

'Long!' Townsend barked at him. Long turned around. 'Whatever it is, move slowly, you understand? Don't give the lawyer and his Dobermann any information. If they think we're moving on Buchanan, you never know what they'll do, and I don't want them involved. This isn't a normal guy we're dealing with, it's a goddamned senator, y'know?'

'I thought justice was blind, Captain.'

'It is,' Townsend replied. 'But that doesn't mean it's stupid.'

'Call the cops up in New Hampshire if you need proof!' Finn shouted. He'd spent the better part of a half hour explaining the situation to Long, but none of it seemed to make a dent. 'They're at Shelly Tesco's house right now, trying to figure out what happened to her.'

'Don't worry, Mr Finn,' Long said. 'I'll call the police up there when we're done. But even if what you say is true – even if she's disappeared, it's hardly proof of a crime. She hasn't even been gone long enough for them to write up a missing person's report.'

'I'm telling you, Buchanan is my father. Elizabeth Connor – my mother – was blackmailing him, so he killed her.'

'Why?' Long asked. 'Having a child out of wedlock is barely a scandal anymore. James Buchanan already has a shady reputation with the ladies; it's not like people think he's Gandhi. What you're talking about happened over forty years ago, before he was even married. How is that blackmail material?'

'Because he's a politician,' Finn said. 'Buchanan knew that a story like this would kill his reelection bid, so he killed my mother. Then, when he realized I was getting close to the truth, he killed Shelly Tesco – the one woman who could prove that he abandoned me as a baby.'

'We don't even know for sure she's dead. Besides, why is she the only one?' Long asked. 'There must be records.'

Finn shook his head. 'They're gone. I had her secretary search for them, but Tesco pulled them yesterday and it looks like she took them out of the office. The cops searched the house, and the file wasn't there. So now all the documentary evidence of the fact that he is my father is gone.'

Long said, 'There would still be DNA testing that could be done.'

'That's my point!' Finn exclaimed. 'Get his DNA tested, and we'll know for sure.'

'You're missing what I'm saying,' Long said. 'Why would he go to all the trouble of having this woman killed and stealing the file if a simple DNA test would provide the same proof? It doesn't make any sense.'

'Because,' Finn said, exasperated, 'he thought the file was the only way that I would find out. He thought that if Tesco was dead and I never got the file, no one would ever link him to my mother or her murder.'

'But you didn't get the file, and you still found out – apparently – that he is your father.' Long sounded skeptical.

'That's only because someone else knew. Someone Buchanan thought would never betray him. He didn't count on that.'

'Who?'

Finn knew the question was coming, and still he had no idea how to handle it. 'I can't tell you that,' he said simply.

'Well, that leaves us in a bit of a bind, doesn't it?' Long said. 'I've got nothing tying all of this together, nothing to support what you're saying.'

'How can you say that?' Finn demanded.

'Look, Mr Finn, I'll check with the police up in New Hampshire, but without more, I don't know what you expect me to do. You need to bring me something I can actually use. No offense, but given the way you've jerked us around in this case, you're the last person I trust.'

'So, that's it?' Finn said. 'That's your last word?'

'For now, yeah.'

'You're making a mistake. You'll regret it later.' It was an appeal to guilt, and Finn knew it meant that he had already lost the argument. Cops were impervious to guilt.

'Maybe,' Long said. He looked so unperturbed, it made Finn furious. 'But right now it's my mistake to make.'

Coale took a wide pass at the police station twice before finding a parking spot a block and a half away with a sightline to the lawyer's car. He was good at what he did, and sometimes it seemed as though he had the ability to become invisible, but tailing someone near the police station had him on edge. All it would take was one slip, and everything would crumble.

His phone buzzed in his jacket pocket. Without taking his eyes off the little MG, he pulled the phone out and pressed the button. He knew who it was.

'You still got him?' McDougal asked.

'Yeah, I still got him,' Coale responded. 'He's at the police station.'

'Talking to Long, no doubt.'

'That's a reasonable assumption. He got here early.'

'And last night?'

The tone of McDougal's questions annoyed Coale. Everything about the man was starting to annoy him. 'At Buchanan's,' he said. 'Then home. He spent some time on the phone with the cops in New Hampshire.'

'So he's got a pretty good idea about your little trip up there,' McDougal said. There was a reproach in his voice.

'I was careful.'

'I wouldn't expect anything less. Still, even if he doesn't have the details, I'm sure he's smart enough to put some of the pieces together. Otherwise, what would have driven him to Long?'

'Are you sure your name won't come up?' Coale asked. It was time to start turning the tables. 'Are you positive the lawyer won't tell Long that you gave him the information about Buchanan?'

There was a pause on the other end of the line. 'I'm sure,' McDougal said. He almost sounded it. 'He knows me well enough to understand what would happen if he mentioned me.'

'What would happen?'

'I'd send you.'

'Sometimes that's enough,' Coale admitted. 'Sometimes not. This isn't about money; this is about family.'

'Money's more important than family to most.'

'Maybe,' Coale said. 'But Finn may not be like most.'

'You just keep an eye on everything,' McDougal said. 'Things are going to start happening quickly. Everything will be just fine if you do your job.'

'When have I not?' Coale said. He clicked off the phone and put it back into his jacket pocket. McDougal was right about one thing, he knew: things were going to start happening very quickly.

CHAPTER THIRTY-SEVEN

Move slowly . . .

That was the advice Townsend had given Long. Good advice, no doubt, but moving slowly had never been Long's style. As he stood at the threshold of the Buchanan mansion on Beacon Hill, he could feel the adrenaline coursing through his bloodstream. It gave him a high like few other things in life. It had been nearly two days since the craving for a drink had quieted to a distant hum in the back of his head. When he was doing his job – really doing his job, not just going through the motions – he didn't need the booze. Didn't even want it, really. All he wanted was the thrill of the takedown. And in this case, the takedown wasn't going to happen if he moved slowly.

The door cracked open. Catherine Buchanan glared out at him. She was wearing a light blue cashmere sweater – technically it was probably azure or sapphire, but to Long it was blue – and her pearls were coiled tightly around her neck. Her hair was styled, her make-up looked professionally applied. For all her perfection, though, her face bore the look of a frightened deer. 'I thought you were warned not to come back,' she said.

'I was,' he replied. 'It didn't take. I figure I still have a job to do, warnings or not.'

She shifted on her feet. 'My husband isn't home,' she said.

'Good,' Long said. 'I didn't come here to talk to him. I came here to talk to you.'

Her lips pursed as she glared back at Long. The fear on her face morphed into confusion. The door opened slightly wider, though, which Long took as a good sign. 'Why?' she asked.

'Because we need to talk,' Long said. 'Can I come in?'

'My husband told me not to talk to anyone.'

'Just for a minute? Please, it's important.'

She hesitated, but after a moment she stepped back and opened the door.

She led him to a sunny glass sitting room off to the side of the house. It was done in yellow, with light, airy floral prints on wicker furniture and a profusion of flowers and plants lining the windows. He could tell immediately that this was her room – her sanctuary.

'What do we need to talk about, Detective?' she asked as they entered the room. She didn't sit. She walked to the window and looked out at a brick-lined patio, keeping her back to him.

'Elizabeth Connor.'

She turned toward him, then looked back out the window. 'You mentioned her the other day. I thought we had that conversation already. I didn't know her.'

'I believe that,' Long said. 'But I've done some digging. Your husband knew her. Your husband knew her quite well.'

'You said that the other day, too. You said she was a supporter.'

'She was more than that,' Long said.

Catherine Buchanan turned to face him fully now, stepped toward him. 'Detective,' she said, the hint of resignation in her voice, 'are you about to tell me that my husband had an affair with this woman?'

He searched her eyes for the pain. He couldn't find it, though. Instead, he saw something much harder. It was as though the pain had been scabbed over. Her eyes had the look of a woman who'd simply turned in on herself for protection. Drawing her out wouldn't be easy.

'Because if that is what you are going to tell me,' she continued, 'you can save your breath. I am quite aware of my husband's extra-marital activities. Everyone is. It is hardly a secret.'

'No,' Long said slowly. 'I wasn't going to tell you that.' He watched her closely as he plotted a new way to come at her. 'I was wrong. Elizabeth Connor wasn't a supporter of your husband's campaign. She just worked for Eamonn McDougal, one of Boston's most powerful mob bosses. McDougal was really the supporter. He had his employees donate to your husband's campaign, and then paid them back. It's a serious violation of the campaign finance laws.'

She shrugged. 'I'm not a lawyer,' she said. 'And I certainly don't know anything about my husband's fundraising activities.'

'No?'

There was silence in the room for a moment. 'Why are you really here, Detective?'

'I was hoping you would help me put your husband in prison,' he said.

She laughed sadly. 'Good lord, I think you're actually serious.' Long said nothing. 'Why would I?'

Long walked over and looked out the window at the same place she had stood a moment earlier. 'My father was a difficult man,' he said. 'A cop. Good man in most respects, but hard. He grew up during a different time. And when he'd had a few too many, he'd get violent.' He could hear Catherine Buchanan suck in a lungful of fear. 'He only came at me once. I don't even know if he remembered in the morning. But my mother . . . well, let's just say he must have remembered some of the times he hit her. It happened too often for him not to remember.'

'What has this got to do with –'

'I like your necklace,' Long said. He was still looking out the window. 'You were wearing it the other day, but down. Not like a choker.' He could feel her hand had gone to her throat. 'Do you mind taking it off?'

He turned to look at her, and her eyes were filled with the rage and fear of a trapped animal. Her hand was still pressed to her neck, holding onto the pearls.

'I could always tell the next day. With my mother, I mean,' Long said. 'You know how? Because he always went for the face and the throat. Whenever my mother came to breakfast in a turtleneck, with her make-up in perfect order, I knew he'd been drinking the night before.'

Her eyes were half-filled with tears now. 'You don't know what you're talking about,' she said.

'Yes, I do. You can't live in a house with that and not know the signs.'

'I can't,' she said, turning away from him. Her voice became distant, dreamy. 'I remember our wedding,' she said. 'It was called "The Wedding of the Century" by the local papers. It may seem hard to imagine now, but back then I was quite a catch.'

'It isn't hard to imagine at all,' Long said.

She raised a dismissive hand. 'You're being kind. But back then, I was something. I was trim and blond and beautiful. More importantly, I was from the right family. A family that made a good strategic match for my husband and his people. I was "Catherine St. James, of the Wellesley St. Jameses". That's how I was described by people. As though my lineage was actually part of my name.' She laughed bitterly, took a deep breath and sighed. 'It was a spectacular wedding, though. Six hundred people. The society pages talked about the place-settings for six months. It was almost enough to make up for the fact that my fiancé had been with another woman the night before.'

'But you married him anyway.'

She turned and looked at him as though he were an idiot. 'Of course,' she said. 'I was Catherine St. James. I had responsibilities. Responsibilities, in many ways, I never lived up to.'

'How so?'

'My husband was from a large family. I was expected to produce children – many children, preferably male. I couldn't. We were married for more than a decade before we had Brooke, and that was it. If my husband has a certain level of anger toward me over that, I suppose I don't even blame him. I blame myself. And so, when you stand there and you ask me to help you put my husband in jail, you must realize how silly you sound. Besides, I could never break up our family.'

'Yeah, I guess you're right.' He looked around the room. 'How can you give up all this? Better to put up with the beatings – call it anger and rationalize it away. Besides, you're in no real danger, right? After all, you're his wife. You're the mother of his child.' He nodded to her. 'You take care of yourself. I'll let myself out.' He crossed to the French doors, then paused. 'There is one other thing you should know, though. Elizabeth Connor wasn't just some woman helping him break the law. He knew her more than forty years ago.'

Catherine Buchanan shook her head in confusion. 'What are you talking about?'

'He knew her even before he met you. In fact, he fathered her child.' He let that sink in for a moment. 'Then he abandoned both of them. The baby was given up for adoption. I think he murdered her.' She was shaking her head furiously now, the tears running down her cheeks. 'You sure you won't help me?' Long thought he had her. There wasn't a doubt in his mind. In another second she would be willing to do anything he asked her to do. In that second, though, a gasp came from behind him, from outside of the room.

'No!'

It was a woman's voice, and Long turned to see Brooke Buchanan standing in the parlor just outside the sun room. He wondered for how long she'd been eavesdropping. From the look on her face, it had been for long enough. 'No!' she choked again.

Catherine Buchanan's demeanor changed instantly. Any sense of vulnerability was gone. She drew herself up and took a deep breath. 'It's time for you to leave, Detective,' she said.

He looked back and forth between mother and daughter. Catherine's tears had already dried, but Brooke's were just starting.

'You can't protect him anymore, Mother. You just can't,' the younger woman pleaded. 'It's time.'

'Detective!' Catherine screamed. 'Unless you have a warrant, I want you out of this house this instant!'

'Mrs Buchanan, Elizabeth Connor was murdered!' Long said. 'Can't you see what that means? She was the mother of your husband's child. She made five sets of calls to your husband and Mr McDougal in the weeks before her death. No one had a better motive to kill her than your husband. If I could just –'

'Now, Detective! Leave now, or I swear I will have your badge before you get back to your desk.'

'Mother, please!' Brooke screamed. 'It's gone on for too long. He can't treat you like this anymore! He can't treat either of us like this anymore!'

'Brooke, shut your mouth!' Catherine yelled to her daughter. She turned back to Long. 'Now!'

He put up his hands. He'd learned years before that no creature was more ferocious than a mother protecting her child. 'I'm leaving,' he said. 'Eventually it will come out.'

'Perhaps,' Catherine said. 'But if it does, it won't come from anyone in this family.'

Peter Mitchell sat in a van outside Joey Slade's office in Dorchester. There were seven of them crammed into the vehicle, all wearing blue windbreakers with BPD emblazoned in yellow. Everyone except Mitchell was armed, two of the cops had shotguns. Mitchell secretly wished they had more artillery. Not because he thought there was any danger – there clearly wasn't – but because he wanted to make the most public statement possible. Shock and awe. It might not work perfectly in war, but Mitchell figured it would be pretty damned effective in the middle of Boston.

He was the leader of Team A, which was tasked with taking down Slade's office. This was where the action was likely to be. They knew Slade was at his desk. Team B was securing the man's home, and Team C was freezing an offsite storage facility maintained by Slade. As the investigation expanded, Mitchell knew there would be other teams. It was his hope – his expectation, really – that Slade would be the wedge. From everything he knew about the man, he was not the sort to allow himself to end up in prison. His sense of self-importance and self-preservation were too highly developed for that. Once he believed a conviction was virtually guaranteed, Slade would roll over like a well-trained dog. And if his involvement in the Boston underworld was as broad as it was rumored . . . well, this was Mitchell's bust, and he might as well start measuring the governor's office for drapes.

He looked at his watch – two o'clock. The operation was scheduled for four. Right now they were simply in place to conduct surveillance so there were no surprises when it was time to move. The air in the van was stale and hot. It stank of coffee breath and nervous sweat, and it was starting to make Mitchell feel ill. He sat up straight and shook off the nausea.

Two hours . . .

He could do that standing on his head, he figured. For the payoff, he could endure just about anything for two hours. Years from now, as he sat in the State House and all those white boys were kissing his ass, he would look back on this moment with fondness. This was the door, and he was about to walk through it.

CHAPTER THIRTY-EIGHT

Finn saw them coming from the window in his office. There were two of them, and they converged on the building from both ends of the street, walking toward each other and meeting in front of the door with military precision. With their dark suits, sunglasses and ear pieces, Finn initially thought they were feds. The hair was too long, though, and after a moment Finn recognized the bodyguard who'd tried to keep him from going into Buchanan's house the day before.

Private security. One step up from common thugs. Loyal, though.

He reached for the phone, ready to dial 911, expecting the door to be kicked in at any moment. Buchanan had already had two people killed, why stop there? And yet it wouldn't make sense to take him in broad daylight, on a busy street. Finn hesitated.

As he watched from the window, the two men never made a move toward the door. They simply stood there, hands folded in front of their crotches, as though they were protecting themselves, staring straight ahead. A moment later a black car drove up behind them. The door opened, and James Buchanan stepped out. The two men parted as Buchanan approached the door and rang the door bell.

Finn was unsure what to do. Looking through the window, a thousand thoughts raced through his mind.

Buchanan rang again.

Finn walked around into the hallway, over to the entryway, turned the knob slowly, and opened the door.

'Mr Finn,' Buchanan said in a formal tone, almost as if he were out campaigning and he was about to explain why Finn should consider voting for him.

'Yes?' Finn was in shock; he had no idea what else to say.

'I thought it might make sense for us to talk.'

Inside the office, the air was electric. Finn's expectations were suffocating. Even Buchanan looked nervous. 'Do you mind if we sit?'

Finn blinked. 'Sure.' It felt inappropriately civilized, and yet he couldn't resist. 'Do you want something to drink? Some coffee?'

Buchanan nodded. 'A glass of water would be nice, thank you.'

'Just a second.' Finn walked out to the little kitchenette and drew a glass of water from the faucet. His hands were shaking the entire time. As he walked back into the office, he set the glass down on a side table near Buchanan to hide the tremors.

Buchanan reached over and picked up the glass, took a sip. He looked around the office. 'You've done very well for yourself,' he said.

'It's not Louisburg Square,' Finn said.

'No, but you built this yourself. I had my people look into your background. You came from nothing. You had every disadvantage a man can have stacked against him, and yet you succeeded. The modern American self-made man. I admire that. I never had the chance to prove I was capable of that; I don't know whether I would have been.'

'I guess that makes me lucky.'

'It's not luck.'

'No? What is it then?' Finn looked hard at Buchanan. 'Breeding?'

Buchanan took another sip of the water. Putting the glass down on the table, he looked back at Finn. 'I'm not your father,' he said.

'Then why are you here?'

Buchanan stood up and paced in front of Finn. 'As I said, I never had to prove that I was capable of making something for myself. Oh, I did an admirable job of protecting my family's wealth and businesses – growing them significantly. Many others in my position have squandered what they were given, pissed it away. But still, it's not the same as building something on your own. As a result, if I am to leave a true legacy, it will have to be through public service.'

'In other words, you're worried about the election.'

Buchanan stopped pacing. 'Yes,' he said. 'I am worried about the election. In times as dangerous as these, the right man in the right position can make all the difference.'

'You as senator? The right man for the right position?'

'For now. In the future . . .' Buchanan raised his eyebrows. 'Who knows where life will lead me?'

'I don't care where it will lead you. I have my own issues to deal with.'

'Yes, you do. *Your* issues. Not mine!' Buchanan's voice was raised, and he pointed his finger at Finn. 'Leave me out of this. Do you have any idea what kind of damage you could do if you continue down the path you seem to have chosen?'

Finn just looked at Buchanan, unsure what to feel about this man who had given him life. This man who had abandoned him once, and now, given a second chance, was abandoning him again. Mostly, Finn just felt sick.

'You say you're not my father,' Finn said.

'And I'm not!'

'Prove it, then. Take a blood test.'

Buchanan shook his head. 'I can't. Don't you see? Once I take a blood test, the story will get out. Once the story is out it won't matter that the test comes back negative. It won't matter that I didn't kill Elizabeth Connor.'

'That's not true.'

'It is true. Most people still think of Richard Jewel as the man who bombed the Olympics. Everyone still thinks that Gary Condit killed Shandra Levy. It doesn't matter that both of them were innocent, and that in both cases they actually caught the real killers. For a man in my position, admitting even the legitimacy of suspicion is the same as admitting guilt.'

'I don't know where that leaves us,' Finn said.

'It leaves you in control of my fate, for now.'

It had been a terrible day at school. The classes Sally usually enjoyed seemed vapid and unimportant; the classes she normally tolerated seemed unbearable. All she could think about was Finn. She'd even asked to skip school that day, but he was having none of it. She agreed to go only because she knew the importance he placed on her education.

As soon as her last class ended, she hopped a bus to the T and rode the train down to the final stop at Lechmere. From there it was only a half mile to Finn's office. She walked with purpose, desperate to know how the meeting with the police detective had gone, wondering whether Buchanan had been arrested. She hoped so. She had little patience for those who abandoned their children.

She saw them as she rounded the corner on Warren Street, closing in on the office. Two men in suits and sunglasses standing with their backs to the doorway, looking out onto the street, their heads swiveling, taking in everything around them. Their posture was condescending, and it annoyed her. The annoyance gave way almost immediately, though, to concern, as she wondered what they were doing at Finn's office.

She quickened her pace.

The man on the left noticed her first. The head-swivel paused, following her, noting her focus. He turned and looked at the other one, nodding to him. Both of them watched Sally as she approached. She ignored them as she reached for the door, but they closed ranks and cut her off.

'Sorry, Miss,' the one on the right said. He was standing on the uneven six-inch granite step in front of the door, looking down at her.

'You will be if you don't let me through,' she replied.

He looked over at his partner and gave a smile that made clear he was not intimidated. Looking back down at her, he said, 'You can't go in.'

'I'm here to see Finn.'

'Not right now, you're not. He's in a meeting.'

'Fine,' she said. 'I'll wait in Kozlowski's office in back.' She reached for the door again, but the one on the left reached down and swept her arm away. 'Don't do that,' she said evenly, staring straight into his sunglasses.

'You believe this?' the one on the right asked his partner. His partner shook his head, but his expression didn't change. 'Mr Finn doesn't want anyone bothering him right now. He's with someone.'

'Let him tell me that himself,' she said.

'He asked us to tell people that.'

'You're lying.' Her heart was beating fast now, and she wondered whether Finn was in danger.

The one on the left was beginning to look nervous, but the one on the right was getting angry. 'I'm not going to tell you again, Miss. You need to leave.'

She looked down at the ground and turned, as if to walk away. She could sense both of them let their attention wander to the rest of the street, assuming the confrontation with her was over. They were mistaken.

Swinging her body back in one quick motion, she lifted her foot and brought it down with all her weight on the top of the right shoe of the man nearer to her. She was wearing her thick, hard-soled boots, and the man's toes were hanging just off the edge of the granite step. The top half of his foot bent forward, cracking one of the bones. He screamed out in pain and his knees buckled.

The one on the left, already uncomfortable, hesitated. It was a mistake. She swung her bag, loaded with textbooks, into his face. It wasn't enough to do any real damage, but it knocked him off balance, and he stumbled off the step.

Sally dashed for the door and grabbed the handle, but she wasn't fast enough. The one with the broken foot had recovered sufficiently to reach out and grab her. His hand came down on top of her head and grabbed hold of her hair. 'You little bitch!' he growled as he pulled her back from the door.

She yelled out in pain and stomped hard again on the man's injured foot, bringing a fresh howl of pain. He let go of her hair and bent over again. She swung the bag into him and he fell into the door. Unfortunately, he managed to catch himself, and as he stood, she could see that his face was contorted in rage. 'Come over here!' he yelled. Reaching out, he grabbed her around the throat and put her in a headlock.

'Let go of me!' she screamed. 'Let go of me now!'

He wouldn't, though. He tightened the headlock, making it difficult for her to breathe. 'You want to play?' he grunted. 'Let's play!'

At that moment, the door behind them opened in, and they both toppled into the office.

'What the hell is going on here?' Finn yelled. He helped Sally to her feet. One of Buchanan's bodyguards tried to keep his hold on her, but Finn stepped on his hand. The man struggled to his feet and started to go after Finn, but a word from Buchanan halted him. 'Maurice!' the senator cautioned.

'They wouldn't let me in,' Sally explained. 'I was worried.'

Finn looked at Buchanan, who nodded. 'I wanted to talk to you in private.'

'This is my office, not yours,' Finn said, angrily. 'You had no right.'

'Given the nature of our talk, I didn't want people –'

'Sally isn't people. She's my . . . she belongs here.' He pulled her over, so that she was standing behind him. 'You need to leave now.'

Buchanan put his hands up, palms forward in a placating gesture. 'I'm going. But I want you to think about what I've said.'

Finn nodded. 'What you've said means nothing. You've got no credibility with me. You want me to believe you? You need to give me a reason, because right now I don't have one.'

CHAPTER THIRTY-NINE

Buchanan was back in his office on the second floor of the house on Louisburg Square an hour later. He felt a sense of vertigo he'd never known before. Nothing looked right anymore; everything was skewed. His chest felt tight, and he was having trouble breathing regularly. Perhaps he was having a heart attack. Perhaps that would be for the best.

He loosened his tie. Early in the day for it, but he thought perhaps it would allow him to breathe better. The call with his lawyer had done little to ease his anxiety. There was no word from within the police department of an imminent arrest, but nor was there any movement to suggest that Detective Long would be pulled from the investigation. Apparently, while few within the department had confidence in Long, fewer wanted to give the appearance of showing favoritism to a politician.

The election was only two weeks off. If he could hold on for just that long, he would survive. The Senate was a bulwark from which a defense could be mounted against just about anything. Only the whims of the electorate could oust him, and only every six years. The memory of the public was laughably short; if he could get through this election, this would all be a distant memory. If Kennedy could survive Chappaquiddick, surely he could weather this storm.

And yet it all seemed to be slipping away.

He didn't hear the door open. He was sitting in his chair, leaning back, looking through the window down onto the square. When he turned, Catherine was there in the doorway, staring at him with that meek-yet-superior look she so often wore on her face. It was a look that enraged him. She would have made a fine martyr.

'What?' he demanded. He did not get up.

She continued to look at him. She opened her mouth to speak, but nothing came out. She looked tired. Tired and old. She always looked tired and old to him now; another thing about her that kindled his hatred. Imagine what he could do in politics with a proper wife and family.

'What?' he said again, this time louder; loud enough to make her jump.

'I'm leaving,' she said.

'Where to?' he asked. 'Off to spend more of my money?' He glared at her, hoping his contempt for her shone through. From her face he was sure it did.

She shook her head. 'I'm leaving,' she said again.

'I heard you,' he said. 'I asked where . . .' He stopped talking as her meaning hit him.

'I'm taking Brooke with me,' she said.

He stood up. His size had always intimidated her, and he could see that she was scared as he walked toward her.

'Like rats from a sinking ship,' he said. His voice was low and threatening. 'With only two weeks until the election.'

She stood her ground, though her posture reflected her fear, leaning back on her heels. 'We won't say anything to the press,' she said. Her voice was desperate, almost a whisper. 'We'll appear on stage at the rallies.'

He nodded as he drew closer. 'Oh, you'll be at the rallies,' he said. 'Because you are not leaving. Not now. Not ever.'

'Yes, we a—'

She started to speak, and he felt the bile rise in his throat. His hand shot out and grasped her around the throat, cutting off her words. It felt good to silence her. It felt right. He moved forward even further, pushed her hard while still holding onto her neck as he slammed her head into the wall behind her. Her gasp was muted by the pressure he kept on her windpipe. He leaned in close to her, so that their noses were nearly touching, so that she could feel the damp heat of his breath on her face as he spoke to her. 'You're worthless,' he said. 'Do you understand that? Worthless. And yet I have stayed by you. Any man with half a brain would have dumped you by the side of the road decades ago, but I didn't. I put up with your worthlessness and your fading looks and your weakness out of pity. And now, after all I have endured from you, you say you are going to leave me?'

She nodded, fighting against his grip. 'I am,' she choked out. 'I am leaving you.'

He held her still by the throat and slapped her hard on the side of the face. He would have punched her instead, but he knew that he would need her on the podium, and welt marks could be covered with make-up; cuts and swelling could not. He longed to beat her properly, as she deserved, to break her nose to drive home his point. Perhaps after the election.

To his surprise, she pushed back against him, slipping out of the grasp of his sweaty hand. 'I am leaving!' she yelled, sliding to her left, making a break for the door.

He grabbed her by the hair, pulled her back. The rage grew, and his concerns about the marks to her face lessened. He threw her head-long into the wall, heard the crack of her skull colliding against the horsehair plaster. It felt good. Pulling her up by the shoulders, he spun her around and swung his fist hard into her stomach, doubling her over. She fell to her knees, gasping and sputtering for breath.

He knelt down next to her, his face close to hers again, his voice low and even. 'You are not leaving me,' he said slowly. 'Do you understand?'

She shook her head, still struggling to breathe. 'I am,' she managed to mouth. She gasped the words over and over again. 'I am, I am, I am.'

He grabbed her by the back of the neck and pulled her closer. He shook his head and he looked straight into her eyes. 'Never,' he said. 'I'll kill you first.'

Long leaned over the sink in the men's room at the station house. He let the water run until it was scalding, dipped his head down, cupped his hands and drew the water to his face. Then he turned off the hot tap and turned on the cold, lowered himself again. If the sink had been large enough, he would have submerged his entire head. He turned the cold water off and repeated the process twice more. He felt defeated, and he'd hoped the alternating extremes would make him feel better. It didn't.

Pulling two paper towels from the dispenser, he dried his face, and headed out. He still had a job to do.

Racine was sitting in the chair next to his desk. 'How'd it go with the wife?' she asked.

He shook his head as he sat.

'Nothing?'

'I thought for a minute she was gonna turn. She was right on the verge.'

'What happened?'

'Her daughter walked in. I could see it in her eyes. All of a sudden, she could picture everything she stood to lose. She walked right up to the edge, but she couldn't jump.'

'Hard to blame her, I guess,' Racine said.

'You think?'

'For that kind of money? Yeah, I think.'

Long frowned. 'He beats her, did I tell you that?'

'No.' Her eyes went wide. 'You know that for sure?'

Long nodded. 'I know.'

'How? Did she admit it?'

'She might as well have. Not that I really needed the confirmation. I know the signs.' He looked at her, and could see the skepticism in her eyes. 'You never lived with that kind of violence. If you had – if the fear had been a part of how you were raised – there's nothing more obvious.'

'And she's still protecting him? God, why?'

'Because that's what people in her position do. It's what almost all families do. It's like watching a bad movie you've already seen. You want to yell at the people on the screen, tell them how it's gonna end. But it never works. The movie always turns out the same no matter what you do.'

'Any chance she'll change her mind?'

'I don't think so. She's gone into protective mode. Once that happens, she'll rationalize it all away.'

'So what now?'

'We keep working the angles. We nail down more information on the campaign finance problems. See if we can turn a few more of Eamonn McDougal's employees. Plus, we see what we can do to get proof that Buchanan is Scott Finn's father. There are a lot of loose threads out there. We keep tugging at them hard enough, this thing's gonna unravel eventually.'

As he spoke, he looked up, and he could see a woman walk into the room. She was tall and attractive and young, with dark hair and features carved from a long, unmistakable lineage. She looked lost, her eyes searching until they met Long's. 'I'll be damned,' Long said.

'What?' Racine looked up, saw the woman. He could feel her tense with a heartbeat of jealousy. 'Who's that?' she asked.

'Brooke Buchanan,' Long said. 'The daughter.'

Racine raised her eyebrows. 'Really?'

'Yeah.'

'Huh.' She looked back over at her. Long could tell that the jealousy was gone. Then she turned to him again. 'Maybe this movie's got a different ending.'

Brooke Buchanan sat in a chair across the table from Long and Racine in an interview room. Her eyes were vacant; she was staring down at her hands in her lap. 'I wish he'd never gone into politics,' she said. 'It was better before. I'm not saying it was good, but it was better. Now, with all the stress my father is under . . .' She looked up at them, then down again, as though looking them in the eyes were physically painful. 'The stress has to go somewhere, right?'

'Your mother?'

She nodded. 'I knew they had fights when I was growing up, but it wasn't very often. I thought that was normal.' She fidgeted with her hands. 'It's not normal anymore.' She took a deep breath. 'I found my mother in her room today. She was hiding. She had cuts on her head, on her face. There's a bad bruise on her throat. He threatened to kill her. From the looks of her, he might have come close today.'

Long and Racine looked at each other. 'She needs to come in,' Long said. 'She needs to report this so we can arrest him.'

Brooke Buchanan shook her head. 'She'll never do that. She's too scared, and she feels like somehow this is all her fault. She doesn't even know I'm here; she doesn't want anyone to know.'

'He will kill her,' Racine said. 'You know that, right? Eventually it will happen.'

She nodded. 'We're out of the house for now, staying with friends for a few days. I'm just afraid she'll end up going back to him. That's why I'm here. I want to see him put away.'

'Has he ever hit you?' Long asked.

'No,' she said. She shook her head vigorously enough to make

Long doubt the answer. 'There have been times when I thought he might,' she said. 'I could see the muscles in his arm go tight, and it felt like he was about to swing, but he's never crossed that line with me. Sometimes I push him, just to see if he will.'

'Why?' Racine asked.

She shrugged. 'I don't know. Maybe I figure if he hits me, he won't hit my mother.' Closing her eyes, she sighed as though she had never been more exhausted. 'Maybe it's just so that we can stop pretending. So we can look at each other for who we really are. Maybe then we could all walk away.'

'If your mother won't come in and swear out a complaint, there's not much we can do, I'm afraid,' Long said. 'How else can we help?'

'That's the question I wanted to ask you – how can *I* help?' She looked him in the eyes. 'You think he killed that woman. Do you know that for sure?'

Long shook his head. 'Not for sure. It's a real possibility, though. A probability.'

'And he really had a child with her, a long time ago?'

Long said nothing.

'I need to know. I don't want anything to happen to my mother. What can I do?'

'Can you get us any information on the campaign's finances? Its donors and bank accounts?'

She shook her head. 'I'm not involved in the campaign. I'm only there when they need the picture of the perfect family. Ironic, isn't it?'

'Anything would be helpful,' Long prodded her.

'I wouldn't even know what to look for.' She frowned. 'What about the other part? Her son. Is there any way I can help figure out whether he's my father's child?'

Long looked at Racine. 'We'd need a sample from Finn as well,' she said. 'It would answer the question, though.'

'How long would it take?' Brooke asked.

'If we get a sample from you and one from Finn today, and if Detective Long pushes the lab we'd have DNA results by tomorrow,' Racine said.

'Do you think he'll do it?' Brooke asked.

'There's only one way to find out,' Long replied.

'Feel better?' Finn asked Sally. He still wasn't very good at reading her moods, and he felt wholly inadequate whenever it fell to him to try to console her. He imagined that the confrontation with Buchanan's bodyguards would have shaken her, and he wanted to show her that he cared. He'd taken her to get ice cream, then brought her back to the office. When he was at a loss, sweets were his fall-back. They'd had a lot of ice cream since she'd moved in with him.

'I wasn't feeling bad before,' she said. 'Good sundae, though. Thanks.'

'You're welcome.'

'What's wrong?'

Finn shook his head. 'I'm not very good at this.'

'Good at what?'

'You just beat up a couple of armed, two-hundred-pound security officers. I don't know what my reaction is supposed to be. Do I yell at you? Point out that if I hadn't opened the door, you would've been hurt – maybe badly? Do I grab you and give you a hug because I'm glad you're okay?'

Sally made a face.

'Then you tell me. Because I don't know what my role is here.'

Sally sucked on her straw, getting down the last of the milkshake. 'I'm not an easy kid,' she said. 'I know that.'

'In some ways, you're the easiest kid there is. I just don't have a lot of room to play the father figure.'

She sighed. 'I don't think I can change who I am.'

'I don't want you to. Hell, I don't even know what a father's supposed to do. I didn't have any role models growing up, so I'm at a loss.'

'Maybe I'm not looking for a father figure. Not in the traditional sense, anyway. Maybe that's okay. When you grow up with a crack addict for a mother and a thief for a father, tradition doesn't mean that much. It's not like we spent a lot of time around the piano singing "White Christmas".'

Finn said, 'So we'll just go with it. Day by day?'

She nodded. 'Day by day.'

The phone rang; Finn picked it up. 'Finn.'

'Mr Finn, it's Detective Long.' Finn felt the muscles in his back tense.

'What do you want?'

'I want a blood sample.'

'Why? Am I a suspect? Are you going to pin something on me, just for fun?'

'It's not like that,' Long said.

'No?'

'We want to check out your theory about Senator Buchanan. We want to know whether he's your father. Who knows, maybe you're on to something. His daughter's willing to cooperate. In order to know, though, we need a DNA sample from you.'

Finn frowned. 'Why the change of heart?'

'Does it matter?'

'It does,' Finn said.

'Why?'

'Because I don't trust you. For all I know, you're just looking to protect him. How do I know you won't just take my sample, throw it away and then tell me you got negative results to get me to drop this whole thing?'

'I guess you don't know,' Long said. 'But that's not how I work. You're just going to have to accept that.'

'Easier said than done.'

'You want to catch your mother's killer? I'm giving you the chance to do that. I'm also giving you the chance to answer one of the biggest questions in your life. Are you ready for that?'

Finn looked at Sally. She was staring at him, a worried look on her face. 'Yeah,' Finn said. 'I'm ready for the answers. I'll be over in a few minutes.' He hung up.

'Cops?' Sally asked.

Finn nodded. 'They're gonna run DNA tests, see if Buchanan's really my father.'

'You think you can handle it if he is?'

'I don't know. I guess we'll find out.' He stood and scrunched the napkins into his milkshake cup. 'You done with yours?' She nodded, and he took the cup from her. On the way out toward the kitchenette, he grabbed the glass of water he'd given to Buchanan.

Out in the kitchen, he threw the cups away and poured the water down the drain. He started to put the glass in the mini dishwasher he'd had installed in the kitchenette, then reconsidered. He held the glass up, looking at the streaks and smudges on the side. Smudges put there by the man who was likely his father. Finn leaned over the sink, looking at the glass, feeling sick and weak. He'd built a life for himself. He wasn't a man used to letting destiny dictate his fate for him. And yet now, it seemed as though everything were out of his control. Life was directing him, not the other way around, and he didn't like it.

He ran the water for a moment, splashed some on his face, wiped it off with a towel. He had to take back the responsibility for his life.

He stood up straight and shook himself. It was time to get some answers once and for all.

CHAPTER FORTY

Shock and awe was an apt description. Peter Mitchell might have wanted more shotguns on the team, but what firepower his people had was utilized to its maximum effect. At precisely four-thirty, three teams moved in unison, swarming over every aspect of Joey Slade's operations. Nine officers stormed Slade's offices, arresting him and securing the premises. All records and computers were confiscated and impounded. Slade himself was led out in handcuffs, as were several of those who worked with him.

By precisely four-forty-five word of the arrest had hit the street. Details emerged in rapid succession, with rumor and speculation mingling easily with fact. A second round of arrests were carried out at six, and by seven o'clock panic had gripped those within Boston's criminal community.

Coale got the call from McDougal at eight. He was sitting in his car outside the lawyer's apartment. Watching. 'You need to be here,' McDougal said over the phone.

'Where's here?'

'My office. Chelsea. I need you now.'

'I still have to finish the job you gave me,' Coale said.

'That job is over,' McDougal said. 'I have a new job.'

'What is it?'

'I'll tell you when you get here.' The man sounded agitated, out on the edge. It was a bad sign.

'Tell me now.'

'When you get here. Drop what you're doing.'

Coale said nothing. He closed his phone and started his car. He gunned the engine and pulled out, heading across two bridges into Chelsea.

McDougal was sitting so still Coale wondered whether the man was breathing. Kevin, McDougal's demented son, was sitting on the couch in the office, looking scared and excited at the same time. Coale knew about the McDougal kid. He didn't like him.

'They arrested Joey,' McDougal said slowly.

Coale nodded. 'Slade. I heard. Bad luck for him.'

McDougal shook his head. 'It wasn't luck. They were tipped. They knew what they were looking for. Cops couldn't pull that off on their own. They had help.'

'You worried?'

McDougal looked at Coale. 'Yeah, I'm fuckin' worried. There were more arrests tonight. Innis. Jackson. Callwell.'

'All friends of yours,' Coale said.

'I don't have any friends. And friendship don't count for shit when you're looking at twenty-to-life. They'll give me up before their lawyers are even sitting at the table.'

Coale considered carefully what to say next. 'If the cops had anything on you, you'd be in jail already.'

McDougal took a quarter out of his pocket, flipped it around on his fingers. 'They're waiting for something,' he said. He sounded so calm it was eerie. 'They've got what they need, they're just dragging this out. Seeing what else they can get on me before they come.'

'What makes you so sure?'

McDougal nodded toward a television on the table next to the couch. It was sitting on top of a VCR. McDougal used one remote to turn on the television, another one to turn on the VCR. Then he pressed play.

The image was static; grainy and indistinct, like an old home movie. A door in dim light, dirty and industrial. There were numbers in the upper right hand side of the screen. A clock. Two days ago. Six forty-three. It took Coale a moment to recognize the scene. It was the front door to the building they were in.

'Yesterday we had a problem with the alarm system. It wasn't working right when Janice came in. The company came out, said the wires had been cut. It didn't make any sense to me, though, because nothing was taken. Then the arrests started.'

On the screen, Coale could see some movement. McDougal was at the door, letting himself in. Sitting in the office, McDougal pressed fast-forward, and the time on the clock spun forward.

'I've got some people on the inside,' McDougal said. 'On the force. They don't know everything, but they know enough. Everything they have on Joey is something I know about. Nothing I'm directly attached to, but everything I've got information on. It's like they picked my mind clean, and they're using it against Joey. That got me thinking about the alarm, so I checked the security tapes from the camera outside.'

On the screen, McDougal exited the building, his movements jerky and fast. In the office he pressed play, and the clock slowed to normal time. Coale could see McDougal's face clearly. Then he walked away, disappearing from sight.

'Keep watching,' McDougal said.

It was only a minute or two before two men appeared on the screen at the door. They were dressed all in black, with dark jackets and watch caps. They were facing the door, their faces away from the camera. One was tall and thin. The other shorter, solid. The solid one went to work on the alarm system. The thinner one seemed to knock on the door. After another moment, the door opened and they stepped inside.

'Police?' Coale asked. 'Maybe feds.'

'The authorities still obey their own rules for the most part,' McDougal said. 'It's one of the things that make this a great country. When they show up, they have jackets with "Police" stamped on them, and they have warrants. All out in the open.'

'Who, then?' Coale asked.

McDougal pressed fast-forward. At the first sign of movement, he pressed play again.

There were three of them when they came out. The two men were accompanied by a young woman. The tall one had files under his arm. They all kept their heads down, though, making it difficult to make out their features. Then, at the last moment before they walked off the screen, the thin one looked up, almost straight into the camera. McDougal pressed pause on the remote, and Coale stared at Scott Finn's face on the screen.

'Not good,' Coale said.

'No,' McDougal agreed. 'Not good at all.'

'What do you want me to do?' Coale asked.

'I want you to kill them.'

Long drove home alone. It was late, ten-thirty. He'd stayed at the office, going over his notes from the investigation, looking to fill in the little pieces that still seemed to elude him. He had the big picture already. If the DNA tests confirmed that Buchanan was Finn's father, it would be a bombshell that could destroy the senator's career. Even without that, Connor knew about Buchanan's campaign finance violations. That would be enough, on its own, to bring the man down. The campaign finance issue also threatened Eamonn McDougal, a man who was notorious for eliminating threats as quickly as they appeared. In so many ways, it felt as though the crime were solved, and yet the picture wasn't complete. There were holes at the edges; Long didn't like holes.

Julie Racine had stayed at the station house with him for a while. She would have stayed all night, but Long wanted to be alone with the case, alone with his thoughts. Besides, he needed to do something on his own, so he'd told her to go home. He would call her later, he said. Maybe in the morning. He stayed another hour, then left for the night.

Interstate Ninety-three was empty, and the trip back to Quincy took less than ten minutes. He pulled off the highway at exit twelve, wound around the off-ramp, past the K-Mart at the edge of Dorch-ester, past the AutoZone and the car dealerships and the candlepin bowling alley. He was less than a half mile from his apartment when he pulled into the parking lot just off Columbus Circle. It was a quiet lot in front of a couple of broken-down warehouses backed up against the marshland by the edge of the Neponset River by Pope John Paul Park. The narrow waterways stank of oil and refuse and sewage.

In front of the warehouses, a run-down two-story brick building fronting the local highway housed Ups n' Downs; a local dive with a neon sign half blocked by the interstate overpass. Two bars – one upstairs, one downstairs. Neither of them saw much action. It was the kind of a place where the regulars came and stayed, and few others dared to venture in. It gave off a defiant atmosphere of defeat and acceptance. Right now, this was where he needed to be.

He walked in, and all six eyes in the place looked up at him. Two of the eyes belonged to the bartender. The others were red and heavily hooded, and looked out from angry faces at the far end of the bar. The bartender glanced at his two patrons and gave them a reassuring nod. He walked toward Long. He was tall, and built like he spent his morn-ings at the gym with free weights. He had a thick head of dark hair and dressed better than the neighborhood required.

'Detective,' he said.

'Nicky,' Long responded.

'Haven't seen you in here for a little while.'

'You miss me?'

'No. Just sayin'.'

Long sat down on a stool. 'Business looks good.'

The bartender nodded. 'Pickin' up lately. It's the economy.' He stood there, scratching a three-day stubble that looked like it was waging a campaign for permanence. 'What do you want?'

Long bowed his head for a moment, breathed in, breathed out. He raised his head and looked at Nicky. 'Dewars. Straight.'

Nicky nodded, walked to the middle of the bar and pulled a bottle off the shelf. Long watched as Nicky tipped the bottle up and a long, thin stream found its way into the highball. Nicky pulled the bottle up into the air, filling the glass much higher than he would for a regular customer. Long was used to it; it was one of the privileges of the badge. Bartenders and strippers treated you right.

Nicky finished the pour and put the bottle back. As he carried the Scotch toward him, Long could feel the tension ease from his shoulders. Just the sight of the drink was enough to make him feel alive.

The bartender pulled a napkin off a plastic tray and put it down on the bar, placing the highball on top of it. 'You wanna start a tab, I assume?'

'You trust me?'

'I gotta choice?'

'Get yourself one, too,' Long said. 'I need someone to toast with.'

Nicky looked at him with uncertainty, but went back and pulled out the bottle again.

Long sat there, looking at the glass while Nicky was pouring another tumblerful. Reaching out, he let his fingers brush the glass, then wrap themselves around it. Lifting it up, he breathed the aroma in deeply enough that his mouth watered. It was enough to give him a buzz, and he reveled in it.

Nicky returned. 'What are we toasting?'

'Not what, Nicky – *who*.'

'Fine. Who are we toasting?'

Long raised his glass. 'My father,' he said. 'My father and all that he stood for. May he and the rest of it stay buried.'

Nicky looked at Long warily, as though regarding a cobra offering kindness. 'Okay,' he said. He raised his glass.

Long clinked his glass with Nicky's and hoisted it to his mouth. The bartender did the same and poured it down his throat. Long let the booze trickle over his lips, like the ominous drip of a flood just topping a dam. Half the glass made it down. He swallowed. Then the dam held. He lowered the glass, set it on the bar. Nicky looked at him. 'Problem?'

Long shook his head. He took a twenty out of his pocket, put it on the bar next to the half-full glass. 'I never said goodbye,' he said. 'I figured it was time.'

Nicky looked at the half-full glass. 'You gonna leave it?'

Long stood up. 'I had something to prove,' he said. He took one last look at the glass, turned, and walked back out to his car.

CHAPTER FORTY-ONE

Finn was at the office later than usual. He'd gone over to the police station to give his blood for the DNA test, and the process had taken longer than expected. By the time he made it back, it was pushing into evening and his mind was reeling. He figured it would be best for him to clear his head of everything going on in his private life. Work would help him with that. Besides, he'd lost so much time in the past few days that his law practice was suffering.

Sally stayed at the office, too. She told him she had homework to do, and she didn't feel like going back to the apartment by herself. Finn had the sense, though, that she also wanted to make sure he was all right. It was an odd feeling, having someone look after him.

By nine-thirty Finn had lost his momentum. 'You wanna get some dinner?' he asked her.

'Sure,' she responded.

He checked the doors to make sure they were locked, and they grabbed their coats and headed out.

They ate at the Family Kitchen on the north side of Charlestown. It was a comfortable spot – low key, good food. Nearly empty at this time of the evening on a Thursday. By the time they finished they were the only diners left, and the staff was shutting the place down. Their waiter's manners remained impeccable, but Finn thought he detected an edge in his voice. He clearly wanted them to leave so he could go home himself. Finn paid, leaving a generous tip to compensate for any inconvenience. It was always good policy to remain on friendly terms at the local establishments.

He and Sally walked out into the cool evening, side by side, down along the edge of the Hill. It was a safe neighborhood, but not too far from the projects to the north. The wind whistled through the empty tree branches, and dry leaves skittered along the sidewalk, chasing their legs, swirling around them menacingly.

'What will you do if he's your father?'

Finn looked at the sidewalk as he considered his answer, following the jagged cracks as they traced the pits and rolls that had heaved through the concrete over the years. No matter how hard people tried to impose order on the world, the world always seemed to have the last word. 'I don't know,' he said.

'It doesn't mean that he killed her. Even if he is your dad.'

'I suppose. He's involved, though. I don't know how for sure, but I know that much.'

She said nothing for a half a block. 'Will you be rich? If he's your father?'

'No.'

'Why not? He's rich.'

'Because even if he's my father, I'm not his son.' He looked down at her. 'I never will be.'

She nodded.

They walked down Bunker Hill Street toward the Mystic River Highway. There was an alley halfway up the block, next to the Spanish and American Grocery Market, just wide enough for eighty-gallon garbage bins piled high with two days' waste. Finn was looking down at the sidewalk again as they neared the opening. He saw the flicker of a shadow passing in the dim glow from a distant streetlight. At first he thought nothing of it; the wind was swirling and the autumn leaves mixed with larger bits of trash, dancing freely along the empty street.

The shadow, though, didn't dance. It stayed put, dark and solid and well defined. A moment later another shadow appeared next to the first.

Finn looked up. There were two men standing on the sidewalk just a few yards ahead of them. One young and short, thick at the neck. The other taller, older. They were facing them. Finn put his hand out in front of Sally. She'd already stopped; she had seen them before Finn had.

They stood there for a moment, and then the younger man took his hand out of his pocket. He lifted his arm and pointed at Finn. Even in the dark, Finn could make out the silhouette of the gun. 'Evening, lawyer-man.'

Finn recognized the voice. 'Kevin?' he said.

'That's right, asshole,' McDougal said. 'You still think I'm a moron?'

Coale remained still. Eamonn McDougal's instructions had been clear: Coale was there only to make sure Kevin didn't make any mistakes. It was time, McDougal said, for his son to learn real responsibility. It was time for him to become a man.

Coale didn't care. One way or another, things were going to come to a head. If this was the way it was to unfold, so be it.

He was standing to Kevin's left, just behind him. Kevin had stepped out of the alley too early, leaving too much space between them and their targets, approaching from the front. It probably didn't matter, particularly with the young girl involved. In other situations, though, a mistake like that could be fatal. It gave the targets a chance to react – to run or to fight. Coale had told McDougal to wait until just after the lawyer and the girl had passed by. Much better to take them from behind, give them no warning. McDougal wasn't listening. He was high on something. His movements were manic, his breathing labored.

Coale heard the hammer pulled back on Kevin's gun. Mistake number two. 'Not here,' Coale said. 'In the alley.'

He sensed the tension in Kevin's arm release. He waved the gun at Finn and the girl. 'Into the alley.' The lawyer hesitated. 'Move now,' Kevin said. His gun was still pointed at Finn. He adjusted his arm so that it was aimed at the girl's head. 'Or I shoot the girl.'

'Let the girl go,' the lawyer said.

'Not until you're in the alley.'

The girl's expression changed. Coale had expected fear. Fear and regret – that was the reaction most people had when a gun was pointed at their head. Not the girl, though. Her expression merely hardened. There was no fear; only anger. Coale admired that. She looked at the lawyer, and he shook his head. 'I'll go,' he said.

'No!' the girl yelled.

'I'll be all right,' the lawyer said.

'Follow him,' McDougal said to the girl.

'You're going to let her go,' Finn said.

'Yeah, we're gonna let her go. But not until I'm done with you. That way I know you'll behave.' McDougal reached and grabbed at the girl, pushing her toward the alley. 'Go,' he said.

All four of them walked into the alleyway. With the garbage bins lined against the wall, they had to enter in single file. Finn was first, then the girl, then McDougal. Coale was last. His breathing was steady, his heart rate normal. Just by looking at the others, he could tell that he was the only one who wasn't hyperventilating.

Past the garbage bins, the alley opened up, and there was room for them to face each other. Finn and the girl turned around, standing close. The lawyer had his hands at his sides. 'We can talk about this,' he said. It was a waste of his breath. McDougal wasn't coherent enough to talk.

'About what?' McDougal screeched. 'About the fact you sold my father out?'

'I don't know what you're talking about.'

Kevin McDougal cackled. 'There was a camera!' he screamed. 'You think I'm dumb?' He stepped forward and pressed the barrel of his gun into the lawyer's chin. He slid it up his face until it was resting against his left nostril, and kept pushing until Finn had to tip his head back to keep the skin from tearing. 'You still think I'm fucking stupid?'

Coale could see the lawyer swallow hard. He didn't beg, though. He kept his eyes on McDougal. 'Let the girl go,' he said simply.

McDougal stepped back, keeping the gun pointed at Finn's face. 'You didn't know, did you? The camera? You thought you'd gotten away with it. Stolen from my father and given over information to the police. You thought he wouldn't find out?' He was babbling, and Coale could see the tendons sticking out of his neck, veins bulging. No matter how things turned out this evening, Coale could see that Kevin McDougal was not long for this world. He wouldn't survive long out on the streets, even with his father's protection.

'Let the girl go,' Finn said again. 'I don't want her to watch me die.'

McDougal cackled again. 'She's not gonna watch you die!' he yelled. He took another step back and aimed the gun at the girl. 'You're gonna watch her die!'

Finn stepped in front of Sally, put his hands up. 'No!' he screamed. 'You said you would let her go!' He was looking at Kevin McDougal for some sign of compassion. He could find none, though. McDougal was a drug-addled psychopath.

'I lied!' McDougal continued laughing. 'You get it? I fuckin' lied!' He had worked himself into hysterics. Had McDougal been alone, Finn thought there might have been a chance. Whatever drugs he had taken had eaten so far through his mind that Finn might have been able to jump him. The gun would probably go off, but he might have wrestled it away from McDougal and been able to save Sally.

The second man presented a problem, however. He was older, but tall and solid through the shoulders. More than that, he was calm. He had his hand in his pocket, presumably wrapped around his own gun. It looked like he had done this sort of thing before, and he was not going to be rattled. The second man scared Finn.

'Don't do this,' Finn said. Maybe if he kept talking there was a chance. He knew it wasn't likely, but he was out of options. 'Listen, Kevin, I didn't give over any information about your father. Your father is safe. I only gave information on others. I did it to get you out of jail. It was all part of my plan.' Finn was talking quickly now, spinning out the story.

'Shut up!' McDougal was shaking his head back and forth.

'Kevin, it's true. Why do you think the police haven't come after Eamonn? They've got nothing. You don't have to do this. Call your father. Tell him. This is what I had to do to get you out.'

'Shut up, shut up, shut up!' McDougal's hand was shaking, the gun wagging in Finn's face. Finn could see his finger turn white from the pressure applied to the trigger.

There was a loud explosion as the gun fired, and Finn's eyes closed, his hands going reflexively to his face, feeling for the hole, desperate to stop the bleeding and to keep whatever was left of him intact.

His face was dry, though. There was no blood, no wound, no pain.

He opened his eyes and looked at McDougal. He was standing there, the gun still raised, his eyes spinning wildly. The gun was so close to Finn's face that it was impossible to believe that he had missed. Even with the drugs, he was just too close.

And then Finn saw it. A fine trickle of blood coming from the corner of McDougal's mouth. It ran down the side of his face, dribbled off his chin. Slowly at first, but gathering speed and volume, until there was a steady river flowing from his mouth, dripping down off his shoes. He gave Finn a curious look, as though he didn't understand what was happening.

Another gunshot rang out, this one hitting McDougal in the back of the head, knocking him forward off his feet, splattering Finn with blood and brain tissue. Blowing whatever life was left from his body. He lay still on the ground, his arm underneath him at an impossible angle, his neck twisted awkwardly, the gun still in his hand.

Finn looked up. The second man still had his gun out, a wisp of smoke trailing from the barrel. It was pointed at Finn. 'Don't,' Finn said.

The gun hovered there, and for a moment it was all that Finn could see. The longer he looked at it, the bigger it became – a huge, heavy instrument of fate, all of the energy in the world concentrated in the dark hole at the end of the barrel, pointing straight at his heart.

He forced himself to look away from the gun, up at the man's face. He was older than Finn would have guessed from the way he carried himself. With hair the gray of an ocean storm and pale eyes just as cold. He was staring at Finn. Or maybe not as much at him as through him. 'Don't,' Finn said again.

Finn saw the man's hand twitch on the gun. The gun didn't go off, though. The man waved it at him. 'Go,' he said.

'What?'

'Go. Now. Take the girl and go.'

Finn reached back behind him without looking, and he could feel Sally put her hand in his. He kept his eyes on the man in front of him, moving slowly, keeping his body between Sally and the gun.

The gun itself remained where it was, still pointed at Finn's torso. He and Sally sidled around the man, up against the brick wall that defined the alley. Finn rotated his body as he passed, always keeping his face toward the man, until he was backing out of the alley with Sally leading the way.

'Who killed my mother?' Finn asked.

The man gave him an uncomprehending look. 'What?'

'Who killed my mother? Elizabeth Connor. Did you kill her?'

It took a moment for the look of confusion to clear on the man's face. With the revelation, he nodded solemnly. 'Yeah,' he said. 'I guess in a way I did. Now go.'

'Why?' Finn demanded. Then he yelled, 'Why?'

'I'm sorry,' the man said. At last the gun came down. 'I started this.' He put the gun in his pocket. 'It's time for me to end it.'

'What do you mean? How do you end it?' Finn was almost tempted to stay. To demand answers. But Sally was pulling on his hand, silently urging him out of danger. 'Was it Buchanan? Did he pay you?' Finn was screaming. 'Did he pay you to kill my mother?'

'Go,' the man said. 'Don't ever look back.'

Finn stared at the man. Then he turned, Sally's hand still in his, and the two of them ran back out onto the street.

CHAPTER FORTY-TWO

It was an hour later – a busy hour for Coale. Nearing midnight now, and the work had only just begun. He flipped open his cell phone and dialed the number from memory.

Eamonn McDougal picked up on the first ring. 'Is it done?' he asked.

'It's done. We need to meet.'

'Put my son on the phone.'

'He's not here.'

There was silence from the other end for a moment. 'Where is he?'

Coale said, 'I didn't know you wanted me to babysit him for the rest of the evening.'

'How did he handle it?'

'He didn't say much.'

'What about Finn?' McDougal spat out the lawyer's name with contempt. 'Did he beg?'

'He said *please*.'

McDougal's laugh was bitter and ugly. 'Good. Bastard.'

'Have you heard anything from the police?'

'No word yet. They must have something, though. Those were my files. Why would Finn have kept my name out of it?'

'He's your lawyer.'

'So? Lawyers have no honor.' Coale could sense no intentional irony from McDougal.

'We need to meet,' Coale said again.

'Tomorrow?'

'No, it can't wait. Tonight.'

'Why?'

'There were complications.'

McDougal's voice turned harsh, accusing. 'What kind of complications?'

'Nothing I couldn't handle. But you'll want to know.'

'My office. Half an hour.'

Coale closed the phone. Meeting at McDougal's office in a half hour wouldn't be a problem for him. He was already there. He'd been there for forty-five minutes. Eamonn McDougal wasn't stupid. His son had been, but Eamonn would be suspicious and careful. No one survived for as long as he had in his position without being careful. But Coale had survived for even longer. He planned on outliving McDougal, even if only for a little while.

A light rain was coming down in the South End as an October storm that had hovered off shore all day took an unusual turn to the north-west, spiraling counter-clockwise and ambushing the city from the north. Long was lying in Racine's bed when they heard the patter of raindrops on the windowpanes. Racine got up and pulled the window shut, stood there for a moment looking out toward the highway.

He rolled onto his side, watching her.

'What?' she asked without turning around.

'Nothing,' he said.

She turned. She was wearing a man's button-down shirt, two buttons done at the center of her chest, nothing underneath. It wasn't one of his. 'Don't give me "nothing",' she said. 'Tell me.'

'Why am I here?' he asked her.

'Ask yourself. You just showed up; I didn't invite you.'

He lay back on the bed. 'Why would you let me in?'

'Because I'm an idiot.'

'I'm serious.'

'I'm not?'

'The department wants nothing to do with me,' he said. 'You know that. You've heard people talk.'

She nodded. 'Yeah, I have.'

'Then you know that they'll take any excuse they can find to kick me off the force.'

'Don't give them any excuse.'

'If I don't give them one, they'll make one up. You really want me tied around your neck when I go down?' He looked at the shirt again, thought about the other guys she could be with. 'I'm just saying, if you want to be with a cop, then I'm probably the wrong pick. My badge has an expiration date on it.'

'What do you mean, "If I want to be with a cop"? What the fuck is that supposed to mean? You think I'm dating the badge?'

'It's been known to happen,' he said. 'And you've dated other cops.'

'Fuck you,' she said. She reached down and picked up his pants, threw them at him. 'Get dressed, and get out!'

He caught the pants, rolled to the side of the bed and pulled them on without saying a word.

'I work with cops,' she said, fuming. She picked up his shirt and threw that at him as well. 'That's who I spend most of my time around, so yeah, I've dated a couple. If you have issues with that, that's your problem.'

He shook his head. 'I don't have issues with it. I just don't want you to get hurt.'

'You've got a funny way of showing it.'

He pulled the shirt over his head. 'Tomorrow the DNA test is gonna come back on Buchanan. If it proves that he's Finn's father, I'm gonna have to go after him. There are a lot of people who aren't gonna like that, and what little solid ground I've got left to stand on is gonna slip out from under me so fast I'll be hip deep in the shit before I know what's happening.'

'So?' she said. 'Why not just leave it alone, then? That's what most guys in your position would do. Walk away and you could probably get through the rest of the crap in the department.'

He felt the muscles in his jaw tighten. 'I can't do that,' he said. It felt like he was losing her just by saying the words. It was probably for the best. Certainly it was the best thing that could happen for her. 'I'm sorry. It's just not the way I'm made.'

She stepped forward, put a hand on his cheek. 'That's why I let you in,' she said.

He put his head down. 'I tried to save him.' The words came out softly. 'Jimmy. I tried, I did. I tried to get him straight, but it was no good. That last night, he was so fucked up. He thought I was going to turn him in, and he panicked. He pulled his gun.'

He could feel her breathing. 'You had no choice,' she said.

'That's what I want to think, but I don't know. It's hard to listen when it's just me saying it to myself. It sounds like a lie.'

She put a hand on his chin, lifted his head so she could look at him. 'Listen to me, then. You had no choice. I know what happened now; it doesn't matter what anyone else says.'

He was looking into her eyes, his desire to protect her and his need to be with her locked in mortal combat. His cell phone rang. He reached into his pocket, held it up to his ear. 'Long,' he said. He listened for almost forty-five seconds, his eyes never leaving hers as she stood inches from him. 'Where?' he finally asked. Then he closed his phone, put it back in his pocket.

'Work?' she asked.

He nodded. 'Kevin McDougal tried to kill Scott Finn and the girl.'

Racine sucked in her breath. 'Are they alive?'

306

'Yeah. Apparently he never even got a shot off. Someone shot him first.'

'Who?'

'Some guy who was with McDougal. Finn didn't know who he was, hadn't seen him before. Older guy, apparently. Dark clothes. Silver hair. Grey eyes.'

'Your ghost.'

Long shrugged. 'Maybe. If so, it looks like my ghost is very much alive.'

Coale was standing in the shadows across the street from McDougal's office in Chelsea. Watching.

McDougal would be careful. Coale needed to know exactly how careful. This was the part of the job he'd excelled at his entire adult life. It was what set him apart. This time it was different, though. This was the last time, and he wanted to go out on top.

The first man arrived at twenty after twelve. He was short and stocky, and he wore a dark hat to protect his head from the rain, which was falling steadily now. Sal Brancaccio. Coale recognized him. He was one of McDougal's best men, which meant that McDougal was taking this seriously. Sal looked around the place, then headed down to the far end of the building, took up a position behind some crates stacked near the water. It was a good spot from which to watch the door. It was dark at that end of the building; dark enough that anyone who hadn't seen him slide into position would have had no idea he was there.

McDougal arrived five minutes later in his big Caddy. The car pulled into the parking lot, riding low, almost bottoming out on the lip. There were three men, big men judging by the stress on the suspension. Two up front, McDougal in back.

The car rolled to a stop, blocking the front door. Two of the men got out – McDougal and the man in the passenger seat. The driver stayed put. McDougal leaned into the driver's side window briefly, giving some final instructions. Then he headed inside. Coale noticed him looking up at the camera mounted well above the door. The camera that had caught the lawyer.

Coale waited another ten minutes, making sure no one else was showing up. No one did. So there were three. Three of McDougal's best, but three was still a small number. A manageable number. Particularly because they thought they had the benefit of surprise. That would make them overconfident. Overconfidence was a leading cause of death in his profession. It was a malady he'd avoided so far.

By the time Long got to Charlestown the rain was coming sideways. The wind was kicking the hell out of the city, tipping garbage cans and spilling their contents, swirling wet leaves into the mix to clog the street drains and gutters until the place was covered in a dark wet smear. Pools of water gathered in the street at the bottom of Bunker Hill, outside the alley where the attack had taken place. The alley itself was a river that would make decent forensics a near impossibility. A tent had been set up over the body, but it was pointless. Like trying to hold back the tide with a shovel.

Finn and the girl were outside the alley, sitting on a bench under an awning halfway up the block. Three cops surrounded them, for their protection and to keep them from disappearing. No one in the group was talking. There was no friendly banter, no threatening interrogation, only the silence of distrust.

Long walked up, shielding his face from the whipping rain until he was under the awning. 'Mr Finn,' he said.

The lawyer looked up, rolled his eyes. 'Thank God you're here.'

'You two all right?'

Finn looked over at the girl. She looked back and nodded. She seemed less agitated than he did. Finn nodded up at Long. 'We're okay,' he said. 'No thanks to you.'

'He tried to kill you?'

'Yeah, he tried to kill us.'

'Ungrateful client,' Long said. 'What happened? He got the bill?'

'This a joke to you?'

Long shook his head. 'Just trying to lighten the mood.'

'You want to lighten my mood? Tell me you've arrested James Buchanan. Short of that, my mood's pretty much gonna suck.'

Long looked down at his feet. The awning was keeping his head dry, but the wind was sweeping the rain up to his knees, and his legs were soaked. He could see water seeping out of his shoes at every shift of his weight. 'You know the senator was involved?'

'Of course he was involved,' Finn said. 'You think McDougal had his own son killed?'

Long shrugged. 'Nothing surprises me anymore. Tell me about the second guy. The one who shot Kevin. Who was he?'

'We didn't exchange business cards.'

'What did he look like?'

'Tall,' Finn said. 'Gray hair, dark suit. Older.'

'Anything else?'

The lawyer laughed bitterly. 'That's all I saw. I was focusing on his gun. You want a description of that? Because I could tell you anything you want to know.'

Long looked at the girl. 'How about you, Miss? Did you see anything else?'

'He had a scar,' she said quietly. Finn turned to look at her. 'On his forehead. It was shaped like a V.'

'Really?' Finn said.

'You didn't notice it?' Long asked.

'I didn't notice it. The gun didn't have a scar, I know that.'

'Did he say anything?' He was looking at the girl when he asked the question. He trusted her memory more than he trusted the lawyer's.

She shook her head. 'Not really. He just told us to go.'

'Why?'

'What?' Finn asked. 'You'd rather you had three bodies on your hands?'

Long shook his head. 'Not really. But it would have made more sense.'

'Thanks,' Finn said.

'Think about it. If this guy is who we think he is, he's a pro. He's also got no conscience. None whatsoever. He's been killing for years, and he knows enough not to leave witnesses. He's never left any before. And yet here he is, shooting a guy in the head in front of two people, letting them get a good clean look at him, and then letting them walk away. Why?'

Finn shook his head. 'I don't know. Maybe he couldn't bring himself to kill a kid.'

Long laughed. 'Trust me, that ain't it.' No one spoke for a moment. The rain continued to batter the sidewalk. 'He say anything else?'

Finn frowned, wiped the rain from his face. 'He said he was the one who started this.'

Long gave this some thought. 'Started what?'

'He killed my mother,' Finn said. 'That's what started it all.'

'You sure?'

Finn nodded. 'It makes sense.'

'Maybe. That it? He didn't say anything more?'

Finn paused before answering. 'He did,' he said finally. He looked up at Long. Long tried to read the lawyer's face, but it was inscrutable.

'What else did he say?'

'He said he was going to finish it.'

CHAPTER FORTY-THREE

The first one was easy. Sal Brancaccio knew what he was doing, but he assumed he would be the hunter, not the hunted. He assumed that he would follow Coale into the warehouse office, undetected. An added layer of insurance, that was all. He had no idea that Coale would be waiting for him.

Once he felt sure that no one else was coming, Coale made his way down the block, staying out of sight. He slipped across the street on the other side of McDougal's building and walked around it from the back, came up behind Brancaccio, who was peeking around the corner, keeping his eyes on the front door. His gun was out, in his hand. He stood still, behind the stack of crates, waiting.

The rain helped. It was coming down hard and fast now, and the noise was thunderous, particularly out by the water. The kind of a rain you had to yell through to be heard. Brancaccio had on a slick dark rain hat that covered his ears. Coale knew that inside the hat all he could hear was the amplified echo of raindrops off oilskin. Sal was good, but not that good.

He never heard a thing, had no idea at all until the knife slid through his throat. One motion, fast and silent. Up under the edge of the jawbone, pulling back and across to make sure that the cut was deep enough and that any struggle would only drive the knife deeper.

There was no resistance. Just a soft gurgle as Sal's hand went to his throat. Coale couldn't see the man's face, but he didn't need to. He'd done this often enough that he knew exactly what he would see. The eyes going wide in terror, the mouth gaping open, the face bloating from lack of breath. Then the line would appear on the throat, thin and dark at first, like a giant paper cut. Any motion, though, would cause the separation, and the blood would flow quickly then, out over the lip of the cut, down the neck, soaking the shirt, running down the chest until the legs would no longer support the body.

It was over quickly. It always was. Sal Brancaccio was dead before his knees hit the gravel. Coale stepped back from the body, looked up toward the car. He gave Brancaccio no further thought. He'd chosen his life. That was more than Coale had been allowed. Besides, there was still more work to be done.

The driver posed more of a challenge. The car served as a protective metal cage, and it was too difficult to attack with a knife unless you were sitting in the seat behind him. There was no way that Coale could get there without alerting him. The camera mounted at the top of the building, trained on the front door, complicated things further. Coale assumed McDougal was watching the closed circuit television feed of that camera from inside. Waiting to see what Coale would do.

He walked back around the other side of the building, up the street. He climbed into his car and drove into the lot, parked his car in between the front door to the building and McDougal's car, facing in the opposite direction to the other car so that the driver's side doors were next to each other. It would effectively block any view the camera might have of McDougal's driver.

He opened his door and stepped out. He patted his jacket pockets as though he were looking for something, tapped on the driver's window. The driver looked at him curiously for a moment, then rolled down the window.

'Yeah?' he said.

'I'm meeting Eamonn inside,' Coale said. He kept his voice as close to friendly as he could. Conspiratorial, even.

'I know,' the driver said.

'You got a match?'

The driver frowned, looking at the rain as it dribbled off the top of the car door onto his sleeve. 'You're gonna smoke in this shit?'

Coale shook his head. 'Inside.'

The driver patted his breast pocket absentmindedly, reached over to the seat next to him. His eyes only left Coale for a second, but that was all he needed. Coale moved without hesitation, his hand sliding out of his jacket, the Beretta nine-millimeter with an AAC M9-SD silencer finding its target. He pulled the trigger twice before the driver could even look back. Two shots to the head. Both punctuated with the loud, dull thud from the silencer. In the rain it would make no difference. The sound wouldn't carry through the building walls. Unsilenced, the shot would have sounded the alarm, but as it was, those within the building would have no clue that anything was wrong. He stood up, gave a salute as though saying thank you to the dead driver, just in case the camera could see any part of him. Then he walked around his car and over to the front entrance.

He tried the door. Usually, when he met with McDougal after hours at the office, McDougal left the door open for him. He was guessing that would be the case tonight, but there was no way of knowing; this night was different from others in so many ways. It would be easier if the door was open. If McDougal was forced to open the door himself, he might look out to check in with his driver, in which case Coale would have to react quickly. If it came to that, he would deal with it, but it would be better to make it inside the building first. It would be cleaner that way.

The doorknob turned easily in his grasp, and the door pushed in.

Halfway there, he thought. Two down, two to go. Then he could turn his attention to the last of his tasks.

He stepped through the door.

McDougal was watching the closed-circuit feed. He saw Coale pull in, up next to McDougal's own car. He could just make out the top of Coale's head as he bent down to ask Smitty, McDougal's driver and part-time bodyguard, a question. He stood up straight after less than a couple of seconds, walked to the door, then disappeared inside.

'He's here,' McDougal said to Jacobs. The man was standing next to McDougal, watching the same video. 'Get into position.'

Jacobs walked to the door that led out to the warehouse. 'I'll be behind the door.'

McDougal nodded. 'Wait for a few minutes after he gets here, then make the call. You understand? Don't do anything unless it sounds like there is a problem. I need to know who else he's working for. If he won't tell me when we're alone, then you and I can spend some time with him and convince him to talk. I want the chance to get it out of him myself first.'

Jacobs opened the door and slipped out, closing the door behind him. The door was cheap and flimsy. Jacobs would hear everything that went on in the office. So would Sal. McDougal had told him to follow Coale in, and to listen at the door that led back out to the reception area. Plus Smitty was out in the car. The three of them could handle one man, even someone with Coale's reputation. In McDougal's experience, reputations tended to be overblown. He couldn't remember the last time he'd met someone who'd lived up to their hype.

He sat down in the chair behind his desk to wait.

Coale walked slowly, carefully through the reception area. There was a closet, and he eased it open to make sure it was empty. He glanced behind the desk. No one. Four doors opened off the narrow hallway that led to McDougal's office. One led back out to the reception area. One was a bathroom. One was the entrance to McDougal's office, and the last one went out to the warehouse. He peered into the bathroom; it was empty. That left just the office and the warehouse.

He took out his gun, unscrewed the silencer and put it in his pocket. Accuracy and speed were at a premium over quiet now. He put the gun in his shoulder holster, kept the holster unclipped, the gun balanced, barely held, ready to be pulled out. He knocked on the door to McDougal's office.

'Come in,' McDougal called.

Coale pushed against the door and stepped inside. McDougal was sitting at his desk, one elbow resting on the desktop, the other in his lap, hidden. Coale looked at him for a moment, surveyed the room. There was no one else there. It was a square space without closets. A sofa was set against the wall, but there was no room behind that for a grown man to hide. That left only the door that led out to the warehouse. It opened inward, the hinges on the far side.

At least he had a good idea where everyone was now.

'Congratulations,' McDougal said.

Coale moved into the room, stood in front of the sofa so that he was on the other side of the hinges on the door to the warehouse. 'For what?'

'A job well done. I just spoke to Kevin.'

Coale controlled his breathing. 'Where is he?'

'He's at his apartment.' Coale could feel McDougal watching him, evaluating his reaction. He didn't care. He'd played the game for too long to give himself away. 'He's going to call us in a few minutes. He sounds more like a man than he ever has. I can't tell you how grateful I am.'

Coale kept his face still, showing nothing. No surprise, no emotion. 'It sometimes happens that way.'

'It does. A man's first kill. The realization that you have the power over life and death is a powerful thing. I remember my first, back in Ireland. I was a child, no more than fourteen. Tommy O'Dea. A local boy who owed me money.' McDougal laughed, an evil chuckle. 'I was scared wet; I didn't want to do it. Once it was done, though, I knew I could do anything. There was nothing I wanted that I couldn't have if I set my mind to it. That's when I left for the States.'

Coale was looking McDougal in the eyes, but he was paying attention to the hand under the desk out of his peripheral vision.

'Do you remember your first?' McDougal asked.

Coale thought about his mother, dying in childbirth. Bleeding out at the same moment she gave him life. 'No,' he said. 'I don't.'

'No?' McDougal sounded surprised. 'Well,' he said, 'I guess when you've sent as many off as you have, it doesn't even make an impression anymore, does it? Like swatting a bug to you. How many has it been? Twenty?'

Coale said nothing.

'Fifty? A hundred?'

'We have some things to discuss,' Coale said.

'We do.' McDougal sat forward in his chair. His hand stayed beneath the desk. 'Complications, you said on the phone.'

Coale nodded slowly. 'Complications. The lawyer said he didn't give any information over to the police.'

McDougal let out a sarcastic grunt. 'We have him on camera breaking into the place, coming out with the files. We know that he did. He was trying to save his ass.'

'He didn't deny breaking in,' Coale said. 'He said that he only gave over material on other people. Nothing on you. He said it was the only way he could keep Kevin from doing time.'

'Did you believe him?'

Coale nodded slowly.

'Wouldn't that be ironic?' McDougal's face turned serious. 'You killed him anyway, right? You didn't let him go, did you?'

'Kevin killed him. You talked to Kevin already, right?'

A shadow of doubt crossed McDougal's face. 'Yeah. I talked to him. He's going to be calling back in a few minutes.' He was still scrutinizing Coale as he spoke.

'So you said.'

The silence hung heavy between them for a long moment. 'Any other complications?' McDougal asked.

Coale shook his head. 'None.'

'So, what else is there to talk about?'

'I'm out,' Coale said. 'I'm done.'

'I hired you to do a job.'

'You did. And I did the job.'

'Did you, now?'

'I did,' Coale said. He crossed his arms in front of his chest, so that his right hand rested on the gun in his shoulder holster under his jacket. 'You hired me to take care of the situation with the Connor woman. I did that. The police found nothing. I took care of the situation in New Hampshire. I took care of the lawyer. I'm done.'

'The police are asking questions about me. They're asking questions about my connections to Buchanan.' McDougal drummed his fingers on the desk. 'That was what I was trying to avoid.'

'Maybe you should have been more careful,' Coale said.

'Or maybe you've not finished the fuckin' job.'

'I'm finished with the job. I'm finished working for you.'

'Are you? You working for someone else now, is that it? Maybe our good senator has offered you more? Maybe you think you can sell me out and save his royal ass?' The fingers stopped drumming. 'Is that what you think?'

'I think you watch too many movies. I think we're done.'

317

The phone on the table rang. Neither man looked at it. Their eyes were locked; neither would look away. McDougal reached out and picked up the receiver without even glancing at it, held it up to his ear. 'Hello?' There was a pause. 'Kevin,' he said, still focused on Coale. 'He's right here.' McDougal held the phone out to Coale. Coale didn't reach for it. His arms stayed folded, his hand inching toward his gun; he wrapped his fingers around the grip. 'No?' McDougal said. 'You don't want to talk to him?'

Coale said nothing. Every muscle in his body was tense, ready.

McDougal let the phone hang down from his hand. 'He's dead, isn't he?' he said. 'You killed my son.'

They both moved at the same time. Coale brought his hand out of his jacket just as McDougal's arm came up from beneath the desk. The guns were in motion. It was like a tribute to the Old West, except that McDougal was sitting, putting him at a disadvantage. It was a critical mistake. They pulled their triggers within milliseconds of each other. Not enough time to be measured by standard commercial timers, but enough to make a difference. Coale's shot took McDougal in the forehead even as McDougal was firing. McDougal's head was thrown back and the momentum of his shot was affected. It wasn't enough to prevent him from getting the shot off, but it was sufficient to disrupt his aim. The slug that would have hit Coale in the center of the chest caught him instead in the muscle of his left shoulder.

The two shots firing at once created an explosion that was deafening in the tiny space. Coale ignored the sound, though, just as he ignored the pain shooting through his shoulder. He spun toward the door to the warehouse, ducking slightly to his left as he did.

It was perfectly planned. McDougal's final man came through the door at the sound of the gunfire. The door opened inward, with Coale on the other side even as it swung open and the man stepped into the room, gun drawn. Coale aimed at the center of the thin, balsawood door and fired seven shots in quick succession.

The door rocked, and Coale heard the familiar grunts and gurgles of a man taking a bullet in the thoracic cavity. There was a loud thud, and the door swung fully open, so that it was flush to the office wall. The man was lying on the floor, his jacket covered in blood. A dark red line ran from his nose, and he wheezed, gasping for breath.

The man's hand was still wrapped around his gun, lying flat on the ground. He looked up, and as he saw Coale, the hand twitched. He was trying to raise it but he had no strength.

Coale walked over and stepped on the hand. He could feel the fingers crack beneath his weight, trapped between his heavy shoe, the butt of the gun, and the floor. The man on the floor winced in agony. It was amazing to Coale that even with multiple slugs having ripped through it, the human body still functioned effectively enough to recognize a new source of pain.

The man looked up at Coale, his eyes pleading.

Coale looked back at him. He shook his head slightly.

He raised his gun, and put a bullet into the man's forehead.

CHAPTER FORTY-FOUR

Long didn't go home. There was no point. Finn's words rang in his ears.

He said he was going to finish it.

Whatever was going to happen was going to happen soon.

He went to the station house, to the detectives' bureau, where his desk had been for the better part of a decade. The place was empty. Even downstairs, it was quiet; not a lot of street action in the city that night. At night, the station house took on an otherworldly feel. An empty, abandoned feeling. It fit his mood.

He stood at the window, looking down on the street from the second floor. The rain continued to fall, and the streetlights sparked diamonds on the asphalt. The steady slosh of tires over the wet streets made him think of the ocean down at Nantasket Beach, where his family went for a week every summer when he was a child. They stayed at a run-down motel across the street from the beach, a quarter mile down from the arcades and the honky-tonks. It had been heaven to him. It was beautiful and clean – a respite from the violence of the rest of their lives. The sound of the waves so close set an even, steady rhythm that calmed everyone.

Tires through puddles seemed a poor substitute.

A hand touched his shoulder. 'You okay?'

He turned to look at Racine. 'Yeah,' he said. 'You?'

She shrugged. 'I figured you'd be here.'

'I've got no place else to go.' As he said the words, he felt their full meaning.

'I know.'

'Kevin McDougal's dead.'

'I heard.' She took her hand off his back, leaned against a desk. 'It's going to get worse, isn't it?'

He nodded. 'It is.' He walked over and leaned against the same desk, next to her. They were shoulder to shoulder, both looking out the window. Lights from a squad car flashed off the raindrops sliding down the glass.

'Is there anything I can do?'

He thought about it for a moment. Then he shook his head. 'I'm not sure there's anything anyone can do.'

Coale made it back to his loft without attracting attention. Soon there would be a full search for him underway. The lawyer and the girl would give a complete description of him, and by morning every cop on the street would have a composite sketch so detailed it would look like a photograph. He took a significant risk letting them go. He hadn't had a choice, though, had he?

He stripped off his shirt. The left sleeve was soaked in blood, and there was a dark red hole on the outer edge of his shoulder. The bleeding had slowed, but it still oozed steadily. He'd been lucky. If the bullet had hit the bone, his mobility would have been severely impaired. That would have made his last task much more difficult. As it was, he would be stiff and sore, but not in a way that he would take notice of.

He pulled out a bowl and a medical kit, filled the bowl with rubbing alcohol. The medical kit had a needle and surgical thread. He put both into the alcohol, dipped a towel in and cleaned the wound. The alcohol on the bullet hole burned, but it was a good burn. A surface burn. Not the nauseous pain that came with more serious damage.

Once the wound was cleaned, he pulled out the needle and stitched the edges together. He had to wipe the blood out of the way several times, but by the time he was done he could already see the wound clotting. He put a bandage on it and put a clean undershirt on.

Resting on the edge of the bed, he breathed in deeply, filling his lungs. He tried to remember the last time he'd had a good sleep. Too long ago to recall. That would not be rectified tonight. He had to pack. By noon he planned to be long gone from Boston. Air travel was out of the question; too many law enforcement types at the airports. He'd drive out of the city. West. Keep going until he couldn't stay on the road anymore, then find a place by the side of the highway. A cheap place. The kind of a place where no one asked any questions. The kind of a place where they assumed everyone was on the run from something. A husband. A wife. A life. He'd figure out where to go once he'd had a chance to rest. As much as it would hurt, he'd ditch the car, get something else to drive; something Midwestern, inconspicuous. But first, he had one more job to do.

He packed quickly. He was a minimalist, and took only what he needed. As he loaded his suitcase he glanced at the pocket where he kept the pictures. He was tempted to pull them out again. Until recently, he'd gone so long without looking at them that the pain had almost vanished. Not vanished, actually, but the scar tissue had grown so thick over the wound that it was almost like the pain wasn't there anymore. It wasn't true, of course. The pain had always been there. Waiting to grab at him at the first opportunity. Waiting for the scar tissue to tear open and reveal the true depth of the wound.

He left the pictures where they were. He would have time to look at them. He would have time to grapple with his past once he was gone. Right now he had to focus.

Early morning was the time to strike – a few hours before sunrise.

That was when the attention of the security guards would be at its lowest ebb. That was when he would have the best chance of getting inside the house undetected. Once inside, he would find a way to get the man alone. He needed time. He needed to make himself understood. That required privacy.

After the suitcase was packed and he was fully dressed, he cleaned the loft – cleaned it like he'd cleaned a thousand places in his long career. People would be coming after him. The police. The feds. McDougal's people. Others. No need to give them any help.

Once he was done, he looked around the place. He tried to remember how long he'd lived there. He had no idea, really. Ten years, maybe fifteen. A lifetime to some. To him, the blink of an eye.

He turned off the light and locked the door. He wasn't coming back. Ever.

CHAPTER FORTY-FIVE

'You should try to sleep,' Finn said.

Sally looked up at him. She was sitting on the couch in the living room, her knees drawn up to her chin. 'You're joking, right?'

'You should try, at least.'

Lissa and Kozlowski were sitting on stools at the kitchen counter. They'd come as soon as Finn called them to tell them what had happened. 'Let her be,' Lissa said to Finn.

He was standing against the wall, and he stared at Lissa, for a moment ready to argue with her. He didn't have the energy, though. He nodded and felt his shoulders sag.

'At least you know now,' Lissa offered. 'That's something.'

'I don't know anything,' Finn said.

'You know who killed your mother. Wasn't that what this was all about?'

He shook his head. 'I don't know who killed her.'

'The man in the alley. You said he told you.'

'He was working for someone. Buchanan. Maybe Eamonn. Maybe both. He might have been the one who actually hit her, but someone else was pulling his strings. I need to know who.'

'You're crazy,' Lissa said. 'You need to let this go.'

'Let it go?' Finn said. 'Kevin McDougal tried to kill me. He tried to kill Sally. We watched as some stranger put a bullet in his head. You think it doesn't matter why?'

'That's right,' Lissa said. 'I don't think it matters why. Right now the only thing that matters to me is that you and Sally weren't killed. The only thing that matters to me is that you're both here right now. I don't know why the guy in the alley let you two go, but next time you may not be so lucky.' She was raising her voice; the baby stirred in his car seat propped on the kitchen counter. She reached in and put her hand on top of him, lowered her voice to a hiss. 'You need to focus on what's important.'

'This is important,' Sally said.

The three adults looked at her, surprised.

'It's important,' she said, 'because I don't want to be looking over my shoulder for the rest of my life. The one thing I know from where I grew up is that shit like this doesn't just go away. Someone tries to kill you once, they'll try again. It's easier to deal with that if you can see it coming. If Finn let's this go now, it'll come back around. Maybe not this week, but sometime down the road.'

The room was silent for a while. The rain was beating against the windows. The baby gurgled softly.

'What do you think?' Finn asked Kozlowski.

He tilted his head. 'If you're really gonna follow this through, don't bother starting with Eamonn,' he said. 'His son was just murdered – I would stay away from him. He's not going to be warm and fuzzy, and you're not gonna get any information out of him.'

'That's a good bet.'

'That just leaves Buchanan.'

'He's desperate for me to drop this,' Finn said. 'He showed up here with a couple of his security people; it seemed pretty important to him to be done with this, and he made it clear that he wasn't going to give me any information. He's never gonna admit that he's my father even if he really is.'

'You don't need him to admit that he's your father. The police are running DNA tests, and they're gonna be able to tell whether he's your father. You need for him to tell you what happened to your mother. You need to know whether he had anything to do with that.'

'And you think he'll just come out and tell me that?' Finn said.

'Maybe. If he was convinced that you wouldn't go to the cops.' Kozlowski looked hard at Finn. 'Let me ask you this: What would you do if you found out he was your father, and that he did have your mother killed? Would you turn him in?'

The question caught Finn short. 'I don't know,' he said. 'I hadn't thought that far ahead.'

'It's not that far ahead anymore,' Kozlowski said. 'It's pretty much right here.'

Finn considered the question. 'I don't know the man,' he said. 'Why would I have any loyalty to him?'

'You didn't know your mother at all, either,' Kozlowski said. 'You seem to have some sort of loyalty to her, though.'

'He left me. He abandoned me.'

'So did your mother.'

'It's different.'

'Why?'

Finn sighed. 'I don't know. Maybe it's not.'

'If he really is your father, could you send him to jail? For good or bad, he's your blood. He's the only father you'll ever have.'

Finn closed his eyes. 'I don't know. I would have to look into his eyes when he tells me. I wouldn't know until that moment.'

Kozlowski looked at his watch. 'Well, you should get yourself ready,' he said. 'Because that moment is coming up in a few hours. First thing this morning, we're going over there.'

Coale left his car near the top of Beacon Hill, a block from Buchanan's mansion on Louisburg Square. It might get a ticket, but it wouldn't get towed, and it would take a day for the police to connect any information on the ticket with events at the mansion. He planned to ditch the car by then.

Walking down Pinkney Street toward the Square from above gave him an excellent view of the Buchanan residence. It was four-fifteen in the morning. The rain had stopped and the streets were slick, reflecting the glow from the streetlights and the moon above. The neighborhood was silent and still, the fall leaves were stuck to the sidewalks from the rain.

He ducked into a small alley that ran off Pinkney behind the house. He knew that Buchanan had security, but to the extent that there were guards on duty at night, they would likely be stationed at the front door. Perhaps they might walk a circuit around the house once an hour, but it would almost certainly be on the hour. Security relied, paradoxically, on set schedules and patterns that allowed those who recognized them to defeat them fairly easily. Most security 'experts' suffered from a tragic inflexibility that provided exploitable gaps.

A wooden fence bordered the property along the alley – six feet tall, with two gates. Peering over the fence, he could see that one of the gates led to the patio off the front of the kitchen. The second led to the back of the kitchen, where a line of trash bins were stacked against the brick wall of a narrow outer passageway.

He jumped the fence out by the garbage. The passageway was blocked off to both the street and the rest of the house. It could be seen only from a small area of the kitchen; at this time of the day, that didn't pose a problem. He had time to work, though he didn't intend to take that for granted. The faster he got into the house, the better off he would be.

The door to the kitchen was an antique. Architects liked to retain as many of the original fixtures as possible on historic homes like this one when they renovated. It retained a touch of authenticity that was essential to the integrity of the place. On the other hand, it compromised areas, such as energy efficiency and safety.

Coale took out a leather case, slipped out his lock pick. He had the lock turned within thirty seconds. Before turning the handle, he brought out a small device with an LCD readout and two wires running to open clips. It was a useful tool that was capable of overriding alarm codes on most current systems. All he had to do was crack the alarm panel and affix the clips to the correct wires within a minute of entry.

He turned the door handle and stepped inside. The alarm panel was just around the corner in the pantry. He found it within five seconds. That left fifty-five. More than enough time.

He pulled out a small screwdriver to prize open the plastic covering. As he started to work, though, he noticed that the alarm panel wasn't beeping. There was no familiar disquieting electronic countdown. He looked more closely and saw that the alarm had not been set. It wasn't unusual; many people took enough comfort from the mere presence of an alarm system and failed to actually turn it on.

Coale put his tools away and surveyed the kitchen. The pale light of the silver moon in the clearing sky was just enough to let him see. The room was huge, bigger than his old loft. He stood there for a moment, listening to the house breathing, using all of his senses to get a feel for the place before he moved on. Once he felt he had the pulse of the house, he moved quickly and silently. He made sure that every room on the ground floor was empty. Then he started up the stairs.

He heard the movement in a room off to the right at the top of the staircase. Down a long hallway, a single light was on, papers were being shuffled. Coale went to the left, checking all of the other rooms on the floor to make sure there was no one else. Then he headed toward the light.

Peering through a crack in the door, he could see the senator hunched over at his desk, going through files. The light came from a green-shaded Tiffany lamp on his desk. His back was to Coale, and the shutters were closed.

Coale pulled out his gun. As he did, Buchanan began to turn. Coale stepped back from the door, listening, aiming the gun at the shaft of light carving through the gap. He heard Buchanan stand, the wooden desk chair creaking as he did. He walked further into the room. Another light was switched on, this one harsher than the subtle, soft tones of the Tiffany lamp. A moment later, Coale heard the familiar dribble from a toilet.

He moved silently into the room, rounded the corner. The door to the bathroom stood open. Buchanan was standing in front of the toilet, his hands below his waist in front of him. His hair was wrecked, the usually perfect coiffure sent askew, standing up at the top of his head, pushed back and to the side.

Coale moved forward to the threshold of the lavatory, extending his arm so that the tip of the silencer rested at the base of Buchanan's skull. Buchanan went stiff, his head coming up, his back going rigid with tension. 'Mr Coale, I presume,' he said without turning around.

'Don't turn around.'

'I wouldn't think of it. Do you mind if I zip my pants?'

'Yes.'

Buchanan took a deep breath. It sounded almost as though his patience had been tried by a small child, and he was now mustering every ounce of forbearance to deal with him. 'Whatever you're being paid, I'll pay more,' Buchanan said. 'A lot more.'

Coale raged internally at Buchanan. He pressed his gun harder into the man's neck, forcing his head down. 'Who said I was being paid?'

Something about Buchanan's posture changed. Coale sensed it. He was a man who was used to being able to solve any problem; to gloss over any unpleasantness, with money and favors. For the first time in his life, James Buchanan was realizing he was in a situation that was completely out of his control. 'Please,' he said. His voice cracked; he sounded weak for the first time. 'Please, we can talk about this.'

Coale eased back on the gun. 'We can talk about this,' he agreed. 'I'm going to talk, and you're going to listen. We are going to talk about this until you understand what you have done; until you understand why I'm here. Then, when we are done talking, I'm going to kill you.' He leaned in close to the senator, spoke softly. 'I wanted you to know that before we began.'

At seven o'clock the phone on Long's desk rang. He was sitting in his chair, looking down at his investigation notes, his elbows on the desk, his head resting on his knuckles. Racine was sitting in the chair on the far side of the desk. The squad room was just beginning to come to life, but it was still quiet, and the phone startled them both.

Long picked up the receiver. 'Detective Long,' he said. He listened for a moment. 'You sure?' He listened again. 'Okay, thanks, Joe. I appreciate you working this overnight.' He hung up. Racine was looking at him, her eyebrows raised. 'The lab,' he said. 'It's a match. Buchanan is Scott Finn's father.'

Racine let out a low whistle. 'Finn was right.'

Long nodded. 'Finn was right,' he agreed.

'Where does that leave us?'

Long shook his head. 'I don't know.'

The phone on the desk rang again. Long looked at it curiously, picked it up. 'Yeah?'

'Is this Long?' came a voice from the other end. It sounded distant; a cell phone with a weak signal, ambient sound from outside crowding out the voice.

'Yeah, this is Long.'

'This is Detective Unger over in Chelsea. I heard through the grapevine you've been working a case that's got something to do with Eamonn McDougal, that right?'

'That's right,' Long said. 'I was out over in Charlestown last night after his son Kevin was whacked. You might want to keep an eye on him over there.'

'Yeah, well, that won't be necessary,' Unger said. 'He's not going anywhere anymore.'

'What do you mean?'

'I mean someone already took care of McDougal last night, maybe early this morning. Three of his guys, too, over here at his office. It's a goddamned massacre.'

Long had no idea how to respond. 'You know who did it?'

'Not yet,' Unger said. 'Seeing as how you've been working on something with him, I was kinda hoping you might be able to shed some light on some of the probables.'

Long thought about it. 'I may be able to,' he said. 'I've got to check a few things out first, okay?'

'Whatever you say,' Unger replied. 'I'm not going anywhere, and neither's McDougal at this point. Just get back to me when you get a chance. This is one we'd like to clear up here. It doesn't look good to have this kind of shit going down and not be able to put someone away. Not that I mind having McDougal off our watch list. Hell, there's a part of me that'd like to find the guy who did this just so I can thank him.'

'I'll get back to you as soon as I can,' Long said. He hung up the phone, looked up at Racine. 'McDougal's dead,' he said.

'Eamonn?'

He nodded.

'Holy crap,' Racine said. 'What does that mean?'

'That means I've got to get over to Buchanan's house, now.'

CHAPTER FORTY-SIX

Scott Finn and Tom Kozlowski climbed out of the little MG in front of the Buchanan house on Louisburg Square at seven-fifteen that morning. They stood there, looking up at the towering residence for a moment before they moved toward it. They walked slowly, almost as if they wanted to delay the inevitable. They were watched by the suited man with the dark sunglasses on the stoop landing at the front door. They stopped two steps below the landing, at a tactical disadvantage. Finn was happy to see, at least, that the man on duty wasn't one of the men he'd already encountered. That might smooth the conversation.

'We need to talk to Senator Buchanan,' Finn said.

The man shook his head. 'He's given instructions that he doesn't want to be disturbed this morning. He's cancelled all his appointments.'

'We don't have an appointment,' Kozlowski said. 'So he didn't cancel us.'

'I'm sorry, sir,' the guard said. 'I can't help you.' He was young and nervous; probably a guy who had tried to get into the police academy and had failed the test. He spoke the way someone who wants to be a cop speaks, but without the confidence that comes from having been the law.

'He's going to want to talk to us,' Finn said. 'He'll be pissed if you don't call him to tell him we're here. You really want to take that chance? Why not at least call up. Tell him Scott Finn is here and he wants to talk about the deal the senator proposed the other day.'

'No can do, sir,' the young man said, though his voice sounded far from confident. 'The senator has given explicit instructions that he is not to be disturbed.'

'You talked to him yourself?' Kozlowski asked.

The guard shook his head slowly. 'I just came on fifteen minutes ago. He called down at five-thirty, left word with the guy who was on before me. Apparently he was up all night.'

'Probably worried about your conversation with him yesterday,' Kozlowski said to Finn. Kozlowski looked up at the young man again. 'You can probably tell we have some pretty important things we need to discuss with the senator. So why don't you press the buzzer and tell him that we're here?'

The guard hesitated. He was starting to look nervous. 'I can't,' he said. He didn't sound very convincing, though. Both Finn and Kozlowski continued to stare at him. 'I'm serious, I could get fired,' he said.

'You could get fired either way, I guess,' Kozlowski said. 'It depends on your judgment.'

The guard looked at the intercom, then back at Kozlowski. It looked like he was about to say something when another car pulled up to the sidewalk directly in front of the house. It was a boxy American-made sedan, so conspicuous on the street that it might as well have had a row of police lights strapped to the top of it.

Kozlowski and Finn watched as Detective Long opened the door and got out. Finn looked at Kozlowski. 'Good news or bad?'

Kozlowski shook his head. 'It's never good news when the cops show up this early in the morning.'

*

'What are you doing here?' Long asked.

'I had some thoughts on health care,' Kozlowski replied.

'Funny.'

'What? He's my senator, right?'

'I have to talk to the man,' Long said. 'You two can't be here. It's part of the investigation.'

'You got some news?' Finn asked.

Long looked at him. He said nothing.

'You came to me, remember?' Finn said. 'You asked me for my blood; now you're not going to tell me?'

'It was positive,' Long said. 'I got the call from the lab a half hour ago. You're his son.'

'No shit,' Finn said.

'No shit.'

No one said anything. Long watched as the lawyer's face displayed a range of conflicting emotions. He wondered what the moment must be like after four and a half decades of not knowing. Most people would break down. Finn's face just went blank. 'You two have to leave,' Long said again.

'Right,' Finn said. Neither he nor Kozlowski moved.

Long climbed the steps, walking past Finn and Kozlowski, until he was standing next to the security guard on the stoop. He ignored the young man and reached out and buzzed the intercom.

'You can't!' the guard protested, his hand reaching up for Long's arm. Long turned on him, grabbed him by the throat and pushed him up against the door. 'You don't want to be touching a cop that way,' he said. 'And I know you don't want to be interfering with an official police investigation, right?' He let go of the man's throat, turned back to the intercom.

'He doesn't want to be disturbed,' the guard choked out. 'He cancelled all his meetings for the morning.'

'Good, then his schedule should be free,' Long said. 'Any way you look at it, though, he is going to talk to me.' He pressed the buzzer again. 'Senator Buchanan,' he said into the intercom. 'It's Detective Long. Open up, sir. I have some important matters to discuss with you.'

There was no answer from the intercom. All four men stood there, looking at the speaker expectantly.

'Senator, open the door,' Long said again. 'I could go and get a warrant, but that isn't going to do either of us any good, sir.'

'Maybe he's sleeping,' the guard said. 'He was up all night.'

Long reached out and hit the intercom again, holding it down for ten seconds. They could hear the obnoxiously loud buzzing from inside. 'Senator, this is police business, open up now!' Long yelled.

A moment later they heard the noise. It was somewhere between a scream and a cry, coming from the second floor. They looked at each other, as if to confirm that they had all heard it. A moment later there came a screech of agony too clear to be questioned. Long pulled out his gun. 'Call 911, now!' he shouted to the security guard. The young man just stared at him, too stunned to move. 'Now!' Long yelled again. This time the guard reacted by pulling out a radio and yelling into it.

'Code red!' he yelled over and over.

Long turned his attention to the door. He leaned back, lifted his foot up, shifted his weight forward and kicked out with all his might, connecting just to the left of the door's handle. The great heavy portal gave a shudder, but didn't budge.

From upstairs within the house came another ear-shattering scream.

Long turned and looked at Finn and Kozlowski. 'Give me a hand!' he yelled.

The two of them joined him at the top of the stoop. The young security guard moved down the steps, fully ceding control over the situation. He was still yelling 'Code red!' into his walkie-talkie. Long, Finn and Kozlowski stood shoulder to shoulder, facing the door. Long gave the count, 'One, two, three,' and then all three of them flung themselves at the door. Finn and Long used their feet. Kozlowski, who was far more solid than either of them, used his shoulder. They all connected at the same time, and the door gave another shudder; this time it was deeper, though, and it was accompanied by a loud cracking sound. It held, but only just.

'One, two, three!' Long counted again. They threw themselves at the door once more, and this time the thick slab of wood gave way, the doorjamb tearing off from the inside.

Long held his gun up and stepped into the house. He turned and looked at Finn and Kozlowski. 'Stay here,' he said.

Kozlowski already had his gun out. He shook his head. 'We're coming in,' he said.

Long started to argue, but before he could get any words out, another scream from the second floor cut him off. He nodded to Kozlowski. 'Keep him out of the way,' he said, motioning at Finn.

Kozlowski nodded his assent and gave Finn a look. 'I'll stay back, but I'm coming up,' Finn said.

'Okay,' Kozlowski said. 'Keep low and don't get shot.'

Long was already moving up the stairs, and Kozlowski joined him. Finn followed a few steps behind. Toward the screams. Toward his father.

CHAPTER FORTY-SEVEN

Coale never heard them coming. He didn't hear the intercom buzzing; he didn't hear them kicking in the door. He was too far gone to hear anything at that point.

Buchanan was sitting on a wooden chair in his study, his hands bound behind his back, his feet tied to two of the legs of the chair. He was bleeding from his mouth and nose, and there were several gashes on his forehead. His head was hanging in exhaustion. He was sobbing.

'I'm sorry,' he kept saying over and over again. It was a plea for mercy not aimed at his current tormentor. He'd concluded more than an hour before that pleas to the man standing before him would be wasted. And so his request for mercy was directed to a higher authority. One to which he was sure he would have his introduction before the morning was over.

Coale was sweating from his exertions. His normally well-combed hair had taken on a wild look, and his sleeves were rolled up. He, too, was talking to himself, muttering his own combination of recriminations and apologies. The cold, calculating demeanor that had served him well throughout his professional life had been shed, and what remained underneath was pure animal fury.

'I'm sorry!' Buchanan screamed, summoning what little strength he had left. Coale turned at him and the hand that held his gun flew from his body, striking Buchanan in the temple, drawing fresh blood.

Buchanan sobbed and Coale kicked him in the chest, knocking the wind from his body. He watched as the senator sat there choking, unable to breathe, spitting up blood as his face contorted in fear and pain. It made Coale feel good to watch it. He supposed that was the final sign of his damnation – that he could take such warm pleasure from what he was doing. It didn't matter to him anymore, though. He'd lived through damnation before.

He used the back of his hand to wipe the sweat from his brow as he thought about what his life might have been. Bending over, he took a deep breath, and slowly some sense of rationality returned.

It was over, he realized. He'd burned through the last of his anger, and the conflagration had taken everything within him. Someone more righteous might have felt cleansed by the experience. Not Coale, though. All he felt was brittle and empty and lost.

He walked over and stood behind Buchanan. The man had served his purpose. He understood, or he didn't; that wasn't for Coale to decide. All that was left was to end the misery. He raised his gun and put the muzzle of the silencer to his temple.

'Police! Freeze!'

Coale looked up. Detective Long was standing in the door, his gun out, aimed straight at Coale's forehead. A moment later the door was crowded with the lawyer and the private detective. Kozlowski was pointing a gun at him as well.

'Drop the gun and step back!' Long shouted.

Coale surveyed the room from the corner of his eye, keeping his focus on Long. He considered his options and concluded almost instantly that he had none. He had no intention of spending the rest of his life in the custody of the Commonwealth.

'Get down on the floor, now, or I will shoot!' Long shouted.

'You're going to have to shoot,' Coale said. 'I'm going to have to shoot, too. Are you ready?'

'Wait, just wait!' Long shouted. He was in a no-win situation, and they both knew it. If he risked shooting Coale, in all likelihood the force from the blast would cause Coale to pull the trigger, killing the senator. But if he did nothing and Coale shot the senator while he was standing there . . . well, no cop could live with that.

'Wait for what?' Coale asked. 'There's nothing to discuss.' He looked at the two men behind Long, saw a peculiar look in the lawyer's eyes. For a moment he felt a wave of guilt rush through him so powerful it almost knocked him off his feet. He pushed it aside, though. There would be no atonement for him. 'Sorry,' he said to the lawyer. 'You were better off without parents.'

'We can talk,' Long said. He was trying to keep his voice calm now, following textbook hostage-situation protocol. Coale figured Long had probably taken some one-day course in it during his career. Rule number one: keep the hostage-taker talking.

Except in this case, the hostage-taker had nothing to say.

'When was the last time you fired your weapon?' Coale asked Long.

'I'm telling you, we can talk,' Long replied.

'It was when you shot your partner, wasn't it? You probably haven't even been back to the range since then, have you?'

'Don't do this.'

The senator was babbling now. Begging for help; crying and apologizing again and again.

'Are you ready?' Coale asked.

'Don't!'

'One . . .' Coale began counting.

'No!'

'Two . . .'

'I'll shoot!'

'Thr—'

Both guns fired at once. Coale stood there, suspended. Time stopped and then rushed forward again. The images came at him, released from places in his mind he'd shuttered so long ago. His father, smiling, running a chamois along the smooth fender of the burgundy Rolls Royce; Morse Pond, out by Wellesley College, where, on off days he would go to swim and to watch the college girls walk to class; the face of the most beautiful woman he'd ever known, and the look in her eyes when she realized, much to her dismay, that she loved him too.

The dark images came as well. The torment of losing his father, of losing everything; scrapping through his early life, fighting for every morsel of food, every bit of respect; his rebirth as a killer of uncommon skill and indifference to human life. All of it interspersed with the faces; too many of them to count. Some crying, begging, pleading; some calling out the names of loved ones as he stood before them with neither judgment not pity. After all, for him it was his only way of living. He had caused so much pain in his lifetime, and yet his final act had been selfless, hadn't it? The last thought that passed through his mind was to wonder, almost idly, whether that was enough for redemption.

He was dead before he hit the floor.

'No!' Finn screamed as the shots were fired. He tried to rush forward, but Long was blocking the door and Kozlowski held him back. He stood there helplessly watching as Long and the man with the scar on his forehead pulled their triggers at the same instant. Buchanan toppled forward, the chair tipping over, the spray of blood and brains coating the floor in front of him. The man with the scar lingered for a moment, a look of bewilderment on his face as the blood trickled down from the hole in his forehead. Then he, too, toppled over, hitting the floor with his full weight.

'Let me through!' Finn yelled.

'Stay back!' Long yelled in return. 'We don't know that he was alone.'

Kozlowski nodded and kept his hand on Finn's chest as Long

advanced into the room. It was a small space, and it took only a few seconds for him to complete his sweep and give the all-clear signal. By then, they could hear the sirens of a dozen squad cars pulling up outside the house. There were footsteps on the stairway, and urgent shouting for ambulances and medical personnel.

Most of it swept over Finn. He was still looking at Buchanan, lying face down on the Persian rug, the pool of blood by his head growing larger by the moment.

He pushed his way past Kozlowski and ducked around Long. Kneeling by Buchanan's body, he reached for his shoulders to roll him over.

'Leave him!' Long ordered. 'The paramedics will be here any second.'

'He's my father,' Finn said simply, as he rolled him over.

He looked better than Finn had expected. The bullet had passed through the top of the skull, entering and exiting above the hairline. There was blood – a lot of blood – and Finn could see the flash of bone in the hairline where the bullet had traveled, but most of the cuts on the man's face had clearly been inflicted prior to the gunshot.

He was alive. That, too, surprised Finn, though it did not appear that the condition would last for long. His eyes spun as Finn rolled him over, placing his jacket under his head. Finn wanted to say something comforting, but he could think of nothing. He just stared at the man, Buchanan staring back, his jaw hanging lax, his eyes losing focus. It felt like there should be something that could be said or done to take so much tragedy and spin a Hollywood ending of reconciliation. It was not to be, though, and a moment later the life fled from Buchanan's eyes. What little muscle tone there had been deserted the body just as the paramedics arrived. Finn stepped out of the way, but he knew that there was nothing that could be done.

He watched them work on Buchanan. Certainly no one there felt authorized to pronounce a United States senator dead, and they continued to pump his chest and bag air into his lungs even as they rolled him out of the room. There were seven responders working on the corpse. *All the king's horses . . .* Finn thought.

No one was working on the man with the scar. One paramedic had spent a brief moment examining the body. It wasn't clear whether he was trying to determine whether he was alive or whether he was important. He diagnosed almost immediately, though, that he was neither, and moved on to help the others with Buchanan.

Finn walked over and looked down at the man who had killed both his mother and his father. Finn replayed the man's words back in his head: *You were better off without parents.* He wondered whether it was true. Certainly nothing that he'd learned about Elizabeth Connor and James Buchanan would recommend either as a candidate for parent of the year. And yet was he really better off without them? He supposed it didn't matter anymore.

He should have detested the man lying dead before him. He should have been able to muster a rage for the ages. What person could take so much from another and not feel the sting of his victim's hate? And yet Finn felt completely numb looking at him. Perhaps it was the fact that he had no emotional attachment to the parents who had been killed. Perhaps it was because he had let Finn and Sally walk away from the alley in Charlestown, giving them their lives. Whatever the reason, he couldn't bring himself to have any strong feelings for the man one way or another.

'You're wrong,' he said to the corpse. 'I would have been better off with parents.' He wasn't sure why he said it. Perhaps it was just to get the last word.

'You okay?' Kozlowski asked from behind.

'Yeah,' Finn said.

'Long wants us downstairs. I'm guessing we're gonna be here most of the day, giving statements and talking to the cops.'

'Yeah. Probably right. You should call Lissa, let her know.'

Kozlowski nodded. 'You sure you're okay?'

'I'm fine. It's not like Buchanan coached my little league teams. He abandoned me, and he probably gave the order to have my mother killed. I'm not exactly feeling a deep sense of personal loss.'

'What are you feeling?'

'You Oprah now?'

'I'm just askin'.'

'Well don't. I'm fine.'

'Good,' Kozlowski said. "Cause you're gonna need the patience of a saint to deal with the rest of this day.'

'No shit,' Finn sighed. 'We might as well get it over with.'

The rest of the day went by in a blur. Finn was asked the same questions a thousand times by a hundred different officers. Every law enforcement agency in the United States was involved at some level. The BPD, of course, struggled to maintain its primary jurisdiction, and had remarkable success given the circumstances. But the FBI and Secret Service would not be denied their place at the table. Even the Department of Homeland Security sent two officers out to make sure it was not the front end of a systemic attack on the nation's government officials.

The story remained the same, though. Unshaken by innuendo and looks of incredulity, all those involved stuck to the truth, and everyone's truth seemed to match up, more or less. It was clear from what the police knew that Elizabeth Connor had been blackmailing Buchanan; maybe McDougal as well. Buchanan and McDougal had been involved in skirting campaign finance limits, and had likely engaged in some sort of *quid pro quo* in the bargain. In addition, Buchanan and Connor had conceived Finn out of wedlock when they were young. Either would have provided Connor leverage, though no one knew which was the angle Connor had taken. There were other unanswered questions, to be sure. How much had Buchanan known about Elizabeth Connor's murder before the fact? Who had given the order to have her killed? Why had the man with the scar, as yet still unidentified, turned so violently against both McDougal and Buchanan?

These were, though, the types of loose ends that were inevitable in cases this messy. Television cop shows give the impression that in the end, with enough effort and intelligence, all is revealed, and the motives and motivations of all involved in a crime are known with certainty. That is not the reality, however. In most cases, even those that are solved, questions remain and uncertainty lingers. No matter how much we think we know about people and their actions, we can never fully explain what drives them to the ultimate acts of violence.

At least Finn and Kozlowski were not required to stay at the Buchanan house for very long. An hour and a half after the questioning began they were taken down to the police station. That was a relief. Shortly after the bodies were taken away, Catherine and Brooke Buchanan had been brought to the house, and the tension was so thick Finn found it difficult to breathe.

He assumed that they had both been informed that James Buchanan was Finn's father. Brooke kept looking at him, bewildered. He couldn't even raise his eyes to her. *He had a sister.* The thought made his hands shake. He wanted to go over to her, but he had no idea what to say. There were too many complications to allow for a clean reunion. She was grieving over their father's death; the father who had abandoned him and likely killed his mother. All he could do was look at his feet and shake his head.

'If looks could kill,' Kozlowski said, sitting next to him.

Finn looked at him, and Kozlowski nodded over toward Catherine Buchanan. She was looking at Finn. Staring through him. Almost as though she were wishing him to vanish; to leave her house and her life and take all the tragedy he seemed to bring to her family.

'Can't really blame her,' Finn said.

'No? It's not like it's your fault.'

'Isn't it?' He looked at his shoes again, unable to bear her look anymore. 'Even if it isn't, I'm still the reason for all this. I'm the reason her world is falling apart. I'm the physical embodiment of everything that was wrong with her husband.' He laughed bitterly. 'I guess I am truly my father's son.'

'That's bullshit,' Kozlowski said. 'She married the asshole. She chose her life. You had nothing to do with it.'

'Maybe not.'

Long walked up, stood in front of them. 'We're done here,' he said. 'We've just got a few more things to take care of down at the station.'

Finn nodded, grateful to be able to get out of the house where he'd never been wanted. He kept his head down as he made his way to the door. He almost made it.

'Scott,' came a voice from behind him. He turned. Brooke Buchanan was standing in front of him. Her face was smudged, and she had circles under her eyes.

'Finn,' he said.

'What?'

'Nobody calls me Scott. Everyone calls me Finn.'

'Oh. Right.' She looked away, and the tears started rolling down her cheeks. 'I'm not very good at this. I don't know what to say.'

'I don't know that there is anything to say.' Finn was desperate to leave.

'I guess not.' She looked away. 'I don't know how to deal with all this,' she said.

'Yeah,' Finn said. 'I get that.'

'I've never had a brother before.'

'I've never had anything before.'

'It's going to take me some time, but when I'm ready, I think I'd like to talk. I don't know when that will be.' She looked guilty. She didn't need to, Finn thought. It wasn't her fault, either.

'If you're ready in the future, maybe we can get a cup of coffee,' Finn said. 'If not, I understand that, too.'

She nodded and started to turn around. Pausing, she turned back and put her hand out. Finn, taking the cue, put his out as well. They shook slowly, looking each other in the eyes. 'It's a pleasure to meet you, Finn,' she said.

'It's a pleasure to meet you, Brooke.'

She let go of his hand and walked away.

CHAPTER FORTY-EIGHT

'Do you inherit anything?'

Sally had a way of cutting through emotional minefields to the practical implications of even the most complicated situations.

The question caught Finn by surprise. 'I don't know,' he said. 'I wouldn't think so. Buchanan must have had a will. Trusts, a tax plan, the whole nine yards. I'm sure his estate plan excludes me.' They were sitting at the office the next day. Finn had gotten back to his apartment the evening before at around six o'clock. By six-fifteen, he was asleep, and he hadn't woken up for more than fourteen hours. It was a personal record.

He was in a panic when he woke up. 'Sally!' he called. 'You're going to be late for school!' He'd run out into the living room, where Sally was sitting in a T-shirt and leggings. 'You're not ready,' he said.

'You serious?'

'What?'

'It's Saturday.'

He took a deep breath. 'Is it?'

'Yeah.'

He rubbed his face, felt the stubble. At least he wouldn't have to shave today. 'I have to go to the office,' he told her. 'You should get dressed.'

'You're going to work today?'

'I need to make sure there are no emergencies, at least. Besides, I can't sit here doing nothing. I'll go crazy.'

'Fine,' she'd said.

Lissa and Kozlowski were already at the office when they arrived. 'You didn't need to come in,' Lissa said. 'I can keep things moving here.'

'You expect me just to stay in my apartment?'

Lissa relented. They all sat and talked for a while. It was a half hour into the conversation when Sally brought up the issue of Finn's potential inheritance.

'I'm sure I won't get anything,' he reiterated.

'I don't know about that,' Lissa said. 'Under some circumstances, if he didn't affirmatively disown you in the will, you may be entitled to a cut of the estate.'

'Seriously?'

'It was on the bar exam.'

Finn thought about it for a moment. 'I wouldn't take it,' he said.

'Why not?' Lissa asked. 'You're entitled. The asshole ditched you when you were a baby. He killed your mother.'

'We don't know that for sure,' Finn pointed out. 'Not to mention the fact that she ditched me, too, remember?'

'All the more reason you should be entitled to something.'

Finn shook his head. 'I didn't need his money growing up, I don't need it now. Taking his money would be like admitting that I couldn't make it on my own. I did make it on my own. Fuck him.'

No one said anything for a little while. When it was starting to get uncomfortable, Sally piped up, 'That's right. Fuck him.' Lissa chuckled.

The phone rang and Lissa picked it up. After a moment, she put the caller on hold, looked over at Finn. 'It's Mark over at Huron Labs. Did you order a rush on some lab tests?'

Finn nodded. 'Not that it matters anymore. It was just some insurance to make sure the cops didn't put the fix in on the Buchanan paternity test.' Lissa and Kozlowski looked at Finn with curiosity, but he ignored them as he picked up his extension. 'Hey Mark,' he said. 'I'm sorry, I should've called you sooner; I don't need the tests anymore. If you ran them, that's fine, just bill me.'

He listened for a moment. 'No, I don't need them,' he repeated. 'I already –'

Mark had cut him off, already giving him the information. Finn leaned back in his chair. 'Say that again, Mark?' he said. He figured he must have misheard. Mark repeated the information.

Finn sat there, staring straight ahead. 'That doesn't make any sense,' he said. 'Are you sure?' Mark said that he had double checked the results. The receiver slipped from Finn's hand, cracked off the desk and bounced to the floor. Finn didn't even notice. He closed his eyes.

'What is it?' Lissa demanded. Everyone in the room was staring at Finn now, worried expressions on their faces. 'What?'

Finn shook his head back and forth, trying to make sense of it all. 'It can't be,' he said quietly to himself. 'It just can't be.'

The drive took three hours. There was midday traffic going through Cambridge, and more out by Alewife. That was to be expected, though in his mental state it was almost enough to send Finn into a rage.

Kozlowski had offered to go with him. Insisted, in fact. So had Sally and Lissa. He refused the company, though. He needed to be alone. He needed to think, to try to put the pieces together.

It had been less than a week since his last trip up to New Hampshire, and yet the landscape on the drive north was severely altered. The leaves were down, now; gone were the beautiful explosions of reds and oranges. A few pockets of dusty brown foliage still clung desperately to the angular limbs of younger trees, but for the most part the battle was over and the war had been lost. The place now felt cold; there was a sense of resignation that winter had arrived, and acceptance that it would last for another six months.

As he approached the highway sign for the exit leading to the Health Center he tensed. It was mid afternoon; the place would still be open. He'd thought of starting there, but realized it made little sense. If she was alive, she wouldn't go there.

He drove on – two more exits, another ten miles. He pulled off the highway and followed the directions he'd printed out before he'd departed, through a small, quaint New England town like a thousand others. White clapboard houses lined the streets, set close upon the sidewalks and backed, often, by a river that ran just off the road. The town seemed trapped by the steep hills through which the river had carved a ribbon of flat ground over the millennia.

At the far end of the town, he pulled down a street into a wooded residential area of small houses. He drove slowly now, looking at the numbers that were only sporadically hung on the houses. It didn't matter; he knew the house instantly without even seeing the number.

It was a small cottage on a corner lot. The leaves that had given up their fight on the trees' limbs had invaded the yard, making it difficult to tell where the grass ended and the woods began. No one had yet taken a rake to the place to clean it up. It wasn't clear to Finn that anyone ever would.

There was a car in the driveway, an ancient hatchback. The back was open, gaping wide like a miniature whale. Bags were stacked next to the car, and clothes on hangers were draped over the tailgate. Someone was clearly here.

The back door banged open, and there was a rustling in the overgrown shrubs that flanked the entryway. She walked around the corner, weary in her step, carrying an armload of clothes. Looking down, she made her way to the car, oblivious to the man sitting in the little MG watching her.

Finn got out of his car. When he slammed the door she looked up. For a moment Finn thought from her expression that she was going to run, but, of course, there was nowhere for her to go. They both knew that. So instead, she put the clothes on the ground. She just stood there for a moment, looking at him. Then slowly, reluctantly, she made her way over to him. 'How did you know I'd be here?'

'There was no body,' Finn said. 'The man with the scar killed a lot of people, but he never hid the bodies. I couldn't see why he would have hidden yours if he'd killed you. I figured that meant there was a chance you were still alive. And if you were, I figured there was a chance you'd come back when you read what happened in the papers.'

'Only for a couple of hours,' Shelly Tesco replied.

'You found your daughter?' Finn said. It was an educated guess.

She nodded. 'He did. The man with the scar.'

'How'd the reunion go? Have you met her yet?'

'No,' she said. 'I know where she is, though. She's out in Ohio. I'm moving there, just to be close to her. Someday I'll figure out a way to approach her. For now, I'm just glad to know she's safe.'

Finn nodded. 'That's good.'

The rustling leaves filled the quiet between them. 'You probably have some questions,' she said at last.

'And you probably have some answers,' he replied.

'Some. Not all.'

He put his hands in his pockets. 'Some is a start.'

Long sat on a bench at the edge of Boston Common, staring at the kids playing on the grass. It was one of those perfect autumn days when the sun stabs through the New England sky with a clarity that can blind. Long closed his eyes and raised his face to the rays, trying to drink in the energy through his skin. It had been two days since he last slept, and it didn't feel as though rest would come any time soon. There was too much to do, and his thoughts were too cluttered and confused to relax.

It had all happened so fast. With the national media and the various different law enforcement branches hovering around the scene of Buchanan's murder, the BPD had closed ranks quickly, eager to create the impression that the investigation into the Connor murder had been handled properly. By necessity, Long was praised by police brass from every microphone that could be commandeered. Overnight he had gone from pariah to star.

He didn't like it.

What he liked even less, though, was the nagging feeling that he was missing something. The entire department was desperate to close the books on the investigation. No one questioned the shooting, and with all the players in the sad psycho-drama dead, there seemed little desire to figure out what exactly had happened. Long understood that, but the questions still nagged at him.

He felt the shadow cross his face. 'How'd you find me?' he asked.

'Just a hunch,' Racine said. 'I figured hiding in plain sight was your only option.'

'Got that right,' he said.

'Tough being a celebrity, is it?'

He opened his eyes, looked sideways at her as she sat next to him. 'I didn't ask for this,' he said. 'And I don't want it.'

She nodded as she slipped her hand into his. 'I know,' she said. She rested her head on his shoulder. 'At least your job is safe,' she pointed out. 'They've got no choice.'

'For now,' Long agreed. 'It doesn't change anything, really, though. I'm still an outcast.'

'Maybe.'

They sat there for a while, neither of them talking. Finally he said, 'Does it bother you?'

'What?'

'That we don't know.'

'Know what?'

'What happened. Why it all went down the way it did. Don't you want to know?'

Racine sat up and looked at him. 'You mean with Buchanan?'

He nodded. 'With all of it. Buchanan. McDougal. His son. Connor. All of it.'

'What more is there to know? Buchanan was a dirty politician who was hooked up with McDougal's mob. Connor knew enough about Buchanan to put him away on a couple of fronts, so one of them hired Coale to kill her. Seems pretty simple. You and the lawyer started pulling at the threads, and the whole thing fell apart.'

'But why?' Long said. 'What made it fall apart? And what sent Coale on his killing spree?'

'You said it yourself,' Racine pointed out, 'he was a psychopath. A killer. Maybe that's all there is to it.'

'Maybe,' Long said. 'But then why did he leave Finn alive?'

She shook her head. 'I don't know.' She leaned back into him. 'All I know is that we have a chance to put all this behind us. You have a chance to start over. Fresh slate.' She squeezed his hand as she closed her eyes. 'Isn't that enough?'

He didn't answer for a moment, and when he did, he spoke very quietly. 'Maybe,' he said. 'I just don't know yet.'

'I don't know who he was,' Shelly Tesco said. They were sitting at the table in her kitchen. She had made coffee. The back door was open, and a breeze blew some leaves in onto the linoleum floor. She didn't seem to care.

'What happened?'

'He came to find out about the file.' She dipped her head as she looked at him. 'Your file.'

'Why?'

'I don't know. He wouldn't say. When I first saw him, I thought he was going to kill me. He had a knife, and a look in his eye that seemed to have no mercy. He didn't kill me, though, as you can tell.

He said that if I told him what he wanted to know, he'd even help me. He told me he knew where my daughter was.'

'How did he find her?'

'He said he convinced the head of the agency that handled the adoption to give him the information.'

'I'm guessing he could be pretty persuasive,' Finn said.

She didn't respond.

'So, what happened?' Finn asked.

She shrugged. 'His information checked out, right down to the birth certificate. So I told him what he wanted to know.'

'Which was?'

'He wanted to know about you. He wanted to know about Elizabeth Connor. I told him what I found. When I was done, he told me to leave. He told me that people would be looking for me, and if they found out that I was alive, they would kill me. He told me where my daughter was and he gave me three minutes to pack. I tore through everything in my closets.'

'And the bloody handprint on the bed?'

Shelly Tesco smiled shyly. 'That was my fault. I was in such a hurry as I was packing that I slammed my finger in the dresser drawer. It bled like you wouldn't believe, but I just wrapped it in a towel, got in the car and took off. He gave me some money.'

'How did you know that you could come back?'

'He told me to watch the news, read the papers. He said it would be obvious when things had come to a head. As long as I stayed away until that happened, he said I'd be fine. I'm still leaving though. It doesn't feel safe here anymore. Even if it wasn't for my daughter, I think I would want to get away.' She got up and poured what was left of her coffee into the sink. 'I need to leave,' she said. 'Is there anything else you want to know?'

Finn looked at her. 'Do you still have my file?'

She was still and silent for a moment. Then she nodded slightly.

'He didn't take it with him?'

'He said he had no use for it,' she said. 'He said you might come looking for it, and that I should give it to you.'

'Will you do that?' he asked. 'And will you explain what it all means?'

She nodded again. 'You deserve that, at least. Let me go get it.'

CHAPTER FORTY-NINE

It was seven o'clock by the time Finn got back to Boston. He called Kozlowski and Lissa to tell them he was going to be later than he anticipated. They demanded to know what was happening, but he refused to say. 'I need to deal with this myself,' was the most he would offer. Lissa cursed a blue streak at him, but there was nothing she could do. Kozlowski said little over the phone. 'I'm here if you need backup,' was the extent of it. Finn told him he would keep that in mind.

It was almost November, and by the time Finn pulled across the Longfellow Bridge from Cambridge into Boston, night had fallen. The days would continue getting shorter for another two months. Finn found it depressing.

He guided the car around the traffic circle where Cambridge Street joins with Charles and spins off onto Storrow Drive. A group of homeless was gathered around the pharmacy across the street from Massachusetts General Hospital. It affected Finn to see such a pocket of poverty so close to one of the richest neighborhoods in the country.

He drove down Charles Street, past the bars and four-star restaurants. Halfway to Beacon Street and Boston Common, he turned left and headed two blocks up the hill to Louisburg Square.

The news crews that had staked out the house for most of the day had packed up and moved on, like vultures grown tired of a carcass picked clean. All that was left was the profusion of cardboard coffee cups and cigarette butts that were scattered around the Square. It looked as though an early snow had hit the area.

The police tape was gone, and the house had been, for the most part, restored to order. In all likelihood the office upstairs where the senator had actually been killed was still closed off, but with three witnesses to the killing it was unlikely that it would stay that way for long. After all, there was no mystery as to what happened as far as the authorities were concerned. There might be political fallout from Buchanan's connection to McDougal, but now that they were both dead, there was no one toward whom the press could direct a right-eous anger. Notwithstanding the need for the twenty-four-hour news stations to feed off tragedy, the story would die as soon as another scandal came around. In a country so prone to violence, Finn figured that wouldn't take long.

He walked up the front steps, rang the doorbell. No one answered. After a moment he rang again. It wasn't until the third ring that there was any sign of life within the house. A voice called out, 'Leave us alone!'

'It's Scott Finn!' he shouted back.

He heard shuffling behind the door. It cracked open. Brooke Buchanan looked at him, frowning. 'I thought the newspeople had come back,' she said. It was not an apology; she didn't seem much happier that it was Finn. 'I told you, I'm not ready to deal with this,' she said.

'I'm not looking for you to be my sister right now,' Finn said. 'I have some questions I need to ask you.'

'About what?'

He hesitated. He had no desire to talk to her on the steps of the house. 'Can I come in?'

She frowned even more deeply, regarding him with suspicion.

'It's important,' he said.

She relented and opened the door, stepping back to let him in. They stood there in the foyer, staring at each other. 'Well?' she demanded.

'I'm sorry,' he said. 'I don't mean to put you out, but I've been driving all day. Is there any chance I could have a glass of water?'

She rolled her eyes. 'Come with me.' She led him back to the kitchen, pulled out a glass, filled it with tap water. 'It's been a really shitty couple of days,' she said to him.

'For me, too,' he agreed. At that, her attitude softened. He took a long drink of the water, considering how to approach the young woman.

She started the conversation. 'So? What's so important that you needed to talk to me tonight?'

'I wanted to know about the tests the police used to prove that you and I have the same father. Did you go in to the police to give them the DNA to test?' Finn asked.

'Yes,' she said. 'I did.'

'Whose idea was it?'

She stared at him. 'I don't understand what you're asking.'

'I mean the DNA tests – were they your idea, or were they the police's idea?'

She shook her head. 'It was their idea. At the time, I didn't even know they thought we might have the same father. All I knew was that my father was mixed up in something bad, and he was hurting my mother.' Her face darkened at the memory. 'I hated him,' she said. 'I think I always hated him. I wanted to do whatever I could to help the police.'

'So when they suggested the DNA test might help, you jumped at the chance?'

'Yes, I did.'

'How did they gather the DNA?'

'What does it matter?' She demanded. Finn could tell the questions were unsettling her, but he pressed on.

'Just tell me, please.'

'They took my blood,' she said.

He nodded. 'And you saw them put it in a vial, mark it with your name?'

'Yes, I did. I was curious about the process – I asked them how it was done and how long it would take. What has this got to do with anything?'

Finn ignored the question, 'I assume your father didn't know you were going to the police?'

'God, no. He would have killed me, I think.'

'Did you tell your mother?'

She shook her head. 'She couldn't seem to let go of my father, no matter what he did to her, no matter how awful things were. She would have tried to stop me. She might have even told my father.'

'Did you tell either of your parents what you'd done when you got back from the police station?'

She nodded slowly. 'I told my mother.' Worry was beginning to break over her face. 'I wanted to show her that we could take a stand against him – against my father.'

'Did you tell her about the DNA test?'

'Yes.' She was white now.

'How did she react?'

'Badly.' Brooke looked so confused and scared, Finn felt sorry for her, but he couldn't stop now. 'Why does it matter? Why are you asking me these questions?'

'Because I'm still trying to figure out what really happened to my mother. What did your mother say when you told her about the DNA test they were going to run?'

She took a deep breath. 'She screamed at me. She told me that I was going to destroy the family. That I was going to ruin everything.'

'Did you understand what she meant by that?'

'Of course I did.' She fidgeted, leaned down on the granite island, the tears flowing freely. 'Look at what's happened since then.'

Finn reached out and put a hand on her back. 'Thank you,' he said. 'I just needed to know.'

'Know what?' Brooke asked. Her voice was raised, almost desperate. 'What did I tell you that could possibly change anything? What did you come here to get from me?'

Finn started to answer, but someone else spoke before he could open his mouth. The voice came from across the room, from the entrance to the kitchen. 'Yes, Mr Finn, what did you come here to get from us?'

Finn and Brooke spun around to see Catherine Buchanan standing at the door. She was calm, composed, perhaps a little weary. The bruises were still evident on her face and neck; she no longer covered them. Finn supposed that was understandable. 'I came here to try to make sense of it all.'

'And have you done that now? Does it all make sense to you now?'

He nodded. 'I think it does.'

Catherine looked at her daughter. 'Sweetheart, I need to talk to Mr Finn alone.'

Brooke shook her head. 'No,' she was weeping openly. 'I don't understand, I'm not leaving.'

'Please, dearest,' her mother said. 'Everything is fine. I will explain it all to you later, but for the moment, I need to talk to him by myself.' She lifted up her daughter's face, kissed her cheek. 'I'll be up in a little while, and we can talk.'

Brooke shook her head, but moved toward the door that led to the stairway. She looked back, and her mother gave a wave that one might give to a kindergartener on her way in to her first day of school. 'Everything will be fine,' her mother repeated.

Once Brooke had left the room, Catherine looked at Finn. 'I'm guessing you have some questions for me, haven't you?'

*

She led Finn into her room – the sun room splashed with yellow florals. It was dark out, but it was still the most cheerful room in the house. As she walked through the other rooms, she'd said, 'We'll have to sell the house, of course.' There was an air of resignation about her. 'It's not financial; my husband had more money then anyone could imagine.' She paused in realization. 'I suppose that means that I now have more money than anyone can imagine.' The thought seemed to surprise her, but she didn't pursue it. 'In any event, I can't imagine staying here now. Not with all the terrible memories.'

'Like the memory of your husband being killed here?' Finn asked.

She looked at him with a tired expression. 'Among many others.' She sat in a low chair with bamboo arms and overstuffed pillows with hand-painted pictures of orchids on them. In another setting, Finn would have found them overdone, but they fit the room, and came off as subtler than they might have. She invited Finn to sit across from her. 'How much do you know, Mr Finn?'

Finn leaned forward. 'I know that your husband was not my father,' he said.

She took the news without any visible reaction. 'How do you know that?' she asked.

'He came to visit me two days ago. He asked me to leave all of this alone.' Finn gave an ironic laugh. 'Maybe we would all have been better off if I'd listened to him. He told me that I was not his son.'

'Well,' Catherine Buchanan said, 'that's what you would expect him to say, isn't it?'

Finn nodded. 'It was, and I didn't believe him.' He stood, paced as he spoke. 'I had his DNA tested against mine.'

She raised her eyebrows. 'Did you? How did you accomplish that?'

'When your husband came to my office, he drank a glass of water. That leaves a residue of saliva on the glass that contains cells from the inside of the mouth. Testing the DNA of those cells is actually a simple process.'

'You're very resourceful,' she said. There was no sarcasm in her voice.

'I almost didn't bother to run the tests. The police told me they were running the DNA tests between me and Brooke; normally that would have seemed like enough.'

'Not in this case, though.'

'No. Not in this case. I didn't trust the police,' Finn said. 'I thought they might try to protect your husband. Cover for him. He's a very powerful man with plenty of connections. I figured they might just tell me there was no match without even running the tests, if only to get me to back off.'

'They ran the tests, though,' Catherine Buchanan said.

'They did,' Finn agreed. 'They told me the test came back positive. Which was why I was so surprised this morning when the lab that I used to test your husband's DNA called me up to tell me there was no match. There is no chance that James Buchanan was my father.'

'So,' Catherine Buchanan said pensively. 'What do you think? Did the police falsify their tests? Were they trying to frame my husband?'

Finn shook his head. 'The test that the police ran was to match my DNA with Brooke's. They wanted to prove that your husband was my father by showing that Brooke and I were siblings. When the test came back positive, *voilà*, they thought they had what they needed. No one considered any other possibility. But Brooke and I don't have the same father.' He looked hard at her. 'We have the same mother.'

CHAPTER FIFTY

Catherine Buchanan looked at him for a very long time. She didn't try to avoid his eyes; she stared straight at him, saying nothing. At last, very quietly and without conviction, she said, 'You don't know that.'

Finn nodded at her. 'Yes, I do.' He reached into his briefcase and pulled out two files. They were government blue, worn and faded. At the sight of them, tears appeared in Catherine Buchanan's eyes.

'What are those?' she asked.

'You know what these are,' Finn said. 'You've seen them before. A long, long time ago. Two files. Two sets of records for two boys born on the same day at the same hospital to young mothers. One died in childbirth; the other survived.' He put one down on the table in front of her. 'This file contains my birth records. See here,' he pointed. 'It lists my name as the one I was given when I was first placed with a family that was supposed to take care of me.' She followed along with him. 'And here,' he pointed again, 'it lists Elizabeth Connor as my mother.'

She frowned. 'So if this lists Elizabeth Connor, what makes you think that I am really your mother?'

'Because it's a lie. The records were switched. Look at the blood types. Elizabeth Conner had a blood type of AB positive. I have a blood type of O negative. That's a biological impossibility. She couldn't have been my mother.' He held up the second file. 'This is a file that contains the birth records of the second child, the one who died in childbirth. His blood type is listed as AB negative. The mother's blood type is listed as O negative. Again, it's not possible.' He lay the folder down on the table. 'Do you see the name listed as the mother? It says Catherine Howard St. James.'

She turned her head. 'That doesn't prove anything. Not conclusively.'

'Maybe not on its own. It could have just been a record-keeping error. But the police DNA test proves that Brooke and I are siblings, and the tests I had run prove that James Buchanan was not my father. That leaves only one possibility.'

Catherine Buchanan closed her eyes.

'We could run a DNA test between you and me to confirm it,' Finn said. 'But we don't need to, do we?'

She shook her head. 'No, we don't.' She opened her eyes, looking down.

'I want to hear it from you,' Finn said.

She could not look him in the face anymore. It took her several moments to speak. 'You have to understand, I was very young,' she said at last. 'Too young. My family was one of the most prominent families in Boston. My father was the chairman of the largest financial institution in the city, and my mother was on the boards of most of the major charitable institutions. They couldn't accept that their fifteen-year-old daughter could have done this to them; that I could have gotten pregnant. If anyone had discovered it at the time, it would have been a scandal that could have destroyed the family.'

'So you gave me up,' Finn said. 'You left me.'

'I didn't want to,' Catherine Buchanan sobbed. 'I was fifteen, what choice did I have? They sent me away. I didn't see anyone in my family for months, and when it was over they took you away. They never even let me see you. I screamed and screamed for days, but they ignored me.'

'You never tried to find me,' Finn said. 'Even after you grew up. With all your money; with all your resources, you never tried to find out what happened to me.'

'I couldn't,' Catherine Buchanan said. She stood up and went to Finn, reached out to him. He pulled away. 'By then I was married to James. They married me off to the most eligible man in the city, one of the first families of Massachusetts. They told me to put it behind me. They told me I had to forget.'

'So you forgot all about me. It was like I had never been born.'

'No,' she said. 'I never forgot. I just buried it. It was always there, I just couldn't deal with it, so I pretended it never happened. It was the only way I could survive.'

'Until Elizabeth Connor surfaced,' Finn pointed out.

She turned away from him. 'Yes,' she said. 'Elizabeth Connor brought it all back in the most degrading way.'

'Blackmail?'

Catherine Buchanan nodded. 'She and I shared that room for nearly two months. We never knew each others' names; that was the way it worked. I was called Lizzie, she was called Jane. She was an awful person, even back then. Rooming with her was one of the worst parts of the whole experience. Her child died, and later my parents paid someone to switch the records – to erase my name so that you would never find me, even if you tried.'

'That's why my letter was sent to her,' Finn said. 'The records listed her as my mother. She must have realized that there was a mistake at the time. She must have suspected that I was your child, not hers. Why would she wait to blackmail you? I sent that letter almost twenty years ago.'

She sat back down again, all the energy drained from her. 'She had no idea who I was,' she said. 'I never told anyone at the home anything about myself. That was drilled into me. *No one must find out who you are.* I don't know how many times my parents told me that before they sent me away. So she wouldn't have known that I was someone who could be blackmailed – who had the money to be blackmailed. Even if she had known, she wouldn't have been able to find me.'

'So why now?' Finn asked. The answer came to him before she needed to answer. 'The election,' he said. 'She saw you because you were at campaign events.'

Catherine nodded once more. 'She recognized me from my picture in the papers, standing next to James, smiling like every good campaign wife should. The first time Jim stood for office, Brooke and I stayed far more in the background. This time, though, the race was much closer, and he said he needed us to help present the look of the perfect family. She knew who I was instantly, and she called me. She started out slowly, saying she remembered me from our time in New Hampshire when we were young. I thought that was clever, at least. Anyone else overhearing us would have had no idea that there was anything ominous or threatening. She said she wanted to get together for coffee. She hadn't finished her first cup before she demanded money.'

'What did you do?'

'I paid her, of course. It wasn't cheap, but she said that was it. One payment and she would walk away. It was a lie, obviously. I suppose I knew it was a lie, even then, but I wanted to believe that there was some way out. I wanted to think she would go away. She didn't go away, though. She contacted me again. And again and again. She became brazen, started calling the house. I think she hated me for my life.' She laughed bitterly. 'Ironic, isn't it? If she only knew how unhappy my life has really been. But all she saw was the money. She thought it was unfair that we had been in the same place all those years ago, and I had lived my life in big houses with fancy cars, and she was scraping by. I realized that last night that she was never going to go away. No amount of money was ever going to be enough.'

'You killed her,' Finn said.

'Yes, I killed her.' She looked relieved to have said the words. 'I don't even remember it, but it happened. I went to her apartment to make one final payment; to try to convince her it was over. She was having none of it. She said that it was never going to be over. She started to paint a picture of what it would be like if she went public. How my husband would react. How all my fancy friends would react. I told her I didn't care anymore. I told her she could go public, and then I would have her prosecuted for extortion. I thought I had a trump card there, but I didn't. She had the trump card.'

'What did she threaten you with?'

'You,' she said. 'She told me that she knew who you were; she knew how to find you. She said, "I wonder how he will feel about the fact that you abandoned him? I wonder if your daughter will ever be able to look you in the face again once she realizes what you did to your son?"' She closed her eyes. 'I don't remember much after that. I flew into a rage. I grabbed the first thing I could find and started hitting her. I hit her and hit her. And yet somehow, it didn't even feel like I was hitting her. It felt like I was hitting myself. All this rage and self-loathing that had built over forty-five years came out all at once. And I kept hitting and hitting until it was out. Then I was alone. Standing in this dreadful, dreary little apartment in a terrible neighborhood over the body of a woman I once knew, who had tormented me. I didn't know what to do, so I ran.'

'How did McDougal get involved in covering it up?' Finn asked.

'That was just chance,' she replied. 'Or mischance, I suppose. It depends on the way you look at it. Elizabeth Connor worked for him, as you already know, and she owed him money. He went by her apartment later that night to collect from her and found her the way she was. She had told him a little about what she was up to, but he thought she was blackmailing my husband – he thought James was your father and that was what she had on him. When he saw her body, he assumed James had killed her. Because he and James were doing business together and she worked for him, he was worried that her murder

367

could cause him a significant amount of trouble, so he called in an expert to make it look like a break-in.'

'Makes sense,' Finn said. He sat there for a while, digesting everything she had told him. He'd suspected it all already, but there is a significant difference between wrestling with suspicions and dealing with reality. She didn't say anything; he supposed she understood at some level what he was going through, and guessed she had a fair amount to adjust to as well. Finally he said, 'I have one more question.' He was almost afraid to ask it.

She looked at him. 'Go ahead.'

He took a deep breath. 'The man with the scar – he could have killed me. He should have killed me, but he didn't. Why not? Who was he?'

She smiled sadly. 'He was someone I knew a long time ago. His name was Billy Gannon. His father was my family's chauffeur when I was growing up. Such a wonderful, hardworking man. He used to tell the children stories out in the garage. The most marvelous, imaginative stories. And Billy was the sweetest, most beautiful boy you could ever imagine.'

'He was a killer,' Finn said.

She shook her head vehemently. 'Not when I knew him. When I knew him he was perfect. Others made him into what he became. He had a tragic story – his father was fired and killed himself. Billy was thrown out with nothing. He disappeared, and we never heard from him again.'

'Why was his father let go?'

She looked him in the eyes. 'Because of me. Because I fell in love with his son.' And then the tears began to flow.

Finn sucked in a breath.

'He was your father.' She put her head down. 'I loved him so much when we were young. I would have done anything for him. After his father killed himself, Billy was thrown out on the street. I was packed off to New Hampshire, and by the time I returned he had disappeared. My family took everything from him. His home, his father, me. He felt so angry and abandoned, he no longer cared how he lived. It was only recently that he realized what a mistake he'd made with his life.'

'Why?'

'I told him he had a son. He didn't know before; I never had a chance to tell him back then.'

'How you find him?'

'I didn't – he found me. That is the great irony of it all. When I fled from Elizabeth Connor's apartment, I was in such a state I left behind the checkbook I had brought with me to buy her silence. Billy found my checkbook, and he came to find me. We hadn't seen each other since he'd been thrown out of my family's house. He'd known all along where I was – who I'd married – but he'd given up on me a long time ago. He thought I was happy. Can you imagine?' She shook her head. 'I told him about you. He was devastated. He felt responsible, and he vowed to protect me and to protect you. And that's what he did. He watched over you to make sure nothing happened. And then, when I told him that James was beating me . . .' She cut herself off. 'I suppose I should have known what that would do to him. Perhaps, deep down, I did.'

Finn stood up. 'I have to leave.'

She rose, reaching out to him once more. 'You can't go,' she said. 'Not yet. Please, we have so much to talk about.'

'No, we don't,' he said.

'You can't mean that. It's been forty-five years.'

'For you it's been forty-five years,' he said. 'For me, it's been fifteen minutes.'

She let her hands drop. 'Of course,' she said. 'Of course you're right.'

'I'll let myself out.'

She nodded. 'What do you plan to do?'

'I don't know.'

'Will you go to the police?'

'I don't know,' he said. 'You killed a woman. Maybe a bad woman, but you killed her nonetheless.'

'I did.'

'I need to think about that. So do you.'

'I will. Whatever you decide, I'll understand. I'm sorry. I'm sorry for so many things. I know that probably doesn't matter.'

'Probably not,' he said.

'I want you to know it anyway.'

'Okay.' He started to walk out of the room. At the threshold, though, he stopped and turned around to look at her once more. 'Did you ever think about me?' he asked. 'Did you ever wonder where I was, whether I was alive, whether I was happy?'

For the first time the tears started flowing down her face. 'Every day,' she said. 'Every single day.'

Long was leaning against his car on the street outside of the Buchanan mansion, looking up at the door, when Finn walked out onto the stoop. Finn was tempted to pretend he hadn't seen him, just walk on by without a word. He knew Long wouldn't let it happen, though. Instead he walked toward the cop.

'A social call?' Long asked him when he drew close. His eyes were clear and penetrating.

'I was going to ask you the same thing,' Finn replied.

They stood there for a few seconds, both taking the measure of the other. Finally Long looked back up at the mansion. 'Quite a place,' he said. 'It could have been yours.'

Finn shook his head. 'No,' he said. 'I would never have survived in that world.'

Long tilted his head at the lawyer. 'You seem pretty resourceful,' he said. 'You made it off the streets, I think you could have made it with the silver spoon set.'

'The streets are different,' Finn said. 'There are rules, and everyone knows them. Up there the rules don't apply. I couldn't live that way.'

'Maybe you just didn't learn their rules early enough.'

Finn shrugged. 'I guess we'll never know.' He stepped away. 'I've got to be getting home.'

Long nodded. 'Must be nice to have a family.' Finn just stared back, saying nothing. 'There's more to all this, isn't there?' Long asked.

It took a moment for Finn to respond. 'Do you have something specific to ask me, Detective?'

Long stared back at Finn, and Finn could hear his own heart beating in his ears. Finally, Long let his gaze drop and he sighed heavily. 'No,' he said. 'Not now.'

'Okay,' Finn said.

'I may be in touch, though. Later.'

Finn looked around at his surroundings. 'I'm not going anywhere.' He pulled his car keys out of his pocket. 'I'll be seeing you, Detective.'

'Yeah,' Long replied. 'I'll be seeing you.'

CHAPTER FIFTY-ONE

'What are you going to do?'

Finn was leaning against the railing that surrounded the roof deck of the penthouse apartment on Beacon Street Lissa and Kozlowski shared. It was a spectacular view, for which it was well worth suffering the chill of the late October evening. Finn didn't feel the cold anymore; he was numb.

Sally asked the question. She, Lissa and Kozlowski had listened quietly in the living room as Finn told them. He told them everything, straight through. No one interrupted him. He needed to talk; needed to hear himself voice all that he'd learned so that he could start to truly digest it. When he was done, he sat there for a few moments in silence before going upstairs to the roof to look out at his city. They gave him some time before they went up after him. There were chairs and a table, and they sat down in the cold. Finn, standing at the railing, heard them, but didn't turn around.

'I don't know,' Finn said.

'She killed a woman,' Kozlowski said. Even with all the change Lissa and his son had brought to his life, his vision was still largely black and white.

'She did,' Finn said.

'She's your mother,' Lissa pointed out.

'She is.'

'What does that matter?' Kozlowski asked. 'We don't have different rules based on who it is we're dealing with.'

'No?' Lissa asked. 'If Andrew breaks the law when he's older would you turn him in? How about me? Would you turn me in?'

'That's different,' Kozlowski said.

'How?'

Kozlowski shook his head and said, 'It just is. We're not talking about someone who raised him. We're talking about someone who abandoned him. It's different.'

'Maybe. It still doesn't seem right.'

'There is no right,' Sally said quietly. Kozlowski and Lissa looked at her. 'There is no right thing to do here. Every option is wrong. There's no point in talking about it in those terms. The only thing that matters is what Finn decides to do. Whatever that is, it's fine, because there is no better decision.'

No one said anything for a while. Finally, Finn began to talk again. He was still looking out at the expanse of the Charles River, and the Esplanade that ran dark along the near shore. In the distance the dome of one of the main buildings at MIT shone bright. The buildings along the far side glowed warm in the autumn chill. 'You know,' he said, 'I used to daydream about my parents – I used to come up with all sorts of stories about why they had left me. Silly, romantic, childish stories borrowed from Walt Disney movies and Grimms' fairytales and King Arthur and all that.'

'It wasn't that far off,' Sally said. 'A little darker, maybe.'

Finn gave an angry laugh. 'A mob executioner and a society killer. Yeah, a little darker, I'd say.'

'That's not who they were when you were born. They were two kids. She was a princess. Trapped. He was the son of a chauffeur, and he couldn't save her. In some ways it is a fairy tale.'

'Without the happily ever after.'

'I guess that's up to you.' Sally walked over to the railing, stood next to Finn, a couple of feet away, looking out at the same view. 'You look at my parents – who they are, what they did, how I was raised – by rights I should be dead or in jail right now. I'm not. I'm not just bits and pieces of their failures. Neither are you.'

He nodded. 'No, I'm not.' He was still looking out over the river. 'It's a nice view from up here,' he said.

'I didn't even know views like this existed a year ago,' Sally agreed.

'So,' Lissa said from behind them. 'What's the answer?'

Finn turned around and looked at Lissa and Kozlowski. 'I can't turn her in,' he said. 'She's my mother. I won't lie for her; if the cops show up and they ask the right questions, I'm not going to risk my life for hers. But I can't go to them on my own.' He thought about it for a long moment. 'That's the best compromise I can come up with. I can live with that.'

Kozlowski nodded. 'Girl's right; there is no right or wrong here. Cops may figure this out on their own. They've gotta be digging into the connection between Buchanan and McDougal. They'll start asking questions at some point.'

'You think?' Finn asked.

'Maybe.'

'Are you going to call her? Talk to your sister, maybe? Try to reconnect with your family?' Lissa asked.

Finn looked around at the three of them. 'I doubt it,' he said. 'I've already got a family.'

ACKNOWLEDGMENTS

I would like to thank and acknowledge:

Trisha Jackson, whose assistance with this book has been invaluable. Thank you so much, I could not have done this without you.

All of the wonderful people at Pan Macmillan who have helped put this together on all fronts, including Thalia Suzuma, Helen Guthrie, Maria Rejt, Ali Blackburn, Stuart Wilson, Eli Dryden, Toni Byrne, Sarah Willcox, Matt Hayes, and Michelle Taylor.

Joanie Hosp, Richard Hosp, Martha Hosp, Ted Hosp and Joan McCormick, for giving helpful comments on early drafts.

Aaron Priest, Lisa Erbach-Vance, and everyone at the Aaron Priest Literary Agency, who are the best agents and friends a writer could have.

As always, my children, Reid and Samantha, as well as family and friends too numerous to mention, but too important to forget – thank you all for your love and support.

Finally, I would like to acknowledge Ann Fessler, with whom I did a book talk and signing at Cape Cod a few years ago. Her book, *The Girls Who Went Away*, was a great resource for the policies and practices involving adoption after the Second World War. I recommend it to anyone who is interested in further information on the subject.